THE TRIGON DISUNITY

"A trilo... ...ting as it is ambitiou...

EMPRISE...

"...has true excitement!"
—Brian W. Aldiss, author of *Helliconia Winter*

"One of those rare books where the ideas, the plotting, the writing, and the characters are all first rate!"
—*Science Fiction Review*

"An impressive debut."
—Julian May, author of *The Saga of the Pliocene Exile*

ENIGMA...

"...is utterly absorbing!"
—*Locus*

"Reminiscent of Arthur C. Clarke at his best."
—*Newsday*

"Intelligent, intriguing and well-written... the reader is left astounded!"
—*Publishers Weekly*

And now, the long-awaited conclusion...
EMPERY

Berkley books by Michael P. Kube-McDowell

THE TRIGON DISUNITY

Michael P. Kube-McDowell

Book Three of the Trigon Disunity

BERKLEY BOOKS, NEW YORK

For Pat, John, Sue, and Pauline,
who have been not just family,
but supporters and friends.

EMPERY

A Berkley Book/published by arrangement with
the author

PRINTING HISTORY
Berkley edition/June 1987

ISBN: 0-425-09887-7

A BERKLEY BOOK ® TM 757,375
Berkley Books are published by The Berkley Publishing Group,
200 Madison Avenue, New York, NY 10016.
The name "BERKLEY" and the stylized "B" with design
are trademarks belonging to Berkley Publishing Corporation.

PRINTED IN THE UNITED STATES OF AMERICA

contents

NORTHERN CELESTIAL HEMISPHERE

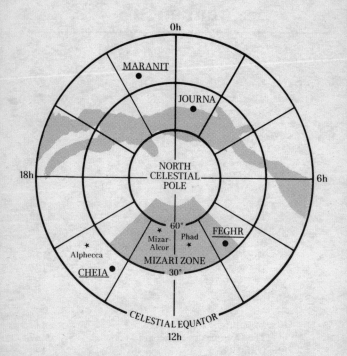

SOUTHERN CELESTIAL HEMISPHERE

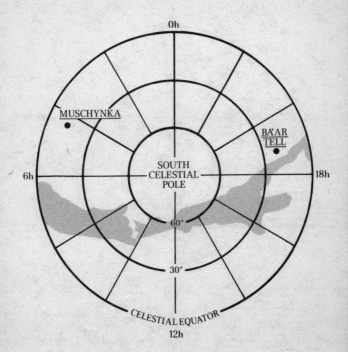

0h

MUSCHYNKA

BA'AR
TELL

6h

SOUTH
CELESTIAL
POLE

18h

60°

30°

CELESTIAL EQUATOR

12h

I.

A.R. 654: THE HUNTER

"It is war that makes the chief, the king, and the state."

—Will Durant

chapter 1

Intruder

Two light-hours from Ba'ar Tell, *Rampart* drifted silently in its asteroidal orbit, primed for a fight. Its sensors were alive, its weapons battle-ready. The prime watch, the best of what was already an elite crew, held down all eight stations on the bridge.

With an electronic chime as herald, a section of the heads-up display on the bubble of Denn Lieter's battle couch reformed. Lieter studied the new data for a moment, then frowned.

"Why are we getting estimated flight tracks on the targets all of a sudden? Aren't the pickets still on them?" Lieter asked quietly. His throat mike picked up the inquiry and relayed it to the other stations.

The answer came from the comtech. "The outer picket in that zone just went silent, sir. Defense Command on Ba'ar Tell is reporting it presumed destroyed. Inner pickets are still too far away for good data."

"If they're going to change course, this would be the time," a calm feminine voice said in Lieter's ear. That was Mills, the battle strategist, on her private captain's line.

"We'll stay put," Lieter said, with more certainty than he felt. "All stations, call down."

"Navcom ready."

"Weapons ready."

"Communications ready."

"Strategy and Analysis ready. . ."

Lieter only half listened to the ritual litany of the call-down check. Moving slowly so as not to trigger the acceleration sensors in the head harness, Lieter twisted sideways in the close confines of his battle couch and looked through the bubble toward the rear of the bridge. As expected, he saw a tall, rangy man in a tan Command uniform standing on the observer's dais.

Before the visitor could make eye contact with him, Lieter turned back to his console. As captain of the *Rampart*, ordinarily Lieter would have been the highest-ranking officer on board. But such was the import of the moment that the observer both outranked Lieter and unsettled him. Harmack Wells, the new Director of USS-Defense, had that kind of effect on people.

Lieter had no doubt that *Rampart*'s machine component was up to the task ahead, but its human component was still unproven. This was the supreme test. Though it was the sole reason they had been built, no Defender had ever been asked to fend off a Mizari attack on one of the Unified Worlds. It was the real possibility of failure that left Lieter's shirt glued to his back with cold sweat, and which made it impossible to forget Wells's watching eyes.

"Interior pickets have reconfirmed the tracks on targets Alpha and Beta," the comtech announced. "DefCom projects a planetary attack vector for both inbounds, confidence-90. *Rampart* authorized for full-force intercept."

Lieter took a deep breath and held it a long moment. "Acknowledged, Rampart authorized for FFI," he said. He tapped a glowing square on a touchboard with his forefinger, and the upper left quadrant of his display changed to a strategy map. "Mills?"

"Yes, Captain. Recommending standard two-target attack."

"Concur. Weapons, begin mode 21 attack immediately."

Within seconds the staccato bark of the fifty-barreled railgun filled the ship: ten barrels per salvo, one hundred rounds per second, sixty thousand rounds per minute. Even through the insulating cocoon of his battle couch, Lieter could hear the insistent, incessant drumming.

Lieter had to imagine the rest: the furious activity of the injectors, reloading each barrel twice a second; the cylindrical pellets hurtling down their electromagnetic channels; the muzzle deflectors tweaking each projectile toward its place in the dispersal pattern. A mode 21 attack meant the pattern Defender crews called the death halo: a five-kilometre-wide cone of high-velocity shrapnel from which no ship larger than a sprint could hope to escape by luck alone.

Devastating as the death halo could be, it was far from infallible. Given enough warning, the intruder could evade it or even turn tail and outrun it. But first, the Mizari had to detect it—not an easy task, since each element of the halo was less than three centimetres in cross section. To all but the very best optical or radar sensors, the halo would be invisible until it was too late.

"We have a telecam view of Beta from Picket I-7," the comtech advised Lieter.

A finger on a touchboard brought the picture up on Lieter's display. The Mizari intruder was a nearly spherical black-hulled object twice *Rampart*'s longest dimension in diameter. No obvious ordnance blisters marred its smoothly curved surface. There was no hint of the savage power that had long ago devastated Earth and earned the Mizari their better known name: the Sterilizers.

But we remember, Lieter thought. *We remember.*

Twenty minutes later the railgun closed the last gap in the death halo and fell silent. *Rampart* coasted on, waiting. The trade-off was distance for energy—the closer the Defender was to its targets, the more watts per square metre the lances would be able to deliver. Unless the Mizari forced Lieter's hand, *Rampart* would wait until the death halo struck the first blow.

"Vector change, Beta," the gravigator announced, his voice betraying a touch of alarm.

"Mills—has he made the halo?" asked Lieter.

"I don't think so, sir. Alpha is still on a collision vector. More likely a change from convoy spacing to attack spacing. Recommend we move with Beta."

"No. At this range we'll just be giving ourselves away. Lances, track Beta." Lieter glanced again at the strategy map and the intercept counter. Less than eight minutes remained before the Mizari and the halo would meet. Lieter's back muscles and sphincter were knotted with tension. "Navcom, prepare to take us toward Beta the moment Alpha hits the halo. We'll make her cross the tee on us—"

"Vector change on Alpha," the gravigator fairly shouted. "They've seen it. Running to the near perimeter—"

"Lances, fire," Lieter said reflexively, the observer behind him forgotten. "Navcom, forty percent forward. Railgun, mode 15. Fire on the run. Mills—is Alpha going to clear the halo?"

As he spoke, the six computer-targeted lances fired. Except as tracks on the strategy map, the stabbing bursts of energy from the lances were invisible. But the picket's telecams showed the result. Great rents opened along the curve of the black sphere as whole sections of the hull boiled away. The first Mizari intruder died quickly and quietly, transformed into a skeleton enveloped in a spreading cloud of molecular metal that had once comprised its integument and sinew.

"Alpha will not clear the halo," Mills said. "They know it, too—they're starting to use some sort of DE weapon to clear a path through."

Lieter's response was terse. "Lances, target Alpha at the projected point of exit. The moment they come through the halo, burn them."

"No need," Mills said. "They're at a bad angle for the pattern. They're not going to make it."

Even as she spoke, the tracks of the Mizari vessel and the halo intersected. Though the pellets were mere inert mass, the combined velocities of target and missile more than made up for any lack of explosives. A bright flower blossomed on the black face of the intruder, then a second and third. Tiny bits of matter flew in every direction. Then an explosion inside the intruder briefly lit the jagged entry holes, giving it the eerie aspect of a candlelit jack-o'-lantern.

A long moment passed, and then a tight cluster of pellets —five or more, Lieter thought, though it happened too quickly to be certain—stitched a line across what remained of the hull, cracking it open like an egg and spilling its contents into cold space. Almost at once the Alpha marker on Lieter's strategy map changed from red to green to signify it had been neutralized.

"Break, break," Lieter said. "All stations, stand down from battle mode. Navcom, let's go have a look at what we did."

There was a burst of happy, self-congratulatory chatter that moved from the comlines to the air as the bubbles of the bridge couches began to retract as one.

"Let's keep the celebration under wraps," Lieter rebuked sharply, looking for Wells as the couch's hold-downs released him. The Director was still standing where Lieter had last seen him, his gaze locked on the blank main display used other than during combat.

Clambering out of the couch, Lieter faced Wells and saluted. "FFI exercise completed, sir. I only wish those had been Mizari ships instead of drone mock-ups."

For several seconds Wells did not react, continuing to stare straight ahead as though he hadn't heard. Then he straightened and nodded in Lieter's direction.

"Be careful what you wish for, Captain. Open warfare with the Mizari is not something to be rushed into."

"I only meant—"

"At least you're not as reckless with your command as you are with your words," Wells continued. "After you've processed the data from the conflict recorders, we'll review the results in detail here. Pending that, please extend my appreciation to everyone involved for their efforts."

"Yes, Director," Lieter said, and saluted again as Wells flickered and vanished. Sensing someone at his elbow, Lieter turned to see Mills waiting for him. "Good work."

"Thank you, sir," she said, fluffing her hair where the head restraints had matted it. "Only, do you have any idea why they were so easy on us? They didn't throw us a single curve. We didn't even come under fire."

"If we had a need to know, they'd tell us," Lieter said, looking back to where the image of Wells had been. "But you can be sure they have their reasons."

Shaking his head and frowning, Harmack Wells stepped out of Telepresence Chamber 041. As he started down the corridor toward his office his adjutant, Teo Farlad, fell in beside him.

"A good exercise," Farlad said. "The crew performed well—"

"Means nothing," Wells said gruffly.

"It means the Defenders can do their job as advertised—"

"I needed a compelling demonstration for the Committee. I

got two big dumb targets that couldn't take a punch, much less throw one."

Farlad's face betrayed his puzzlement. "We gave the drones every reasonable capacity. Their battle computers weren't constrained—they just didn't make the halo and *Rampart* until it was too late."

"Is assuming the Mizari DE weapons couldn't break through the halo a reasonable assumption? Is assuming their ships were that vulnerable to our lances reasonable? The Chancellor isn't stupid. She knows when she's being flim-flammed."

"But, sir—we don't know what their weapons and defenses are capable of. There's no way to simulate—"

"For sixty million Coullars I expected more than target practice."

"There'll be more rehearsals, with other variables—"

"Hopefully some will resemble the real world. In the meantime we'll have to figure out how to sell that fantasy to the Committee." They were approaching the central hub of the USS-Central station, a nine-story open atrium filled with light and greenery.

"I do have some good news for you," Farlad said, eager to repair the damage. "It's why I met you—I was coming to tell you."

"So stop puffing yourself up and tell me," Wells said, squinting across the hub at a group of people walking toward the entrance to the Resource wing.

"I've come up with another Thackery document—"

"Hardly earthshaking news."

"This one is something special—something he wrote *after* he left the Service—"

"Put it in my private file and I'll have a look at it," Wells said, signaling for silence and stopping. "Isn't that Comitè Sujata?"

Farlad peered in the direction Wells pointed and fixed on a tall, long-limbed woman wearing a half blouse and hip wrap in the Maranit style. "Yes, sir. With Whitehall of the Arcturus research colony and his facilitator."

"I thought you were going to get back to me with some useful information on her."

"Her bio is as complete as I can make it—"

"I still need to know how she's likely to vote on Triad."

"She's gone with the majority on the monthly Defense appropriations."

"Not good enough. We haven't brought any new defense initiatives before the Committee in the six months she's been sitting on it. It doesn't require any special commitment to confirm the status quo."

"I gave her the Triad briefing material the second week she was here. But she's put off talking with me about it a half dozen times. Maybe if you approached her directly—"

Wells's answering tone was that of a man nearing the limits of his patience. "I don't expect her to be a factor. I just don't want any surprises. We go to the Committee Thursday. Have something for me by then."

Farlad swallowed hard. "Yes, sir."

"And come by my office as soon as Lieter relays the combat data. We'll take up the Ba'ar Tell matter then," he said, and walked away toward the Defense wing. Wearing an exasperated expression, Farlad watched him go, then started across the atrium in pursuit of Sujata.

The body language of the two combatants could not have been more different. Richard Whitehall, a bullnecked colony manager whose appearance was at odds with his prim antiquarian name, had taken over a chair in the Resource Director's office with the restless authority of a bear staking claim to his den. In the chair facing him, Janell Sujata sat lightly, legs crossed discreetly, hands fingertip-to-fingertip in her lap, a model of quiet self-assurance.

"I'm sorry," Sujata was saying. "That's simply the way things are."

"Tèrira pa nèti, par es," Whitehall said gruffly, locking his arms over his chest.

"The truth is, I would like very much to help you," Sujata continued in an even tone which implied she had not understood the Shinn curse, though she had. "But your problem isn't with Resource, it's with Defense. Every cargo packet in the octant is tied up with the buildup of Boötes Center and the Sentinel Support Node. There won't be any ships free to increase the frequency of the Arcturus packet runs until Defense releases them back to Transport."

Standing while the others sat, the short, round-bodied facilitator interposed himself physically as well as diplomatically between the Comitè and the Arcturus manager. "Mr. Whitehall noted that there was excess capacity in the Lupus Octant, and wondered if it wouldn't be possible to transfer one or more ships—"

Sujata smiled wanly. "If it were, Defense would take them as well. You have to understand that they have first claim on the resources of the Service."

"Mr. Whitehall would like you to understand that certain commitments were made to the Arcturus colonists as well."

"And those commitments are largely being met, through the Museum program—"

It was a measure of Whitehall's frustration that, though raised under Liam-Won's fiercely chauvinistic monarchy, he nevertheless addressed Sujata directly. "Is this what the Committee meant us to be, a dumping ground for broken-down ships and useless personnel?" he demanded. "Have we volunteered to be shuffled off and forgotten?"

Sujata was not cowed by Whitehall's accusing tone. "Mr. Whitehall, I should not have to be the one to remind you of the Arcturus project's history. The management of Boötes Center initiated your colony primarily as a means to increase their own ship traffic and accelerate the Center's growth. But Boötes Center is now under a military governor whose prime concern is the Mizari, not the health of the Arcturus colony on Cheia—"

The facilitator risked an interruption in the hopes of restoring decorum. "Mr. Whitehall is well versed in Cheia's history. His concern is for the present and the future."

"Then he would do well not to accuse his only friend at Unity of being his enemy," Sujata replied. "If my predecessor hadn't chosen Arcturus as the site for the Museum, Mr. Whitehall would have had far less help and much more to complain about. Or would he rather the colony were without the people and matériel the Museum ships brought out on their final voyages?"

The facilitator glanced nervously at Whitehall and read his expression. "Mr. Whitehall only wishes to make certain you understand that the present situation is not optimum."

"I understand that the lack of inbound traffic has affected Cheia's growth plan. But I repeat, your problem is primarily with Defense, indirectly with Transport, and ultimately with the Mizari."

"And that is all you are able to offer Mr. Whitehall?"

Sujata spread her hands wide, palms up. "That and my promise we'll continue sending mothballed ships to the Museum as fast as they come into our hands, with as long a cargo and passenger manifest as they'll bear. The Defense branch is building its own freighters even now. When they start to come on line, you should see an improvement in the packet schedule."

"Mr. Whitehall would be more at peace if that promise bore any specifics," the facilitator said gravely as Whitehall began to rise from his chair.

Though she did not seem to hurry, somehow Sujata was standing first. "Perhaps Mr. Whitehall would see the whole matter in a better light if he reminded himself that instead of being chosen to receive a unique asset like the Museum, Cheia might instead have been blessed with the Sentinel Support Node and all the interference from Defense that goes with it."

"Fècuma," Whitehall muttered as he moved past her. An impolitic smile tugged at one corner of Sujata's mouth, but she politely hid it behind one hand as she showed the men to the door.

Coming from Ba'ar Tell, it was inevitable that Wyrena Ten Ga'ar would find Unity Center overwhelming. The communal cabin on the packet *Moraji* had been a new enough experience in itself, but at least she had had the company of others from her own world on the first leg, to Microscopium Center.

M–Center was a greater shock, and one for which she had no cushion. The great space station, which had begun life as an Advance Base in the era of expansion, gave her her first taste of what her father disparagingly called Terran hive-living. Inevitably, Wyrena got lost repeatedly in M–Center's eighteen levels during the three-day layover, confused to the point of tears by the quad-level-sector address system and the maze of look-alike corridors.

From M–Center inbound to Unity, *Moraji* carried a more ethnically diverse group. Fully half the twenty beds were filled by Service staffers near Wyrena's own age. She found them loud, mannerless, and intimidating. Two Ba'ar men were aboard, one a minor official of the Centrality and the other a student. But neither was from her home city of Farnax, and though she would have been willing to forgo clan rules for conversation and companionship, they made clear that they were not.

Also aboard was a stiff-necked delegation from Daehne, whose attitude toward the rest of the passengers fluctuated between paranoia and condescension. Two of the Daehni made open sexual demands on Wyrena, which she escaped granting less because of her own will than because of the intervention of a member of the USS tutelary commission traveling with the Daehni.

"Nothing personal," the commissioner told her. "They just resent the fact that Ba'ar Tell has a Committee Observer and Daehne is still on the outside looking in. To get the best of a Ba'ar—especially a female—well, you understand."

After that Wyrena kept to herself, with little to do but think about the decision she had made, already afraid she had made the wrong choice. She smoothed over her fears by painting her trip as an adventure and turning her hoped-for reunion with Janell into a girlish fantasy. Someone who met the ship would know Janell, or know someone who did. Or perhaps Janell would even be there waiting, having found out somehow that she was coming—

But Unity was no outer world to which ships came calling only four or five times in a year, and where traditions of hospitality dictated each be received with high ceremony. *Moraji* was just another inbound packet, and the bewildered Ba'ar woman aboard her just another visitor. The harried-looking guest liaison who herded all the non-USS passengers through the terminal seemed far more interested in rushing them through processing than in welcoming them individually. After passing her identity and solvency checks, Wyrena was set free to fend for herself.

Despite having spent most of the last three days inbound planning what she would do, the next hours were better forgotten: it was the bustle and confusion of M–Center again, only worse. Her first act was to commandeer the first free com node she saw. Facing an unfamiliar technology, she gratefully and hopefully accepted the unit's patient prompts.

Then came the first surprise. On Ba'ar Tell no one who owned a talkwire ever left it unattended; etiquette demanded that someone answer every call. But Janell was "Page Off-line—Message Only."

"Where is she?" Wyrena asked plaintively. "When will she be back?"

But however humanlike the voice, she was talking with a machine, not a sympathetic house retainer. "The address is

UC-R-S100. No other data is available," the com node advised her. "Would you like to leave a message?"

Wyrena did not want Janell to hear the news that way, from a frozen voice caught in an electronic trap. She would wait until she could witness the reaction she could not predict.

"No message," she said.

"Thank you," the voice said sweetly.

Wyrena spent two hours wandering the lower levels of Unity in search for R-S100 before the forlorn expression etched into her face prompted another woman in the same lift to take pity on her. It was then she learned that she was looking in the wrong place. UC-R-S100 was an address not at Unity but at a satellite station trailing Unity in orbit by a few thousand klicks. *USS-Central, Resource Wing, Suite 100*.

Wyrena's benefactor helped her find the commuter node and get a seat on the twice-hourly UC shuttle. But then she was alone again. The canisterlike shuttle was claustrophobic, the view of the Earth from its window-simulating displays vertiginous, and the forty-minute flight almost unendurable.

When the shuttle finally docked, she followed the other passengers onto a spiral escalator. Three upward rotations later it delivered her into the middle of a towering atrium large enough to enclose the eight-story Counciliary Hall in Farnax. Dazzled by the architectural wonder surrounding her, several minutes passed before she noted the five great corridors corresponding to the Center's five spokes and the USS's five branches: Transport, Survey, Resource, Defense, and Operations. With tentative steps she crossed the atrium to the Resource wing and started down the central corridor.

Inside was a lift node, with its ranks of doors and electronic Directory. Beyond, a security station barred the way down the corridor. Beyond that, Wyrena saw a glass-walled waiting room where a woman sat working, a man sat waiting, and three office doors stood closed. The glass wall bore a perplexing legend:

SUITE 100

OFFICE OF THE DIRECTOR

USS-RESOURCE

Janell had been head of the USS office on Ba'ar Tell, but the circumstances under which she had left—could she be working for a Comitè now?

Confused, Wyrena summoned up her courage and stepped up to the security station. "I need to see Janell Sujata—"

"Show your card."

Wyrena did, hopefully.

The officer barely glanced at it. "Not cleared. Have an appointment?"

"No—"

"Would you like to request an appointment?"

At that moment one of the doors inside Suite 100 opened, and three figures emerged from the room beyond. The first two Wyrena did not know, but the one trailing behind—

"Janell!" Wyrena called out impulsively.

Sujata peered out through the glass, her face flashing annoyance at being addressed in public by her private name. Then she saw the woman standing by the Security desk, and the annoyance evaporated.

"Wyrena?" she exclaimed, disbelieving, and crossed the space between them with swift strides. "Wyrena!"

They hugged fiercely for a moment, wordlessly absorbing the sensory reality of each other, relearning familiar scents and softnesses. Then the men who had come out of the office with Sujata brushed by them in leaving, and the reminder of their presence brought on a spontaneous rush of self-consciousness. She pushed Sujata away, only to have her guilty impulse confirmed when she saw the frankly curious way the man seated in the waiting area was studying them.

Sujata caught the shamed look in her eyes and laughed. "This is Unity, not Ba'ar Tell," she said gaily. "You don't have to worry about offending people."

Pulling Wyrena close again, Sujata kissed her gently but knowingly, an unhurried, fullmouthed kiss of lovers separated and reunited. Eyes closed, Wyrena forgot her guilt, and this time it was Sujata who finally broke the embrace.

"Come on," Sujata said, taking the younger woman's hands. "My quarters are upstairs."

As they turned to go, the man who had been waiting stood.

"Comitè Sujata, I really must see you," he said in a clear, commanding voice. "Director Wells is very eager for your reaction to the materials I left with you last month."

At the man's tone Wyrena hesitated. But Sujata did not even look back. "Another time, Mr. Farlad," she called over her shoulder. "Another time."

• • •

There were a half dozen items queued up on the com register for Wells's attention: a progress report on construction of the new headquarters; a quarterly budget statement; the latest recon survey from the Sentinels; and other less urgent minutiae.

Relegating the rest to a holding file, Wells took a few minutes to review the recon survey. It was both the most important and the most predictable item on the list. He knew before starting that there would be no real news in it; were anything unusual to happen on the Perimeter he would be notified immediately and directly by means of the tiny transceiver implanted below his right ear.

As always, the first item in the report was the deployment update. Only eight of the ten Sentinels were on station; *Muschynka* and *Gnivi* were still in the yards at Lynx Center for general overhaul.

I'd love to replace all five of those old survey ships, Wells thought as he read on. *They were a poor bargain right from the start.*

Next came the rotation schedule for the Sentinels' twelve-person crews. The tender *Edmund Hillary* was en route with relief crews for *Maranit* and *Feghr*. All the other crews were well within the stringent fatigue criteria employed on the Perimeter.

The penultimate section dealt with the condition of the eight hundred listening buoys oriented toward the Ursa Major cluster and popularly known as the Shield. As might be expected with two Sentinels in port, the inspection schedule had slipped a bit, and an unusually high fifty-three buoys were abnominal in one parameter or another. But there was no pattern to the failures, nor any real gap in the coverage. The situation bore watching but did not justify heightened concern.

Lastly there was a summary of the data collected by the buoys. The buoys' receptors were capable of simultaneously and continuously monitoring everything from low-frequency radio on one end of the spectrum to microwaves at the other. The raw data was sieved in real-time against a long list of alarm triggers, then relayed via dedicated Kleine links to the Strategic Data Center, which occupied two levels of the Defense wing.

What finally reached Wells was a list of anomalies, tagged

by time and buoy, along with the explanation for each and a rating of the degree of confidence with which that explanation was proffered. In this instance, as was generally the case, it was a short list. By now the only real secrets of the quarantined zone were those that lay beyond the capacities of the receptors.

Foremost among them the Mizari themselves.

Somewhere in the Ursa Major moving cluster, the Sterilizers waited. Almost certainly the suns of the Mizar-Alcor system—the Horse and the Rider of Arabian astronomy, the traditional test for acuity of vision—shone bright in their sky, but they might call other worlds home, as well, worlds orbiting Alioth or Merak or Megrez or Phad. Even the most far-flung members of the cluster, in Draco and Leo Minor and Ursa Minor, could by now be host to the murderous Mizari. On the star map in the Committee Chamber, all sixteen members of the cluster were black-flagged.

Wells could not think of the Mizari without surrendering at least part of his conscious energies to a well-considered and deeply rooted antipathy. It had been sixty thousand years since humans and Mizari had last had contact, but for Wells that dusty history was as vivid and immediate as if he had witnessed it. The vast span of time only heightened his outrage at a crime so long left unavenged.

With no more provocation than the appearance of a single Weichsel iceship near their triple binary system, the black star of the Mizari had struck back across the light-years and destroyed the human civilization now known as the Founders. The punishment was so out of proportion to the offense that Wells could find no way to rationalize it. It had been deliberate, cold-blooded, unblinking genocide, an attempt to erase from existence an entire sentient species. Had the Mizari known of the colonies started by the Weichsel explorers, the attempt would doubtless have been successful.

And had it not been for Merritt Thackery's pursuit of, and contact with, the ethereal D'shanna and the revelations that resulted, the foraging survey ships would inevitably have blundered into Mizari space once more and given the bastards a second chance.

Which we will never give you, Wells vowed. *Never again will we allow ourselves to be victimized.*

But it was a vow that was still mostly bluster. No one knew

better than Wells how precarious the strategic situation was. No one knew better than he what a woeful misnomer it was to call the elliptical array of buoys a Shield. It was psychologically appealing, and the geometry of their deployment even suggested such a shape. But the elements of the Shield were unarmed and completely passive, mere receptors for the energies that reached them and the information that might thereby be gleaned. Even active radar was considered too risky, too intrusive.

The Sentinels, which looked after the buoys as shepherds might look after sheep, were warships only in name. Carrying only a single-barreled railgun and a single terawatt lance turret each, they might hold their own in a duel against ships of their own kind, but in cold truth were little more imposing than a shepherd waving his wooden staff.

Put bluntly, if the Sterilizers came out now, USS-Defense would be helpless to stop them. That fact had become the unifying focus of Wells's life, gnawing at him and driving him on. He was ashamed of the timidity forced on him by the weakness of the Unified Worlds, furious at those who refused to see the threat. The specter of the Sterilizers cast a shadow over everything that humankind was and did, and nothing was more important than beating back the darkness.

"Busy?" a cheery voice asked, intruding on Wells's brooding. Even without looking, Wells knew who his visitor was—the distinctive tenor voice and presumptuous entrance were sufficient identification. Wells reflexively purged the screen of his terminal, then settled back in his chair with his hands folded in his lap.

"Observer Berberon," Wells said. "What a surprise. What brings you over from Unity?"

Felithe Berberon beamed, as though merely being recognized was the highest form of flattery. "Oh, this, that, the little details that so fill up one's calendar. But when I heard, I had to come up and congratulate you."

Wells's gaze narrowed. "Congratulate me on what?"

"Why, on your successful test of the Defenders, of course. I'm sure the Committee is going to be delighted with the news—you're ahead of schedule and I'll wager you're under budget as well. Excellent, simply excellent."

Working to keep a scowl off his face, Wells replied. "I'm

glad you're pleased. We're ready to declare the Defenders operational, in fact." It was bad enough to be reminded that he had thus far been unable to ferret out Berberon's sources inside Defense, but Wells had no patience for Berberon's endless ingratiatory chatter.

"Of course, I understand perfectly," Berberon was saying, "though I understand the attack drones didn't put up much of a fight, did they? Still, I assume you'll have some spectacular video of the war for Thursday's Committee meeting?"

What nerve, Wells thought, and almost said. *I don't care how many years you've been here, you're only an Observer. You can't even vote on appropriations.*

But the liquid-voiced senior member of the Terran Observer Delegation had some influence on the Committee— there was no doubt about that. Even if you never knew exactly where he really stood, there was no point in going out of your way to offend him. No matter how smarmy he was—

"If we can put it together by then, and the agenda allows," Wells said.

"Oh, I'll see that there's time for you. Count on it," Berberon promised breezily. "Well, I won't keep you, Harmack. See you Thursday."

Swallowing his spittle, Wells nodded acknowledgment as the door closed on Berberon. He allowed enough time for Berberon to clear the outer office, then touched a contact on his terminal. "Lieutenant Holloway? Have someone find out who Berberon talked to before he came here. Get on it right now."

"Another leak, Director?"

"Yes, another leak, goddamnit," Wells said, scowling. "And I want it plugged fast, before something important gets compromised."

chapter 2

In the
Private Heart

After the spontaneous moment of reunion, there was awk-
wardness. Though she hated herself for it and strove not to
show it, Sujata found that Wyrena's reappearance in her life
felt like an intrusion. However warmly remembered, the Ba'ar
woman was part of a life episode already put away as complete. She belonged there, on Ba'ar Tell, in the past. Not here.

There was no mistaking that Wyrena was uncomfortable,
too. All the way to Sujata's quarters, Wyrena was on the
verge of blurting out either an apology or an explanation. The
same insecurity that prompted the urge quelled it.

But alone, naked in each other's arms, they rediscovered
the wordless communion which they had known on Ba'ar Tell.
The erotic glow enfolded them and carried them off to a private place. And after, with the distance between them erased,
talk came more easily.

"I shouldn't have come." The words were said in a small
voice muffled by the pillow into which Wyrena's face was
pressed, as if they were not really meant to be heard.

Sujata smiled to herself and shifted so that she could reach
out and stroke the bare skin of Wyrena's back. "Why not?"

"I couldn't know you'd become this important—"

"Nor could I," she said, remembering. The whole structure

of the Service had changed while she was in the high craze to Unity, and, with it, the selection procedures for the high staff positions. "But what does that have to do with us?"

"They'll use me against you—you'll lose influence—"

Sujata understood the younger woman's distress. Ba'ar Tell was a world of rigid rules and roles. There was no place for the kind of relationship she and Wyrena had enjoyed, and, in the end, that was what had separated them.

"That isn't how things work here," Sujata said, tracing small circles with her forefinger at the base of Wyrena's spine.

"The way that man glared at us—"

"What, Whitehall? He's from Liam-Won. There isn't much he approves of here."

Wyrena rolled on her side and propped her head on her hand. "But this isn't your home, either. Are you sure you really know these people?"

Sujata sought Wyrena's hand with her own. "This place is not without its prejudices. But the people who matter understand that who I share my bed with doesn't affect how I do my job. And the others can't reach us. No one will pressure you here. No one will judge."

Wyrena looked away, and Sujata knew that they had reached a delicate area. "My father was not wrong to do what he did," Wyrena said at last. "He could not have done otherwise."

"What about me?" Sujata asked. "Were you angry with me for agreeing to leave?"

"No—oh, no. If you didn't leave, my family's position would have been damaged terribly."

"But no one outside the family knew—"

"In time they would have," Wyrena said soberly. "Besides, even if you had stayed, we never could have seen each other. Just as we never got to say good-bye."

"You allow him that much power over you, simply because you were living in his house—"

"You don't understand. He would have forbidden it, and I would have had to obey him. I was bound just as he was."

"You said you loved me." This was said in a teasing, testing voice.

"Oh, Janell—I do. But even for you—"

"Conflict is hard for you to deal with."

"Conflict is the consequence of selfishness."

It had the sound of an epigram, and it was one. "The Philosopher's First Canon."

"Yes. A very early lesson in my schooling."

"So, then, why did you leave?"

Wyrena was slow to answer, as though there were still some uncertainty in her own mind. "Because I missed you. And because I wanted to know what it was like to live outside the rules, the way you did. A Ba'ar woman's dreams are for her mate and sons. I wanted to dream for myself."

Sujata opened her arms, and Wyrena came to her. They cuddled close, the feel of skin against skin comforting. "Ever since I left, I've been afraid," Wyrena said. "Afraid that I'd waited too long and I'd find you gone, headed for some other world or outpost, and I'd never catch up. Afraid that you wouldn't want me—that I hadn't been as important to you as you'd been to me. I never was able to tell you—"

"Your mouth was otherwise occupied," Sujata teased. "No, go on, finish."

"I had never met anyone like you. No woman on Ba'ar Tell can ever hope to be self-minded the way you are. You know the word they use—"

"Ka'ila'in."

"And it's not only the men who would call you that but the women too. The reason they curse the *ka'ila'in* so harshly is that they are afraid of them, for different reasons. But I thought you were wonderful—"

"I never felt that from them—"

"You are not Ba'ar. You were allowed to be different," she said, and kissed the curve of Sujata's right breast. "No, if I were going to be angry with you, it would be for refusing to understand how great the risk was. Do you see why I'm loath to take your word that neither of us can be hurt for the same thing here? Are we really safe, Janell, or is it just that you wish we were, like on Ba'ar Tell?"

Sujata's fingers played in the soft hair streaming down Wyrena's back. "We're safe, Wy—from others. We can still hurt each other if we're cruel or careless or fall out of love."

"I won't let that happen."

"Nor I," she said, and kissed her forehead. "But explain, please—how were you able to leave? Surely your father objected—"

"Oh, but he didn't—because appearances were maintained. My father knew my feelings but never acknowledged them to me. Still, without a word being said, he saw that everything was taken care of. You see, I left, not in disgrace, but with honor. I came at the invitation of Ambassador Wen, who promised me a place in his office."

Sujata wrinkled her nose, puzzled. "But Wen is gone—Elir Ka'in is the Ba'ar Observer now. Surely your father knew how much time would pass. Ba'ar Tell is nearly fifty cees out—"

"Of course he knew."

"So he kicked you out."

"But gracefully and with my needs considered."

"Amazing, the games you Ba'ar play."

Wyrena smiled. "We have an art for compromise and accommodation which you never did understand."

"There's something in the Canons about that, isn't there?"

"A great deal of something," Wyrena said. "I knew you weren't listening when I explained it."

"Because you were distracting me at the same time," Sujata said playfully. "Now you'll have more time to teach me."

Wyrena laughed in her throaty way. "Especially since there is no place waiting in the Ba'ar Tell Observer's office."

"I shouldn't have much trouble finding something for you if you want."

Wyrena lifted her head to look into Sujata's eyes. "Must I?"

"No. But if not that, then what?"

"If I could just stay here—be here for you—not have to face them—would that be all right?"

"There's no reason to hide from them—you said you wanted to live outside the rules, didn't you? But if that's what you want—"

"It is," Wyrena said, and snuggled closer.

The next morning, Wells found Farlad waiting for him in his office anteroom. The adjutant came to his feet as Wells came through the outer door, then followed him into the inner office.

"Expected to see you yesterday," Wells said as he disappeared momentarily into the kitchenette. He reappeared a moment later with a glass of ice water in one hand. "What happened?"

"Operations was having trouble with the Kleine transmissions—the data didn't come in clean until just a few hours ago."

Wells's forehead became creased with concern. "What kind of trouble?"

"Noise. Interference. Dropped bits. The error algorithms had a busy night."

Frowning, Wells settled into his chair. "I don't like that. I don't like that at all. Reliable Kleine communications are key to our battle command and control. Were you given any explanation for the problem?"

"No, sir. According to the senior comtech, they don't know why it's been happening."

"Been happening? Then this isn't a one-time problem?"

"Apparently not, sir. She said it's been cropping up more and more often, especially in the octants where there's a lot of ship traffic."

"Which means Boötes and Lynx."

"Among others."

"That's even more disturbing," Wells said, his expression grim. "If we were to lose the ability to communicate with the Perimeter—I want a full report on this fast. How often it happens, how long it lasts—everything. If we can't put an end to it, we may have to revise our C3 procedures."

"Yes, sir. I'll put in the request."

Wells settled back in his chair. "So what about the Ba'ar Tell exercise? Have you figured out yet why I'm not impressed?"

"Frankly, sir, no. The Defenders are tough little warships. I'd hate to have to lead an attack against them."

"I'm not impressed because that exercise was a fantasy. We weren't attacking the Mizari, we were attacking ourselves." Wells touched a contact and activated his terminal. "I'm not the only one that recognizes it, either. Berberon was in here yesterday and got in a few digs about us beating up on straw men."

"Berberon? How did he find out about the test?"

"That's a separate problem. The point is, he wasn't impressed." Wells leaned forward and rested his elbows on the desk. "Teo, my predecessor in this office made a career out of underestimating the Mizari. I wouldn't like to see you repeating his error."

Farlad took a seat across from Wells. "I'm afraid I don't

quite understand your thinking. If you're convinced the Defenders can't fulfill their mission, why did you continue the program? Why did you accelerate deployment if you don't believe there's any strategic value?"

"Not all strategies are directed against the enemy," Wells said quietly. With a sideways glance he scanned the columns of numbers that had appeared on the display. "I think perhaps we can carry this off, Berberon notwithstanding."

Comprehension dawned on Farlad's face. "The Committee—"

"If I were to have come in four years ago and scrapped the Defenders, telling the Committee that they were useless, we would have been forced to spend the next twenty years building something to replace them."

"I still don't see the value—"

"Consider the deployment of the Defenders. Three for Earth. Two for Journa. One each for Ba'ar Tell and Maranit and Rena-Kiri."

"Protecting the five most populous Worlds," Farlad said slowly. "All of which are represented by Observers. And if the Observers believe that their home worlds are safe—"

Smiling faintly, Wells interrupted. "Only when they feel safe will they allow us to focus on building a weapons system that would allow us to carry the fight to the Mizari."

"Triad." Farlad shook his head. "I always thought it was a little crazy to base a Defender at Ba'ar Tell, way out in one of the safe octants, before we placed one at Liam-Won, practically in the Mizari's backyard. Now I see—Liam-Won has sixty-one million inhabitants, while Ba'ar Tell has well over a billion."

"That was one consideration," Wells said, nodding. "Another is that while Ambassador Ka'in is well liked and respected, Prince Denzell is an obnoxious prig who has even alienated Comitè Vandekar, his planet-kin."

"So while on the one hand we assure enough votes to approve Triad," Farlad mused, "at the same time we make clear that it's good to be our friend."

"Just so."

"The only thing that puzzles me is that Triad can't have any deterrent value unless we reestablish contact with the Mizari. And even if we do reestablish contact, we don't know what level of threat would be a deterrent to them."

"We can be sure the Defenders would not be," Wells said,

then paused. "But you're right—we simply have to learn more about the Mizari. We can't be confident that we're secure until we do."

"Director Lycom was considering a proposal to send drift probes into the quarantine zone—"

"And then cower behind the Sentinel line for another two hundred years, waiting for them to reach Mizar-Alcor? That might have been fine for Lycom but not for me. Don't trouble yourself to mention it again." Wells's answer was reflexive rather than angry; he was staring past Farlad with an unfocused gaze, most of his attention elsewhere.

"No, sir," Farlad said. "Comitè, have you read *Jiadur's Wake* yet?"

"Hmm?"

"Thackery's book. I told you about it yesterday."

"No."

"I really urge you to take a look at it soon. There are some perspectives in it we haven't seen anywhere else in the record—"

"Suggestion noted," Wells said, returning from his reverie and straightening up in his chair. "When will the video abstract of the Ba'ar Tell exercise be ready for prescreening?"

"It's being edited now. Should be no more than another hour or so."

"I'll want to see it as soon as possible. We need to make it easy for the Committee to say yes to Triad."

"I'll go down and check on it as soon as we're finished here."

"I think we're finished. Oh—what about Sujata?"

"I haven't been able to see her." Farlad held up his hands as though to fend off criticism. "Not my fault. She hasn't been in her office since midday yesterday. But that doesn't mean I don't have something new to tell you about her. I'm not sure that it'll be of any practical value, but let me tell you what's been occupying her. . . ."

Felithe Berberon frowned to himself and stared down at the hallway floor as he waited, listening to the chimes sound on the far side of the apartment door. *Why did the Chancellor want to see me here*? he wondered. *The last time I was here was the party Chancellor Delkes threw after resigning—was that seven years ago or eight*?

The soft whir of the security camera brought his head up

again, and he flashed a vacant smile in its direction. A moment later the lock unlatched with a buzz, and Berberon stepped forward and into the apartment.

Inside, it was about as he had expected, considering the personality of its occupant: elegant, practical, uncrowded. Unlike some of her predecessors, the Chancellor clearly maintained the suite as a comfortable retreat, not a showplace for entertaining. Other than the sheer size of the suite, the only real touch of luxury was the viewpit, with its cushion sculpture and floor-to-ceiling windows, which occupied the far end of the rectangular greatroom. *Arvade had that installed,* he recalled fondly. *I was young enough to enjoy it then.*

"Hello, Felithe," said Chancellor Blythe Erickson as she crossed the greatroom toward him, her white silk caftan flowing gracefully with her strides. She locked fingers with him in the formal greeting that said "equal," stepped close to brush her cheek against his in a gesture that amended it to "friend," then turned away.

"Thank you for coming up tonight," she said, recrossing the room and retrieving a glass half filled with ice and an amber liquid.

"Is there enough of that for two?"

She gestured at the bar. "You're welcome to choice of the house, so long as you promise not to compromise your judgment. I need you at your best tonight."

Berberon smiled. "Since alcohol works only on the higher brain functions, I am hardly in any danger."

"You are immodest in your modesty." Pausing, she stared through the bottom of her glass at the floor. "Felithe, I'm about to tell you some things you are not supposed to know, because I need to ask your opinion. Do you have any objection to my doing that?"

"No—except it may not be necessary. I find I know many things I am not supposed to know."

"Does the catalog include something called Triad?"

"A rather large entry, I am embarrassed to admit."

Erickson shook her head and smiled wryly. "I might have expected it. You always know things that no one else does."

He bowed in mock ceremony. "One of the few and decidedly minor compensations for having been here thirty-five years."

With her drink replenished and his drawn fresh, they settled in the viewpit. The Chancellor settled gracefully on the padded floor near the center window, knees together and bare feet tucked beneath her. Berberon sat uncomfortably cross-legged opposite her.

"How can I help you, Blythe?"

"I believe that Wells is planning to bring the Triad proposal before the Committee tomorrow."

That rumor was not meant for your ears, Berberon thought. Someone has been indiscreet. "I would not be surprised if that were true," he said, nodding.

"Do you know how the vote will go?"

"How can I say, Madame Chancellor? I am only an Observer, not a Director. I cannot even vote myself."

"Now you dissemble too much. Surely you have a sense of their leanings—"

"No better or worse than your own." He hesitated, then added, "I must tell you that when it happens, tomorrow or another day, I will myself speak in favor."

"Felithe! Why?"

He shrugged at her expression of dismay. "You know that Wells has many friends, friends who are in a position to cause the Terran Council a great deal of grief."

"It seemed to me that the Nines have been quiet lately. Are they still a problem?"

"The Nines will be a problem until they grow up or die off," Berberon said with uncommon depth of feeling. "They are arrogant, self-important elitists who've decided they will only tolerate sharing Earth with their inferiors if they themselves are in charge." Checking his outburst, he smiled sheepishly. "Forgive me. You did not ask me here to listen to me carry on about matters that are outside your concern."

"Yet it seems that your problems with the Nines affect us here."

"They affect my public posture only. I cast no vote in Committee. It's your Directors who will decide whether Wells gets what he is asking for, and you after them."

"I'd hoped to enlist you to speak against him. Or at least to offer him no support."

Berberon lifted his hands in a gesture of helplessness. "How can I? My charge is to befriend him, to assist him in obtaining what he wants. Thus the Council hopes to buy off the Nines and focus their attention elsewhere. And there are other considerations as well. Thirty percent of Earth's industrial product is related to Defense expenditures. Wells's buildup has helped us considerably."

"So to keep the money flowing and the workers busy, you would give a man who feels as Wells does that kind of power—"

"Alone he is not a threat to our interests," Berberon said softly. "Collectively the Nines are."

Erickson pressed her body back into the cushions and stared out the window, as though seeking to withdraw from him. "I invited Felithe Berberon to my apartment, but it seems I got the Terran Observer to the Committee instead. Can you never speak for yourself?"

Sighing, Berberon drained his glass and set it aside. "My own thoughts are irrelevant. I've survived here this long because I obediently advocate what I am told to advocate."

"Even when you disagree?"

Berberon cocked an eyebrow and shrugged. "If my wisdom were better thought of, I would be *on* the World Council, not representing it."

"Felithe, please—am I wrong to mistrust Wells? To want this weapon never to come into existence?" There was honest anguish in her voice.

It was Berberon's turn to stare out the window as he carefully composed an answer. "I am convinced that Wells is sincerely interested in the security of the Unified Worlds. If I may revive an archaic word, he is a patriot. That is both his strength and his weakness. As for Triad—perhaps it is my age that makes me so fearless. I hope the Mizari are gone, extinct thousands of years ago. But if they are not, I would like to know that we will fare better against them the second time."

"Then your own beliefs are not so far from official policy as you might have wanted me to think."

Berberon's smile was rueful. "In this instance, perhaps not, after all."

Eyes downcast, Blythe drew her knees up to her chest and hugged them. "I suppose I've known this has been coming since he joined the Committee." She raised her head and met Berberon's gaze. "Thank you for coming by, Ambassador. You can see yourself out?'

She seemed lonely; perhaps that was inevitable for one in her position. If he were a younger man, or a different kind of man, he might have stayed and tried to fill that need. But it was not the kind of thing Felithe Berberon did, not the kind of relationship he formed. He had learned that lesson decades ago: that as expediency demanded, he could find himself tomorrow lining up against a friend made today. Knowing that, he had kept his distance and been rewarded for his discipline. Through the years Chancellors and Directors alike came and went, while Berberon carried on just the same, his tenure unprecedented and unequalled.

But as he left the executive complex, a part of him wondered against his will whether he knew how to stop playing the role in which he had submerged himself for so long, and whether he would have had what Erickson needed within him to give.

"Archive," Erickson said softly, curled up alone in the viewpit of her darkened apartment.

"Ready," answered the netlink.

"Terran history. Nines. Statement of purpose. Exclude references previously accessed. Primary sources if available."

"No contemporary primary sources available. I have twenty-four speeches by founder Eric Lange from his campaign for supervisor of Sudamerica District 5."

"Oldest entry. Context."

"Year 610 A.R. A public rally in Montevideo, Sudamerica. Estimated attendance, six thousand. Source of reference, Earthnet polinews archive."

"Show me," Erickson said, settling back firmly against the cushions.

The greatroom lights dimmed further, and a flatscreen video element in the viewpit's broad window came to life. "There were warnings," the image of Eric Lange said to the overflow crowd in the seedy public hall. "William Clifford, a man who would be here tonight had he not lived nearly a thousand years ago, a man who was in every way one of us, saw what was coming.

"'A race which is fixed, persistent in form, unable to change,' he said, 'is surely in peril of extinction. It is quite possible for conventional rules and habits to get such power that progress is impossible, and the race is fit only for death. In the face of such a danger, it is not right to be proper!'

"Clifford was right—but no one listened. We went on taxing the winners so that losers could be made equal. We went on legitimizing the claims of the have-nots and would-nots and could-nots. We went on elevating mediocrity. And we taught our children that that was what it meant to be civilized."

There was a light in Lange's eyes that seemed to burn through Erickson's objective remove, and his voice had the compelling power of honest conviction. A powerful speaker, yes, but no demagogue, she thought. Every word spoken from the heart, every idea the product of introspection—

"They will ask us what we stand for," Lange said. "We will tell them. We believe in survival." He was cheered.

"They will ask us what we want. We will tell them. We want the freedom to grow." The cheers resounded.

"They will ask us what we offer. We will tell them. We offer change—change for the better if we can, but if not, then change for its own sake. We have a right to live in interesting times. We have a right to struggle, and if we are worthy, to greatness."

The audience told him, with six thousand massed voices, that they agreed. Lange smiled an uncomfortable, embarrassed smile and waited for them to quiet.

"They will ask us our name," he began again softly. "And we will tell them. We are the not-average. We are the non-followers." As he continued, his voice rose, and the sound of voices crying "Yes" rose with it to reach a roar. "We are the un-mediocre. We are the movers. We are the dreamers. We are the builders and planners. We mastered fire. We invented writing. And we colonized the stars. We are the Nines. We are the Nines. And we will not be denied our birthright."

The images played in Erickson's mind long after she closed the archive file and shut off the netlink. It was still "tonight" for Lange, still the pinnacle of his triumph. There was no hint there of what would come just three months later.

How would it be different if you hadn't been killed, if those who reacted to your message with fear instead of cheers hadn't dragged you from your house and silenced you? she wondered. *At the very least the Nines wouldn't have felt the need to go underground, and we would have known who we were fighting.*

Would you have approved of them as they are now? Would you have embraced the same goals? I hear the origins of their agenda in your words—it's all there. But is what they want what you wanted? I believe you truly meant to lift us up, but what they do promises to drag us down—

• • •

Tipping back his head, Wells drained the tall glass of ice water, then refilled it and drank half. As he wiped his mouth with the back of his hand, he noted the clock and was surprised to see that it read 20:40.

Returning to his seat, Wells viewed one last time the seven-and-a-half-minute unnarrated clip of the Ba'ar Tell FFI exercise. The first edit had been too slick, too theatrical—too patently intended to end all debate over the Defender's effectiveness. This one, the third, was better: the overview of the Defender system and strategy he had ordered added at the beginning made everything that followed more effective.

"Save," Wells said. "File to Wells, Defense Archives, Committee Chamber. Level One voice-lock."

"Done," replied the terminal.

Now—what else needs my attention before I leave? He ran through a mental list as precise and complete as if it had been written down and came up with only one item: Farlad's new Thackery document. *I'll give it ten minutes,* Wells thought. *That probably will be enough.*

But first he touched the com key. "Ronina."

The terminal needed no more guidance than that. On its own it quickly sought out her com address from his directory and placed the call. When she came on, her voice contained a gratifying note of surprise and pleasure. "Mack—how nice. I've been hoping you hadn't crossed me off your list."

That was one of Ronina's few unattractive features—her propensity for prompting him for reassurance, for setting him up to offer some verbal endorsement of her status. As he usually did, he ignored the cue. "I'll be done here in a little while—"

"I'll take that as an invitation," she purred. "Do you want to come here or should I go up to your apartment?"

"Mine, I think."

"I'll be waiting for you—and thinking wicked thoughts."

Then, clearing the screen of his notes for the next day's presentation, Wells called up his private files, an act that required voice-password and retinal identification. There was a brief pause as the decryptor failed to keep pace with the system's file retrieval speed, and then the menu popped up on the screen.

The file was named, unambiguously, MERRITT THACKERY. Shortly after becoming Director of Defense, Wells had begun a search of Service records for any and all anecdotal accounts by Thackery of his encounter with the D'shanna he called Gabriel and of what Thackery saw while on the spindle.

There turned out to be hundreds of such documents. It was impossible to believe that anyone anywhere had ever been more intensively interviewed and debriefed than had Thackery after his return from the spindle. There were literally thousands of hours of interviews: normal, under time-expansion hypnosis, and using endorphin memory-enhancement therapy. Had Service physicians known how to dissect Thackery's brain and suck out the memories directly, Wells did not think they would have hesitated to do so.

The documents told Wells what every schoolchild knew, and little more. Then in the drive core of the shattered Survey ship *Dove,* Gabriel had reached out from the spindle and taken Thackery back with him across the barrier. That from the vantage of the energy matrix of the spindle, Gabriel showed Thackery the echoes of the ice-age Earth-based civilization that had founded the heretofore inexplicable human colonies.

Traveling downtime on the spindle, Thackery witnessed the Mizari's savage attack on the Weichsel civilization. He learned the danger that awaited in the Ursa Major cluster, and he brought that warning back to the matter-matrix, once thought the only reality. And in doing so he had become the best-known personage in human history. Thackery's miraculous translocation persuaded the skeptics, as it had the Survey brass, that the story he told was not fantasy, however fantastic.

But the things that Wells wanted most to find, even needed to find, simply were not there. There were no details about the Mizari, no glimpse of their world or even themselves, no hint of what moved them or, even more importantly, what their vulnerabilities might be. Not trusting the task to anyone else, Wells had plowed his way through more than two thirds of the documents in a search for even a handful of clues about the Mizari.

He had not found even one.

Farlad's flagnote for *Jiadur's Wake* indicated that it had been written after Thackery's retirement and represented the last contact between the Service and the onetime Director of the Survey Branch. When Thackery had offered the text to the Earthnet for distribution, they had routinely referred it to the Committee for clearance. Clearance had been summarily denied—and rightly so, Wells saw immediately—on grounds of executive privilege and internal security.

It began:

I am Merritt Thackery. If you think you know me, you do not. I have seen the videos of my life, and it was not so. The creators of those images grafted the places and faces of my life onto another person, a stronger, more self-confident person, a person who might well have been due the acclaim that I have accrued. That person was admirable, even heroic, and his story entertaining. But it was not me, and it was not my story.

When I returned to Earth, I was asked what I did, and I told them. I was asked what I saw, and I told them. But I was never asked what I felt, and when I offered it myself, there was little interest. Somehow that was deemed not worthy of study, or thought too subjective to be trustworthy. What they wanted, and therefore what they got, was the testimony of a witness, not the experiences of a man.

So the story that the Service eventually released, and the creative talents of the Nets transmogrified, was but the skeleton of truth, lacking the sinew of emotion to animate it, the tissue of humanity to smooth over the awkward joints. The truth is this: What I did could have been done as well by another. And there have been times when I wished that it had been.

If you prefer your histories simple and your heroes untarnished, read no farther. But if you prefer the truth, whatever shape it takes, then read on, for it is for you that I have written this.

Farlad was right—I've found you at last, Wells thought with satisfaction. He touched the com key. "Ronina."

"I'm here, sweet. Will you be long?" She answered in video mode, posing before the terminal in a translucent cat suit that revealed creamy white skin down nearly to her nipples and hid very little elsewhere.

But even that sight was insufficient inducement to change his mind. "Go home. I won't be coming back to the apartment, after all," he said, and cued forward to the first chapter.

chapter 3

Sword

It was nearly four in the morning when Wells finished reading. He had moved from the desk to a couch and traded the fixed terminal for a hand-held slate. His eyes were weary, and when he set the slate aside, he dimmed the room's lights for their sake. But he was nowhere near sleep, for his mind was full of what he had just read.

The tone of the manuscript was mocking, cynical, almost embittered. Despite it, or perhaps because of it, *Jiadur's Wake* sang, and Wells had found himself drawn in.

Though not strictly chronological, most of the first half of the text dealt with the early history of the Service, beginning with the Reunion of Earth with its daughter world, Journa, and continuing through the Revision, which had closed out the Phase II explorations in which Thackery had taken part.

His portrait of the Service was blunt and unflattering, pointing up the flaws and foibles of both the organization as a whole and the individuals who comprised it. But he was no more kind to himself. Speaking frankly of his initial lack of commitment, his later selfishness, his subsequent obsession, Thackery laid waste to his own popular image as a self-directed hero.

Wells was not obliged to accept Thackery's own harsh appraisal of his worth. Clearly Thackery had succumbed in his later years to the imposter syndrome, that self-destructive suspicion that one's success is due to luck and accident, not personal merit. Even great men grow weary, Wells thought.

But Wells accepted enough of Thackery's self-deprecation at face value to lay to rest a nagging puzzle. From the time he first began to study Revision history, Wells had been haunted by the conviction that there was more to the story than was being told.

Wells could not believe that Thackery had not demanded to see the Mizari homeworld, to divine their nature. All he would have had to do is look out from the spindle and he would have seen them, as he had seen what they had done to Earth, as he had seen the death of the Weichsel ship, which in turn had brought on the death of the Weichsel. Thackery must have done so; the Service must be concealing what he learned. Of that Wells had been certain.

That certainty had been one of several motivations that had led him to a career in the USS. If there was more to learn, the Service was the natural custodian of that knowledge. To share in it, he would have to become one of them. To learn, then, that even the Service knew nothing more had only compounded his consternation. The months-long search through the Thackery file had been motivated by the hope that they contained data lost or overlooked.

Now, as Thackery the man rewrote Thackery the legend, it was easier to understand. Thackery had been afraid. He had been overwhelmed by what he had seen—no shame in that, surely!—and his time on the spindle had been cut short by his own inability to deal with the revelations granted to him. Consequently the things that Wells needed to learn, Thackery had never known.

But the D'shanna knew. Looking out from the energy-matrix that flowed from the universe's beginning and guaranteed its end, the D'shanna could provide perfect knowledge of the Mizari: what they were, where they were, and how they could be dealt with. The D'shanna could do at any time what Thackery had failed to do in his only opportunity.

Yet in the century and a half since the Revision, no such collaboration had taken place. Thackery had reported that of all the D'shanna only Gabriel had taken note of the human species and an interest in its plight. And Gabriel had been crippled by the time of his encounter with Thackery and thereafter had either "died" or gone far uptime on the spindle to rejoin his own kind and replenish himself. Either way, Gabriel was beyond reach.

These were the givens: that Thackery's experience had been unique and unrepeatable and that the D'shanna could not be counted on to do any more than they already had.

But *Jiadur's Wake* told Wells that Thackery's feelings toward the D'shanna had not been sufficiently taken into account. One passage near the end illumed that more clearly than the rest:

> . . . Somehow, because of our need for heroes, I have been credited for that which Gabriel did. If there was sacrifice, the greater sacrifice by far was his, for he owed us no loyalty save that which his morality imposed upon himself. For that reason, if there was nobility, it was Gabriel's, not mine. My interests were selfish, his selfless. The human race has never had a better friend. Nor have I.

> For, while I was on the spindle, Gabriel and I were intimate in a way that I had never before nor have ever since experienced with another human. It was a quality of relationship that is beyond depiction, beyond description, just as the spindle itself cannot be understood solely in terms of the matter-matrix. Without masks or barriers or deceptions each grasped and accepted the essence of the other. It was the purest moment of my life, a high, clear note of joy.

> Gabriel gave us life, knowledge, and identity, perhaps at the cost of his own. And I, our feeble ambassador, was able to give him nothing in return. . . .

Wells had been searching for what had been overlooked, not hidden. None of the memory aids used in Thackery's debriefing could make a man say what he did not want to say. It was assumed throughout that Thackery was a willing subject, eager to share everything that he knew.

But was that true?

A dark suspicion was forming in Wells's mind, a slippery, shadowy thought that resisted his efforts to dislodge it. *Where were your loyalties, Thackery? What didn't you tell us? Perhaps that you could call Gabriel at will? Did you think to protect him from further demands, or perhaps insure that no one would intrude on that most perfect relationship with that most empathic mind?*

It was a shocking, almost treasonous thought—that Merritt Thackery, the most outstanding figure in Service history, the architect of the Revision, had been compromised by divided loyalties, had held back information because of the bond he felt with an alien being.

A radical thought, indeed. But as Wells lay in the darkness and reflected, it was a thought he could not stop thinking.

Wells's presence in the suite at seven in the morning surprised Farlad. "You're in early, sir."

Weary enough to find that observation funny, Wells chuckled deep in his throat. "In a manner of speaking, yes."

"Have you been up all night?"

"I have."

Farlad's gaze narrowed in concern. "Are you going to be all right for the Committee meeting this morning?"

Wells laughed. "I haven't required more than five hours of sleep a night for more than twenty years. It'd be a sad commentary on my fitness if I couldn't go without even that for a day."

"Yes, sir." Farlad hesitated, then went on. "If you're ready to hear it, I have a little more data on that communications problem. It seems that, quite unknown to anyone outside Operations, the quality of our Kleine transmissions has been steadily deteriorating—enough so that they've had to reduce the standard rate of transmission three times in the last six years. I've asked the supervisor of communications to come in and give you a full briefing."

"Do they have any idea what's causing it?"

"No—only that they're now confident that it isn't a hardware problem."

"Meaning that it's something happening between the transmitter and the receiver."

"Yes, sir."

"But the signal is piped directly through the spindle. The interference would have to originate there."

"Supervisor Ruiz believes it's related directly to the sheer volume of traffic—that we're approaching the carrying capacity of the system. There's a good correlation between the degree of interference and the level of traffic in a particular octant."

Wells shook his head. "Unless he can support his belief with more than a correlation, we're obliged to take a darker view of this business—officially, at least."

"Are you suggesting that the Mizari could be responsible?"

"They could be," he said, steepling his fingers and touching them to his chin. "Perhaps they've learned how to access the spindle or how to project some instrumentality there." He paused, his expression thoughtful. "There's also the possibility it may be the D'shanna."

"Trying to communicate? Or trying to cut off our communications?"

"It doesn't have to be either. It could be a meaningless consequence of their normal activity. It doesn't matter. What would matter is if they're there—if they've taken note of us or could be made to take an interest. We could use an ally, Teo—someone who can get us the information we need without alerting or alarming the Mizari."

"The D'shanna certainly *could* do that. But why would they? According to Thackery—"

"I am not sure we can trust Thackery's assertions on the subject. After reviewing his manuscript I find myself wondering if he remained in contact with the D'shanna after returning to Earth, or at least knew how to contact them at will."

"I find that hard to believe."

"Nevertheless, I want to know what happened to Thackery's personal datarecs—his notes, diaries, logs, anyplace he might have recorded his most private thoughts."

"I presume he took his personal recs with him when he resigned. There may be some record of the download—"

"There is. Two hundred gigabytes worth."

"P.D.'s aren't archived. They're gone."

"But *he* had them. That's the track I want to follow."

"Impossible," Farlad said, shaking his head. "Thackery filed a comprehensive no-disclosure request with Earth's Citizen Registry three years after he resigned. I can't even get confirmation on a date of death."

Wells scowled. "Damned Privacy Laws—what the hell is the use of a planetary information net if you can't get anything out of it?"

"I can't blame Thackery. He was apparently hounded by all

sorts of mystics and religionists who wanted his blessing or his secrets or to have his baby."

"If we couch the request as a Defense need-to-know—"

"I did, sir. They wouldn't release any information, citing the Right of Privacy. They wouldn't even confirm that they *had* any information."

"Route the request through Berberon."

Farlad shook his head. "Sir, I've dealt with these people before. It doesn't matter. Thackery requested that his records be closed, so they are closed, end of discussion. Earth citizens have that right, sir, as you well know. Even Berberon wouldn't be able to help. And in any case, if there really was anything sensitive in his files, Thackery would have ordered them destroyed after his death."

"I suppose so," Wells said. He pursed his lips and glanced at the clock. "I can shower here before the Committee meets, but my dress uniform is upstairs in my apartment—"

Farlad took the hint graciously. "Be back with it shortly," he said, and left the room.

But rather than head for the comfort room, Wells went to his desk. He dialed the number manually, since it was forbidden to have it recorded anywhere. Even the dialer's traffic log would be purged by commands from the other end as soon as the connection was made.

The phone rang twice, then stopped. No one spoke, but he had not expected them to. "This is Harmack Wells, Eighth Tier," he said, and hung up.

A moment later the phone buzzed softly. Wells touched a contact and settled back in his chair.

"Alcibiades went out for the evening," said the caller.

"And saw a play by Aristophanes," Wells replied. The callback and code exchange were special concessions to the need to protect Wells from being charged with a proscribed affiliation. Had he been an Earth-based civilian, as most Nines were, no such precautions would have been necessary.

"Good morning, Mr. Wells," the undertier said. "How can I help you?"

"I have an Aid Referral request."

"Go ahead, sir."

"Do we have persons placed where they can access secured data in Earth's information net?"

"Of course, Mr. Wells."

"I need to get around a Registry blackout and locate the personal datarecs of former USS Director Merritt Thackery. If they're archived anywhere, I want a copy. If not, I want to know what became of them. Can you help?"

"One moment." After a few seconds the undertier came back on the line. "Yes, we have some avenues we can pursue. What priority shall we assign to it?"

"Highest."

"Yes, Mr. Wells. Will a progress report every six hours be sufficient?"

"Yes, thank you."

"If he's left any traces, we'll find them," the undertier promised.

Sujata breezed into the Chamber Room of the Unified Space Service Steering Committee later than she had planned but still with ten minutes to spare. Her circular alcove was on the far side of the sunken central arena, one of six on that level—for the five directors and the Chancellor. Six similar alcoves, reserved for the Observers, looked down on the arena from the upper level.

Giving the aggregation of Observers, Directors, and senior aides milling about the chamber only a cursory glance, Sujata circled the room to her seat. She had just begun to descend the three steps that led to her alcove when hands touched her shoulders from behind and a familiar voice whispered at her ear: *"Fraxis denya—natalir pendiya nalyir en entya, ne fraxis.* So you do still exist—I heard rumors that you'd fallen down a hole and been lost."

Reaching up to grasp the trespassing hands, Sujata looked back over her shoulder into the knowing smile of Allianora of Brenadan, the Maranit Observer. *"Sarir pendiya bis penya, Allianya*—gossip sits badly on your tongue, Allianora," Sujata answered in the same mellifluous language and salacious spirit.

"A surprise, since so much sits well there," said Allianora in English, eyes twinkling. "Ten minutes ago I had a chance to wager whether you would tear yourself away long enough for the meeting. Not having yet seen your pillow mate, I was forced to decline. When do I meet her?"

"When you promise to behave yourself around her."

Allianora laughed huskily. "Perhaps you're wise to keep her hidden away, at that."

"In truth, it's on her account more than mine that we've been so reclusive."

"I think you'll be glad you came out," Allianora said, looking past Sujata to the other side of the room. "Considering who's chosen today to return to the fold, this might well be amusing." She gave Sujata's hands a squeeze, then continued on to her own alcove a quarter-turn around the upper level.

A more attentive survey of the chamber gave Allianora's parting comment meaning. Sujata had taken part in fifteen Committee meetings since her appointment, and never before had all six seats on the Observer level been filled. Sujata was accustomed to seeing one, two, even three of the Observers' alcoves empty.

But today, even Prince Denzell of Liam-Won and Elder Gayla Hollis of Rena-Kiri, the most frequent absentees, were present. Both had been known to complain that their presence there was meaningless and ceremonial and that their time was better spent trying to influence the servicrats directly.

The complaint was not without merit. Though each Observer was routinely allotted ten minutes for free commentary, that time came at the top of the agenda, often leaving them in the position of addressing decisions made during the last meeting rather than those at hand. And Sujata could not deny that more than one Director held that the real business of the Committee began after the last of the Observers had spoken.

Denzell had one other, more personal grievance. In line with the closed nature of Committee meetings, Erickson would not permit the use of facilitators in the Chamber—a significant ruling, since three women held seats in the arena. Though the stricture predated Denzell's arrival (and despite the example of his worldkin, Operations Director Anjean Vandekar, who had managed to adapt), Denzell maintained that the Chancellor was practicing "cultural terrorism" by forcing him to speak directly to her. Sujata had no sympathy for the Liamese Observer on that particular count.

As Sujata settled in her chair a small, hooded console opened clamshell-fashion and placed itself in reach of her right hand. On it was the hexagonal debate manager—a representation of the Chamber with a small lightbar in the center and twelve request-to-speak lights arrayed around it. Like the Observers, each Director was budgeted a certain amount of time, usually thirty minutes. They controlled that time by means of the debate manager, holding or passing the token in whatever manner they desired.

She logged in absently, studying Denzell's brooding eyes and deeply lined face and wondering what had brought him back. As was the customary practice of the Committee, no agenda had been circulated. But obviously there had been either leak or lobbying, though neither had reached Sujata.

Chancellor Erickson then appeared at the doorway, resplendent in a free-flowing Shinn remembrance gown. She smiled briefly at Comitè Rieke and Ambassador Pawley Bree, who were standing by the door talking in hushed tones, then descended to her alcove. That started both a migration and an exodus, as the Observers and Directors moved toward their seats, their aides toward the door.

When all movement stopped, two alcoves on opposite sides of the arena remained vacant: Transport and Defense. Loughridge and Wells came in together, last but not late. The sandy-haired Loughridge laughed as though Wells had made a joke just before they entered, and then the two parted company and headed for their alcoves.

Erickson followed them to their seats with her eyes, then reached for her console. The double doors at her back slid shut, and the slender metal rod of the Committee secretary—not a person but a program—rose from the floor at the very center of the arena. Since the log the secretary compiled was actually made by means of sensors located in each individual alcove, the rod was more of a courtesy, a visual reminder that what transpired would become part of the Committee's archives.

"Log begin," the secretary announced. "A meeting of the Steering Committee of the Unified Space Service. Present: Chancellor Erickson, Observer Berberon—"

"Cancel. It's obvious that everyone is here," Erickson interrupted. "We will take the roll as read."

"A pity," Berberon said from his place on the upper level to Erickson's right. "My disbelieving eyes would have welcomed confirmation that the elusive Prince Denzell has rejoined us at last."

By dint of personality, position, and seniority, Berberon took it as his right to interject his thoughts at will. Despite the rigid rules on debate management under which the Committee operated, his wry comments and gentle barbs were usually well received. This was no exception: a ripple of laughter rolled through the room, leaving several smiles in its wake.

But Denzell did not share the others' amusement. "I would remind Observer Berberon that his time begins when the light on his console begins glowing, not the far dimmer light in his head," he said, glowering at Berberon.

"Observer Denzell has a point—if we might at least observe our own rules at the beginning?" Erickson said. "Observer Berberon, if you would like to continue on this or some more pertinent subject, you have the token."

"Thank you, Chancellor," Berberon said, rising from his chair. "As much as I would enjoy further colloquy with my friend the Prince, I am aware that we have much to do this morning. In the hopes of furthering us along that path and in full confidence that you will welcome hearing what he has to say, I cede my commentary time to Comitè Wells."

Sujata perked up; this was an unusual, though presumably permissible, departure from routine.

"I thank Observer Berberon for his courtesy," Wells said as all eyes shifted their focus to him. "I can't promise that all of you will welcome everything I have to say today, but we should at least be able to start out in agreement. As of this morning, the Planetary Defense Force has been declared fully operational—"

Applause interrupted Wells—it seemed to start with Loughridge, but several others who shared or understood the custom quickly joined in. Wells waited patiently until the noise waned, then he continued. "We took this step after conducting a final certification exercise in the Ba'ar Tell system earlier this week. With the Chancellor's indulgence I would like to show you the results of that exercise."

As the Chamber's lights dimmed, a hexagonal section of the floor at the center of the arena rose slowly until the metre-tall screens on each of the six faces were fully exposed. The "exploding star" logo of the Defense Branch appeared in white on the black screen, then dissolved into a polar map of the twelve-planet system.

"The exercise involved a simulated attack on Ba'ar Tell by two Mizari intruders," Wells narrated. "All elements of the Defender system were involved: the deep-space pickets, the C3 center on Ba'ar Tell, and the mobile weapons platform—in this case, the *Rampart*—"

Sujata studied the screen intently as Wells continued.

Preoccupied by the enormous task of gathering up the unraveling threads of the bloated and inefficient Resource branch, she had made a conscious decision to postpone the rest of her education. Since there was little Resource could do for Defense that Wells was not busily preparing his branch to provide for itself, Defense matters had gotten the shortest shrift. Consequently much of what she was seeing was new to her.

"The attack drones were given every reasonable capability —the supercee speed of a Sentinel, the firepower of a Defender, the detection gear of a Shield element," Wells was saying. "The battle-management computers on board the drones were given free rein to attack any and all elements of the system when detected. However, *Rampart*'s drift mode deployment successfully concealed its position and enabled it to strike the first blow—"

It was an impressive display of carnage, even on the small screen. Most compelling were the screen-filling views of dissolving hulls and splintering bulkheads captured by the relays mounted on board the drones. Though it was merely one high-tech robot destroying another, it was nevertheless a level of violence to which Sujata had never been exposed. She found it as disquieting as it was fascinating.

At the height of the attack, she averted her eyes, and was startled to find Wells studying her with cold curiosity as he continued his narration.

She found herself unable to look away for a long moment. What do you want? she wondered, feeling invaded by the directness of his interest. Then the chamber lights began to brighten, and she looked away to see the now darkened screens retreat into the floor.

"We will, of course, continue testing and learning," Wells was saying. "But from this point on, the goal will not be development but honing our operational readiness."

Bree, the Journan Observer, spoke up. "Comitè Wells, what is the status of Defender deployment?"

"Six of the eight Defenders that have been authorized are complete," Wells told him. "The second Defender for Journa and the third for Earth are nearing completion under an accelerated construction schedule."

"And are any further Defenders planned?" asked Denzell from across the Chamber.

"No."

"Then what use will be made of the shipbuilding capacity brought into being for this project?"

"As funds and facilities become available, new cargo carriers are being built for the Defense branch. I reviewed our plans in this area at a meeting several months ago."

Denzell's cheeks colored at the implied reproof, but he had nothing to say—or was given no opportunity to say it. Meanwhile Erickson had gained the floor. "Comitè Wells, do you mean to say that you are fully confident the Defenders can blunt a Mizari attack?" she asked. "Or does this represent some lower level of confidence related to their mechanical readiness?"

"We are more capable and secure than we were. We are less capable and secure than we should be," Wells said gravely. "I will have more to say about that when I control my own time. I'm afraid I have consumed all of Observer Berberon's."

Ambassador Ka'in spoke up then. "My time is next, and I will gladly forgo it so that we may pursue the Chancellor's question. How much confidence should we place in the Defenders, Comitè Wells? How much security do they represent?"

"I'll warn you in advance that a complete answer to that will be time-consuming."

"I will be happy to pass the token as well, if necessary," said Elder Hollis.

"Thank you," Wells said with an acknowledging nod. "I'll be as concise as possible. We have to start by considering the tactical and strategic situations separately. The Defenders were built to fulfill a specific tactical need—protecting a heavily populated planet from attack. We think they're now ready to do that.

"The strategic situation is much more complex. Now we have to protect not one planet, but thirteen F.C. worlds, the Cheia colony, and nineteen other systems where there's a human presence—plus the hundreds of unarmed packets and sprints traveling between them.

"The goal of strategic planning is to prevent not just a given planetary assault, but *any* attack on any element of our community. And I'm obliged to tell you that the tactical competence of the Defenders has absolutely no impact on the strategic situation.

"Obviously, the Mizari can still attack any installation that lacks a Defender force. But even beyond that, they have nothing to lose in attacking Ba'ar Tell or Maranit or Earth, even if the attack initially fails. All that they risk are the forces directly involved. Defenders are effectively restricted to operations in and near a single star system—"

Sujata's hand went to her console at that comment and logged a request-to-speak.

"—which means that the Mizari homeworlds are safe. They could, in fact, send one assault force after another against one of the Worlds until they wear down or puzzle out its defenses. At present, we couldn't even reinforce the besieged World, much less carry the fight back to the Mizari."

Sujata's token began glowing, more quickly than she had expected. "Comitè Wells, I regret the ignorance that underlies this question, but I'll get no wiser if I stay silent. Why can't a Defender attack a Mizari homeworld?"

Wells smiled. "That's a good question, not a foolish one—in fact, you anticipate me. There are two answers. First, the Defenders lack supercee capability. Because of crew time, the practical limit to their operational range is a rather severe one—perhaps half a cee. That's why they were built in the systems where they were deployed, even though that required creating shipbuilding capacity almost from scratch in more than one case."

The token was still lit, so Sujata pursued the issue. "Then what I don't understand is why they were designed that way."

"Trade-offs," Wells said. "I offer you as a counterexample the Sentinels, which are supercee-capable but comparatively lightly armed. Our ship designers are pushing against a technological ceiling. The S-series drive in the Defenders draws as much power from the spindle as we are able to channel and control. Without a breakthrough in materials science that would allow us to open the tap wider, we have to budget a fixed amount of energy among the competing demands."

The token went black, and Wells looked away from Sujata to his larger audience. "But, for the sake of argument, let's say that we acquire the technology to build a new class of vessel with the firepower of a Defender and the speed of a Sentinel. You might think that we'd then have a weapons system capable of attacking a Mizari homeworld.

"You'd be wrong, for—and this is the second answer to

Comitè Sujata's question—it's vastly more difficult to attack a planet than to defend one.

"I understand that to nonmilitary people this seems counterintuitive. But the truth is that planets are easy to hit, but hard to hurt. Planets are like the boxer who gives you his belly knowing he can take it long enough to zero in on your jaw. They have no weak points—no hollow shell to shatter, no finely tuned systems to scramble. Point weapons such as lances are virtually useless. Only a weapon of mass destruction could be effective. And there is no such weapon in our arsenal.

"We have the Sentinels and the Shield to monitor our frontier. We have the Defenders to secure our homeworlds," Wells said. "But we have no sword. We have no way to persuade our enemy not to pick a fight—or to punish him if he does. We can defend—but we lack the power to destroy.

"Nearly two years ago my office circulated to the Directors a proposal for a new weapons system that would fill this strategic gap and give us, for the first time, a deterrent threat. Recognizing that the first priority had to go to direct defense of the major Worlds, we offered the plan for consideration, not action. But now that the Defenders are in place, we must move forward."

"It's time for us to forge a sword. It's time to build the Triad Force."

You're quite a salesman, Harmack Wells, Sujata thought, her fingers dancing over her touchboard and filling the tiny display with data. *Now let's see what it is you're selling*.

chapter 4

Triad

PROJECT PROPOSAL: TRIAD FORCE

Section 1: Summary Overview

1.0　Strategic Role of the Triad Force

1.1　　Triad would provide a long-range planetary assault option not currently available to Unified Space Service planners. This option is seen as essential to establishing a credible deterrent posture.

2.0 Composition of the Triad Attack Group

2.1   A Triad attack group would consist of three vessels:
> * Two (2) supercee-capable lineships equipped with AVLO-S main drive and AVLO-C translational drive
> * One (1) supercee-capable carrier.

3.0 Armament of the Triad Attack Group

3.1   Triad lineships would be equipped with a compound neutral-particle/laser lance of at least one (1) terawatt (measured at aperture).

3.2   Triad carriers would be equipped with appropriate surface assault weapons, including, but not limited to, static mass bombs, fission weapons, fusion weapons, and/or other technologies that may become available (see section 6.0).

4.0 Mission Outline

4.1   Triad strategy requires a high-velocity short-duration assault commencing immediately after the attack group elements drop to subcee velocities.

4.2   The lineships will employ direct approach vectors diverging no greater than sixty degrees, providing a central zone of overlapping coverage. After deploying decoys and other countermeasures the lineships will engage any and all planetary defense systems and attack surface-point targets related to planetary defense.

4.3   The carrier will employ a direct approach vector to the central target zone, decelerating to the appropriate entry velocity of the armaments prior to release.

5.0 Parameters and Procurement

5.1   The initial size of the Triad Force is proposed at five attack groups.

5.2   The following shipyards are accredited at the required technical level and would be candidates for construction contracts: Boötes Center, Lynx Center, Perseus Center, Journa (Yard B), Earth (Yards 102 and 105), Maranit.

6.0 Alternative Weapons Technologies

6.1 Maximum effectiveness of the Triad concept depends on successful development of the Danfield Device, a nonexplosive weapon of mass destruction based on AVLO technology. It is theorized that in the absence of flux coils and other moderating devices, an AVLO spindle tap of unrestricted size opened for one nanosecond or less would yield an intense burst of energy across the electromagnetic spectrum. The yield is estimated to be two orders of magnitude greater than the largest available fusion weapons.

6.2 Basic research related to the Danfield Device is currently being conducted under the authority of the Defense Research Office, with the concurrence of the Command Board.

THIS RELEASE AUTHORIZED UNDER CODE
41–1–425–R

Harmack Wells
Director
USS–Defense

(MORE FOLLOWS)

There were times when Felithe Berberon found himself feeling a grudging admiration for Harmack Wells—for his unwavering internal compass, for his almost self-righteous sense of purpose, for the intellectual and emotional commitment he brought to anything he did. Since those were also the qualities that made Wells so damnably difficult to deal with, the feeling never lasted long. But it was real enough while it lasted, even if it did leave Berberon feeling faintly disloyal.

This was one of those times. The meeting was going splendidly for Wells. The Comitè was in his element, holding forth in loving detail on the system he had diligently shepherded through the approvals process since joining the Service as a defense strategist more than a dozen years ago.

Berberon reflected that he was perhaps the only person in the room—Wells excepted—with a sense of what had led to that moment. Triad had become Wells's personal charge almost by default. When first proposed, none of the senior Defense staff was eager to embrace it, in part because the timing was wrong—the Defender program having just hit full stride —and in part because of difficulties within the Affirmation.

The new Elder of Rena-Kiri was then refusing to recognize certain guarantees contained in the Affirmation of Unity signed by his predecessor. He could do so with impunity, in part because the Affirmation specifically reserved him that right, and in part because the Unified Worlds, then as now, were not unified at all. The Affirmation created no executive machinery by which other signees could respond in concert.

Even so, Elder North's repudiation of Rena-Kiri's responsibilities under the Affirmation was so hard-edged that it divided the other worlds into two camps, one that saw the Renan action as a threat to the Affirmation generally and one that saw it as a defense of the principle of planetary independence. There was a real fear that Triad would be seen by the latter group not as a strategic deterrent, but as a tool by which the majority would enforce discipline and move the loose twelve-member planetary confederation toward some more rigidly structured federalist body.

Any such suspicion on the part of the Renans (or the three other worlds that sided with them) was ludicrous on its face, of course. The Service was not an arm of the Affirmation but an independent, self-supported, and self-directed organization. And no Chancellor, certainly not Chancellor Delkes, would have approved any such use of any such weapon. Nevertheless, because of the perceived potential for diplomatic disaster, Triad was not merely ignored. It was actively squelched. Berberon himself had helped see to that.

Though not there at the conception, Wells soon adopted the Triad proposal as his own. Each time he advanced in the Defense bureaucracy—and he had advanced with uncommon speed—he brought Triad along with him, refining it, updating it, winning over key skeptics, emphasizing the Mizari threat, until now he stood just one step away from final vindication.

All the more marvelous to watch because you really believe it, Berberon thought as he listened.

"The Danfield Device will effect the most concentrated release of energy known outside a stellar core," Wells was saying. "Picture an amount of energy equal to that required to boost a Sentinel to supercee, but released in less than a millisecond. If the device is triggered on the way down, the energy outflux will boil the atmosphere off the planet like peeling the rind off an orange. The shock wave and windstorm alone will shatter anything less dense than a granite mountain for five thousand kilometres in every direction."

Wells paused a moment to let that image register on his audience. "If the device penetrates to the surface, even some of the mountains are at risk. No artificial structure, whether on the surface or below, will be left intact. The planet will ring with Force 8 aftershocks for weeks. The Danfield Device won't destroy the planet, but it almost certainly will eliminate any Mizari occupying it. It would even be effective against a species based on a gaseous world similar to Jupiter."

Berberon noted Sujata blanching at Wells's description. *A horrible weapon,* Berberon agreed silently. *Horrible enough in itself—more horrible to see the invention that gave us the stars and each other subverted this way.*

"And the ships that deliver this device—how will they survive? Or will this be a mission for volunteers' honor?" asked Elder Hollis, reclaiming a moment of his commentary time.

Berberon's face twisted into a grimace. The reference was to what Berberon considered a particularly distasteful concept of martyrdom drawn from the pattern of armed conflict that had dominated even recent Renan history.

Wells shook his head. "Even with the best available shielding, the Danfield Device will have to decelerate to less than tencee to penetrate the atmosphere," he said. "The Triad ships will have enough time to move safely into the blast shadow of the target planet itself."

Berberon requested and quickly was passed the token. "On what far horizon does this hopeful mirage lie, Comitè?" he asked with studied innocence, though he knew the answer before asking. "How many miracles must your scientists work to bring it into existence?"

Wells nodded slightly. "A fair question, Mr. Berberon. I'm happy to say that due to advances over the last year, and the last three months in particular, the problems involved in building the Danfield Device are now solely engineering ones. There are no fundamental theoretical hurdles."

"That is welcome news indeed, Comitè," Berberon said pleasantly.

But the tone of the meeting changed dramatically a few minutes later, when control of the token passed to Denzell. "We of Liam-Won are pleased that these powerful ships have proven such a wise investment," Denzell began, his expression showing anything but pleasure. "We would be more pleased if one were defending our world.

"Would you explain again to me, please, why the sixty-one million people of Liam-Won are not worthy of protection? Must I give you all a lesson in astrography? We are just thirteen cees from the Perimeter. Does the Comitè expect the Mizari to pass over us and come looking for a more challenging target?"

"If Observer Denzell wants answers, he will have to grant my request-to-speak—" Wells attempted to interject.

"You have choreographed enough of this already, you and your grinning accomplice there," Denzell said, pointing at Berberon. "We know the answers. You leave us out there as bait, undefended, tempting, to dangle before the Mizari and coax them into the attack that will give you the war you want so badly."

The charge was preposterous on its face, yet Berberon felt obliged to come to Wells's defense. "If the learned Observer were still capable of reason, I am sure he would realize that Triad will do more to assure Liam-Won's safety than any number of Defenders could," he said with a politeness that was in itself an insult.

"How easily that comes to your lips, with not one but three Defenders orbiting overhead," Denzell shouted. "Yet we are the ones at risk—"

"You forget that the Mizari know the way here," Berberon said, the chill in his voice authentic. "It was our world they scorched, our ancestors they exterminated."

"Were the Weichsel not our ancestors as well?" Denzell demanded angrily. "Were they not the Founders of all the Worlds—"

"Break!" Erickson said sharply, and both men fell abruptly silent. "Observer Denzell, you have challenged Comitè Wells on a personal level. He has a right-of-reply."

"Thank you, Chancellor," Wells said without waiting for Denzell to acknowledge the point of order. "I am afraid the Observer is beyond persuasion, but I will address myself to his audience. Nearly all our people are already protected. What Prince Denzell asks is not reasonable—"

Denzell reentered the debate with an emphatic interruption. "Before Comitè Wells silences me again by consuming all my time, I must protest his lies. I ask only for fairness—that you place at least one Defender in each inhabited system. Nothing more than that."

"Do you understand the price?" Wells asked, his voice still calm. "To directly protect that last one half of one percent of the Affirmation's human population will require an investment at least equal to that which we have already made. And we'll have to give up the real security of the Triad Force at the same time. We'd be paying a very high price for very little."

"Someone must speak for those who are not here," Ambassador Bree said, taking up Denzell's theme. "The fact that more than ninety-nine percent of our kin live on five worlds is irrelevant. Those who call Liam-Won or Dzuba or Pai-Tem home value their lives as much as any on the five major worlds. Perhaps more importantly, each world still harbors a unique and irreplaceable expression of the human potential. I would not like to see us say as a matter of policy that a culture of seventy thousand is less valuable than one of seventy million."

Wells shook his head. "Ambassador, beginning work on Triad would say just the opposite. It would say that we are willing to fight for what is ours, that we will pursue every avenue to guarantee the security of the Affirmation."

At that point the lights on Berberon's console told him that Wells was, for the first time, controlling his own time. *It's over,* Berberon thought in Denzell's direction. *Watch as he lays you open so gracefully that you cannot help but admire the skill, even as you bleed.*

But first Wells let several moments of silence slip by as a means of collecting the full attention of the Committee. When he was satisfied, he resumed talking, this time with all suggestion of pleading removed from his voice.

"Prince Denzell is not being realistic," he said matter-of-factly. "That vulnerable half percent of our population is scattered over twenty-two different systems. Would he have us build twenty-two more Defenders when five Triad groups would provide far greater security and flexibility for half the cost or less?"

"Prince Denzell is also not being honest. The human world

that is most at risk is not Liam-Won but Feghr—Feghr, located not merely near the Perimeter but beyond it, virtually on the doorstep of the Mizari Cluster. The last of the First Colonization worlds—on our maps since the Revision, spiritually and genetically our kin but still ignorant of our presence, still prisoners within the restricted zone.

"Why? Because we have been so weak, our fear of the Mizari so great, that we would rather sacrifice them than disturb the Mizari again. With Triad in place we need not be so timid. With Triad in place, we could restore Feghr to its birthright.

"But the question of cost and the problem of Feghr are secondary issues. If this very moment we received notice from the Sentinels the Mizari were crossing the Perimeter—something that *could* happen, at any moment of any day—we would have only two options. To flee to the sanctuary of our Defender-protected worlds and prepare for a siege we cannot win—or to fall to our knees and submit to their will—whatever that may be.

"Triad will create a third option—through which we will be able to preserve our several cultures, our beloved homeworlds, and our self-respect. Chancellor Erickson, in the name of our own survival, I ask for a poll of the Committee on this question."

"Seconded," Loughridge said quickly.

Four-one or five-zero, Berberon predicted silently.

"Are you convinced that there has been enough discussion?" Erickson asked, her tone oddly cautionary.

What are you thinking, Blythe? Berberon wondered apprehensively. This has a greater momentum than you realize—

"It's a simple enough issue," Wells said. "We can choose to be helpless or choose to be secure."

"Is that how you want the question worded?" Erickson asked with just a hint of ridicule.

For the first time Berberon saw annoyance on Wells's face. "I put the question: Should the USS immediately begin development of the Triad Force?"

"Very well," Erickson said. "We will see what all of us have to say."

"A poll of the Committee on the question offered by Comitè Wells," said the secretary. "Defense—how do you vote?"

"I vote yes," said Wells emphatically.

"Defense votes yes," said the secretary. "Survey—how do you vote?"

Rieke had been silent until that moment, but her feelings about the Defense branch in general were no mystery and her vote, therefore, no surprise.

"I remind the other Directors that half of the Sentinels, all of the Sentinel tenders, and all of the Reconnaissance vessels are former Survey ships," Rieke said. "I am left with just eleven major vessels to carry out geophysical and archaeological studies of two hundred systems with ten thousand planets. Survey has been emasculated, and Transport and Resource are being bled dry—all to feed the appetite of this war machine Comitè Wells is creating. Enough and too much. I say no to this madness."

Unmoved by Rieke's impassioned preface, the secretary pressed on. "Survey votes no. Resource—how do you vote?"

"I find merit in the arguments raised by both Comitè Wells and Ambassador Bree," Sujata said slowly. "But my duties within my own branch have kept me from learning as much about Defense matters as I feel I should know before expressing an opinion. Therefore I beg the indulgence of both sides and reluctantly abstain."

That was unexpected. Interesting, Berberon thought. Are you truly that conscientious or is it merely that you wish to avoid being caught on the losing side?

Transport was next, but Loughridge's affirmative vote was a foregone conclusion. That left Vandekar to decide whether Wells would win a three-to-one victory, or lose on a two-two null vote.

Vandekar's eyes were directed downward as he answered the secretary's call, thereby avoiding both Wells's and Denzell's expectant gazes.

"Like Comitè Sujata, I do not find the choice as simple as Comitè Wells feels I should," Vandekar said in his reedy voice. "Like my planet-kin Aramir Denzell, I fear that should war come, Liam-Won must inevitably be a battleground. Positioned as we are, we can expect nothing else. Therefore any move that might increase the chance of war—even a war we might eventually win—cannot meet with our approval. For this reason we would oppose any mission to Feghr. To hear Comitè Wells say that with Triad such an endeavor might be risked chills me."

Denzell was smiling confidently at this point, but when Vandekar continued, the smile quickly vanished.

"But I have had to remind myself that I do not sit on the Committee as the representative of Liam-Won," Vandekar said in a tone appropriate for an apology. "I regret the position in which Comitè Rieke finds herself and her branch. I understand fully the suspicion of Prince Denzell that all worlds are not being treated equally. I sympathize with Ambassador Bree's profound observations on the intrinsic value of each member of our community. But we have limited resources. We cannot do everything worth doing. We must make choices."

He paused, more for breath than for effect. "And I am persuaded that the better choice for the greater community we serve is to make Comitè Wells's metaphorical sword real. I vote yes on Triad."

"A report on the question," said the secretary. "Three in the affirmative, one in the negative, one abstention. The proposal is recommended to the Chancellor."

Affirm it, Berberon urged Erickson silently from behind. Don't be foolish. Triad itself means nothing. The compromise of interests is what matters. Don't upset the balance.

But when Erickson failed to respond to the secretary's report with her usual businesslike briskness, Berberon knew that she had decided otherwise.

"Perhaps there have been too many words said in the matter already," she began. "Even so, I will add a few more in the hope that you will understand the action I am about to take.

"First, I believe we have a moral obligation to station a Defender not only at Liam-Won but also at Dzuba and Shinn, Daehne and Muschynka, even Sennifi, our willful isolate. I view this as a service we are extending to the various Worlds, no less than the packet schedules we set or the Kleine nets we manage. Until now we have worked very hard to avoid dividing the Worlds into the haves and the have-nots. If these vessels were worth deploying anywhere, they are worth deploying everywhere."

His lips pressed into a thin line of displeasure, Wells shook his head as a father might react when his child disappointed him.

Berberon sank back into his chair and masked his face with a hand. Blythe, you are buying more trouble than you know, he thought sadly. For more than just yourself.

"I am also concerned," she continued, "that the kind of decision Comitè Wells proposes we make is one that a collective body of the Worlds could justly make, but which we cannot presume to make on their behalf. The shift of strategy embodied in merely creating Triad represents a revision in the Service's historic role that I cannot endorse.

"By means of the Shield and the Defenders, we presently provide the planetary leaders with the time and security they would require to respond to any threat from the Mizari. In the absence of any preexisting mechanism for consensus among the Worlds, to build and operate an attack force implies that we have arrogated to ourselves the right to decide when and under what circumstances that force should be used. This is something we cannot do."

A disaster, Berberon moaned. *Blythe, you have ambushed me.*

"Lastly I reject the sense of urgency with which this proposal is offered," Erickson said. "There has been no contact between human and Mizari in sixty millennia. The people of Feghr have survived without knowledge of us for an equally long time. I see no reason why we need anticipate or initiate change in either area. We don't even know that the Sterilizers themselves still exist. We proceed only on the assumption that since we have survived this long, they have as well. But it *is* an assumption, as likely to be wrong as right."

"Nothing that powerful disappears of its own accord," Wells said, scowling. "Not without something more powerful coming along to push them off their pedestal."

"A correct and commendable attitude for one in your position, Comitè," Erickson replied evenly. "It serves us well for you to cast things in the worst possible light. But I am not obliged to share your view. I hereby table the Triad proposal and set aside the Committee's poll." She glanced down at her console. "The token has passed from Comitè Wells. Comitè Rieke, I believe you have some other matters to bring before us?"

chapter 5

The Consequences
of Honor

Wyrena lay on her stomach at the edge of the tile, resting her chin on her folded arms and watching Janell circle the pool. The first few laps she had been furiously intense, legs thrashing the water, arms slashing down through the surface in a manner that created more spray than speed. The hard walls splashed the sound of her passage around the room such that when Wyrena closed her eyes, it had seemed as though there must be a half dozen other swimmers keeping Janell company.

But she had worked out whatever hateful energy had possessed her, and for the past ten minutes Janell had been gliding and gamboling gracefully. Wyrena watched her dive deep and lost sight of her in the reflections of the lights overhead. A moment later Janell surfaced within arm's reach and shook her head to spray Wyrena with droplets from her hair.

"Are you sure you don't want to join me?" Sujata asked, smiling and panting slightly as she clung to the edge with one hand.

"Did you ever see a woman swimming the whole time you were on Ba'ar Tell?" There was a hint of impatience in the question.

"I didn't see *anyone* swimming. Is there a pool in the entire city of Farnax?"

Wyrena shook her head. "There may not be one on the planet."

"Doesn't anyone know how to swim?"

"Of course we know how. There is a river-bathing ceremony that is part of the *mala'nat*—the renewal."

Sujata smiled conspiratorially. "From which we absented ourselves because the house would be empty, as I recall. Is there a reason I wouldn't have seen women particularly?"

"Because it's forbidden under the Code of Conduct."

"Forbidden? Whatever for?"

"Because we poison the water."

It was said earnestly, so Sujata stilled her initial impulse to laugh. "Just by being women?"

"Yes. When the *fraili* die or the crops grow sick, it can always be traced back to a woman swimming in the river."

"Really," Sujata said with a straight face, pushing off backward and coasting away on the power of a slow kick. "May as well come in if that's the only reason. Undoubtedly I've poisoned it pretty well already."

Wyrena sat up. "I don't ridicule your faith," she said indignantly.

"That's because the Maranit faith isn't cluttered up with silly rules," Sujata said, cupping a hand and sending a sheet of water in Wyrena's direction. Most of it fell short, though the leading edge came close enough to cause Wyrena to jump up and retreat a step.

Laughing, Sujata changed directions and came paddling back. "You really should spend some time in here yourself. It's the best way to build up your leg strength. When we go downwell to Earth and you feel that full one gee, you'll wish you had."

"Are we going to Earth?" Wyrena asked, a note of anxiety in her voice.

"Absolutely and unquestionably, just as soon as I can get away. Aren't you curious? I've been wanting to go downwell ever since I came here, but there was always something more important—if less fun. Now I'm glad I was too busy, so we can discover it together. It'll be more fun with you along. If I don't have to push you in a sedan chair, that is!"

Sujata had reached the stairs and came rising out of the water, droplets cascading down her sleek skin and the shiny fabric of her suit. Wyrena met her at the top with a towel and a kiss. "I have so much to learn here yet," Wyrena said. "The thought of facing a world with that many people on it leaves me breathless."

"You'll have time to catch your breath. We won't be going anytime soon," Sujata said, toweling off her matted hair. "I have too much catching up to do just now."

With those words a hint of the inner unrest Sujata had taken into the pool returned to her face.

"Why can't you talk to me about your meeting?" Wyrena asked plaintively.

Sujata shook her head. "Because that's the rule. And because officially nothing happened."

"You were gone four hours—"

"That's not unusual for the Committee."

"Four hours and nothing happened?"

"Only decisions to do something count. There weren't any."

"And everything else is a secret?"

"The Directors can tell their aides—the Observers can tell whatever authorities selected them. Everyone else is shut out." Draping the towel over her shoulders, Sujata inclined her head toward the door. "Come on," she said with a grin. "I need to shower off the poison."

With a sheepish smile, Wyrena fell in beside her. "Maybe it's just our way to avoid getting our long hair wet—"

"Now there's a reason that makes sense."

Later, enclosed in the privacy of Sujata's suite, Wyrena made another attempt to draw her out. "Was it what wasn't passed at the meeting that upset you?"

"No—"

"Something made you upset. It's still in your eyes when you're not using them to lie."

"I was upset at myself, for being caught unprepared." She frowned and shook her head. "I should have made time for Farlad." Noting Wyrena's puzzlement, she added, "The man who was in the waiting room the day you arrived."

Wyrena retreated into the corner of the couch, her face suddenly ashen. "Then it's my fault—that's why you won't talk about it with me. Because of me you shamed yourself. You see, I was right—I shouldn't have come. The third day and already I've given you reason to be angry with me."

"I'm not angry with you!" Sujata said, reaching unsuccessfully for Wyrena's hand. "You didn't do anything wrong—"

"If that was so, you'd share your unhappiness with me," Wyrena said, her small voice brimming with barely contained emotion. "Who could I tell? Who do I even know? You shared with me in Farnax and never heard of any of it from other than me. Isn't it so? Why have you stopped trusting me?"

Sujata slid along the couch and drew Wyrena into her comforting embrace. "Little one, I haven't stopped trusting you," she said soothingly. "But to prove it I'd have to break one of the rules I swore to follow. Unless"—Sujata drew her head back far enough that she could look into Wyrena's eyes—"unless you were working for me, after all."

Wyrena's eyes showed skepticism. "It would only be a fiction of convenience."

"Why? I need a sounding board. I'm still learning. We'll learn together."

"If you think it would work—"

"Of course. And I have an open req for an administrative assistant. Please—you wouldn't be forced to have contact with a lot of people. The person you'd see the most of would be me."

For the first time since the conversation had begun, Wyrena smiled, a warm, dazzling, faintly admiring smile. "If you really want me to, I will. When do I start?"

"Officially when I've filed all the approvals. Unofficially you start right now."

In the next ten minutes Sujata outlined the highlights of the meeting, including her own vote and Erickson's action. Like the well-bred Ba'ar woman she was, Wyrena listened without interruptions.

"I don't understand why the Chancellor could do that," she said when Sujata was done. "How can she simply set their decision aside?"

"Don't think of the USS as a government. Think of it as a corporation with no stockholders. It's only accountable to itself. And internally everyone is accountable to the Chancellor. The Steering Committee is technically there only to advise. That's why we use the terms we do—a poll of the Committee, not a vote. A recommendation to the Chancellor, not a decision. She usually takes the recs, of course. But the only thing that we ever do that carries any authority is a Vote of Continuance."

"The Chancellor is a very powerful person, then," Wyrena said thoughtfully.

"That she is."

"I'm surprised the Worlds allow this to continue."

Sujata chuckled softly. "The thing is, it didn't used to matter, when all the USS did was run the orbital stations and operate the survey ships. And now that it does matter, no one quite knows how to bell the cat. I'm told there was quite a fuss about forty years back. That's when the rules were revised to admit the Observers. But that's as far as reform got. The Service still charts its own course."

"And the Observers don't have any real say."

"Except in a vote of Continuance," Sujata agreed. "Though I gladly would have traded seats with an Observer today. The thing of it is, I very nearly voted yes. Wells was so persuasive, so confident and professional. But after hearing the Chancellor's reasons I realized how selective his version of the issue had been."

"I see now why you were upset."

"I hate being caught like that. I should have realized when Farlad kept harping on it that it was important to them, even if it wasn't to me."

"When emotions run high, you cannot make friends without making enemies. You did the right thing by abstaining."

Sujata shook her head. "This time my conscience demanded I not vote. The next time it will demand I do."

"Maybe this is the end of it."

"I don't think so," Sujata said forlornly. "This is going to come up again—and I don't know what I'm going to do when it does."

The star dome was deserted except for the two shadowy figures near its center. One lay full-length on one of the recliners, his attention focused upward on the tiny nodes of light that seemed to lie just beyond the seamless synglas. The other sat upright on the edge of a nearby chair, his attention focused on the first. Starlight alone betrayed the troubled expressions both men wore.

"She said she doubted they existed," Wells said. "I could hardly believe I'd heard it. I feel them there, Teo. It's as though there were a chill in that part of the sky."

Farlad's gaze flicked upward briefly and found the familiar

outline of Ursa Major. "It's irresponsible of her, of course. But only two firm yes votes—that isn't much cause for optimism."

"I prefer to focus on the fact that there was only one firm no vote."

"What I meant is that the Chancellor isn't likely to change her mind if that's the most support you can muster. We can continue funding the research from other accounts. It's just not time to build yet."

"That's not acceptable."

"She sits for renewal in less than two years," Farlad reminded. "She may step aside then. Or we may be able to lay the groundwork for replacing her."

"Two more years wasted—two more years vulnerable—"

"It will take a dozen years or more to build Triad once we have the go-ahead, longer than that to deploy the groups to advance bases. Against that—"

"Against that two years is still two years more in which the Mizari could act and we couldn't. I'm disturbed enough about the window of vulnerability forced on us by the system's lead time. I won't tolerate opening it still wider for no good purpose."

"I understand that, sir. I just don't see that we have anything to say about it just now."

To that Wells had no immediate reply. He lay perfectly still on the recliner, folded hands resting on his taut stomach, gazing out at the stars of the Great Bear. Then, in one smooth motion, he swung his legs over the side of the recliner and came to his feet.

"Thank you, Teo. I'll see you in the office tomorrow," he said briskly, and started off toward the exit, his long strides carrying him quickly across the floor.

"Where are you going?" Farlad called after, jumping up.

"To see that Comitè Sujata is prepared to render a vote the next time," Wells called back. "It was negligent of me not to see to it sooner."

"What point is there to that? The Chancellor can set aside a four-to-one vote as easily as a three-to-one."

Wells paused and looked back. "Why, you said it yourself, she knows our support has some softness. Perhaps she'll see things differently when she feels more alone."

Farlad glanced at the faintly glowing face of his watch. "It's late. Sujata will be in her suite by now, surely."

Wells waved a hand in the air. "Just as well. Sometimes the surroundings in which something is said affects how it is heard."

Whenever Janell was away, Wyrena rattled around the apartment aimlessly. There were no rituals or rhythms to the household, no well-defined place for her yet. With a touch of the anxiety that came with custom violated or ignored, she felt a need to be needed, to be useful. But beyond some trivial straightening and putting-away, there was nothing for her to do.

Moreover, Wyrena felt unnaturally alone. Janell's way of living was machine-dependent and streamlined to a degree that Wyrena, raised in the highly social complexity of a Ba'ar family enclave, could not have previously imagined. The formalized interplay in which she was so skillful, the carefully delineated roles in which she was so comfortable, had been left on Ba'ar Tell. She had failed to realize how much she would miss them.

Now there was only Janell. *I cannot lose her,* was the fearful refrain of her thoughts. *If I lose her, all time will be like these empty hours.* From lovers' games Wyrena vowed to build them a comfortable web of ritual. From her lover's cues she would carve out a complementary selfhood, making each necessary to the other, making each complete through the other.

Janell's concession earlier that day to share what had troubled her was a beginning. The rules and dynamics of the Committee were fascinating, not unlike an undisciplined Ba'ar enclave. It was the aspect of Janell's life for which Wyrena had felt the greatest immediate affinity, in which she could most readily foresee being useful.

Yet even in this most important task Wyrena had already made errors. She had been clinging, possessive, wanting instead of giving. Janell had said as much when she went off to discharge her responsibilities to words and numbers and machines, though the work center of the apartment surely contained everything she would need.

"Must you leave? Can't you work here?" Wyrena had pleaded.

"I can—but with you here I won't," was the answer. There was no question where it placed the fault for this particular separation.

Janell had showed her how to use the net and fill a wall

with light and images, but nothing in her experience had trained her to fill time with passive watching. Her solitude weighed on her, the more so because she did not know how long it would last.

By the time the door page sounded, Wyrena was dozing in the chair where she had settled to await Janell's return. She was momentarily taken aback by the unfamiliar noise, then followed it with tentative steps to the entryway. The tiny display by the door controls was black, but a yellow light above it was flashing. Her hand went out, and the page fell silent as the door slid open.

"Janell?" Wyrena said hopefully.

Instead of Janell, a strange man stood there with arms crossed over his chest, almost filling the doorway with his frame. For several long seconds, while she stood frozen by uncertainty, he raked her with piercing, deep-set eyes.

Then his arms fell to his sides and the rigidness left his pose. "Greetings of the evening," he said pleasantly, bowing from the neck. "I ask harmony on your house and family, and the blessings of the endless river on your lands."

Her heart leapt at the familiar phrasing. "At our door is the end of your road, and at our table the end of your hunger," Wyrena said reflexively, stepping back from the doorway. "Are you from the Tell?" she added hopefully.

"I'm afraid not," the stranger said as he stepped past her. "But my position has allowed me to learn some of its customs." Reading the lack of recognition in her eyes, he said, "I'm Harmack Wells."

So this is Wells! she thought admiringly. *Just as Janell led me to believe, one who lives with confidence and walks with strength.* Bowing, she said, "Comitè Sujata has spoken of you."

"I'd like to talk to her, if she's not in bed."

Either Wells had not learned as much as he claimed or he had abandoned it in favor of the looser local mores, for the question fit badly with Wyrena's rules of propriety for visitors. "No," she said finally, struggling past her slack-jawed indecision.

"Ah," Wells said, eyeing her nightdress and rumpled hair. "I apologize for disturbing you. I trust you'll tell her that I was here?"

Belatedly Wyrena realized her inarticulate answer had

misled him. "I meant to say she's not here," she said hastily. "Janell went to her office. You can find her there."

"I see. Thank you." He took a step toward the door, then turned and looked back at her. "My manners fail me at times. Let me welcome you to Unity and Earth. I understand you've only recently arrived?"

"Five days ago."

Wells nodded. "You'll forgive my curiosity, but I find myself wondering what kind of Ba'ar woman comes here alone."

"I am not alone," she said defensively.

"Forgive my error. When you greeted me, you seemed hungry for the familiar. Here and on Unity there are many men from Ba'ar Tell, equally hungry. I thought perhaps to make your presence known to them."

"That is not necessary," Wyrena said, looking away.

"I would be happy—"

"I told you, I'm not alone!" Wyrena could feel him watching her, could sense the probing gaze and the mind behind it.

"Te da'arit?" he said softly.

The question was impertinent but phrased in the male obligatory. She had to answer. "Yes. I love her."

"Do you practice the Canon?"

"Of course."

"And what of Comitè Sujata? Has she learned the Canon too? Does she understand the woman's true role, the beauty of silent compromise, the imperative of accommodation?"

"I try to teach her, as I can—by word and example."

"Is she a good student?"

When she did not answer, Wells moved closer, until she could almost feel his warm breath on her face. "You said that she had spoken of me. Has she spoken of the work she does, the problems we face?"

Wyrena turned her back to Wells—an insult which, regrettably, he probably would fail to take the meaning of—and said nothing.

"Listen, little *ka'ila'in,*" Wells said softly, his lips but a hand's breadth from her ear. "There are things you should know. Your Janell has important decisions to make in the days ahead. She has risen to a position of great honor, a position whose responsibilities she takes to heart. But persons of conscience are sometimes paralyzed by decisions of consequence. If she should share her struggle with you, I would like to know that you will counsel her in accord with the Canon. I would like to think that you will help her steer a course of compromise."

Surprised by Wells's words, Wyrena turned to face him. "I would do that for her anyway, to bring her peace."

"Of course," Wells said, holding her gaze almost hypnotically. "But you need to understand that there's more at stake than her peace. If the wrong decisions are made, or no decision at all, the consequences won't stop at the border of this little world you share with her. Do you understand?"

Wyrena searched his words for a threat, yet found only a warning. Nevertheless, she felt the threat all the same. "Yes, I understand."

"And you'll remember, when the time comes?"

"I will."

"Then it won't be necessary to tell Janell that I was here," Wells said, bowing. "Good night, Wyrena Ten Ga'ar."

It was not until after he had gone that she realized she had never told him her name. *There is the threat,* she thought. *It is in the things he knows without being told. It is in his eyes, which look at me as if they see my essence. He is not Ba'ar, but he knows us. Knows me. Oh, Janell—come home soon and make me forget his eyes.*

Felithe Berberon glanced back and forth between Wells and Erickson and sighed. Enough hostile energy was flowing back and forth across Erickson's meeting lounge to make him loath to step between them. *For this I gave up talking to children?* he thought mockingly.

The "invitation" from Wells had come late, only that morning. When it reached him, Berberon was already in his single-seat courier, being whisked through Unity's maze of travel tubes to a meeting with a group of Council Scholars—Terran youths being honored for their academic achievements with a week of ceremony at Capital, the island seat of the World Council, and a three-day trip to Unity, the orbiting seat of the Service.

In truth Berberon had been half wishing for a reprieve from that yearly responsibility. He had no quarrel with recognizing talent, as far as that went. But in recent years the program had become little more than a recruiting exercise, run by the Nines for their own benefit but paid for with Coullars. Worse, the planners seemed to think that the Scholars' greatest need in life was to meet with as much of the orbital officialdom as possible.

They bring these kids up here, he had been thinking, *most of them for the first time, ostensibly the brightest and best of their generation, and proceed to herd them from one activity to another as if they didn't trust them to plan as much as a minute's free time. The kids'd appreciate it a lot more if we'd let them loose at the transship terminal with a couple hundred Coullars and what amounts to a three-day liberty.*

Then the message had come, popping up on the courier's com like an unwanted houseguest. "Felithe—I am going to see the Chancellor at ten to see if we can't find some common ground on Triad. Teo suggested, and I concur, that it might be well if you were to go along. Perhaps you can play the peacemaker."

Hearing it the first time, Berberon had groaned audibly. He had much to lose by going, more to lose by not going. Without much enthusiasm he redirected his courier toward the shuttle terminal and arranged for the Terran Unitor to stand in for him with the Scholars. He did not think that there was much chance he could play peacemaker. More likely referee. Or if things get particularly bloody, witness.

Erickson had received them civilly, if not cordially. That atmosphere lasted exactly as long as it took for them to reach the privacy of the lounge and close the door behind them. "Felithe, I suppose I'm not surprised to see you here, though I am disappointed," Erickson said as she settled in a chair. "Comitè, I presume this has something to do with Triad. I would have thought enough was said on that subject yesterday."

Wells remained standing. "I want to see if we can't establish a time frame for bringing in Triad that would satisfy your objections."

"I'm afraid that's not possible," Erickson said stiffly.

"Please, Blythe," Berberon had said, spreading his hands wide. "Let's not start from unnecessarily rigid positions. Your rejection of the proposal yesterday was conditional, not final. In that light—"

"I'm very much sorry if I led anyone to think that," she said. "I should have been more explicit."

Berberon had made one further foredoomed effort to smooth the waters. "Reasonable people can always find room for compromise. Isn't it said that government is the art of compromise—"

But Erickson cut him off again. "I should not have to remind you that the Service is *not* a government. I have no intention of compromising. I will not allow Triad to be built."

"Would you rather the Mizari overwhelmed us?" Wells asked harshly.

"No—but I don't think that's the choice."

It had gone downhill from there. Berberon had rarely seen Wells so passionate; he had never seen Erickson so resolute. Predictably neither made any headway with the other.

"The whole point of Triad is to make the prospect of war so terrifying that they can't conceive of starting one," Wells was saying. "We don't have to fight a war. We just have to make sure they know we're *ready* to fight one."

Erickson answered first with a scornful look. "We're too ready, as far as I'm concerned. Don't you know the history of that idea and where it almost led us? Why don't you come to the Committee with a proposal to build an ambassador ship? Why not build a *Pride of Man*?"

"Because the only way to negotiate with them is from a position of strength."

"I would have thought that the logic of mutual survival would overcome such thinking."

"We have no reason to believe they're interested in *mutual* survival. We have very good reason to believe just the opposite."

Erickson waved a hand at him in dismissal. "We're not even in communication with them. We don't know why they did what they did. We don't know if the conditions that prompted them to do it are still in place."

"So should we forgive and forget until they come after us again?"

"What alternative are you offering? Your talk of deterrence sounds like a childish need to frighten those who frighten you. What if fear is foreign to their nature?"

"Every sentient understands death and what it means."

"So what's your intent once Triad is built—to make Contact for the sole purpose of threatening them?"

"Reestablishment of an interface between the Mizari and ourselves is inevitable."

"I like that—'reestablishing an interface.' It sounds so perfectly benign. What you mean is, we'll prod them with a stick until they wake up and then beat them senseless."

Patiently Wells shifted to another tack. "Chancellor, please understand that I recognize valid reasons for believing the Mizari either don't exist or are no longer a threat. This is a subject on which reasonable minds may disagree. But when you don't know which course is right, you have to look at the price of being wrong. If you're wrong, it could cost us everything. If I'm wrong, all it costs us is a little time."

"Do you really think that this is doing nothing more to us than that?" she demanded. "That gearing up for total war amounts to nothing more than putting railguns on cargo packets?"

Erickson's words came with a rush, passion breaking through frost. "You already have the greatest share of our internal appropriations. In just forty years Defense has grown larger than any other branch and threatens to become larger than all the others combined. We now extract Planetary Service Assessments from everyone who can pay them—what are they but a war tax? The billions of Coullars you've pumped into the Sentinel and Defender programs have stoked the economies of the industrial worlds to the point that we've begun to affect planetary politics. Isn't that right, Felithe? What do the Observers care if you cry wolf, as long as you whisper *profit* in the same breath?"

Berberon shrugged. "There is no shame in having a selfish interest so long as you also have a more noble one."

Erickson came up out of her seat and threw her hands high in the air in frustration. "And which interest accounts for the messages I've received since yesterday from the Journan Elector and the Maranit High Mistress? Which one accounts for Felithe's presence here?"

"Chancellor," Wells said gently, "I quarrel with none of your observations. These are facts that anyone can see. But they'll all be instantly irrelevant if the Mizari attack while we're still powerless to retaliate."

Erickson settled back into her chair, propping her chin on one fist as she avoided looking at either visitor. "Are we so sure of ourselves that we would never strike at them first?"

"The sole purpose of Triad is to *protect* the human community," Berberon said.

Erickson turned on Wells. "And if you learned that you

could attack them with impunity and destroy them before they could respond, you wouldn't persuade yourself that you were only protecting us and go ahead and give the order?"

Wells hesitated only a moment, but it was enough for Erickson. "Just as I thought," she said, verbally pouncing. "The problem is not the weapons. It's the reason we think we have for using them."

"No prudent commander limits his options in advance," Wells said with quick anger. "Yes, a unilateral attack has to be considered a possibility. But it wouldn't be a first strike. They struck first, a long time ago."

"Enough," Erickson said, raising one hand. "Everything you say only confirms my initial decision. There will be no Triad while I'm Chancellor. I won't be the one to put the Service on a war footing. You're welcome to take your case to the individual planetary governments and try to persuade them to turn the Affirmation of Unity into something more substantial, something that can bear the weight of this kind of decision."

"You overlook the likelihood that the worlds may be happy to have the Service deal with this, that in us they have exactly the central government they want," Wells said.

"If so, they're going to have to spell it out," Erickson said curtly. The audience was over.

All the way back to his office in the Defense wing, Wells said nothing. He was too busy at first stilling the spurious emotions that had been stirred up in the conflict, and too busy after that digesting its substantive outcome. Neither explicitly included nor dismissed. Berberon trailed along, respecting Wells's silence but regarding him with a combination of curiosity and apprehension.

Farlad met them at the door to the suite. "What did she say?" he asked hopefully.

"She said no," was Wells's succinct reply as he crossed the room and settled on one of the lounges. He stared at the floor as he massaged the back of his neck, aware that the others were watching him expectantly. "Teo, I'm even more grateful to you now for your suggestion," he said at last. "It's very important that Observer Berberon was there to see that display."

"She did close the door rather firmly," Berberon said with a weak smile in Farlad's direction.

Wells nodded, his expression grave. "More exactly, she left us with no choice but to ask a Vote of Continuance on her."

His face registering shock, Berberon shook his head vigorously. "Triad isn't a recall issue."

"It is for me."

"Harmack, yesterday's votes on Triad mean nothing in this context. Chancellor Erickson has been a first-rate administrator. No one has a grievance against her personally."

"I have no grievance against her personally myself," Wells said, raising his head to meet the Observer's gaze. "But her attitude is reckless. It was one thing to be timid when we had no other choice. But only a fool or a coward would continue that posture now."

"Blythe is neither a fool nor a coward," Berberon said, a noticeable edge in his voice. "She took the stand she did on principle."

"Perhaps," Wells said in a tone that conceded no such thing. "Regardless, she's wrong."

"Harmack, this can't be the only way we can go," Berberon said pleadingly.

Wells stretched out his legs and settled back against the cushions. "Actually I think she expects it. She as much as invited it. She acknowledged that the reaction has been critical. She made it a personal issue. She challenged us to show her that the Worlds stand with us. This will show her very clearly."

Farlad sounded a note of caution. "We need to count the votes very carefully before going ahead with this. She may know she can withstand this and is hoping to hang you out to dry publicly."

"Vote-counting be damned," Wells said with a sidewise glance at Berberon. "I've got a principle at stake here too."

Berberon had found his way to a chair. "And who will you replace her with if you win? Yourself?"

"I've no interest in being Chancellor."

"Who, then? You won't sit for Rieke. Erickson won't sit for Loughridge. Sujata hasn't the experience. And Vandekar —well, Vandekar shouldn't even be a Director, much less Chancellor. Like as not, you'll go through all this only to elect Erickson all over again."

"I don't necessarily agree with your opinions of the candidates," Wells said with equanimity. "What I would value is your opinion of where the requisite fourth Observer vote is most likely to come from."

But rebellion had bubbled up from some heretofore unknown reservoir and taken command of Berberon's tongue. "You'd better worry about where the first vote is coming from first," he said, coming to his feet. "This time you want too much."

Wells sat upright slowly, holding contact with Berberon's defiant eyes. "I've never demanded anything from you, Felithe, least of all that you compromise yourself," he said in a measured tone.

"Oh, not directly, no, that would taint the relationship," Berberon said sarcastically. "You call your puppeteer, and the World Council dances, and the words come out of my mouth. You bloody Nines! Well, this time I won't have it."

"How little you understand us," Wells said quietly.

"You should wish that were so," was Berberon's harsh-edged reply. "I'll stand against you with my vote, my voice, and all the debts I can call in. I supported your advancement to the Committee, Harmack, and I've done you a hundred smaller favors since then. But this time you're wrong. Blythe Erickson belongs in the Chancellery, and Triad be damned."

When Berberon was gone, Farlad cast an apprehensive glance in Wells's direction.

Wells caught the glance and returned a wry smile. "No, I'm not going to retract what I said earlier. This wasn't your fault."

"Did you know that he knew?" Farlad asked cautiously.

"Yes and no," Wells said. "He's never said anything before, but I always assumed he believed I was a Nine. We are not that hard to pick out of a crowd, after all."

"This makes matters awkward."

"I doubt he has adequate proof to ask for my dismissal. *You* would have trouble proving it, even as a Second-tier Nine."

"I meant his opposition."

"Ah. It changes only the difficulty of the objective, not the objective itself." Wells shook his head and laughed softly. "Of all the surprises—even Berberon has principles. Who would have thought he was hiding a diamond or two in his shit all these years?"

• • •

The laughter helped, but nonetheless Wells's equanimity was bruised by three so closely spaced setbacks. Before long, he sent Farlad away and sealed himself within the cocoon of his suite to mend.

There were times it seemed as if he had been fighting the same fight forever, that the nits and gnats who kept coming forward to spar with him were determined to wear him down before he could ever face his real opponent. The only cure for that weariness of spirit was to retreat for a few hours, to take time to simply *be*.

Wells had one totem, one source of material comfort. From a voice-locked drawer he retrieved a small jeweler's box, such as might hold a ring or a pair of earrings. Inside was a thumb-nail-sized gold trigon comprised of three discontinuous bars. Besides Wells, only the metalsmith who had made it knew it existed. Only Wells knew what it was: the symbol of Triad, an insignia for a nonexistent command.

But he knew the kind of men that would wear it, the kind of ships they would employ, the task they would undertake. They would wear the gold triangle, not along with the traditional black ellipse but in place of it. It would be a symbol that set them apart, that raised them up. Looking at the example he held in his hand, he did not consider such thoughts to be mere wishes or hopes. The tangible, tactile reality of the gleaming emblem somehow made it easier to believe in that which was still unrealized.

As Wells was returning the insignia to its case his implant transceiver penetrated his meditations with the seven-tone signal that announced a page from the Nines. He had been half expecting it, since the third of the promised progress reports was overdue. But the voice he heard was not that of the researcher, or even a messenger, but of one of the most senior members of the Eighth Tier: Robert Chaisson.

A brilliant political historian with polymathic knowledge of pre-Reunion society, Chaisson was one of the five overtiers who had recommended Wells's promotion to Eighth. At that time Wells had regarded him as the most likely candidate to join Eric Lange, the movement's martyred founder, on the Ninth Tier. Four years later Wells understood the sociodynamics of the Eighth Tier well enough not to expect that, but he was still vaguely uncomfortable to have Chaisson treat him as an equal.

"How are you, Harmack?" Chaisson asked cheerfully.

"I'm well, Robert. Busy. A bit tired. Our paths haven't crossed for a while now."

"You have to get back down to Earth now and again."

"I do, actually. It's just that I never seem to have the time to come over to the Americas."

"Maybe you just need a more compelling reason," Chaisson said, continuing on before Wells could decide if the comment was said in pique or jest. "I understand you had a setback in Committee yesterday."

It was no surprise that Chaisson knew; he had a web of contacts in Capital. "A temporary problem only, I expect."

"I am glad to hear you so optimistic. Though it *is* disappointing in a way—I thought perhaps I would have a chance to lift your spirits. I'm calling to tell you your search has borne sweeter fruit than you imagined."

"Thackery's personal recs still exist?" Wells asked hopefully.

"Presumably."

The answer did not seem to make sense. "What do you mean?" Wells asked, less insistently than he would have if he had been talking to anyone else.

"It would be unusual to purge them while you still might need them, wouldn't you say?"

"Damn you, stop playing. What are you trying to say?"

Chaisson laughed, a soft-edged sound like a bird's wings fluttering. "That Merritt Thackery is alive. He's living alone in the Susquehanna Valley, on property listed in the name of J. M. Langston."

Wells felt his legs weaken under him even as his heart began to race. "Alive? How? He resigned as Director the year before I was born. He was old then, and that was forty-three years ago!"

"Not as old as you seem to think. Don't forget that he did fieldwork even after the Revision, almost right up to when he resigned. Directors weren't time-bound then—that reform came later. Brian Arlett, the Fourth Tier who handled your request, says that biologically Thackery's no more than a hundred and five—hardly remarkable. And there's always been speculation that his journey through the spindle turned his odometer back, so to speak. There was even a cult of the Immortal centered on him—short-lived, though." Chaisson chuckled deep in his throat at his own joke.

"I can hardly believe it," Wells said, holding his head in his hands. "How can he have hidden from everyone for forty years and we find him in forty-eight hours?"

Chaisson laughed again. "You know the answer to that. We cheat. We can milk the databases in ways no legitimate user can. Arlett can tell you more, if it matters to you. He's waiting to come on the line and give you a full report. My only role here is to steal his thunder."

"Has Thackery been contacted? Does he know we've found him?"

"No to both. He hid himself purposefully and well. Arlett didn't think we should give him a chance to destroy what you're after."

"He's what I'm after—now."

"The sentiment still applies. And besides—just as I wanted to be the one to tell you, I thought you would want to go see him first yourself."

"I do, absolutely." He glanced across the office at the clock. "I should be able to get downwell within the hour."

"No hurry," Chaisson said breezily. "A couple of Third Tiers are watching him. He won't go anywhere without us knowing it."

"Thank you."

"Not me. Arlett saw to that, too. He really has done an excellent bit of service for you. You are planning to promote him for this, I assume?"

"Of course."

"Just wanted to be sure you weren't so excited that you forgot," Chaisson said cheerfully. "Brian's a good kid with a lot of potential. I've been aware of him for some time. Oh, and Harmack? When you're done with Thackery, let me know. I should very much like to talk with him myself."

chapter 6

Refuge

Had he been there for any less urgent purpose, the dirt road
might have been enough to make Harmack Wells turn back.
Just as it had been described to him, it was the sort of road
seemingly designed to enforce privacy. Unmarked, over-
grown, and eroded, it offered no promise that anyone lived at
the other end of it, much less the man who did.

But neither the steep slope nor the washboard surface of
the road was an impediment to Wells's slim-profiled skeeter.
He guided the vehicle slowly through the shadowy tunnel until
it ended, widening out into a clearing barely large enough to
turn a nonflying car around in. The leaf-and-needle carpet
covering the clearing showed no sign that another vehicle had
ever disturbed it.

Leaving his skeeter parked on the road, Wells continued
upslope on foot, on a path barely discernible from the rest of
the terrain. Until entering the Pennsylvania Protectorate, he
had not realized so much undomesticated forestland still existed in the densely populated eastern half of North America.
Not that he had spent any time wondering about it: His last
several visits had been confined to Capital and Benamira.

The canopy of leaves was so thick and the path so undulat-
ing that it was impossible to see the house until he was on top

of it. It was a Swann self-contained, half buried in the hillside and cloaked in a shell of natural wood planking so light in color, it looked as though it were freshly cut. So disguised, it almost seemed to belong there.

Below the house, on the sunny south slope, was a sprawling ornamental garden, a living quilt of yellow and red and white blossoms. On the steepest parts of the slope the flower beds were terraced and the wood-slat walks became stairs. The detailed planning and diligent care evident in the garden made a sharp contrast with the neglected road and forest path.

Movement in the garden drew Wells's eye: a man, his back to Wells, kneeling on one of the upper tiers. Wells picked his way to the nearest walkway and followed it upward. Drawing closer, he took note of the man's thinning silver hair, the tray of tools resting to one side, the trowel being energetically wielded in one gnarled hand.

As Wells reached the same level as the gardener, the creak of the walkway boards under his full frame announced his presence. The man glanced up, then brushed moist black dirt from his hands and sat back on his heels. A thick, close-cropped white beard masked what would have been a familiar visage.

"I do not welcome guests," he said. "Please leave the way you came." There were many years and much travail in the lines of his face but a clear and determined light in his eyes.

Wells stepped toward him. "Do you know who I am?"

"No," said the old man, sniffing as though to say he also did not care.

Wells drew another step closer. "I know who you are." When the old man continued to silently regard Wells with open annoyance, Wells went on, "I know all about you. The Great Revisionist. First Ambassador to the D'shanna. Director of—"

"Spare me my biography," said the man, turning away and plunging his hands into one of the tray's several compartments. He deposited a double handful of peat in the hole before him, then sighed and hung his head at an angle. "I had rather hoped I had been forgotten."

"Hardly," Wells said, approaching within a metre. "Though, like most of my generation must, I thought Merritt Thackery was dead. Or do I take you wrong? Is that what you want?"

Thackery said nothing as he pressed the soil into place

around the last of a new cluster of zinnias, kept his silence as he gathered up his tools and took the tray in hand. Turning his back on Wells, he started up the sloping walkway, his strides made deliberate by age.

Wells followed Thackery at a respectful distance. When Thackery went to place his tray in a large wooden storage box nestled against the house, Wells jumped forward to lift the heavy lid. But Thackery made no acknowledgment that the younger man was even there.

"I mean I know *everything* about you," Wells said as Thackery washed his scarred hands under an outdoor spigot. "Even things you may not know. And things you may not want others to know."

But still Thackery showed no spark of interest, almost as though he were deaf to Wells's words. He wiped his hands casually on his trouser legs, then moved toward the door.

Not being recognized had been an affront; being ignored drove a needle deep into Wells's ego. "Do you think this is all it will take?" he called out angrily. "Are you waiting for me to get tired of being ignored and go away?"

"No," Thackery said, pausing on the threshold. "I am waiting for you to stop trying to impress me and tell me what you want."

"Then you'll talk with me?"

Thackery's eyebrow lifted in surprise. "You would have had to go to a great deal of trouble to find me. I know, because I went to a great deal of trouble not to be found. You didn't intend to let me refuse, did you?"

Wells stared a moment. "No."

Thackery nodded. "Then you'd better come inside."

The house had been as completely reworked on the inside as it had on the outside. Only the positions of the sun jacket, the regen inputs, and other elements of the environmental system marked it as a Swann. Many of the interior walls had been removed, and several ceilings raised, so that instead of several small rooms, there was a single elongated and irregularly shaped chamber. At one end a spiral staircase led to a rooftop observation deck, visible through the sloping high-wall glass of the sun jacket.

It seemed almost like the great hall of a castle from a new medieval age. Aside from the light fixtures, virtually none of the common home technology was in evidence. Nowhere did Wells espy a netlink projector, or even a furniture grouping oriented for a concealed one. And to reinforce the impression, despite all the glass, the interior seemed shadowy and somber.

They settled in soft chairs by a window that looked out on the tree-covered valley. "Perhaps I *should* know who you are," Thackery said.

"My name is Harmack Wells."

Thackery gestured in the air with one hand. "I'm afraid I've rather completely eloigned myself from the affairs of the world. Your name is not one I have heard before."

"Four years ago I was named Director of USS-Defense."

"Ah," Thackery said, his hand going to his chin. "That explains some things. Not all, by far. How did you find me? No one in the Service knows where I am."

Wells smiled. "I have access to resources beyond those the Service can call on."

"And what are those?"

Wells hesitated. For all the information he had gathered on Thackery, the man had already surprised him more than once. Wells had expected Thackery to vigorously resist the intrusion; that was why Wells had come himself, and alone. Yet Thackery's easy concession was no victory. Wells still had to prove himself, and one of the tests would be honesty.

"I am also an Eighth Tier member of the Nines," said Wells.

It was an admission Wells rarely made to those outside the organization. A conflict-of-interest clause in Service contracts prohibited membership in certain types of partisan organizations and any sort of involvement with planetary politics. The Nines were at the top of the blacklist.

Contract notwithstanding, Wells was admitting not only to membership but also to a very high level of involvement. Consequently he was not surprised when Thackery frowned and looked away, out the window.

Wells continued, "As you might expect, a number of our members work in information science. They were able to access the payment records from your Service trust and your primary credit account. Following the money is usually a good way to find someone."

Thackery turned back and regarded Wells with a level gaze. "Then it's the Ninth Tier that sent you? Or does the

Chancellor of the Service now condone its Directors coming downwell to violate the Privacy Laws and harass Earth citizens?"

"Certain issues transcend such considerations."

Thackery scowled. "That's the kind of arrogance I've come to expect from the Nines. I've long suspected you believe that Council law applies only to others. This episode demonstrates that I was right."

Wells felt himself tensing. "Perhaps you should wait until you hear why I sought you out before judging."

"I've been waiting since you first disturbed me," Thackery said, folding his hands on his lap.

His irritation on the rise again, Wells wondered when he had lost control of the encounter. "I don't know what you know of the strategic situation—" Wells began.

"Nothing, and I have even less interest."

"Can I continue?"

Thackery waved a hand. "Of course."

"When I became Director of Defense, I inherited a passive establishment capable of doing little more than warning that an attack was coming. We had no way of blunting another attack. We still have no way of carrying the war to the Sterilizers."

"An oversight you no doubt intend to correct."

"The only way to assure our own peace is to be ready to go to war."

"If you say. What have I to contribute to this?"

"We need to know more about the Mizari. As a matter of political necessity, we need conclusive proof that they still exist. As a matter of military intelligence, we need to know what they are like and what they are capable of. It would be best if we could acquire both without reminding them of our own existence."

"Why come to me? All I know of the Sterilizers can be found in the reports I made."

"I know that. I've read *Jiadur's Wake.*"

Thackery raised an eyebrow in mild surprise. "Then you are one of the few," he said with some bitterness. "But that still doesn't answer my question."

"I need your help only to contact the D'shanna. They can provide us the rest of what we need."

Thackery seemed to shrink into his chair like a turtle withdrawing into his shell. "There is nothing I can do for you."

"You have to," Wells pressed, sensing Thackery's vulnerability. "No one else has ever been on the spindle. No one else has ever contacted the D'shanna."

"I do not have the information you seek. I know no way to do what you want," he said stonily. Then his expression softened to one of wistful reflection. "And if I did, I no longer have the confidence of purpose to trust myself to know the right thing to do with it."

"I have the confidence. Trust me."

Thackery sank back into his chair, slowly drew his legs up, and twisted to one side, a trembling hand hiding his eyes. "This is the world you built," Thackery said wearily, "you and your kind. I neither know nor care about your squabbles. Please go away."

With those words the last remnants of the idolatry Wells had once felt for Thackery melted away, and with them, Wells's inhibitions. "You're human. You're bloodkin to the whole Affirmation. How can you favor an alien over your own kind?" he demanded.

"My own kind?" Thackery said with a bitter laugh. "No one anywhere is like me. I waited too long to retire—about four centuries too long. There's not one person on Earth who's seen half of what I have or understands what seeing it did to me. I don't belong here."

"Where do you belong, then?" Wells asked cuttingly. "On the spindle, with Gabriel? Is that why you've isolated yourself, so no one will know when you go away with him?"

Suddenly Thackery was on his feet, shouting. "If I knew how to return there, do you think I would still be here? Do you think I haven't called out to the sky ten thousand times hoping Gabriel would answer, that he would return and take me back? Why do you think I've clung to life this long?"

As though his legs had gone to rubber beneath him, Thackery slowly slipped back down into his seat and buried his face in his hands. Wells looked away, embarrassed for the man.

The courtesy also helped mask Wells's own fierce disappointment. He did not want to believe Thackery, for that would require him to abandon hope for an ally against the Mizari. But Thackery's pain was no pretense; Wells did not doubt that he had tried to make contact and failed, not once but many times. Even so, Wells could not help but play one last card.

"Director—"

Thackery looked up.

"I'm going to leave now. You've made your attitude clear. There's something I have to make clear to you. I'm afraid it won't be possible to protect your secret. There is a whole generation who knows you only as a name. They will be curious to see you as a man. Many will want more from you than I do."

"That threat was implied the moment you appeared," Thackery said, his face and voice regaining the gruffness they had projected in the garden. "It makes no difference. I have nothing to tell you."

Wells pursed his lips and nodded. He extracted his long frame from the chair and stood there for a moment, looking down at Thackery. "You were once a hero to me," he said, a bare hint of the sadness he felt escaping with the words.

Thackery raised his head and met Wells's gaze levelly. "I trust you know better now."

"Yes," Wells said, and turned away.

Somehow the walk back down the hill to his skeeter seemed endless.

For a long time after Wells left, Thackery sat in his chair and thought the things he had not said.

If being with Gabriel on the spindle had been the high point of his life, it had also served to make the years that followed seem all the more hollow. Not thirteen years restructuring Survey for its new, more limited role, not his final mission to Rena-Kiri, not his brief stint as Director of the Service had been enough to make him whole again. The degree to which he was lionized following the Council's announcement of his discoveries only accentuated his empty feelings.

After his resignation he had begun an emotional odyssey, a search for a community in which he could be comfortable, to which he could experience a sense of belonging. He tried to inject himself into one Terran subculture after another, commune and clan, archaicist and mysticist, hoping to find minds attuned to his own perceptions of existence.

But the respectful deference of people who might otherwise have been his friends, the endless attempts by smiling influence-peddlers to place him in their debt, the ingrained misperceptions of what he had actually done, the shallowness and temporality of their vision of the world, all worked to deny him what he was seeking.

It was then that he began work on *Jiadur's Wake,* naïvely hoping to free himself of the burden of his own fame. When it was rejected—he could not view the decision to censor it in any other light—he considered it a rejection of himself and turned his back on them.

In fact, the only lesson of enduring value that emerged from that time was one of rejection—that he was a foreigner, an oddity, an alien. There was no one else like him anywhere. Acceptance of that lesson had brought him at last to the Susquehanna.

There had been little enough pleasure in the four decades since he had retired, but most of what there had been, he had found here, in his woodland sanctuary. Now it had been violated, and Thackery knew he could not stay. But where he could go, he did not know. One thing was clear: There would be no sanctuary for him now anywhere on Earth.

His deepyacht, *Fireside,* had been downwell for a long time, but he had provided for its upkeep by means of a testamentary trust. He had had no conscious reason for doing so, beyond the natural inclination of a sailor to care for his ship. She had no great sentimental value to him, as he had made only one voyage in her. She had no practical value so long as he wished to maintain his pseudonymous hermitage.

Now the ship beckoned to him, offering escape. But where could it take him that Wells could not reach? To regain what he had lost, he would have to leave not only Earth but also the Affirmation. To attempt that in a deepyacht too closely resembled suicide.

It was several hours before he hit upon an alternative, but when he did, its rightness compelled him to embrace it. The first step required but a phone call. "Prepare *Fireside* for space," he said. "I'm going out." The word *again* was so strong in his mind that he wondered if he had said it.

Thackery had not quite admitted to himself until Wells had torn it from him that his time in the Susquehanna had been a vigil. If he was to fail to find a place in the human community, if he was to be denied reunion with Gabriel, he could at least choose not to surrender his remaining life to those hurts.

He had had enough of being lonely; now it was time to be alone.

Three hours after leaving Thackery, Wells rode an empty twelve-seat executive shuttle out of Newark back to orbit. The Brazilian orbital injector was closed twenty-four hours for maintenance, and he preferred enduring the extra gees and extra cost of the any-field shuttle to either waiting or going halfway around the world to the still operating African or Far East injectors. He briefly considered accepting the forced layover and flying west to see Chaisson, but in the end he decided he had left too many matters hanging to justify more time away.

Almost until he boarded the shuttle Wells had been unable to look past his disappointment at the outcome of his visit. But as the swollen-bodied vehicle lumbered upward, vibrating in sympathy with its roaring chemical engines, he at last put the disappointment behind him.

The whole business had been false to his basic beliefs. He was embarrassed remembering the threat he had made, the emotional barbs he had attempted to lodge in Thackery's conscience. It had been so tempting to hope that Thackery could pave smooth one of the most difficult parts of what lay ahead.

But despite what Berberon thought, and even if the same could not be said of the Nines generally, coercion was not Wells's way. It was usually better that something not be done at all than be done by unwilling hands. And it was always better to take responsibilities on oneself than to drop them into the laps of the unprepared.

Seduced by the prospect of a quick and easy solution to the problem of scouting the Mizari, he had allowed himself to be distracted at a time when more essential matters had required his full attention. Now Triad had been derailed, Berberon alienated, and Erickson alerted.

As the sky outside the shuttle's windows faded quickly from blue to violet, and then to black, Wells took advantage of the privacy of the passenger cabin to make two calls, closing out his business on the surface.

The first was to Chaisson. The historian was off-line, so Wells left a brief message: "Richard—the business with Merritt will take some time to complete, and I don't think it will withstand any extraneous contacts. Please put off indefinitely any plans to see him, and treat his existence as the strictest possible secret." Tradition would give the request the force of an order.

The second call was to Arlett. "We're going to have to keep watching Thackery, and you're going to have to coordinate it," Wells told him. "Anybody who doesn't already know that he's there isn't to find out. Anybody who does know is under interdict."

"I understand, Mr. Wells. Nobody comes to see him except you."

"I won't be coming back to see him," Wells said. "But so long as he stays in that house, I want him left undisturbed. If he should leave, that's another story. I'm to be alerted immediately, and he's to be monitored as intensively and invasively as we're capable of. Barring that, though, leave him be."

"I understand. Sir—if I might ask about the possibility of promotion—"

"No. Never ask, Brian. And never make it part of your decision to lend service. Do for yourself and the things you believe in and not for the rewards that might come."

"That would be easier if it were always clear how the things we are asked to do serve what we believe in."

"It would be clearer if you did not always expect it to be easy," Wells said sharply.

"Yes, sir," Arlett said in a subdued voice.

In fairness, finding Thackery was service at least equal to that on which many promotions had been granted, and doubtless Arlett knew that. But he also doubtless knew that the jump from Fourth to Fifth brought with it so large a measure of additional authority—including the right to recruit new First Tiers and the first, albeit limited, authority to place referral requests—that it was not uncommon for the overtier involved to "load up" on the candidate.

Wells was content to let Arlett think that was the reason and grumble to himself if so inclined. To grant a promotion now, Wells would have to make known to the community of the Nines the service that had won it, and that he was not prepared to do. He would sustain a small, short-lived injustice in expiation of a larger one, so that he might quell his conscience and quiet his backward-looking curiosity, and so focus his efforts on shaping the still malleable future.

That business dealt with, he made one final call, to Kioni.

He felt within him a growing restless energy, an impatience with the endless jockeying of move and countermove, pawn traded for pawn—an eagerness to press on to the endgame. There was no cure at hand for the root cause, but he was not above treating the symptoms.

Kioni was much preferable to Ronina for such matings. She was much less his physical ideal than Ronina, small-breasted where Ronina was well gifted, thick-thighed where Ronina was long-limbed. But Kioni allowed him to come to her without promises and to touch her without touching, in whatever way he chose and whenever he pleased. They came together as animals, in mutual selfishness, and parted as strangers, in mutual satiation. Or so he had come to expect of her from their half dozen previous encounters.

She was waiting in his bed when he arrived, and she did not disappoint him.

chapter 7

Recall

Felithe Berberon had fully expected to hear from the World Council concerning his report on the challenge to Chancellor Erickson. But he had not expected to be ordered to Capital three hours after transmitting it.

Nor was the order a welcome one. For a variety of reasons, it had been more than seven years since Berberon had been on Earth. One reason had to do with personal biology. Berberon was allergic to more than two hundred varieties of atmospheric flotsam and did not care either to flood his body with mind-dulling drugs or to go without and spend his time downwell feeling as though his chest were in a vise.

An even larger factor was that the trip down and back quite thoroughly terrorized him. Having no comforting faith with which to sanguinely accept his own mortality, Berberon chose to avoid placing his life at even minimal risk. That was not possible where spaceflight was concerned—particularly the orbit-to-ground and ground-to-orbit regimens.

True, shuttle crashes were rare, and failures of the orbital injectors even rarer, but when accidents did occur, there were never any survivors. As he habitually reminded those amused by his phobia, "Bags of protoplasm make notoriously bad meteors."

A final consideration was that, thanks to three decades in reduced gravity and an aversion to exercise for its own sake, he was now thoroughly maladapted to a full gee field. Climbing a ramp or stairway on Earth left him panting, his heart beating angry protest against the exertion. Too, the altered environment clashed against his learned reflexes, turning his gliding steps into graceless stumbles. And what were pleasingly rounded body contours in orbit became loose, sagging folds of flesh on Earth; the first day down, the man in Berberon's mirror was a stranger.

In light of such considerations, and not being notably sentimental about verdant hills and pristine brooks, Berberon had gladly forgone many opportunities to return to his homeworld. The last event he had thought important enough to come downwell for had been the election of Jean-Paul Tanvier as World Council President. Being present at the inauguration and endearingly visible during the social functions that surrounded it had doubtless been a factor in Tanvier retaining Berberon as Observer, especially considering that one of the President's aides had been angling for the post for himself.

This time he had been given no choice.

Mercifully the worst part of the trip was already behind him. He had come in through Algiers Port of Entry, the shuttle popping its double sonic boom over the Strait of Gibraltar and making its final heart-pounding energy management turn over the western Mediterranean. Only when the spaceplane stopped rolling did he unclench his teeth and relax his viselike grip on the padded body harness.

A Council airskiff had been waiting for him there. As quickly as his overnighter could be retrieved from the cargo claim, he was aloft again. Flying fifteen hundred metres above the water, the skiff made a dogleg around Sardegna and then skimmed across the Tyrrhenian Sea in a beeline toward the Italian peninsula and the Adriatic beyond. Now, with the rounded ridges of the Apennines ahead on the horizon and the coastline passing below, the skiff began to climb. Capital lay just twenty minutes away.

Still troubling Berberon was the question of why he had been recalled. Other than purely social functions, which this surely was not, there was no interaction that could not be handled technologically, no information that could not be passed by means of the secure channels of the net.

The only reasons Berberon could think of for bringing him

down to Earth were symbolic ones. Recall without explanation was in itself a naked reminder of the Council's authority. And Tanvier's insistence on breathing the same air as he did could be an attempt to reinforce through the ancient language of biological programming just who was in charge. Body-language dominance displays were transmitted poorly by the net, and pheromones and fear-sweat not at all.

But there had been nothing in Berberon's message that should have prompted a rebuke. He had not mentioned his admittedly indiscreet blowup with Wells, offering instead a prediction that Wells would attempt to have Erickson removed, along with his own appraisal of why that was undesirable.

Which meant that almost certainly a version of that regrettable conversation had reached Tanvier by another route. If so, then there was one more possible reason for the recall—that Tanvier was going to remove him from the Observer's office.

Before Berberon could evaluate the question to his satisfaction, the skiff was suddenly over water again and Capital was in sight.

The once free-floating artificial island had been permanently located in the shallows of the Gulf of Venice for the better part of a century, ever since the practical difficulties of maintaining it had begun to outweigh the symbolic value of a Capital not physically "belonging" to any traditional nation-state.

At first, it had been moored still afloat. Later, when the *bora*-whipped waters of the Gulf and the unpredictable seiches of the Adriatic continued the structural assault begun in the free-roaming years, Capital had been elevated out of the sea on pillars in a feat of engineering arguably more remarkable than the city's construction.

Berberon had always found it both ironic and appropriate that the island city had ended up in sight of the ruins of the City of Canals. Both Capital and Venice were centers of economic and political power for their eras, and both had made a devil's pact with the sea—acquiring a unique beauty and character even while sowing the seeds of self-destruction.

After decades of fighting subsidence and flooding, Venice had succumbed to entropy and neglect in the Black Years preceding Reunion. Capital's end was even now being preordained by efficiency analyses, which pointed up the undeniably high cost of the endless maintenance of an architectural white elephant and proposed moving the seat of government elsewhere.

But until the Council turned analysis into action, Capital would continue its life as a modern reincarnation of *La Serenissima*.

The airskiff delivered Berberon to the elevated passenger-only landing deck on the west edge of the city. From there an open-air slidewalk carried him to the security checkpoint at the entrance to the Council Hall. By the time he reached it, he was gasping for breath despite the drugs he had taken that morning.

On the other side of the checkpoint an aide-courtier was waiting to escort him to the meeting. From the route they took, Berberon knew almost immediately that their destination was one of the four sumptuous lounges on the sixteenth floor of the Hall, each of which looked out to a different compass point through a broad expanse of seamless synglas.

Being taken there instead of to the regular Council chamber confirmed Berberon's suspicion that he would not be facing the full seventeen-member Council but its unofficial inner circle: Tanvier and the five High Ministers. They were waiting there for him, seated as though they had known his arrival was imminent, talking quietly among themselves.

Berberon knew them all in varying degrees. The closest he had to a personal friend in the group was Aram Wolfe, the High Minister for Economic Planning, who was the oldest of the six by several years. The two women, Hu and Aboulein, were nearly strangers; Hu by dint of a retiring personality and Aboulein because she had been in office less than a year.

The blunt-spoken Breswaithe regarded Berberon with a certain amount of personal antipathy; presumably it arose from incompatible personalities, since they often agreed on matters of policy. By contrast, Berberon had had several heated disagreements, public and private, with President Tanvier, most notably over his strategy for appeasing the Nines. Yet Tanvier was enough of a professional that those conflicts had never taken on personal dimensions.

Dailey was the hardest to take, for he held the seat Berberon thought by rights should have belonged to him. Worse, the chisel-featured North American seemed somehow to charge every look and utterance with his self-satisfied awareness of that grievance.

There was one chair left unoccupied, and Berberon eased

his weary-limbed frame into it gratefully as the ministers shifted their attention from each other to the newcomer.

"Capital is enjoying a cool summer, I see," Berberon offered conversationally.

"Do you think so?" Tanvier asked lightly. "Perhaps you have become too thoroughly acclimated to Unity. I know I always find it oppressively warm there."

His control of the meeting established, Tanvier paused and glanced down at the slate in his lap. "We've reviewed your most recent dispatch with a great deal of interest," he said, looking up. "As you well know, Felithe, no Chancellor has faced a Vote of Continuation since Delkes withstood three of them early in his first term. And no Chancellor has lost a Vote since Ryan Bodanis was shown the door in 'twenty-four."

"Quite true," Berberon said.

"Then you understand why I thought it would be a good idea for you to come and review the process with us, for the benefit of those of us whose political memories don't reach back that far." Tanvier smiled at Aboulein as he spoke.

At first blush, Berberon was insulted by the request. There were probably fifty political analysts, including at least five who were experts on the USS, with offices within ten minutes of the conference room. Any one of them could have easily provided what amounted to a second form polisci lecture. And what's more, it was their job.

But a moment's reflection persuaded Berberon that perhaps Tanvier was more concerned about security than professional courtesy. In any event, there was nothing to be gained by demurring.

"A brief review before we move on to the particulars of the present situation would very likely be time well spent," Berberon agreed. "According to the revision of the bylaws adopted in 640—"

"Excuse me, Observer Berberon," Aboulein interrupted. "I am one who requested your appearance here. I've read the bylaws, as I hope every Councilor has. What is not clear to me is whether the high officers of the Service actually follow their own rules."

"Oh?"

"After all, with the autonomy granted the Chancellor and the degree of secrecy that surrounds Committee decisions, it would be very difficult for the Service Court to make a case against the ruling oligarchy, even if they were inclined to do so. I would very much value your observations along that line."

Berberon nodded, his pride somewhat assuaged by the young Mideasterner's redefinition of the question. "I understand that it's hard for the members of a body such as the Council, with all the elaborate checks and balances under which it operates, to see what restrains those who hold power more absolutely. And it's true that from time to time, as in any large organization, there exists a distinction between the way things are officially done and the way they are really done.

"However, in this particular area the bylaws have always been very carefully observed. The Chancellor's term is ten years. The only way to remove her before that time is through a Vote of Continuation, the rules for which are very specific. Wells or any other Comitè can ask for a Vote of Continuation at any meeting or request a meeting for that purpose. He will be allowed to state why he believes a change is desirable. The Chancellor will be allowed an equal amount of time—be it five minutes or five hours—for rebuttal.

"Once the statements are on record, the Committee votes secretly, with no further discussion. Once the Committee's vote is recorded—but not announced—the Observers are polled publicly, in order of seniority."

"So you would vote first," Breswaithe observed. "Would you say that that gives you any useful influence?"

"Of course. The process was meant to allow those with the longest perspective to set the tone," Berberon said. "Where was I? Oh, yes—for Erickson to be removed, a majority of both the Committee and the Observers—each counted separately—must vote against her."

"So Chancellor Erickson could conceivably alienate eight of the eleven concerned and still stay on," Dailey said. "I find that remarkable."

"Remember that before Atlee's reforms, the chief executive of the Service could not be removed at all. The Service has always been interested in long-term stability. These rules were meant to protect against frivolous concerns being used against a sitting Chancellor," Berberon said.

"It still strikes me as reckless and politically naïve," Dailey said.

"You apply a false standard," Berberon said firmly. "Fundamentally it is not a political system. It is an administrative one—"

Tanvier interrupted, imposing a truce on the skirmishing parties. "You haven't addressed the selection of a replacement."

Berberon nodded. "True, I have not. But then, there is little I can say, because the Observers—which is to say the Worlds—have no role in it. Should a Chancellor lose a Vote of Continuation, he or she becomes a temporary member of the Committee. The Committee then meets daily in private— no Observers present—until one of its members is elected Chancellor, again on a majority vote. But, of course, a majority is now *four* votes, not three. You see the potential for stalemate, I trust."

"The former Chancellor could conceivably wield considerable influence in choosing her successor," Aboulein suggested.

"That's often been the case at the end of a term, when the same procedure is followed," Berberon agreed.

Wolfe joined the discussion for the first time. "How do you see things proceeding should Erickson lose the vote?"

There was something unspoken in the question that troubled Berberon, prompting him to answer more bluntly than he otherwise might have. "You can count on at least six weeks of posturing and bloodletting before a replacement is chosen," he warned. "It'll take that long for everyone to stop promoting their own cause and come together for the common good."

"Not unlike the College of Cardinals," Tanvier observed.

"Except that the ghost of the last pope gets to vote—and may even get to succeed himself."

"Is that your prediction in this instance?" Tanvier asked.

Berberon shook his head. "I don't think it's possible at this time to predict who will emerge as the new Chancellor."

"Could it be Wells himself?" Wolfe asked with a note of concern.

"I'm reasonably confident that Chancellor Erickson would be able to block that." Berberon turned his eyes on Tanvier as he continued. "But I would prefer not to see it get that far. No matter who is eventually elected, Wells is certain to have more influence than he does now with Erickson. By successfully removing a Chancellor who opposed him, he will have warned others against doing the same."

Continuing, he addressed himself to the group as a whole. "This is one of several reasons why it's very important that Erickson win this vote. I have already talked with Ambassador

Ka'in about it, and I will see Ambassador Bree on my return. Wells will be lobbying them as well, of course, but I am reasonably confident that at least two of the other Observers will stand with me."

Tanvier contemplated his hands, folded and resting in his lap, as he replied. "I'm afraid that we do not share your appraisal of the situation, Felithe."

"In what respect?" Berberon demanded.

It was Breswaithe who answered, stepping in in a manner suggesting that it had been prearranged. "There are consequences to this business that you've overlooked or minimized. The efficiency and effectiveness of the Service will be affected by the time spent haggling over elections, as well as by the long period of readjustment that is bound to follow."

Berberon stared at Breswaithe disbelievingly. "I don't see where the prospect of weakening the Service argues for Erickson's removal. I would think the opposite were true."

"We believe that having the Service in internal disarray, however briefly, works to our advantage," Breswaithe said quietly.

"*Who* believes that?" Berberon demanded, giving Breswaithe a scathing look. "Oh, I know the Nines do, because of their paranoia about an interplanetary government. They'd love to see us seize control of the USS and end any drift toward federalism. But who else in their right mind? The USS is the glue that holds the Unified Worlds together."

No one spoke, and Berberon searched their faces for explanations. "Is that it? Is annexation officially on our agenda now?"

"Nothing as extreme as that," Tanvier said, gesturing in the air with one hand. "But I am increasingly uncomfortable with the degree to which we are dependent on an organization as potentially—ah—unpredictable as the Unified Space Service. This would seem to offer an opportunity to gain some additional leverage and thereby reduce that dependence."

"We seem to be having some trouble finding the right words," Berberon said with a tightness in his throat. "You say the USS is unpredictable, and yet it seems that what you're really saying is that you don't control them. And what you see as undesirable dependence looks to me like a perfectly benign interdependence."

"Honorable minds may differ on the latter," Hu said.

Berberon stared. "When did this Council turn isolationist?

How are we harmed by ties with the Service or the other worlds?" he demanded challengingly. "Tell me how that diminishes anything except the chances of the Nines gaining the kind of control that they seek."

Wolfe made one feeble effort to cast events in a better light. "If Wells is truly as potentially disruptive as you have lately been arguing, perhaps you can look on this as an opportunity to throw an obstacle in his path."

It was painfully clear that the matter had been fully discussed and the decision made even before Berberon had been recalled to Capital. "It won't be an obstacle," Berberon said angrily. "You're doing him a favor. Perhaps I've misread this from the start. Is that fleet he's building to be Earth's rather than the Service's? Has some deal been struck under which he's to become Chancellor and give us what would be too much trouble to take? If so, then for life's sake tell me now. I operate best when I have the maximum available information."

"No such deal exists," Tanvier said, less convincingly than Berberon would have liked. "Certainly annexation has been discussed in High Council. And I won't say that the possibility has been ruled out. But for the present we will content ourselves with more modest goals—such as control of our own spaceports and of ground-to-orbit travel. Erickson has been unequivocal in her refusal even to negotiate such a transfer. Hopefully her successor will be more reasonable."

Berberon sank back into his chair. "You'd better spell out what you expect from me, then. This is not the game I thought we were playing."

"I fully intended to," Tanvier said amicably. "Your instructions are to stand mute on the question of the recall of Chancellor Erickson."

Berberon shook his head in disgust. "I tell you again, it is a mistake of the first order to consciously try to weaken the Service."

Tanvier refolded his hands in his lap. "That may be, from their perspective. But your first obligation is to us, Felithe. Please do not make us think that you have been away so long as to have forgotten it."

Janell Sujata had had to leave much of Maranit behind when she came to Unity the first time, as a member of one of the early tutelary classes from that world. She had left behind the familiar pastels of the heath, the faintly gingerish scent of maranax on the summer air, the noisy camaraderie of the kinderhouse. But by bringing her lifecord with her, she felt as though she somehow had brought all of that and more with her.

Five years later, when she and two others from her class had chosen to stay in what her home tongue called the world of outsiders, she had given up still more. Contact with the outside was too new for Maranit to have a legal concept of planetary citizenship, but that did not mean it had no sense of community. By staying behind, the three gave up a claim to belonging as tangible as any in law. Sujata of Murlith signed her first Service contract as Janell Sujata, put away her *feya*-cloth hipwraps, and faced the fact that opportunities for *xochaya* would be few and far between.

It was not all sacrifice—far from it. She had learned by then that the Service was eager to dilute the dominance of Earth and Journa by assimilating representatives from other worlds. It was the key reason why they so willingly brought in hundreds of young colonials, then clothed, housed, fed, and educated them at Service expense. Having had the chance to evaluate them at length and in detail, at the end of the tutelary period the Service coaxed and wooed and eventually hired the best of them.

That was the other thing Sujata learned: that she was good at doing the things the Service needed done. She had a knack, more trained than inherited, for making groups function smoothly—not by inspiring them, not by mastering every last detail of their task herself, but by reading the strengths of each individual and placing them where they could be most effective.

In the world of outsiders there was opportunity for one with such a skill. On Maranit the road to the top was congested with other aspirants. Kinship and friendship and personality often counted as much as ability, and in those categories she had no special advantage. Seduced by praise she deserved but rarely heard, she stayed.

Perhaps because of her lineage, rather than despite it, she had been well rewarded. Her first job had been as a minor project leader during the construction of USS-Central; her portion had come in ahead of schedule and within the conservatively set budget. From there she had gone to Microscopium Center as an associate deputy manager of base operations.

Two promotions later she had moved on to Ba'ar Tell as Director of the Service's office there. At each stop she had become more a part of the Service and less a part of Maranit.

But throughout she had kept the lifecord, and if she had had fewer chances to wear it those years, that was not to say that it had become any less important to her. She still faithfully cared for it: the core of the sugar-brown necklace of intricately woven and knotted hair was now nearly twenty years old, but was still as silky and supple as when it had been part of her uncut tresses at age twelve. She had been late to menarche and so had welcomed the chance to begin work on her lifecord when it finally came.

And she still faithfully observed the requirement to add to the lifecord yearly, so that the record it contained might be complete. According to tradition, the fragile strands held the memory of each hour and minute of that person's life. When that individual died, the lifecord was treated with more reverence than the body and was commonly kept by the family as a memorial.

Inevitably, anthropologists had come to dissect Maranit customs. With the imperiousness of superior knowledge, they had announced that while hair did indeed contain a continuous record of health and diet, dead protein offered neither the mechanism nor the structure to preserve emotion and experience. Like most Maranit, Janell Sujata found she did not care. What matter if a lifecord was not really a vault of memories, so long as when she contemplated it and touched it, she remembered?

Concealed by the loose Shinn-style blouse she wore, Sujata's lifecord was around her neck now as she walked through the corridors of Unity's diplomatic section. Hanging from the cord was a smooth-surfaced pendant made of what seemed to be a finely grained wood but was in fact a tiny piece of Maranit itself. She had chipped her heartstone from the mother rock in Murlith the same day her hair was cut for the lifecord. Like all new heartstones, it had broken off jagged and ugly, characterless. The beauty it had since acquired had come solely from her.

If the lifecord was a testament to accumulated experience, the heartstone was a test of character. Many a young girl made her fingers bleed trying to accomplish too much too quickly. It had taken Sujata eight years to work her stone, hand-rubbing its roughness smooth, imprinting her soul on its malleable heart. Only then had she been proud enough of her stone to hang it from her lifecord and so proclaim herself an adult.

Lifecord and heartstone together—the merging of learning and experience with commitment and inner strength—made for the most precious and the most private possession a Maranit woman owned. Sujata had never allowed Wyrena to see it, or even to know that it existed. Created by Maranit sensibilities, it was fit only for Maranit eyes.

She turned onto a wide boulevard flanked by yard apartments whose front doors opened not onto a sterile corridor but to a private patch of landscaped life lit from a high-arched glassine ceiling. The ground cover and flowers chosen by Environmental Maintenance were egocentrically Terran, to be sure, but the effect was still pleasing. Had the whole block that contained it not been security-restricted, Gegenschein Way would likely have been featured on the standard Unity tour.

As she came up the walk toward the entrance to one of the apartments, the door slid open and a woman stepped to the opening.

"Come in, Sujata," Allianora said, and stepped aside to admit her.

Wordlessly they readied themselves, shedding jewelry and blouses, scrubbing away makeup. The ritual of *xochaya* was familiar to each separately, even if they were relatively new to each other. It was not uncommon for sisters or close friends to sit down together weekly, or lovers daily. Sujata's relationship with Allianora fit none of those categories, and in the three months since her arrival the two women had performed *xochaya* only three times.

That was admittedly more Sujata's doing than Allianora's. As the senior ruler, Allianora had made the customary offer on first meeting, and Sujata had accepted, as politeness demanded. But whether due to the difference in age, Sujata's separation from her own traditions, or simply as a matter of random incompatibility, they learned that time that Sujata did not read Allianora well. *Xochaya* required mutual trust, involved mutual risk, but could not promise mutual rewards.

With a long-time mate on her diplomatic staff Allianora could gracefully sustain an occasional unequal match. Sujata was too aware of the one-sidedness to avail herself often of Allianora's generosity. But there were times, like this, when the need was too great.

Bare to the waist, hipwrap knotted on the private right instead of the public left, they sat down on opposite sides of a low table decorated with elaborate abstract carvings. Sujata placed her hands side by side on the table, palms down, fingers parallel, thumbs touching tip to tip. Allianora did the same, completing the cradle. Allianora's hands reminded Sujata of her mother's: the skin life-toughened, the ring finger almost as long as the middle. Closing her eyes, Sujata focused on her own breathing until it became deep, peaceful, and regular. The heartstone dangled between her breasts, swaying like a metronome and pacing her body's fundamental rhythm.

Sujata opened her eyes to find Allianora studying her closely. The focus of Allianora's gaze was not Sujata's face but just below. Sujata showed her acceptance of the scrutiny by returning it. Opening herself to Allianora's reading, Sujata reached out with her eyes toward what Maranit artists called the "second face"—the breasts, lifecord, and heartstone of another. Together they spoke the pledge:

> *Selir bi' chentya*
> *Darnatir bi' maranya en bis losya*
> *Ti bir naskya en bis pentaya*
> *Loris bir rownya*
> *Qoris nonitya*

> I lower my mask
> Open my heart to your eyes
> My ears to your words of guidance
> Expose the flaws in my essence
> Make me whole

Breaking the cradle, Allianora reached out with her right hand and closed her fingers around Sujata's heartstone. Closing her eyes, she explored its sinuous surface with her fingertips, as if drawing through them the residue of Sujata's unresolved emotion. After several minutes she released the stone and sat back on her heels.

"You are unhappy," Allianora said, opening her eyes. "The little one has complicated your life."

Sujata sighed deeply. "She's working so hard to get close to me that she's driving me away. She is endlessly solicitous. She apologizes anytime she imagines she has displeased me —and she imagines it often."

"Her need follows the path of dependence."

"But she wasn't like this before," Sujata said, taking her own heartstone in hand. "On Ba'ar Tell she was confident, playful. She came to me, not the other way around. Nothing would have happened between us if that hadn't been true."

"This is your world, Sujata. It frightens her."

"Why should she be frightened? I'm as new to this Unity as she. But I find nothing frightening here."

Allianora smiled. "Because you have something important to do. You have worth-making tasks enough to occupy you fully—as they did before she came. But you are her whole life now."

"I know that," Sujata said resignedly. "But I don't want to be."

"Because of the responsiblity you feel toward her?"

"It's an unhealthy way to live, for either side."

"Don't judge so harshly. None of us can fully escape that which we learn with the uncritical mind. You were able to introduce her to a new pattern because she was secure that the old was there for her to flee to. It was a game, an adventure. She was testing herself with the forbidden, and it took hold of her. Now she is here, without that security. All she has is the old patterns driven into her as a child."

"She never showed me this face before."

"She had no need to. What you describe is the way in which Ba'ar Tell women are taught to hold their mates. What you despise, men cherish because it brings gratification to them and peace to the household. If she is true to the pattern, you will never hear her complain, no matter how unhappy she becomes. One of the rules of compromise is to swallow your own unhappiness."

"She has shown that already," Sujata said unhappily. "Allianora, I cannot share my home with this sort of woman."

"Then do not."

Sujata said nothing, and Allianora nodded. "I know. If you have conscience, you are as much a prisoner of her dependence as she is. How deep are your feelings for her?"

"For the Wyrena I knew six months ago, very. For this stranger using her name and face—"

"You know the choice, then," Allianora said. "You can turn her out, solving your problem by increasing hers. Or you can swallow your own unhappiness long enough to help her to grow, against her will. That way you may rediscover the Wyrena you thought you knew—"

That was when the interruption came: a grating buzz in Sujata's right ear and a louder, more musical message alarm sounding from Allianora's terminal in a far corner of the room. As Allianora rose from the table Sujata's right hand went to the small depression behind her ear. With a practiced motion she pressed the skin-covered stem twice: once to silence the alert and once to retrieve the message.

"Comitè Janell Sujata: Chancellor Blythe Erickson wishes to advise you that a special session of the Steering Committee, Unified Space Service, has been called for 20:00 hours, Day 134, A.R. 654, in the customary place. Comitè Janell Sujata—"

As the message began to repeat, Sujata pressed the stem again to silence the transceiver and looked to Allianora, now standing by her net. "I presume yours is also about the Committee meeting?"

"Yes," Allianora said, standing at the net and studying the display. "How very odd—at night, and with only an hour's warning."

"So it is unusual? I wondered." Sujata stood and reached for her blouse. "Are you going to go?"

"Are you?"

"I have to," Sujata said matter-of-factly. "And I'll be doing well not to be late. Could you call down to the terminal and reserve a seat? Or two, if you're coming."

"But we weren't finished. I hate being interrupted. I don't like leaving *xochaya* with so much still to talk about and so little resolved—"

Sujata flashed a helpless, resigned smile. "What can we do? The Chancellor calls, for whatever reason."

Erickson had not intended that four days would slip by between the decision itself and its execution. In reflecting on her meeting with Wells and Berberon, only one course of action had recommended itself to her, and it was one best carried out quickly. The problem was that the Committee would not stand still.

In calling a meeting, Erickson needed to give only an hour's notice, not the three days that was her custom. For this particular session she determined from the start to give Wells as little time as possible to work on the rest of the Committee. But key individuals kept placing themselves more than an hour away—most notably Wells himself. By the time she was ready to move, he was already gone, on his way downwell in the middle of the night.

By the time Wells returned the next day, Sujata had left to spend a long day reviewing productivity and safety problems with the staff of the Cluster B processing station, half a million klicks away—a good three hours even traveling by high-gee sprint. Then it was Wells's turn again, off inspecting the sentinel *Guardian,* under construction in Yard 104. His shuttle was due back at Central in slightly more than twenty minutes; when it docked, all five members of the Committee would be on-station for the first time in four days.

Wells's trip to Earth troubled Erickson deeply. On orbit she could keep close tabs on anyone wearing a transceiver. She had no such authority on Earth, and her informal sources had returned few details of Wells's brief visit. Aside from his general destination and the time elapsed between his landing and return, she knew nothing, had no clue who he had seen or what his business there might have been. It took little imagination to concoct ominous answers. She could only hope that, confident the next move was his, Wells had moved slowly enough to leave her an opening.

Ka'in was the first to arrive, followed in short order by Rieke and Loughridge. Erickson sat in her alcove and made small talk with Rieke, using the Survey chief as a buffer against the curiosity of the others. As the others wandered in by ones and twos, both speculation and complaint were effectively squelched by Erickson's presence, though an occasional stray comment reached her ear from the corridor outside.

Wells arrived with five minutes to spare, looking somewhat worn and wrinkled from his travels and sporting a smear of lubricant along the right forearm of his Service blouse. He nodded politely to Erickson as he took his place, then turned his attention to the slate he carried.

Those who had lingered outside in the corridor seemed to interpret Wells's arrival as a signal that the meeting was about to start. They followed him in en masse, moving to their seats in a strange kind of silence.

Sujata had been the farthest away and so was, unsurprisingly, the last to straggle in, breathless as though she had run all the way from the terminal. When 20:00 hours came, Prince

Denzell and Elder Hollis were nowhere to be seen, but that did not matter; only the five who shared the center with her would have anything to say about what happened next.

"First, I want to apologize for finding it necessary to call all of you away from whatever was occupying you this evening," Erickson said, slowly scanning their faces. "I promise you that although what we are about to consider is important, it will not require much of our time. The sole purpose of this meeting is to consider a Chancellor's Request for withdrawal by a sitting member of the Committee. No other business will be discussed."

There was a stirring, but Erickson did not pause long enough to allow it to become an interruption. "The reason cited in defense of this Request is Chancellor's privilege. Although all authority does proceed from the Chancellorship, the fact is that the Director of any branch has considerable discretionary power. It is not possible for the Chancellor to exercise thoroughgoing and continuous oversight.

"Nor should it be necessary. The Chancellor has the right to know that the executive officers acting in her name are also acting in accord with her stated objectives and principles, even if they should personally disagree with them. It was evident the last time we gathered here that a fundamental disagreement exists between Comitè Wells and myself. Unfortunately I no longer have full confidence that Comitè Wells accepts the condition and principle I just described.

"I want to make perfectly clear that I am requesting the withdrawal of Comitè Wells solely on the basis of Chancellor's Privilege. I do not mean to imply in any manner or degree that Comitè Wells is unfit for his post or to suggest he has deliberately abused his authority—nor do I believe that either of those is true. Comitè Wells has been a dedicated member of the Service, and I would like to see him continue with the Service in a different capacity."

Erickson touched her console, and the secretary took over. "Comitè Wells, the Chancellor has requested that you voluntarily withdraw from your position as Director of Defense and a member of this Committee. Do you accede to this request?"

"I do not," Wells said firmly.

"Comitè Wells declines to withdraw," confirmed the secretary. "A vote on removal is in order. Comitè Wells, do you wish to make a statement?"

"I do."

"You have one minute and twenty seconds."

Wells took several of those seconds to compose his thoughts, pursing his lips and staring at the recording pylon in the center of the arena. Then he straightened up in his seat, folded his hands across his lap, and raised his head to look directly at Erickson. He spoke softly at first, but his eyes were hard and unyielding.

"I appreciate the Chancellor's effort to spare me public humiliation by couching her demand in the least contentious terms, by cloaking it in the most admirable principles," Wells said. "I am only sorry that my conscience will not permit me to do the same."

Shifting forward in his seat, Wells continued in a voice suddenly steel-edged and commanding. "The fact is that this vote has nothing to do with Chancellor's Privilege," Wells said. "This vote is about survival. If you vote as Chancellor Erickson asks, you are voting for timidity, for weakness, for vulnerability. You are voting to prolong the terror with which we've already lived for more than a hundred years. You are voting, should it come to that pass, for our dream to become a nightmare, for our people to again die screaming under the weapons of an alien race."

He sat back in his chair, gripping the armrests tightly with his hands. "If you don't believe that can happen, if you're confident the Mizari are nothing more than the boogeymen in a sixty-thousand-year-old scare story, then you should vote as Chancellor Erickson wishes you would. But if even part of you knows or fears, as I do, that the Mizari are still a threat to us, then there is only one way you can vote and only one course the Service can take—"

"Comitè Wells's time has expired," announced the secretary. "A vote on removal is ordered—"

"—which is for us to rise to their challenge and defend the human community with every tool at our disposal," Wells concluded emphatically. "*That* is what this vote is about."

Hearing him and looking at the faces of the rest of the Committee, Erickson felt a chill of foreboding. Her request had been reasonable, dispassionate, proper—and a waste of time. In his first few words he had shunted aside the substance of her appeal. The rest of his words fueled and then exploited their anxieties.

I made the mistake of thinking it was enough to be right,

she thought regretfully. *But he answered with symbols, with emotions that undercut reason. It wasn't a fair fight—how could I win?*

While Erickson and Wells locked gazes, the question appeared simultaneously on the consoles of the other four members. All that was required of them was two small movements of the hand: one touch to vote, another to confirm. It took very little time.

"By a vote of one to three," the secretary announced impassively, "the removal of Comitè Wells is not agreed to."

Even anticipating the outcome, it was a blow to hear it confirmed. As Rieke's dismayed gasp betrayed her vote, Erickson lowered her head and momentarily closed her eyes. When she looked up again, Loughridge was gloating openly, his face split by a mocking grin. Wells sat impassively in his alcove, his eyes on his folded hands. If he felt either relief or the exultation of victory, neither made it to his face. Erickson doubted that she was doing as thorough a job of hiding her feelings.

"The meeting is adjourned," she said hoarsely.

For a long moment no one moved. Then Berberon scuttled out, shaking his head as he went and starting an exodus that left Erickson and Wells alone in the chamber.

"I think—I think it would be a good idea if we talked," she said at last.

"I agree," Wells said quietly.

"Not tonight. Tomorrow sometime. I'll leave a message with your office."

Wells bowed his head politely as he stood. "I'm at your disposal, Chancellor. Tomorrow."

She did not look at him as he climbed to the upper level and left the chamber through the doors at her back. But when he was gone, she touched her console and the doors closed to enforce her privacy. For a long minute she sat as though frozen, taking her breath in shallow, noisy gulps and fighting the wave of despair that threatened to overtake her.

But shortly there came a moment when resistance and surrender seemed equally pointless. In that moment she slipped to one side in her chair, covered her eyes with a hand as though ashamed, and began to cry—a chest-heaving, almost tearless possession that filled her with fury over her own helplessness to prevent it.

It took twenty minutes for Erickson to collect herself sufficiently to think about going home. Even then there was no spring in the steps that carried her up out of her alcove, no life in the downcast eyes that guided her to the doorway. The doors slid open obediently at her approach, but when she tried to pass through them, she was brought up short by a man who stepped out from the shadows along the far wall and into her path.

"What is it?" she asked wildly, her head whipping up as she tried to focus on the face.

"I'm sorry if I startled you, Blythe," Felithe Berberon said gently. "But before you talk to Wells tomorrow, you should talk with me."

"I'm going home," she said in a fragile voice. Lowering her head, she started to brush past him.

"Not alone," he said, catching her bare arm with one hand.

She stared at him with eyes still bright with moisture, uncomprehending.

"I can help, Blythe," he said pleadingly. "Please let me."

In a rush of ascetic self-flagellation, she nearly refused him. But the touch of his hand on her skin was a reminder of a closeness she had long forgone, one which at that moment was compellingly appealing. She knew that was not what Berberon was offering; knew, too, that he was not one whom she would have sought out for the role. But there was an earnestness in him that she had not much seen before. And this night, this one time, if he could even just hold her and manage to be tender, he could at least make sleep come more easily.

"Come with me, then," she said at last, pulling free and leading the way toward the lift node.

Mercifully, he *was* tender. And in the morning, before they talked, he made breakfast for them both.

chapter 8

The Chains
of Power

Brian Arlett sat on the lift flange of his rented skeeter and peered across the deserted flight apron toward the deepyacht. The ship rested in the upright launch position on the apron in front of its berthing bunker, which was the largest of the five strung along the west edge of the port. Several pieces of ground-support equipment were arrayed around the ship, but they were still and silent. The only sounds Arlett heard now were occasional cries from orbiting seabirds; he could not even hear any sound from the sea as it lapped gently at the beach just three hundred metres away.

"Anything yet?" he asked aloud. The words were picked up by the implant mike and relayed through the open channel to 9-Net.

"Sorry, Brian," came the reply. "No answer. I'm trying to get an overtier to authorize a direct page. That's not too easy, since you won't let me tell them what this is about. If Wells was so eager to hear from you, he should have set up a net pass-through."

"Keep trying," Arlett said with a sigh.

Standing, Arlett brought his scanner up to eye level and trained it on Berth 5. Over the last hour the steady stream of orange-clad techs making their way between the bunker and the ship had dwindled away to nothing. Now the only people in sight were the officious-looking Customs agent at the foot of the access ramp and the small clot of techs standing idly between the yawning doors of the now empty bunker.

"This is Wells," a voice said in his ear.

Reflexively Arlett straightened up before answering. "Mr. Wells, this is Brian Arlett. I have an update on Merritt Thackery. There is some urgency to it or I wouldn't have insisted on a page."

"Yes, Brian. Go ahead."

"He took us a little by surprise—left his house this morning before seven in a land cruiser and went straight to the Lancaster County Airport. The spotter notified me, and I caught up with him in Florida. We're now both at Port Abaco, in the Bahamas."

"Port Abaco—what's he doing there?"

"Apparently trying to sneak out the back way, sir."

"I thought the launch facilities there were shut down several years ago."

"So did I," Arlett said. "But if I understand the port manager correctly—he has a damnably thick accent and refuses to repeat anything—under Service space law, no ship that received proper authorization to land and is up-to-date on its berthing fees and taxes can be refused permission to lift again."

Wells clucked. "That's correct. That provision was added after there was some trouble with the Daehne trying to appropriate an archaeological vessel. So what you're telling me is that there're some ships there that haven't moved since the port was closed?"

"Yes, Mr. Wells—three of them. Two are antiques. I don't think they could move even if the port still had the kind of support facilities they require. But the third is another story. It's a free-landing deepyacht named *Fireside,* and it's sitting out on a lift pad looking like it's ready to go."

"*Fireside.* Well, I'll be damned. That's Thackery's ship. How close are you? Can you see what's going on?"

"I'm sitting about a half a klick away on the north edge of the field. Thackery was aboard his ship for twenty-five minutes, but then he came out again and talked with some of the tech people before disappearing into the berthing bunker. I haven't seen him for a quarter of an hour."

"Where is *Fireside* supposed to be headed? What did the port manager say?"

"I don't think he knew, and I haven't been able to get into the right system to find out myself," Arlett said, pacing alongside his vehicle. "But either Thackery's having trouble with Customs, or Transport must have rejected his flight proposal. The port manager was expecting *Fireside* to lift at ten local time—which would have been about ten minutes after Thackery got here. But it's past eleven already."

"Those are *our* systems that you're trying to get into," Wells said dryly. "All flight requests are filed with USS-Transport." Wells fell silent for a moment, then added, "I'm going to go off-line for a moment. Hold on there while I check this out."

It was not the call that Wells had been expecting that morning, but he was glad he had been there to receive it live. His lips pursed pensively, Wells muted the link and turned to his terminal. "Quicksearch. Let me have the DFAR abstract on deepyacht *Fireside*," he said, propping his chin on his folded hands.

The abstract popped up on the display a moment later:

Vessel: FIRESIDE (Y-400317)	Type: Class B Deepyacht
Registry: Earth	Manufacturer: Adara (Journa)
Ownership: Private	Drive: AVLO Compact, Series III

Proposed Flight Plan:
  Originate: Port Abaco, Earth
    Requested Departure: IST AR 654.118.21:00
  Destination: Port Helixis, Arcturus New
                             Colony
    Estimated Arrival: IST AR 676.311
  Passenger Manifest: Merritt T. Langston
  Cargo Manifest: Personal Effects (Classes A1,
                             C, D3)

Transport Flight Approval Request #652-AB-00001
Action: Referred to Defense Traffic Office
Defense Flight Approval Referral #DFAR-E122341
Action: Rejected

What did you expect, Thackery? Wells thought. *You know that Arcturus is in the Boötes Octant. Surely you realized that we screen everything going that way—that Transport would have to get permission from Defense to let you go. And we don't approve much except for the regular packets and our own internal operations. That's why you're still sitting on the ground there.*

Shaking his head to himself, Wells reopened the link. "Are you there?"

"Yes, Mr. Wells," Arlett acknowledged.

"I've found out what's holding him up," Wells said. "I'm not sure yet how I want to handle it. I'd like you to stay where you are and call back if there're any developments. I'll want to know immediately if they start to move Fireside out to the flight line or back into the bunker. If Thackery leaves, you leave with him."

"I understand," Arlett said.

Wells broke the link and sat back in his chair. *You could have stayed in the Susquehanna. I would have seen that you were left alone. But you didn't know, did you? I threatened the very opposite. But I hoped you would wait until you saw if I was really going to follow through on it.*

A quick check with Boötes Traffic Control told him that there were six ships en route to Arcturus, ranging from a freighter less than a cee from grounding at Helixis to a packet barely six weeks out from Boötes Center. Would it make any difference to add *Fireside* to that stream?

Objectively considered, it was not a particularly dangerous run. At a distance of thirty-seven cees Arcturus was barely halfway to the Ursa Major cluster and a full thirteen cees within the Perimeter. Moreover, the trajectory that led to Arcturus lay thirty degrees south and west of the nearest black-flagged star—

The only thing holding Wells back was Thackery himself. *Can I trust him to go there and only there?* All traffic in the octants adjoining the Perimeter was subject to strict lane discipline. Would that be enough to insure Thackery's compliance? Wells could not keep Thackery on Earth, even if he wanted to. All Thackery had to do was file a new request with a different destination, and he would be gone—

Wells realized belatedly that he was searching for a reason to let Thackery go, trying to justify in his head a decision already made in his heart. The Traffic Office has sound, conservative guidelines. They followed precedent. Why overrule them?

Perhaps it was guilt over having chased Thackery from his hiding place. Perhaps it was yesterday's victory over Erickson and the anticipation of her surrender that inclined him to be generous. Wells did not know, and it did not seem important enough to wring his hands endlessly. Why shouldn't he be able to go to Arcturus New Colony if that's what he wants? he thought.

"Defnet. Traffic Office," he said.

A woman responded. "Traffic, Lieutenant Lezak."

"This is Director Wells. Voice Authorization Check."

There was hardly any pause. "Confirmed, sir. How can I help you?"

"In regard to #DFAR-E122341—"

"Go ahead, sir. I have it up in front of me."

"You are to approve the request, subject to the normal corridor and communications restrictions for the Boötes Octant. Correct the request to reflect an IST 22:00 departure and see that an amended report is sent over to Transport immediately."

Never having seen a deepyacht lift, Arlett did not immediately know whether, when the techs started returning the support gear to Berth 5, that meant the launch was imminent or had been scrubbed.

The first unambiguous sign was when Thackery emerged from the bunker and began to cross the open pavement toward *Fireside* with brisk, purposeful strides. Arlett immediately paged Wells, but by then things were happening very quickly. The Customs agent gave Thackery a quick, cursory, final inspection, then hurried off toward the cavernous bunker. Thackery scrambled aboard his ship and sealed the hatch behind him. A high-pitched hiss and wail coming from the ship conspired with the growl of the closing bunker doors to shatter the silence of the port.

It seemed an eternity before Wells responded to the page. "Yes, Brian," he said at last. "What's happening?"

"Mr. Wells! She's going to lift—"

At that moment the whistle of the compressors turned into an angry whine, and a fierce but flameless blast of air from the liftjets blew a cloud of limestone dust outward from the base of the ship. The ground shook, sending dozens of speckle-furred agoutis scrambling from nests and burrows they had never had any reason to think unsafe.

Within a minute the leading edge of the jet blast reached where Arlett stood, forcing him to turn his head away and shield his eyes from the hail of tiny grit. When he looked back, *Fireside* was already its own height off the ground, liftjets screaming as they fought the dead weight of the fuselage that enclosed them.

The painfully slow ascent made Arlett wonder if something was wrong, if the ship was about to lose what seemed to be a precarious balance and come crashing down into the sea. But the deepyacht continued to climb, accelerating steadily, if unspectacularly. Arlett tracked *Fireside* with his scanner as long as possible, until the ship seemed to tear a hole through a bank of clouds and then vanish beyond them.

"Did she get away all right?" Wells asked calmly.

"I—I suppose so, sir," Arlett said in a shaky voice. "I can't see her anymore."

Inexplicably Wells sounded pleased. "Thank you, Brian," he said. "Please consider yourself released. You acquitted yourself quite well during this whole matter, and I have decided to put through a recommendation for your promotion to Fifth Tier."

"Thank you," Arlett said uncertainly. "But I honestly don't understand. I thought you would want to stop him—"

"At one time I would have," Wells said. "But he's not important anymore."

A night's rest or reflection, or both, had put the starch back into Erickson, Wells concluded. After keeping him waiting most of the morning, she had one of her aides call him to her office with a message that was far more like a summons than an invitation. When he arrived, he was shown into an empty conference room and kept waiting again.

Now Erickson had joined him, slate in hand, and he could see by the set of her jaw and the firmness of her mouth that her self-confidence, or at least a convincing substitute for it, had returned. She swept through the room en route to her chair, offering no detectable greeting except to indicate with a wave of the hand that he should sit.

"Do you still plan to ask for a Vote of Continuance on me?" she asked bluntly when they both were settled.

Wells was less surprised by the question than by the tone in which it was asked. Whether she had guessed, or Berberon had told her, hardly mattered. "Has last night's vote given you any cause to rethink your position on Triad?"

"No." Her answer was flat and unapologetic.

"In that case, the answer to your question is yes."

"About as I thought," she said, nodding. "Tell me, Comitè Wells, what did you expect out of this meeting?"

He smiled faintly. "I'm afraid I've already had to discard my expectations."

"You thought that I had asked you here to work out the ground rules for an accommodation."

"Yes," Wells admitted.

"Under what terms?"

Wells shrugged. "I thought you might offer to allow the construction of Triad—"

"While you allow me to remain Chancellor?"

"Yes."

"Would you have accepted such a proposal?"

"It would have merited close examination. But it seems you have no intention of making such an offer."

"True. My principles are not that flexible. I will not preside over your vision of the Service. I would sooner resign than carry out policies I don't believe in."

Wells sat back in his chair and folded his hands on his lap. "Then resign."

"I'm prepared to—if we can agree on my successor here today."

Wells shook his head. "The time when the head of the Service could handpick his or her successor is past. Why should I strike a deal with you when I can have you removed and then choose a replacement to my own liking?"

"Because it isn't that easy, and you know it."

Wells did, but was not about to concede the point. "What will be different from last night, except that I'll also be voting?"

"Nothing. They will be just as reluctant to remove me as they were to remove you. They may be perfectly happy with you doing what you do best and me doing what I do best, even if we end up fighting because of it."

Wells shook his head. "I see one vote to retain you, no more."

"I see three—and one of them should be yours. You

wouldn't have the budget and the program you do if the rest of the Service weren't well run and fiscally healthy."

"Maybe that's how we should vote," Wells said. "But it's not how we *will* vote."

Erickson showed a faint smile. "Perhaps not. But what makes you think that any majority you whip together will stay intact once the Chancellery's open? Every one of them will be thinking about their own chances—and why not? There's nothing *you* can give them. They're already all one step from the top. Why should they go for someone else at your say-so?"

"Because they have a clear idea of the direction we need to take."

"That's wishful thinking. If you were going to put yourself up for the Chancellorship, you might hold them together— might possibly, if you fought for it hard enough. But you don't want to be Chancellor."

She was not supposed to have known that; it was to have been a concession she would think cost him more than it did. Now it had been devalued. *It had to have been Berberon.* "Did I say that?" he asked lamely.

"Why would you, when it's to your advantage if I think otherwise? But you implied it when you talked about a replacement who was 'to your liking.' And besides, you wouldn't want to trade spending all of your time directly involved in what you think most important for five Branches' worth of administrative duties."

"No—but I'd take the post myself before letting someone who thinks as you do have it," he said warningly.

"You can only be talking about Rieke. I'm realist enough to never have considered her as a possible successor—just as you need to be realistic and understand that Loughridge can never be approved as Chancellor."

There was no point in denying that that was his intent. "Why not?"

"Because *I* won't allow it."

"What makes you think it's up to you?"

The faint, annoying smile played on her lips again. "You're still being too idealistic. It's much easier in this kind of situation to muster votes against someone than for them. It's going to be a long time before anyone puts together four votes and ends it. And, you know, you may not be the one that does it."

"If it took a month, six months—a year, even—it would be worth it."

"Would it be worth having the World Council of Commissioners nationalize our ground facilities?"

Wells gaped in disbelief. "What are you talking about?"

"The orbital injectors, all sixteen operational ports—I don't need to inventory our investment for you."

"They wouldn't do that—"

"They're itching to do that, and more if we give them the opportunity. Why are you surprised? Your friends downwell have put this bug in their ear. The Commissioners want us fighting, Harmack. They want to take advantage of us while we're distracted. And how long do you think it would take King Parath and Elder Barsihlev to decide that Liam-Won and Rena-Kiri ought to do the same? I wouldn't put it past the First Mistress of Maranit to follow suit, once she saw everyone else getting away with it."

"They wouldn't get away with it."

"No? What are you going to do? Make war on our own people?"

"Of course not. But economic pressure—"

"So we refuse to send anything down while they're controlling the ports. Who can stand that the longest?"

"We're self-sufficient. And they depend on us. We sell them twenty times what they sell us—"

"Which means suspension of trade hurts us twenty times as much as it does them—more, really, since they number eleven billion to our one million. It's fiscal suicide for a net exporter to suspend exports. Didn't you ever study macroeconomics?"

"There would be things we could do. We could cut off communications—"

"All you would accomplish is legitimizing their anxiety about us." Hands resting on her knees, she leaned forward in her chair. "Let me tell you what you'd do: nothing. And then you'd learn how to get along without the income we've been generating by charging them for the privilege of doing business with us. Do you think they don't know that the landing fees and transshipment levies far exceed the actual cost of running the ports? That money paid for the Defenders—just try to build Triad without it."

"And the alternative—"

"I already told you. I resign—and a neutral candidate agreed on between us now becomes Chancellor."

"How do you know I won't turn right around and get rid of the new Chancellor too?"

Erickson settled back in her chair. "I'll take that chance. My guess is you're only going to be able to stampede them once. You try this again six months down the road and they're going to start to think the problem's with you."

Regrettably that, too, conformed to Wells's own appraisal of the situation. "I get to build Triad?"

"Probably," Erickson said, her voice registering her unhappiness about it. "But I can't promise it. That's not part of the deal. You'll have a chance to make your case to a new face. I can't tell you what they'll decide when they're sitting here."

"That doesn't make this very attractive for me. Maybe I should just take my chances with the Committee and the Council."

"Go ahead—if you really believe in taking chances. Here's how it adds up: You don't know that you can replace me. Even if you do, you don't know that you get to pick my replacement. And even if you do, it won't come easily or quickly—and the planetary governments will be gnawing away at us the whole time we're squabbling."

Appalled by the prospect, Wells shook his head. "I can't believe that you're willing to see us pushed to the wall over a point of personal pride."

"You had better believe it if you want to prevent it," she said coolly. "Harmack, I love the Service. I don't want to see it crippled by bureaucratic fratricide. I don't want to see it preyed upon by little men with little minds—"

"But you're threatening to let both those things happen."

"Yes—if you try to seat yourself or Loughridge as Chancellor. I'd rather see the Service chopped up by the Worlds than see you in command of a combat force with no checks on your authority."

Wells considered that for a moment. "Who do you propose, then?"

"The list of candidates isn't terribly long. Vandekar has the most experience—"

"No," Wells said emphatically. "He's too much a monarch's minister."

"What do you mean?"

"The Liamese are bred to believe that authority comes by blood and divine right. Vandekar is uncomfortable sitting at the top of the ladder, as though he doesn't believe he truly belongs there. You can see it in the way he handles Operations, always looking for someone else to make the decision. The Service would end up being led either by King Parath or by no one. And what you said earlier was right—for Defense to be strong, the rest of the Service has to be strong too."

"That narrows the list to one."

"I know."

"And?"

Wells tipped his head back and stared up at the ceiling. It was less than he had come here expecting—less, even, than he had thought assured of a week ago. The whole question centered on Triad, but it had gotten enormously more complicated than that. All he had was one uncertainty to weigh against another. Even so, the scales were tipping heavily in one direction.

"Each of us delivers our vote and one other," Wells said slowly.

"Yes."

"You bow out quietly, and we cheat the World Council out of their opportunity for mischief."

"Yes."

"And neither of us tries to attach any preconditions to the nomination. We both take our chances."

"That's right."

Wells pursed his lips. There are no unqualified victories, after all, he thought. Erickson will be gone—the Council will be frustrated—

At last he nodded. "All right. I can live with Sujata."

"Then it's time to find out what she thinks," Erickson said. "Do you want to be there?"

"Of course."

"Let's break for lunch," Erickson said, rising. "I'll ask her to come in at thirteen."

"Fine," Wells said. "Except I think we'd best go to lunch together and agree how much we're going to tell her."

Curiously, the only three times Sujata had been inside the Chancellor's suite had been prior to her appointment as Director of the Resource Branch.

On returning to Unity from Ba'ar Tell, she had been invited in for what seemed on the surface to be a formal welcome back from the Chancellor to a moderately important servicrat. A week later, she had been called back for an undisguised and far more thoroughgoing interview for an unspecified job. The third occasion, which came three days later, had lasted only long enough for Erickson to tell Sujata of her appointment to the Committee.

But that had been the end of it, rather than the beginning. Except for the periodic Committee meetings, Erickson was content to communicate her concerns and requests by memo and phone. So coming as an exception to Erickson's insular management style, the summons to Erickson's office itself loudly proclaimed that something both important and out of the ordinary was to happen.

Forewarned, Sujata managed to sit quietly while Erickson, with Wells a silent spectator, announced without embellishment that she was leaving the Chancellor's office, and how would Sujata feel about stepping into the vacancy?

But the outward calm with which Sujata received those words was not reflected inside her. While listening, she recalled the Maranit game of tossing a seedpod from a ghirlu plant back and forth in a circle of children. Eventually the pod mistook the shaking it received in the course of the game to mean that the late-summer winds had begun and thereupon obediently exploded, splattering anyone nearby with its cache of sticky, foul-smelling seeds.

Sujata viewed the offer of the Chancellorship with the same apprehension felt by a Maranit child preparing to make a catch on a well-shaken ghirlu pod. *And we always tried to toss it to someone we didn't like. . . .*

Knowing Erickson and Wells would take her slowness to respond as a natural consequence of surprise, Sujata allowed herself a moment to try to read them. She focused first on Wells but found the Defense Director's expression as unrevealing as ever. Sujata was always discomfited dealing with a male as skilled at self-concealment as a Maranit highwoman; under the present circumstances her unease was magnified.

Looking back to Erickson, Sujata saw a weariness in the Chancellor's eyes. You may be doing this voluntarily, but you are not doing it willingly, she thought. What's going on? "Why me?" she said at last.

"Because you're the best candidate," Erickson said.

"Best how?" Sujata said skeptically. "I'm the least experienced member of the Committee. I've barely begun to master the workings of my own branch, much less that of the rest of the Service. I'm still thirty years out of sync—both with what's happening here and out in the Affirmation. How can you say that I'm most qualified?"

Wells answered. "She didn't. She said that you were the best candidate."

"Would you explain to me the difference?"

"The Chancellery is a post you grow into," Erickson said with philosophical detachment. "No one comes to it qualified —I certainly didn't. You come to it with potential."

"Which you've demonstrated you have," Wells added.

Flattery from Wells? An even more flagrant warning sign. "Even so—I can't believe the Committee would rather have me as Chancellor than you," Sujata said, looking straight at Erickson.

"That's not the choice facing them," Erickson said, "since I'm resigning."

This time Sujata looked at Wells. "I don't understand why. The Committee would never remove you—"

Glancing sideways at Wells before she began, Erickson replied, "I've been in this post for eight years. As rewarding as it is, it is also very demanding. The time has come for me to do other things."

The glance, which Sujata caught in her fringe vision, had the effect of negating Erickson's words. *Neither one of them is going to be honest unless I force them to be,* Sujata realized.

"So you and Comitè Wells have agreed that I should be the new Chancellor. It hasn't been that long since I read the bylaws—I thought this sort of thing was up to the Committee. How is it that you two are making the decision for us?"

Now Erickson and Wells exchanged glances, as though neither was eager to be the one to answer. "Because there are considerations that are not obvious to you right now," Erickson said at last. "The integrity of the Service is best served by a smooth transition."

"There is nothing underhanded in our trying to guarantee that that's what takes place," Wells said.

"Why are you both trying so hard to hide what's really involved here?" Sujata demanded. "What you're telling me would make a fine face-saving press release. But I'm not a netcaster. I'm the one who's being asked to stand in for one side in a scrap. This has nothing to do with being tired or with a graceful succession. It has to do with you two and Triad. Isn't that right?"

"I *am* tired," Erickson said tersely. "And there are reasons other than the cosmetic why the transition must be smooth."

Wells began, "It's true that we have had—"

"Continue to have," Erickson said quietly.

"—profound differences," Wells said. "But at the moment we are in agreement—that you should be the next Chancellor of the Unified Space Service."

"So you've struck a compromise, then," Sujata said.

"Yes," Erickson acknowledged. "And since you insist on addressing it, you should know it's a delicate compromise and that you are a key part of it."

"Or would be—if you agree to our proposal," Wells said. "But you don't seem eager to do that—"

"I find that more reassuring than disturbing," Erickson said before Sujata could answer. "I've learned to be suspicious of those who are too eager for power."

Wells ignored the dig. "You clearly are not flattered by the offer. I would have thought that to be asked would be a pleasant surprise, no matter whether you were disposed to accept or not. Would you mind explaining why I was wrong?"

"You wouldn't approve me if you didn't think I was going to be either ineffective or sympathetic. Why should I be flattered?"

"Not at all," Wells said, gesturing with his right hand. "I would be delighted if you proved merely to be realistic. What matters most is that you bring to the Chancellery the same quality of administration you've shown in all your previous billets."

"That is my hope too," Erickson said.

Liar, Sujata thought. You don't realize—your face is so open. You give away so much. You show things that Maranit highwomen share only in *xochaya,* if then. "I don't know but that Resource isn't too big for me to manage," she said. "How can I take on an even greater responsibility before I find out?"

"By trusting our judgment," Erickson said. "By putting the Service's needs above your own anxieties. Comitè Sujata, if you say no, it will in all likelihood precipitate a difficult time for the Service. It would be unfair to lay the responsibility for that on you. But you *can* prevent it—by saying yes."

"Do I really have a choice?" Sujata asked. "I was under the impression that I was being drafted, not asked to volunteer."

"Of course you do," Wells said. "If you tell the Committee you don't want to be Chancellor, you can be sure they won't elect you, our compromise notwithstanding. You have a choice."

Yes—the same choice I always had during the game. To catch the ghirlu and risk it dying in my hands—or to let it drop and risk being thought a coward. "I want to think it over."

"I would insist on it. But please, do not take too much time deciding," Erickson said. "If you do, I'm fairly certain Comitè Wells will lose his enthusiasm for the compromise—"

"In all probability," Wells said.

"—and we'll all have to start looking at the less attractive options," Erickson finished.

"I'm not the kind that takes forever to make a decision," Sujata said, standing. "I'll let you know before long."

chapter 9

The Path
Regained

Janell Sujata did not know where her footsteps were taking
her. Her legs carried her along of their own volition, taking
this corridor, that lift, picking a path through the animate ob-
stacles that were other pedestrians. She moved as though pursued, as though she feared being caught from behind, except
that she never stole a glance back over her shoulder.

Instead, her gaze was focused on the far distance. She saw
without seeing, in the sort of trancelike state that suggested
she was following a path so familiar that the instructions for
retracing it had been added to her repertoire of reflexes. Except that, as often as she had gone walking in Unity, she did
not know where she was.

After leaving the Chancellor's suite, Sujata had avoided
her office and her apartment. Several of her staff knew where
she had been and would want to know what had transpired at
the meeting, but Sujata instinctively moved to protect her own
decision-making process from the opinions of others, especially those with a vested interest. *None of the complexities
affect them. They'll think it's wonderful and expect to move up
with me. How can I tell them and then face their disappointment if I refuse—*

At home waited Wyrena—a good listener and a valuable

sounding board, except that this time she was part of the problem too. The farrago of thought Sujata yearned to scatter on the table for scrutiny included things she could not disclose to a plainwoman, and she was not confident of her ability to selectively hold up the mask just now. *And how can I tell Wyrena that I was glad to leave Ba'ar Tell, why I was grateful for a chance to return here—*

It was Allianora she needed to talk with, Allianora to whom she could unburden herself freely. But Allianora had not answered Sujata's page, and the Maranit Mission Office would not tell Sujata where the Observer was. The first dismayed Sujata, the latter aggrieved her. *I am a highwoman too,* had been her unexamined thought. *My claim on her is as important as any.* Recasting her need as possessive jealousy, she had gone straight to the Unity shuttle, blindly determined to track Allianora down.

Learning no more from visiting the Mission in person than she had by calling, Sujata had gone next to Allianora's home. There had been no answer to the door page, which should have ended Sujata's search. Enough time had passed for her to have shaken the impulse that had brought her there, enough time to recognize its essential foolishness.

But she knew a name, spoken once by Allianora and filed away by Sujata in the reflexive way that a Maranit highwoman hoarded personal information, the name of a young Mission staffer whom Allianora often blessed with her company. It was an easy matter to learn the address attached to the name, a matter of a few minutes brisk walk to reach the residential block that contained it. Everything was too easy, too fast. Even Cajiya answered the door page too quickly for Sujata to ask herself what she was doing there and turn away.

"I want to see Allianora," Sujata had said stiffly.

"She's not here," Cajiya had said, surprised.

Then, in a loss of control that was painful to remember, Sujata had pushed her way past the young servicrat and searched the apartment herself before she was satisfied that she had been told the truth. At that moment of realization everything she had done became clear to her, and she had wanted to hide, to disappear—anything to escape having to retrace her steps past Cajiya and subject herself to Cajiya's judgmental gaze.

"She went downwell," Cajiya said quietly as Sujata neared

the front door again. "Something about a festival in Majorca." She said it in such a way that it was an apology, and the apology an insult.

That was when Sujata's flight had begun, a flight that could not succeed because her pursuer was her equal in speed and endurance. She did not look back because the demons that were chasing her were inside her mind and memory's eye.

The walls on either side of the corridor fell back, and the pathway split to become a balcony encircling a small atrium. Sujata slowed, now knowing at least generally, if not specifically, where she was. The minor atria were the anchor points for the residential blocks, linked by fifth-level slidewalks to the city core and other major nodes. If she wanted to make her way home, she could now do so easily.

She came to the balcony overlooking the gallery and looked over the edge. Three floors below, a play was in progress, the kind of slapstick comedy that played well on an open-air proscenium. The high, affected voices of the actors and the laughter of the audience carried up to where she stood alone.

Would that I could sit down there among them with nothing to think about but the last joke and the unfolding story. I've allowed myself so little time for self these last six months, denied myself in the expectation that I will receive a greater measure later.

Sujata knew her own pattern: to plunge into the task with an obsessive fervor, establishing her presence and authority and shaping or reshaping the group to her liking, then to pull back and let people do their jobs. A technically minded friend had once offered her a useful analysis by analogy: The design and engineering of a complex system with many moving parts was a time-consuming process, but one hour of anticipation saved a hundred hours of correction. A well-constructed machine should run without supervision, requiring only occasional maintenance to insure its efficiency.

In the same way, Sujata endured the sacrifices of the "design" phase because of the rewards of the "maintenance" phase. But Wells and Erickson had only seen the first half of the pattern. They did not understand that it was not the responsibility to which Sujata responded but the recognition that came with accepting it.

No wonder Wells and Erickson chose me. But I never

meant to live like this. Do they know how much time I've had to spend in sprints just to begin putting Resource in order? Do they know what I'm expecting in return? No—I would never let them. But still, I'm six months into repairing one fiendishly complex machine with the end nowhere in sight, and they want me to leave it to take on an even more dauntingly complicated one—
plicated one—

In a flash of self-revelation Sujata saw that her resistance to the proposal that Wells and Erickson had laid before her and her problems with Wyrena were of a piece. Both threatened, though on different scales, to push further into the future the arrival of the rewards of her labors.

It's not Wyrena that's changed, she thought as she climbed the ramp to the fifth-level slidewalks. *I have. When we met on Ba'ar Tell, I felt free to indulge myself. The Ba'ar Tell office was already in order. I could give her first claim on my time because I needed so little to keep things running smoothly. But here I have my hands full. Here I push her away to protect my single-mindedness—and feel guilty even as I do because I know that what she wants is nothing more than her due.*

She let the slidewalk carry her toward the city core and her thoughts carry her toward an inevitable conclusion. *Work is not life—it's what gets in the way of living. But there are some tasks so large that once you accept them, you risk never getting back to what, until then, you thought was most important. Wyrena and I can talk. Now that I understand, I can make her understand, and we can work out an accommodation. But what accommodation can I possibly make with the Chancellery?*

Six months, and she had not yet even made a first visit to the surface. Nothing was keeping her from ending that skein. With her travel rating she could go to the terminal at any time and bump someone off any Earthbound flight. Her papers were in order. She had already accumulated nearly three weeks of compensatory time. Either her personal or her Director's accounts could easily stand the expense. Nothing kept her from going except the knowledge that one visit would be at once too little to satisfy her and too much for her future resolve.

A gibbous Earth was large in the windows of the UC shuttle terminal. Sujata arranged for her seat, then settled in a chair to savor the view. Africa appeared to her as a dusty-brown film overlaid by broken white clouds, a mere crust seemingly afloat on a liquid-blue sphere and being chased by approaching night.

This is the mask of the Mother, she thought as she looked out, *beautiful, serene, timeless. But she wears her past on her secret face like any highwoman, in the intricate weave of the living mane she wears, the sheen and shape of her heartstone. There are wonderful ancient places down there, valleys rich with millions of years of growing, a hundred thousand species each of which is kin to me. This is what I came back for—to touch her and read her and take her inside me—*

The first call chime announced the shuttle ready for boarding, and Sujata reluctantly tore herself away. *When will I know you?* she thought sadly as she rose from her chair. *When is there to be time for me?*

Wyrena Ten Ga'ar looked flushed and uncomfortable from the moment the link was completed and her face appeared on Wells's display. *"Lodanya* Wyrena, this is Harmack Wells. Do you remember me?"

"Yes, Comitè," said Wyrena, averting her eyes according to custom. "I remember you. I regret to tell you that Comitè Sujata is not here—"

"I know that, *keefla,"* he said, watching her face closely. The Maranit term described one who has given up homekeeping to become a mistress. Said with its original inflection, it was a term of affection between a man and his lover. Said with a different inflection by one woman about another, it was a pejorative. Said that same way by a man, it was a rebuke.

As he had expected, Wyrena accepted the rebuke and apologized. *"Fraxir marya.* I did not mean to presume."

"I called not to talk with Comitè Sujata but with you— about Comitè Sujata. The last time I spoke to you, I warned you that she would have difficult decisions to make."

"I remember."

"Good," Wells said. "Those decisions are on her now. She has been offered the Chancellery of the Service."

Wyrena's eyes came up, and Wells read both surprise and elation in them. "Yes, Comitè. I understand."

"I hope you do," Wells said. "But we'll take a few moments to make certain you see the ramifications for all the parties concerned. When you do, I am sure you will be able to help her make the right choice."

• • •

Wells's call prepared Wyrena to address the political dimensions of Sujata's dilemma. But when Sujata returned to the apartment, it was the personal dimension that received primary consideration, and for that Wyrena was completely unprepared.

On Ba'ar Tell they had had neither the need nor the inclination to talk self-consciously of their relationship. They had simply enjoyed each other as much as the time they could steal allowed. Wyrena had always presumed that Sujata, too, understood that emotions were to be experienced, not analyzed. The giddy excitement and self-devouring pain that were the two sides of love were not things that could be frozen and dissected with a psychological scalpel.

She loved Janell because she could not help but love her, because being with Janell was the most uplifting state of being Wyrena had known. Such a feeling could not have its genesis in anything except the complementary perfection of the other and the rightness of sharing life with them.

But now Sujata insisted on offering reasons for things that could have no reason except beyond their inarguable reality, taking something that was seamless and beautiful and tearing it apart with cold and calculating analysis.

Her life in the Ga'ar enclave had been full of rules and reasons—do this to make yourself useful, do this to make yourself desirable—and the result was a life of artifice and counterfeit emotion. Now Janell was as much as saying that what they had shared was equally counterfeit, equally tainted by matters far removed from the simple equation of two hearts in synchrony.

Just tell me what you want, she thought anxiously, *not why you think you want it. It's enough to know that there is something I can do for you. To be asked is reason enough.*

But as Sujata went on, Wyrena learned to her distress that she could not reach and heal the hurt Sujata had inside her, because Sujata wanted things that Wyrena could not give her. There was a rival for Sujata's time and perhaps for her affections as well—a rival whose appeal Wyrena found inexplicable.

"I want to be able to spend two or three months out of the year on Earth, wandering here and there," Sujata protested. "But how can I do that as Chancellor? Look at Chancellor Erickson. After eight years her life consisted of office and

Committee and home, one tightly circumscribed circle. The job nearly consumed her."

By the end of an hour, Wyrena saw clearly the direction in which Sujata was moving. She also knew by then that she had a better reason to try to turn Sujata than any Wells had provided. But Sujata had offered no opportunity for Wyrena to influence the decision, and Wyrena had found no ways to create one. Sujata was telling, not asking—talking, not listening—as she moved inexorably toward the cusp.

For that reason Wyrena viewed the unexpected sound of the door page as a welcome interruption. Without waiting for Sujata's approval, Wyrena bounded from her chair to answer it.

The man Wyrena saw in the monitor displayed the dandyish affectations she had come to associate with Terran high fashion: tightly curled hair hung girlishly at shoulder length, a lacy jabot setting off the visitor's blue silk blouse. Despite having been chided by Sujata for her ethnocentricity, Wyrena still felt a reflexive flash of scorn on seeing such a spectacle. Misbehaving Ba'ar Tell boys were sometimes dressed in their sisters' clothing for punishment; why a man would choose to dress himself that way, she could not discern.

But this once, her gratitude for the interruption suppressed that judgmental impulse. "Greetings of the house," Wyrena said buoyantly.

"And to you. Would you be so kind as to tell Comitè Sujata that the Terran Observer would like to see her?" the visitor said, beaming unctuously at the camera.

By that time, Sujata had followed Wyrena as far as the end of the entryway. "Let him in," she said, and turned away.

Berberon bobbed his head in salute as the door opened. "You must be Wyrena Ten Ga'ar, the Director's new aide," he said politely. "I am Felithe Berberon, Terran Observer to the Committee."

"In here, Felithe," Sujata called from the other room.

Answering Berberon's bow of the head with a welcoming smile, Wyrena let him past, then followed him into the great room. They found Sujata seated where Wyrena had left her a few moments earlier.

"Good evening, Director," Berberon said. "I hope I haven't disturbed you—"

"No."

"I thought you might grant me a few minutes to speak privately with you."

"About what?"

Berberon glanced sideways at Wyrena, raising an eyebrow questioningly.

"If it's the Chancellery, she knows," Sujata said. "We've been talking about it."

Nodding, Berberon edged toward a seat. "Then, of course, she should stay. I was given to understand you are having some difficulty deciding what to do. I thought I might be able to help."

"How?"

"By providing you with information you are not likely to have received elsewhere."

"She doesn't want to take the post," Wyrena said.

His eyes betraying his alarm, Berberon looked to Wyrena questioningly, as though wondering whether she were ally or enemy. Then he turned back to Sujata. "Am I too late, then?" Berberon asked. "Have you already decided?"

"No," Sujata said. "Not entirely. But Wyrena is right. I don't *want* the post."

"But you may take it nonetheless?"

"All I can say is that I haven't decided not to," Sujata said.

"I will take that as a positive sign," Berberon said with a hopeful smile.

Sujata did not answer the smile. "So what does the World Council have to say on the subject of Chancellor Erickson's successor?"

"I am not here representing the Council," Berberon admitted.

"Oh? Then who sent you here? Wells? Or Erickson?"

"Neither. Though I, too, want to see you take the post, I do so for separate and personal reasons."

"Do you plan to offer as selective a version of the truth as they did?"

"No. I will be honest with you—perhaps uncomfortably so."

"Then please sit down," Sujata said. "I would welcome some honesty."

Relieved, Wyrena waited until Berberon had selected a chair, then settled herself behind and to the right of him, out of the range of his peripheral vision. It was the traditional place for a Ba'ar woman at a talk circle, but more than habit dictated her choice. Had Wyrena made herself part of the circle, Berberon would have been obliged to divide his attention between Sujata and herself. This way he could focus his attention on Sujata exclusively.

"You can begin by explaining why Chancellor Erickson is resigning," Sujata said, drawing her legs up and tucking her knees under her chin.

"It's really quite simple. Blythe doesn't think she can beat Wells on Triad."

Sujata shook her head. "But why resign? Shouldn't she go out fighting, making as much noise as possible? Shouldn't she force him to use a recall vote and not just quietly absent herself?"

Berberon smiled. "Is there such a thing as gambling on Maranit?"

"No—but I've come across it enough times since leaving there. Why?"

"I once watched a gambler facing bankruptcy bet his last dozen chips on a weak hand. Later I asked him why he'd done that, when he could have held on for several more hands hoping for something better. He said that if you're playing to win, and not just to postpone leaving the table, sometimes you have to take a chance before the chips are gone. That's what Blythe is doing. Having you made Chancellor is the best she thinks she can get."

"But she's the Chancellor. She's Director Wells's superior. He has to take her orders."

Berberon shook his head. "Wells is different. He has leverage of his own."

"Why?"

"Because Wells is a member of the Nines."

Sujata frowned. "I have encountered the term several times since I arrived here, but I don't really understand what it refers to—or why it matters."

"How to describe them?" Berberon said with a sigh. "The Nines are part philosophical clique, part political party, part activist cadre. They are the champions of the individual in this generation. They believe that competition is the ideal way to allocate wealth and power in society."

"I don't remember hearing of them when I was here before, as a tutelate. Or, for that matter, at M-Center or Ba'ar Tell."

"Perfectly understandable. They were founded here forty-odd years ago and have little or no presence elsewhere. They are uniquely Terran, though there are some parallels between their beliefs and the self-reliance code of the Rena-Kiri."

"What does the name refer to?"

"To their conceit. To the rank they have given themselves. They consider themselves the elite, the intellectually gifted, the morally superior."

"You disagree, it seems."

"Yes. Before I offer further opinions of the Nines, you should know that my antipathy toward them is personal and long-standing. I was recruited by them thirty years ago. Though I take no pride in saying so, I qualified easily. But I was horrified by what they advocate."

"Why? What do they want?"

Berberon sighed again. "Their complaint is that they are being held back from reaching their ultimate levels of achievement by a social order biased against excellence."

"And is it?"

He shrugged. "Any society that tries to protect its weaker members must set some limits on the power of its stronger members. The Council has worked hard to still the competitive element in our nature and to blunt and channel it where it cannot be stilled. It's not easily done. You may have difficulty understanding this, coming from Maranit."

"What do you mean?"

Berberon pursed his lips. "What fraction of the membership of the Nines would you guess is male?"

"Why, I don't know. Wouldn't it reflect the sex ratio on Earth—fifty percent or something near it?"

Berberon shook his head. "Our best guess is that at least eighty percent of the Nines are male. The Nines aren't overtly sexist, mind you—the numbers reflect the sexual bias in what they have to offer."

"Explain."

"I hope to," he said, settling back in his chair. "You see, at least in *our* post-Founding culture, male competitiveness is linked to the programming for sexual selection. Achievement translates into opportunity for reproduction. Look at Wells and his little harem—he's a perfect example of what I mean. If you look into what we know of our history, you'll see that it's always been that way. Wealth and power, achievement of virtually any variety, have been the green light to mating."

"If that's programmed into human males genetically, what

explanation do you offer for Maranit? All positions of authority are held by highwomen, and the men accept this and always have."

"Just so—because you have found different ways of satisfying the unique biological imperatives of the sexes."

"I do not know what you mean by 'unique biological imperatives.'"

A frown flickered across Berberon's face. "Simply that in terms of their sexual strategies, men and women are very nearly two different species."

"Curious. Is this your opinion, or do Terrans consider this a fact?"

"It's a basic principle of sociobiology," Berberon said with a hint of defensiveness. "May I speak personally?"

"Go ahead."

"Since sperm are plentiful and represent a trivial investment, the fundamental male strategy is to mate as widely as possible—a strategy that puts every male in direct competition with every other male, since every female is a potential mate."

Wyrena found Sujata's expression cautionary. "And what are the women thought to be doing while the men are fighting over them?" Sujata asked.

"Following their own strategy. The female investment in reproduction is much greater than the male's, which means that the female strategy must necessarily be different. First, to be selective. And second, to see that her issue is well provided for. There are many exceptions to this, of course—nurture has its say as well. But this is the underlying pattern laid down by nature."

"According to Terran science."

"According to Nature herself. You can see it in hundreds of species and thousands of human cultures."

"Not on Maranit. Our pattern is completely different."

"But do you understand why you are different?" Berberon demanded. "Because Maranit women have had control of their own fertility for thousands of years. Because you've never tried to make your males responsible for supporting the young you choose to bear. And because you let your men mate freely with the female underclass. Don't you see? Maranit culture is as completely entangled with the sexes' biological programs as ours. But your version escapes the destructive male competitiveness that has always marred ours."

"Maranit is hardly without conflict and competition."

"But you highwomen reserve that to yourselves. Your competition springs from a more benign instinct. You compete to find better ways to preserve and provide. It's a struggle where even the losers win. Earth and Maranit represent opposite swings of the pendulum—one, ours, in which male, sex-based competitiveness and the behaviors that result from it are at their peak, and one, yours, in which they are mercifully almost nonexistent."

Wyrena sensed growing resistance in Sujata. "Even if your speculations are correct, what has any of this to do with the question of my becoming Chancellor?"

"Everything, if you heed its import—nothing if you do not," Berberon said somberly. "Perhaps you know that shortly before the reunion we were on the verge of doing to ourselves what we so hate the Mizari for doing—destroying human life on a global scale. It sounds like madness and it was. The madness is part of us.

"That time the fission blanket saved us from ourselves. But we're back to shouting across the glade again, making the ape threat-display to the Mizari—except with our latest technology of death instead of upraised arms and snarls. The sorry truth is that the behaviors that come with the male sexual strategy translate poorly to a culture that can build fusion bombs and DE weapons."

Sujata was shaking her head, arms crossed over her chest. "This is all very difficult for me to credit. And even if what you say is true, where is the mind? Surely we've learned something in all this time."

"The biological program can be overridden, but it can never be banished or forgotten. It's always running, always pushing, always testing," Berberon said grimly. "And the wonderful human rationality that can check a primal impulse is just as good at constructing justifications for following it instead."

Sujata held up her hands, palms out. "We've expended a lot of time on this, and I don't see the relevance, even if I accepted the premises. I'd like to move on to other things."

For the first time Berberon showed impatience. "You don't have to accept what I say about ethnology. Look into it yourself when you have the opportunity and draw your own conclusions. But what matters to me is that, for whatever reason, you Maranit have learned how to live without war. I do not know whether the lessons you have learned are transferable or not. I only know that of all the worlds, yours is the only one of which it can be said, and you are the only member of the Committee that comes from such a heritage."

"Surely that's more of a liability than an asset? I'm the least prepared to evaluate what Wells says he must have or must do," Sujata said. "These kinds of questions are completely alien to my experience. Why do you think I had so much difficulty making a decision on Triad? If I were Chancellor, I would be completely dependent on Wells. You might as well have him as Chancellor."

"You feel inadequate to pass on questions of military strategy?"

"Yes—"

"Then you have embraced the fiction that military decisions require more than ordinary clear thinking and good judgment," Berberon said, rising out of his chair and gesturing dramatically with one hand. "What does it matter if you can't cite the Thirteen Principles of Sun Tzu or the elements of Delbruck's Strategy of Exhaustion? Janell, our bloody history has given us many lessons in how to win. But a soldier knows no more than you do on the subject of when to fight."

"Somehow I doubt that Wells would agree with you."

Berberon settled back into his chair. "I think perhaps he would. Certainly Carl von Clausewitz would have. Clausewitz is one of those names you feel so crippled by not knowing— he is regarded as the father of modern strategic thought. 'War has its own grammer,' Clausewitz said, 'but not its own logic.' That's from his classic treatise, *On War*. I believe you'd find Wells has a copy of the original German edition in his library."

For the first time Wyrena felt as though Berberon had scored heavily with Sujata. Confirmation of sorts came with her response.

"So perhaps I'm not disadvantaged," Sujata said slowly. "There's still Wells and the Nines. How am I to be any more effective against them than Erickson was?"

Berberon sat forward. "Let's consider why Erickson had trouble. You must begin with the understanding that the Nines are not a monolithic organization—they hardly could be, considering their basic beliefs. And they never could be a mass movement, filling the streets with their supporters. Nevertheless the World Council fears them."

"Because they disagree on public policy?"

"No. Because one of their goals is to eliminate the Council, and it never pays to ignore or underestimate a self-declared enemy."

"Why would they want to remove the Council? Wouldn't a simpler goal be to control it?"

"Except that the Council itself can close off that avenue through the appointment process. There are also philosophical objections. They consider the Council to be false to its origin, which was the meritocratic Pangaean Consortium ruled by a single strong leader. The Nines despise government by committee and consensus. Given a chance, they would replace the Council with their version of Plato's philosopher-king and reinstitute what they euphemistically call an 'opportunity society.'"

"Presumably the Council has some strategy for preventing this from happening."

"Yes. By turning their attention elsewhere while we work to break the back of this destructive pattern of socialization."

Light dawned in Sujata's eyes. "By turning their attention to the Mizari—"

Wells nodded. "There is only one thing that goads the Nines even more than living under the rule of the Council. As egocentric and individualistic as they are, they are also fiercely proud of their humanity. And because they are proud, they are also protective. They have become the most vocal advocates on Earth of a strong military posture."

"Which at this moment is symbolized by Triad."

"Yes. And as long as the Council assists them in this area, they are unwilling to risk the initial chaos that even the most peaceful revolution must bring. They will tolerate us as long as our policy in this area is 'right.'"

"So this is why you've been Wells's ally on the Committee."

"Yes. The Council has actively cultivated the Nines's xenophobia. In a real sense they created Wells. Unfortunately they built too well. The fear has begun to feed back on its creators."

"You didn't expect Wells to become this powerful."

"No," Berberon said, shaking his head. "Certainly not this quickly. Though it's not that he himself is so powerful. It's that our fear, which he understands and uses perfectly, has made us weak. The strength of the Nines is in ideas, symbols that have the capacity to reach beyond their own membership and change the way people act. And the most powerful of those symbols—about loyalty and strength and victory— reach right past the mind to the emotions."

"So how do I control him?"

Wyrena had not understood everything that Berberon had said—parts of it had been so foreign to her view of life as to be incomprehensible, and other parts simply had been outside the scope of her education. But she knew what Wells wanted. She understood clearly enough that if Sujata became Chancellor, she would need Wyrena all the more. And she knew that, with Sujata vacillating at last, it was time to throw her weight on the scale.

"By giving him what he wants," Wyrena said, loudly enough to assure that she would not be ignored. Sujata and Berberon both started, confirming Wyrena's suspicion that that they had forgotten her presence. Berberon twisted around in his seat. his eyes offering gratitude for her allegiance.

"What did you say?" Sujata asked.

"Give Comitè Wells what he wants," she repeated, emboldened. "Let him build Triad. There is more to the Service than Defense, and more to fighting a war than simply building the weapons. Give Comitè Wells his head on this and manage the rest as best you can."

"The rest—"

"Yes. Make the Chancellery strong and the Service flourish. Invest yourself with the kind of authority Comitè Wells will respect. He's vulnerable to the same kind of appeal he makes to others, because he believes. You could do it, Janell. I can help. Women of Ba'ar Tell know things about power too."

"Your friend is right," Berberon said, turning back to Sujata. "The only course left is to give Wells what he wants. The new Chancellor will have to give him Triad. The Committee has made that clear."

"How can that be called 'controlling' him?"

"Wells is influential now. But it will take years to build the Triad force," Wyrena said. "Fear fades. Sometime in that span a chance will come to turn him."

"There is always that hope," Berberon said. "As well as the hope that we will discover that the Mizari are extinct."

"But what a waste—of time, of material, of labor—"

"We can afford to let Wells build Triad, and the weapon system after that, and the one after that," Berberon continued. "What we can't afford is to let him start a war."

"That's a very thin line to draw."

"Yes. Appeasement is always a dangerous game to play. But as I said, we are out of options. That's why I want you as Chancellor. The final authority is in this office, not his. And you are the only one I have any confidence will say no when he comes asking."

"You expect me to hold the office a long time, then. As Wyrena has pointed out, it will be a decade or more before Triad will be ready."

Berberon nodded. "I would hope your tenure is one day longer than Wells's."

"And if I don't become Chancellor?"

"Then Wells will soon have not only Triad but also the authority to use it, a prospect that frightens me more than I can say."

For a moment Sujata said nothing. "And if it's the Mizari and not the Nines we should be worrying about?" she asked finally. "What if the right answer turns out to be yes?"

Berberon grimaced. "The right answer will never be yes. The concept of war only applies between relative equals. No one calls it war when you pour boiling water on an anthill. The Mizari were unimaginably more powerful than us sixty thousand years ago. If they still exist, it would be a miracle if the gap were not even wider now. Don't waste time worrying about the Mizari coming looking for us, because there'd be nothing to do but lay down and die if they did. Worry about us getting cocky and going out looking for them."

Sujata rested her chin on her folded hands and stared at the center of the floor. For long seconds no one said anything. Wyrena caught a glance and a nervous smile from Berberon.

"All right," Sujata said at last. "I'll take the post."

"Thank you," Berberon said, rising. "I wish I could promise you won't regret it—"

"I would never expect such a promise," Sujata said. "My eyes are open. But I have some conditions of my own. The first is that you get Erickson to wait a week. I want to go downwell, by myself, for a few days before the change takes place."

"I understand," he said, bowing his head politely.

"The second is that you commit yourself to staying in the Terran Observer's Office as long as you expect me to stay in the Chancellor's suite. I know that to some degree that's up to the World Council. But as long as they'll have you, you'd damn well better stay. You share the responsibility for creating this crisis. You should share the responsibility for trying to shape this stalemate that you think will be a solution."

Berberon nodded his acquiescence. "As you note, I am not my own master. But I promise you that as long as I am able, I will be here, and I will help you however I can." Bowing to Wyrena, he began backing toward the door.

"Observer Berberon—that gambler," Sujata called after him. "What happened?"

Berberon smiled somberly. "Not that it matters, but he lost to a stronger hand."

From the moment he had first been informed of its terms, Berberon had been aware of a disturbing window of vulnerability in Erickson's pact with Wells. Under the Committee's procedures Erickson would have to forgo her post first, making her irrevocable concession before Wells was obliged to answer in kind. There was at least a possibility that Wells would renege, offering Loughridge or even himself for the vacancy.

Erickson did not share Berberon's fear. She was confident that Wells was not only properly chary of the fight she had promised and the threat from Tanvier's quarter, but essentially honorable. Wells was to second Erickson's nomination of Sujata; the vote would be a formality.

Berberon would have welcomed an infusion of the same confidence. But the moment Erickson announced her resignation to a mostly startled Committee, Berberon's stomach began to churn. As he led the Observers from the room and the chamber doors closed behind them so that the Elections Committee could begin its work in secrecy, his anxiety soared. His rubbery legs carried him barely a dozen steps down the corridor, at which point he collapsed onto the benchlike sill of a hexagonal window overlooking the Center's main atrium.

His presence drew the others to that part of the corridor. Berberon was surprised to see how thoroughly the knowledge of what was to happen had been contained. Like Loughridge and Vandekar, whose incredulous faces had betrayed them as the two directors who had not been apprised in advance, all of the Observers except Berberon, himself, were stunned by Erickson's resignation. They had filed out in silence, looking wonderingly at each other and back into the arena, their steps as uncertain and tentative as those of a child testing thin ice.

Now they were finding their voices—though, too proud to admit they had been caught by surprise, they had little more than idle chatter to offer.

"I'm not surprised," Prince Denzell declared, though he had no audience. "She should have been removed years ago. She was clearly unfit to be Chancellor."

"Odd—I seem to recall you allying yourself with the Chancellor just a couple of weeks ago," Ambassador Ka'in said quietly.

"Even the incompetent must sometimes be right, by chance alone," was Denzell's stiff-necked reply.

Allianora came and shared the sill with Berberon. "How will we know when they're done?"

"There'll be a recall page," Berberon said in a shaky voice.

"It's all right to leave, then?" Hollis asked. "They don't expect us to wait here?"

"No," Berberon said.

"Good," Hollis said gruffly, and stomped off toward the lifts.

Allianora looked around her uncertainly, then started to rise as if to leave. Berberon checked her movement with a hand on her forearm. "This will either be short or very long," he said. "We may as well wait a bit."

It was barely ten minutes, but it seemed to Berberon to be an hour. Heads turned as the chamber doors opened, and Berberon and Allianora rose from their seats expectantly. A moment later Erickson emerged, her back straight and head high, her expression dignified and controlled. Without as much as a glance in their direction she walked off down the curving corridor in the opposite direction, away from the executive offices and toward the residential block.

Knowing what it was she was walking away from, Berberon found Erickson's retreating figure a poignant, forlorn sight. He felt a strong urge to follow, but resisted. It was unlikely she would welcome company just now, and his need to know that all had proceeded according to plan was even stronger.

The recall page came as they were already moving back toward the open doors of the chamber. As they filed back in and took their seats on the upper level, they saw that the remaining members of the Committee were in their customary places, with the Chancellor's alcove empty. Sujata sat with head lowered as though in a private world. Among the others there was much intent examination of hands and nails, interspersed with many furtive, curious glances. No one spoke until a breathless Hollis rejoined them a few minutes later.

"What's happened?" he demanded from the doorway.

"Nothing. And nothing will until you come log in," Berberon answered with faint impatience.

Moments after Hollis settled in his alcove the status light on the recorder pylon changed from amber to green.

"By a vote of the Elections Committee," the machine intoned, "the nomination of Janell Sujata as Chancellor of the Unified Space Service is confirmed."

Berberon started the applause, which had a curious quality. As small as the group was, it was possible to distinguish varying degrees of enthusiasm, including the merely polite. Denzell did not join in at all.

Recalled from her introspective reverie, Sujata climbed out of her alcove and made the long walk around the periphery of the room. When she had settled in the seat so recently occupied by Erickson, she looked slowly around the room before speaking, making eye contact with each Observer and Director in turn.

"To those who supported my nomination, thank you," she said. "To those of you who did not, I ask only that you will give me a fair opportunity to prove you wrong."

Berberon was encouraged. Whether she truly felt that way or not, Sujata was projecting surprising calm and self-assurance. *I think she's going to be all right—*

"I won't keep you here very much longer today, though you can count on seeing me often from now on. But there are two things that deserve some attention. The first is the vacancy on the Committee. I'll begin conducting interviews immediately. If you have any candidates you would like to recommend, please forward their names to me promptly.

"The second item is Triad. Director Wells?"

"Yes?"

"The Defense Branch's current proposal for a force of five Triad attack groups is not acceptable. I would like to see a revised budget and procurement schedule for a three-group force at our next meeting. Also, I find the description of your proposed operational communications, command, and control for Triad inadequate. Please submit a revised specification that provides more detail and clearly reflects the final authority of the Chancellor's office."

"Certainly, Chancellor Sujata," Wells said with a little bow of his head.

"That's all, then," Sujata said. "I'll be seeing each of you individually, and I'll see all of you back here next Tuesday."

She rose, and others with her, beginning the exodus.

"No!" Denzell shouted, his face twisted by fury and contempt. "Wells! How can you allow this? She is worse than the last one! Not just a woman but a Maranite—her woman-organs ripped from her—bedding her aide without shame. What kind of person is this to lead us? Someone who has committed reproductive suicide. What does her kind care about the future?"

Though the appeal was to Wells, he merely crossed his arms on his chest and regarded Denzell quizzically. All other eyes went to Sujata. Above and beyond the unprecedented breach of etiquette, Denzell's histrionics were the first overt challenge to the new doyenne, and everyone froze in place as they waited to see what she would do.

Her gaze locked on the breast-beating Liamese, Sujata allowed him to rant on for a few more sentences. Then she pounced on his first hesitation for breath, saying lightly, "We all must make allowances, Aramir. I trust you will forgive me my cultural baggage, just as I will not hold you responsible for the ritual lobotomy you obviously endured."

The tension was broken by laughter, led by Berberon's distinctive chortle and Loughridge's basso guffaw. Even Wells's face was split by an ear-to-ear grin. Seeing the last, Denzell stormed off, purpling and sputtering to himself.

A repartee worthy even of me, Berberon thought with satisfaction. *She's going to do just fine. Yes, she's going to do just fine.*

Farlad found Wells in the star dome, lying on a recliner near the center of the room and staring out at the stars of Ursa Major. The moon, at first quarter, was just moving into the field of view, its brilliance overpowering the star field around it and lending a death-white cast to the interior of the dome.

"Yes, Lieutenant?" Wells said as Farlad approached.

"I thought you would want to know. We just got confirmation in the office of Chancellor Sujata's request for proposal. It's official. You've won."

"This is just the beginning," Wells said in a faraway voice. "I've been playing chess simultaneously with two opponents. Now the weaker has been eliminated. Now there is only one to concern myself with."

"Yes, sir."

"I've been lying here thinking about Thackery. A great man, Teo. A great man despite his flaws. But he left the job half finished. No fault of his, mind you—there was no opportunity to do more. We have that opportunity," Wells said. "Teo, you, and I are going to live to see this stalemate broken."

"Sir?"

Wells sat up and swung his legs over the side of the recliner. "Rashuri gave us the Reunion—Thackery the Revision. But only when there has been a Reckoning will what they started be complete."

Farlad's frown was barely detectable in the moonlight. "It's difficult for me to see that happening in our lifetime, sir."

"There are ways to cheat time, Teo. I began this expecting to finish it."

"You've accomplished a great deal just seeing Triad through to this point."

Wells shook his head slowly. "There's a great deal left to be done between now and when the Triad groups are ready. A great deal left to be done before we're ready to face the Mizari."

"Perhaps that won't be necessary, sir."

Wells stood, and the moonlight made his features and tall, lean frame seem sculpted of gray stone rather than flesh. "If we find them, we will have to fight them," he said firmly. "And we *will* find them."

II.

A.R. 660: THE HUNT

"Il faut, dans le gouvernement, des bergers et des bouchers."

—Voltaire

chapter 10

Eyes Bright
With Purpose

"I go amongst the buildings of a city and I
see a Man hurrying along—to what? The
Creature hath a purpose, and its eyes are
bright with it."

—John Keats

"I want to thank you for taking the time to come over," Harmack Wells said to the woman keeping pace at his side.

"No trouble, Director. It's my job to deal with this sort of
thing when the Chancellor is off-station," Wyrena Ten Ga'ar
replied.

She had come to Unity as little more than a girl, but had
grown enough in spirit that "woman" fit her more comfortably
now. Six years of responsibility, responsibility that had expanded almost faster than she had been prepared for, had
worked a change on her. The pattern and habits of her Ba'ar
heritage were too deeply engrained to be erased, but they had
been softened by a new confidence and self-assurance.

Still, sometimes new faces or places brought back an echo
of how she had felt when she first arrived: insecure, intimi-
dated, painfully deferential. And there was one old face who
could do that to her still—Harmack Wells.

They were walking down a corridor deep in the bowels of
USS-Central, in a section rarely seen by outsiders. The decor
consequently lacked the plush and polish accorded the public
areas. The walls were covered in a calming, but bland, light
blue impervacoat, and the uncarpeted composite floor bore the

147

scars and black streaks that were the telltale signs of vehicular traffic.

Ahead, the corridor divided. "This way," Wells said as they neared it, catching Ten Ga'ar's elbow and steering her toward the left branch. "Just a little farther to the lab."

"Thanks. You'd think I'd know this whole station by now," Ten Ga'ar said. "The Chancellor never gets lost. I still do. If you left me down here, I'd be a week finding my way back."

"This is tech country," Wells said. "Nobody ever comes down here except the whitecoats."

A few paces ahead on the right, a door opened and a low-slung cargo trolley trundled out and began to make a wide turn toward them. Sensing their presence, it paused until they were past, then continued on its way with a faint whirring sound.

"You could always hitch a ride with one of those," Wells said, smiling and jerking a thumb over his shoulder. "Here's the lab," he added, angling toward the next door.

The sign beside the door read, SYNTHETIC MODELING APPLICATIONS LABORATORY.

"I wouldn't have asked you to come down here, except that this is the only full-scale holo simulator in a secured area," Wells said, waiting for her to catch up. When she did, he stood aside and allowed her to enter first.

Beyond the door was a modestly sized and relatively uncluttered room. A single two-seat console faced a large synglas window, and three low equipment racks stood along one wall. The sole tech seated at the console wore gray coveralls and a black-and-red shoulder emblem Ten Ga'ar did not recognize. He came to his feet as they entered.

"Everything is ready, Director," the tech said, saluting.

"Thank you, Joel," Wells said. "We'll go right on down."

Wells led the way through another door and down a narrow passage on a steeply sloping ramp lit only by small lamps at knee height. After a dozen or so steps Ten Ga'ar found herself in a large, dimly lit chamber, which was spherical except for the small, level area in the middle of the floor where she and Wells were standing. Looking up, she saw the synglas window of the control room halfway up the wall to her right.

"Voice cue, please, Joel," Wells said.

"Yes, Director," was the disembodied reply. A moment later the window dimmed to black, and the chamber grew even darker.

Wells turned to face Ten Ga'ar. "What I wanted to talk to the Chancellor about—and will still need to, probably—concerns the Kleine communications system. Maybe it's just as well that I have you to practice on, because of the complexity of the problem."

"If the problem is anything other than procurement or security, I'm afraid you're doomed to lose me," Ten Ga'ar said with a wry smile.

"I'm afraid the problem is technical. But I don't intend to offer a technical explanation," Wells said. "I'm as likely as anyone to defer that sort of thing to an expert. I just want to see if I can give you a useful handle on the situation."

"We can try, anyway," Ten Ga'ar said agreeably.

"For the sake of our sanity we'll keep this two-dimensional," Wells said. "You know that the Kleine is used throughout the Service as the primary long-range communications system. The only such system, really, if you're talking about any distance farther than a few cee-seconds."

"All the ships still carry wideband EM transmitters, don't they?"

"And narrowband laser relays, too, but about the only time they're even used is in-system or when a ship's disabled. The Kleine is used everywhere, all the time. How much do you know about how it works?"

"Enough to sit down at a com node and send a message somewhere—nothing more than that."

Wells nodded. "Then we'll start from the beginning. I'll invite you to think of an infinitely large billiard table—"

As he spoke, a fine grid of intersecting green lines appeared, just overhead and parallel to the floor. Some trick of reflection made it seem as though the phantom bisected the chamber and continued infinitely outward.

"This represents the boundary between the matter-matrix of the Universe, down here where we are, and the energy-matrix of the spindle, up there above us. The boundary—that is, the table—isn't completely planar," Wells continued. "Here and there you find a conical depression—"

Several dozen such depressions, each with a smoothly sloping symmetrical shape reminiscent of the bell of a brass instrument, appeared in the construct.

"—almost like pockets out in the middle of the table. At the bottom of every pocket is an AVLO generator—either a ship drive or a station power unit like we have here." A number of the depressions, apparently representing ships in flight, started to crawl slowly across the mesh field. Wells continued, "Sending a Kleine transmission is like shooting a billiard ball up out of one of the pockets with exactly the right force and velocity so it crosses the table and drops into the pocket where the intended receiver is located."

All across the grid, bright orange spheres began arcing up out of the various depressions, "rolling" across the mesh surface, and then plunging back down into a neighboring depression.

There was something elegant and graceful in their motions, but Ten Ga'ar forced herself to attend to the point of the illustration. "A receiver-addressable system," Ten Ga'ar said.

"Exactly."

"And the problem is?"

"That it's becoming harder and harder to get the messages where they're aimed."

Ten Ga'ar's face creased with concern. "Why is it happening?"

"In objective terms, we don't know. The problem is on the spindle, where we have no way of making direct observations. By analogy, though, it's as though the surface of our billiard table were gradually getting rougher—wrinkling, developing tiny tears, warping."

It was clear by now that the simulator was closely attending to Wells's words, for as he continued to explain, each new aspect of the problem was played out on the construct overhead. Ten Ga'ar watched, fascinated, as the grid began to distort, sending the orange spheres careening unpredictably.

"No one understands why it's happening—whether the four hundred years we've been using the Kleine has, in effect, worn down the table; or if it's a matter of too many pockets in the table, so that the farther the message is going, the more likely it'll be deflected; or even a matter of too many balls on the table, so they keep colliding.

"Kleine messages aren't billiard balls, of course—they're packets of energy, and the analogy breaks down at that point. Getting a message to its destination isn't an all-or-nothing proposition—what happens is that the energy becomes diffused and the information content is degraded."

"Is there anything you can do?"

"On its own, Operations instituted error-checking protocols on all communications about ten years ago. Of course, the error-checking procedures themselves can be affected by the interference, so that at times the data may come through clean but end up needing to be retransmitted because the checksum itself got hit. And all the error-checking and retransmission represent overhead that slows down the rate of data exchange —the more so, the worse the interference gets and the more complex the data-integrity precautions become."

"Did you say the interference is getting worse?"

"Yes. Right now we're managing, but the rate of deterioration has us concerned," Wells said. "Concerned enough that we've restricted Kleine traffic in the Lynx and Boötes Octants and done everything we can to hold down the number of ships operating there."

"Has that helped?"

"Not appreciably. End simulation," he said, and the grid vanished. "I don't need to tell you how important reliable Kleine communications are to everything we're doing," he continued, leading her back up the passage to the control center. "If data from the Sentinels on the Perimeter can't reach us, we're as good as blind—with no way to know what's going on out there and no warning if what's going on isn't to our liking. And, of course, it would be impossible to coordinate any sort of response if we can't reach all the elements of our forces swiftly and reliably. Thanks, Joel," he added with a nod to the tech as they left the lab.

Ten Ga'ar did not need to be persuaded that the situation was serious. There were implications that went far beyond military readiness. Except for the Kleine, the Worlds and the ships that served them were all isolates in time. The Kleine bound them together.

Only the Kleine gave the concept of "now" more than a local, parochial meaning. Without it, the Affirmation could not exist. No number of ships could replace it. By ship, Journa was ten years away, Ba'ar Tell a quarter-century. Neither commerce nor a sense of community could survive the loss of the Kleine.

"You said that Operations knew about this for ten years, and you've apparently known about it for at least a while," Ten Ga'ar said, falling in beside him as they headed back the way they had come. "Why are we only hearing about it from you now? Why did you wait this long to alert us to the problem?"

"A fair question. I feel a bit uncomfortable defending our silence. I guess part of the answer to that is that it wasn't a problem at the outset, just an operational nuisance, the kind of technological idiosyncrasy that every complex system displays," Wells said. "Another part is that we had no reason not to think the interference wouldn't plateau at some manageable level."

They reached the lift nexus, and Wells used his priority key to call a car.

"So what do we do now that there is a problem?" Ten Ga'ar asked as the lift doors opened to admit them.

There were two others on the lift already, and Wells shook his head. "Later."

"We can go to my office," Ten Ga'ar said.

"Mine is closer," Wells said, in a manner that ended discussion.

They rode in silence, Wells studying the lift status display and Ten Ga'ar studying him. Wells no longer terrified her, but she still respected his power. *I should have insisted on my office,* she thought in self-reproach. It was a constant struggle not to simply surrender on some level to his aura of command. *Still,* she thought, *I think I'm handling myself pretty well on this one.*

Looking away from Wells, Ten Ga'ar became aware that the other riders were eyeing Wells and her curiously, with questioning glances and barely concealed sniggering smiles. When they left the lift four levels up, she laughed. "You don't think they thought—hearing only what they did—"

"I certainly hope so," Wells said with a straight face. "My reputation can use the boost."

Ten Ga'ar said nothing, but Wells's jest started her thinking. In all the time she had known him Wells had lived alone, but clearly by choice rather than by necessity. With his burning eyes, trim physique, and quiet authority, Wells projected a message to which many women responded strongly. Ten Ga'ar herself felt it, and she had heard more than a few others on the staff admit to the same reaction.

Wells had taken advantage of that attraction to enjoy a series—and, at times, a multiplicity—of casual matings. In the language of her homeworld, he was *ga'fla*—one who beds, but does not wed. Ten Ga'ar counted among her friends two women who had been on his string and one who hoped she still was, and knew that their commitment to and hopes for the relationship had always been greater than Wells's.

Even knowing Wells's reputation, each had been convinced that she could offer him something unique, something that would make her his chosen. Though Ten Ga'ar was polite enough not to force them to face it, the reality was that all Wells wanted from them was what any woman could give him. He consciously and consistently chose not to involve himself on any other level.

But for perhaps as long as half a year, Wells had apparently been pulling back from even that minimal involvement. Ten Ga'ar became aware of it when Kilaoqe came to her, distraught that Wells had stopped asking for her and wondering if Wyrena knew who had stolen his attentions. After harvesting what they could from the grapevine and finding others wondering the same, they concluded it was someone Wells was seeing during his periodic brief visits downwell.

Wells's small, self-conscious jest opened the door to an entirely different view of the matter. Consciously and deliberately, Wells had allowed his intimate relationships to quietly expire, like so many neglected houseplants. Ten Ga'ar had an idea how long ago he had made that decision. What still wasn't clear was why.

Before Ten Ga'ar's silence became conspicuous, the lift disgorged them on Level 1. Corridor traffic prevented them from resuming their conversation until they reached Wells's office five minutes later.

"You were asking about what we do now," Wells said as they settled in facing chairs. "The only long-term fix that any of our people can envision is building a system of automated relay stations. The interference increases with distance, so the plan would be to lay out trunk lines, with active repeaters every ten cees or so grabbing every message, cleaning it up as necessary, and firing it along to the next. We're also looking at instituting communications controls at the same time."

"The independent shipowners aren't going to like that," Ten Ga'ar observed. "They're unhappy enough having to submit to Service traffic control. If you start telling them they have to channel all their transmissions through us as well, they'll be in the Chancellor's office crying foul before you can finish a sentence."

"They'll have to live with it, though. At the moment every Kleine unit can direct-link to every other Kleine unit, and the number of possible connections has just completely gone around the bend. In the beginning that kind of unrestricted communications was a boon, but it's becoming a nightmare.

"By consolidating everything along a set series of links and doing some traffic management at the same time—every major user being allocated certain blocks of time to originate messages, with Defnet having a priority claim at all times—we should be able to get around these interference problems."

"If you want to volunteer to do the selling job on the Independent Shipowners Association, you're welcome to it," Ten Ga'ar said. "How many trunk corridors?"

"At least eight, with possibly an extra one each for the Perseus and Microscopium Octants and a dedicated one for Defense in the Mizari Zone."

"With an average of five repeaters for every trunk, that's more than fifty relays—"

"Eighty-four, with backups and branch links."

"—every one with its own AVLO generator, station-keeping servos—would they be manned?"

"Probably only the Defnet trunk. But there'd have to be maintenance ships for the rest of them. You're right—it's a big project, and expensive as hell. Just looking at the logistics, not the design and construction, it'll take thirty-five years to bring it into being. And from the pace the Kleine signal is degrading on the longest runs—here to Ba'ar Tell and the Perimeter—we should have started ten years ago."

Her face showing worry lines, Ten Ga'ar shook her head. "Did you mean to imply earlier that there's a short-term solution?"

"No," Wells said, "But there's a short-term precaution we need to take."

"What's that?"

"Move my office and staff out to Lynx Center."

So that's what this is about, she thought, looking askant at Wells. "The bylaws require the Chancellor and members of the Committee to stay time-bound to the Terran system for the duration of their appointment."

"I'm aware of that. A special exemption will have to be made."

"The Chancellor will be reluctant to make one. There's a good reason Atlee wrote a travel restriction into the reforms.

We don't want a repeat of the abuses the old system permitted, the worst of which was Thackery being promoted to Director of the Service while he has in the craze returning from a field assignment."

"I'm aware of the problems Atlee was addressing," Wells said. "But the fact is that we face the prospect of losing direct communications with the Perimeter before the relay system can be deployed. That would seem to be an important enough reason to make an exception. My moving to Lynx Center should guarantee that we experience no window of vulnerability."

"Why not just use Lynx Center as a temporary relay point until the trunk system is ready in that sector?"

"I intend to. But don't you think it'd be prudent to shorten the command chain where we can?"

"The Chancellor will have to make that decision," Ten Ga'ar said.

"Of course," Wells said agreeably. "Do you know where Chancellor Sujata is?"

"Of course," Ten Ga'ar said, rising from her chair to signify that the discussion was over. "Is this important enough to call her back from Earth?"

"Important enough, certainly. Urgent enough—umm. How much longer is she supposed to be downwell?"

"The Chancellor is due back next Monday."

Wells mused. "No. We'll respect her privacy. But it's certainly important enough to be at the top of the list when she comes back."

"Done."

The black-grained beach was deserted except for its native inhabitants and a solitary woman, sitting cross-legged just above the tide line. Bare-breasted and clutching a pendant dangling from her necklace, she rocked slowly to and fro as she chanted to herself:

Selir bi' chentya
Darnatir bi' maranya en bis losya
Qoris nonitya . . .

Sujata opened her eyes slowly and looked seaward. Her other senses were already nearly overloaded: the brisk breeze exploring her skin, the tang of the salt spume in her nostrils, the cacophony of rushing and splashing water in her ears. She added to that the sight of endless waves punishing the faces of craggy black sea stacks, which stood defiantly against the battering of the sea.

She had only begun to sample all of Earth's textures, and yet this place had drawn her back. The interface between water, land, and air seemed to her the most magic of the many magic places she had discovered.

Once, farther south on the same shore, she had come across a seal rookery at twilight and had sat awestruck on a cliff overlooking the beach as thousands of sleek, black bodies struggled ashore and clustered together on the sands for the night. The air had been full of their barking and their wet, musky scent; later, when she climbed down to the beach and walked among them in the darkness, she had sensed their self-awareness and primal circle of community.

Sujata wondered at times whether she would have felt the same affection for Maranit had she undertaken a similar odyssey there. Maranit had seas and forbidding mountain ranges and deserts. But on Maranit the highlands of the First Continent were an island of life on an otherwise unfriendly world, like an infection that had not yet overwhelmed the patient's body. The rest of Maranit, as well as it was known, was barren.

But on Earth there seemed to be no environment so hostile that it did not harbor life. Life clung fiercely, possessively, to the Earth. On the top of some of the sea stacks, trees grew, stalwart remnants of an ancient forest carved up by the sea's advance. Other sea stacks wore a cap of white guano that marked where gulls and terns roosted. The turbulent waves broke on a beach that was home to a hundred species, from tiny amphipods buried out of sight to the sandpipers that skittered along the changing water line.

Half shrouded by a late-forming sea mist, the disc of the sun was dipping down toward the broken horizon. As it dived between the silhouettes of two of the largest sea stacks, a chime sounded from Sujata's implant transceiver. Reluctantly she rose from her cross-legged repose and walked up the beach to the edge of the marrat grass, where a small carrybag rested.

She took from the bag a Journan-style *daiiki*—a full-sleeved, ankle-length caftan dyed in muted rusts and ambers

—and drew it around her. As she began buttoning the garment's long front closure she began to hear a new note over the sound of the sea: a sound that was artificial, mechanical, and therefore alien to the place. A few moments later she saw the airskiff angling toward her, its landing lights bright against the darkening sky.

The skiff landed a few dozen metres from where Sujata stood, and a moment later a young man clambered out of the cabin.

"Sorry I'm late, Chancellor," he called as he crossed the sand toward her. "I misjudged the headwinds coming west over the Rockies—should have gotten off earlier from Philadelphia."

"That's all right, Joaquim," Sujata said, lifting her bag to her shoulder and going to meet him. "I'm never in a hurry to leave here."

Two of the three seats in the airskiff's small passenger cabin were already occupied by Katrina Evanik and Laban Garrard, recent additions to her staff. Evanik, dark-haired and round-faced, was from Journa; Garrard, slender and sallow-complected, was Dzuban. Their contracts called them staff consultants. In fact, they were field observers with advanced degrees in cultural psychology and certificates from the Survey Branch's Human Studies School.

Like Sujata, Evanik and Garrard had been on Earth for the last six weeks, but with a nearly opposite purpose. Where Sujata had isolated herself hoping to find the pulse of Earth's natural community, her handpicked sociologists had immersed themselves in its human community.

"Hello, Katrina, Laban," Sujata said as she settled between them. "How did things go?"

"I thought it was very productive," Evanik said. "I only wish it wasn't necessary to leave this abruptly." The skiff lurched abruptly as Joaquim guided the skiff back into the air.

"I understand. But we're looking for a series of snapshots. We haven't the resources to make feature films," Sujata said. "Laban? Did you think your time well spent?"

"I told you before we came down here that I'm not comfortable with this methodology," Garrard hedged. "I still don't see why we can't go to the Council's Data and Evaluation people. The chances are they already have what you want to know on file."

"I'm not interested in having my data filtered through the Council's particular set of prejudices," Sujata said. "And I doubt they would have what I want available, in any case. These people studied and probed and judged my world—and yours, and Katrina's—as though Earth represented the ultimate expression of humanity. I don't think they're prepared to look at themselves with an objective eye."

"I seem to recall that the anthropologists were under the aegis of the Service—"

"The Service has always reflected primarily Terran culture and attitudes," Evanik said.

Garrard glared crossly at his colleague. "Even so, what the Chancellor has us doing can't be considered a properly formulated research program—"

"I asked you to find out what Terrans are thinking and saying about Wells, the Mizari, and the possibility of war," Sujata said. "That seems perfectly clear to me."

"But all you're going to get is a limited sample of completely anecdotal evidence. There's no way to construct any sort of useful hypothesis from that sort of data—"

"I already have my hypothesis," Sujata said. "What I need is for you and Katrina to be my eyes and ears. I want you to watch and listen for the things I would be watching and listening for if I were free to go where you can and make the kinds of contacts you can make," Sujata said. "Which brings me back to my original question. What did you find out?"

"I'd prefer to wait until I've had a chance to review and edit my notes," Garrard said stiffly. "I hope you will allow me to be at least that professional."

Before the frosty silence that followed could become too uncomfortable, Evanik spoke up. "Did either of you hear about the war rally in Munich?" she asked.

"I wouldn't have," Sujata said. "Dr. Garrard?"

"It would be easier to say if I did if I knew more about what Dr. Evanik is referring to."

"Katrina?"

"It was on the fourteenth—a spontaneous noon-hour rally," Evanik said. "There must have been three thousand people—"

"Is that your estimate or the authorities'?" Garrard said, interrupting. "What did the authorities say?"

"It's my estimate. I saw at least one camera crew there, but if there was any mention on Earthnet, it was blacked out locally. That's why I wondered if you'd heard about it."

"No," Garrard said. "I heard nothing. Though it should be easy enough to find out what the net carried."

"Was it the rally itself or the reason for it that was so unusual?" Sujata asked.

"Both, really. From a communications rationale there's no reason to bring people together physically when Earthnet can relay the information content to any number of people up to and including the entire population. And the Council frowns on what it calls 'unstructured mass associations' for anything other than live entertainment events, since human beings are not at their rational best in large multiples of a hundred."

"How did these people get a permit, then?"

"Apparently they didn't," Evanik said. "There was no prior announcement, no publicity, just the rumor that someone named Robert Chaisson was going to be there. At eleven-thirty the plaza was empty—at noon it was packed. It was all very old-fashioned. No Orator's Screen, no dais. Chaisson simply climbed to the highest spot in the plaza, set up his loudbox, and spoke to them."

"What was his agenda?"

"His main point was that he thought the Council should immediately begin building a standing army of at least half a million men. And he wanted the Council to urge the other major worlds to do the same. He asked the crowd to press Dailey, the Commissioner for Eastern Europe, to propose it to the Council. He also urged the young men in the audience to prepare themselves to serve, and to tell Dailey they were willing to volunteer. He was a very effective speaker, by the way. Very bright, very articulate."

"Why would Earth need a self-defense force?" Sujata wondered aloud. "Does this mean they've no confidence in the Defenders?"

Evanik shook her head. "Exactly the opposite. They have complete confidence in the Defenders—though Chaisson did say that Earth shouldn't be content to have the Service do its fighting for it. But he wasn't talking about a self-defense force. He wants an offensive army—to attack the Mizari. The words he used were 'to root out the vermin wherever they're hiding and make space safe for mankind again.'"

"How did they respond to him?"

"They stayed. They listened. That line about the vermin got a big roar of approval. And they booed the Peace Corps when they came to arrest him."

"Ah. That explains it," Garrard said, settling back in his seat. "As a general rule, the net doesn't publicize criminal activity."

That didn't begin to explain it, Sujata thought. They had to know it would be blacked out. So who was it meant for? Tanvier. The Council. It had to be. And they *would* take note, and they would start to worry. "The Nines are restless—" And then Berberon would come knocking. But why now? What do they want now?

Perhaps just the obvious. "Worry about us getting cocky and going out looking for them," Berberon had warned her. Maybe it was time to start. . . .

The Chancellor's conference room was more crowded than Berberon could remember seeing it. Even allowing for Sujata's passion for face-to-face accountability, it was an unusual gathering. The Chancellery embraced a richly populated bureaucracy, and most of the principals were on hand.

Berberon recalled how in the first year or so of Sujata's stewardship many senior Chancellery staffers had experienced panic on discovering that their new boss expected them to be able to present their ideas in person and to answer questions off the cuff. Sujata would not let them hide behind memos and arms-length electronic consultations.

Nor did she respect the traditional and fiercely defended fiefdoms that had been carved out in the name of division of responsibility. She expected everyone, not merely the staff analysts, to embrace the larger picture and offer insights. And she encouraged them to disagree, not only with each other but with her as well. In short she had brought the art of the dialogue back to the Service.

The gathering was a crisis conference in everything but name. In the three weeks since Sujata had returned from her leave, most of the resources of the Chancellery had been marshaled for an intensive review of Wells's latest proposal. Now it was time for answers to the questions she had posed. The witnesses sat elbow-to-elbow at the far end of the room, waiting to be called on.

Since he did not share her authority, Berberon was not

seated at the main table with Sujata, Ten Ga'ar, and Regan Marshall, the Vice Chancellor. But he had been given full access to Wells's formal proposal and understood that the session was as much for his benefit as for Sujata's. By his actions eight years ago, Berberon had shouldered an extra burden where Wells was concerned.

First up was the chief of Data and Library Services.

"You've reviewed the Defense Branch's report on Kleine interference?" Sujata asked.

"Yes, Chancellor."

"Is it accurate?"

"I consulted the Operations Branch records in an attempt to see if there were inaccuracies or omissions. I found none."

"In your opinion the report contains an accurate history of the problem?"

"Yes, Chancellor."

"And you found no evidence that any coordinated effort was made to suppress knowledge of the problem?"

"I found no such evidence. Judging from the number of individuals who knew of the problem and when and how they heard of it, dissemination followed a natural dispersal pattern."

"Who knew? Any of our people?" asked Marshall.

"I've located seven individual Chancellery staffers who had some awareness of the problem, but they all viewed it as a technical matter with no policy consequences, and all had been reassured that Operations was addressing it."

That answer could hardly please Sujata, but she made no comment and dismissed the chief. Next up was the supervisor of the Office of Technical Coordination.

"Franklin, may we have your evaluation of the proposed trunk communications system?"

"We don't really have much to look at so far, Chancellor. What we have is a statement of design intent, not a fully engineered solution," the supervisor said, resting his folded hands on his round belly pontifically. "But the theory is consistent with our understanding of the physics of transmatrix links."

"Why can't we just increase the strength of the transmission and get a better signal-to-noise ratio?" asked the chief of the Office of Financial Management.

The OTC supervisor turned to face his colleague. "Ken,

this isn't like trying to be heard across a noisy room. You can't simply talk louder. We're not pushing energy. We're just aiming it."

"Does Lynx Center have the capacity to serve as a temporary relay point between here and the Perimeter?" Marshall asked.

"Not at present."

"When could they have it?" Sujata asked.

"Considering that they're already beginning some preliminary tests, there's a very high probability they could begin to assume that function in five years."

"And Perimeter Command?"

"A few years longer. They don't have the facilities Lynx does."

"Won't that solve the problem?" asked the finance chief. "It's taken us three hundred years for the problem to become significant. Seems like bringing up just two relay stations between here and the Perimeter should buy us quite a lot of time."

"You don't cut the interference by a third simply by cutting the distance into thirds," the OTC man said with a hint of impatience. "The baseline interference on even the shortest link is already high enough to require special data-handling protocols. By the time the Lynx and Perimeter Command relays come on line, we'll be lucky if we're no worse off than we are right now."

"Let's take a closer look at the time parameter," Sujata said. "The schedule proposed for deployment of the repeater system in the Lynx and Boötes Octants—is it realistic?"

"Optimistic, I would say. Token-passing communications have never been attempted on this scale. There are bound to be some difficulties."

"So you agree that there is potentially a window during which we will be out of touch with the Perimeter."

"Completely out of touch, no. But suffering from severely impaired communications, yes. Real-time voice and video will probably be impossible, even with sparse matrix techniques."

"Thank you, Director," Sujata said.

Over the next hour they heard from several other witnesses concerning the financial and logistical feasibility of the repeater system. Then Sujata dismissed all those who had testified, leaving only her committee liaison and the High Justice of the Service Court awaiting their turn.

"Those of us who remain are the only ones who know that Comitè Wells has recommended moving the Strategy Committee and certain officers in command of the Defense Branch, including himself, to Lynx Center," Sujata said. "I'd like for us to now focus on that part of the proposal. Justice Kemmerman, would you please offer your interpretation of Section 74.1?"

"The bylaws are very clear on this," the silver-haired justice said, speaking slowly. "Section 74.1 specifies that no member of the Steering Committee may take any action that would remove himself or herself from the system-local time track or place himself of herself out of real-time communication with the remainder of the Committee for more than fourteen consecutive days. In effect that means that Wells can go to the moon or Mars, but he can't go to Lynx—not as Director of the Defense Branch, that is."

"Unless the bylaws are changed," the liaison interjected.

"Yes. There is that option, if you wish to take it and you can muster a unanimous vote of the Committee. Though I would discourage you from tinkering with the long-term stability of the Service to meet short-term needs."

The liaison turned to Sujata. "Chancellor, you have to weigh the desirability. But as a practical matter, in my opinion the Committee would be willing to approve a change exempting only the Director of the Defense Branch from Section 74.1."

"I wonder," Marshall said. "Chancellor, I might remind you that three of the Directors are colonials like yourself, who might be very interested in being free to make a visit home without having to resign from the Committee to do it."

"You may well be right, Regan," Sujata said. "Justice Kemmerman, is there any way to let Wells go without changing the bylaws and throwing the door wide open for everyone?"

"I'm afraid not."

"What about the Chancellor's emergency powers under 32.33?" Ten Ga'ar asked.

Kemmerman frowned. "It's a gray area," he acknowledged grudgingly. "You have a certain latitude under the emergency-powers clause, but the Committee is always in a position to disagree as to whether the situation qualifies as an emergency."

"Would the Court feel obliged to initiate any action on its own to stop the transfer?"

"You're asking me to speak for all five justices—not just for myself—and to render a decision before the fact," Kemmerman said. "I really am not in a position to do either."

"Let me put it another way," the liaison said. "Has the Court ever intervened against a decision by the Chancellor without having first received a petition from a member of the Committee?"

"No," Kemmerman said. "That has not happened."

"Then, Chancellor, I'd say that if you took the precaution of getting the Committee's approval by means of an advisory vote, you should be safe from any repercussions."

For the next quarter of an hour the group brainstormed possible ways of providing for an interim exercise of power. Then Sujata excused both the High Justice and the committee liaison, leaving only Berberon, Marshall, Ten Ga'ar, and herself in the room.

"It sounds to me as though everything hangs together except Wells's reason for going," Sujata began. "Our experts don't foresee a complete loss of communications with the Perimeter. Building the repeater system would be enough of a response to the situation."

"Wells does have a certain obligation to look on the dark side," Marshall pointed out. "He may well think a loss of communications is a real enough possibility that prudence requires moving the command forward."

"He may," Sujata said. "But for the moment let's assume otherwise. Can anyone think of any reason that hasn't already been stated here why Wells may see this as a desirable move?"

"Symbology," Berberon said.

"Explain."

Berberon dragged his chair forward to join the others at the table before continuing. "Being on the Perimeter is not particularly attractive duty. There aren't many creature comforts on a Sentinel, and very few more on a tender. The crews are small and the ships are crowded. There's a mind-numbing sameness to the work. Instead of going back to Lynx Center, the rotations now take the crews to Perimeter Command, which is just as spartan as the ships they come off. They never get that now-I'm-back-in-civilization feeling. And on top of everything else there's a sense of isolation, of vulnerability— particularly so now that they can look back here and see the worlds enjoying protections they don't have."

"Meaning the Defenders."

"Yes. But for Wells to bring a fleet flagship into a forward area as much as says, 'We're strong. We're safe here.' And privations are less onerous when they're shared."

"I agree—but I think it goes further," Ten Ga'ar said. "Chancellor, I've watched him, both with a Ba'ar woman's eyes and with the tools that you have taught me. Comitè Wells has a warrior spirit. It is in his walk, in the way he dominates a room by his presence. It is the reason for the mask behind which he hides. To fulfill that spirit, to be honest to his essence, at some time he must walk into the arena to be tested. I think this is why he asks to leave us. The rest is only pretext."

Sujata locked eyes with Ten Ga'ar. "If you're right, is walking into the arena enough?" she asked softly. "Or does he have to fight and defeat an opponent too?"

"Chancellor, I do not know."

"Probably Wells, himself, doesn't know," Berberon said. "The Renans have a saying, 'No one hates war more than a warrior. But no one loves victory more than the victor.' It's a conflict every soldier wrestles with in times of peace. Once war has begun, of course, they do not have the luxury of being philosophical. More fundamental concerns come to the fore—like survival."

Staring at the center of the table, Sujata chewed at the tip of her thumb thoughtfully. "If I believed that the Perimeter might become isolated by this interference problem," she said at last, "I never would consider letting Wells go there. I never have caught him in a lie or found him to follow the letter of the law while violating its spirit. Yet, though I trust him, I would not want to tempt him. That much of what Wyrena says I have seen in him myself.

"But Franklin tells me that I can count on always being able to get a priority message through to the Perimeter. As long as that link exists, the last word belongs to the Chancellor. It seems as though I am free to let Wells go but not obliged to. So should I?"

It was the question Berberon had been waiting for, and he pounced on it without hesitation. "Yes, Chancellor, absolutely. This is what we've been asking for—a chance to neutralize Wells. It's a seventeen-year run to Lynx. Seventeen years to take back what we gave him. Seventeen years the Committee will be free from his influence."

"Doesn't he know that too? Why would he throw away the position and the power he worked so hard to achieve, unless he knew he were going to get even more?"

"Power is only a means to an end. He would give it up when he's achieved that end. I think Wyrena is right. Wells is so enamored of the thought of riding to the front on a white charger that he's willing to separate himself from his allies downwell."

Sujata looked to the Vice Chancellor. "Regan?"

"I'm really not convinced that romantic notions of gallantry or symbolism from the days of trench warfare have anything to do with Comitè Wells's proposal. As for a hidden agenda, I don't see what good he can do for his friends there that he can't do here," Marshall said. "And as for trusting or tempting Wells, I don't see what harm he can do us there that he can't do here. Let him go. Let him take himself out of the picture."

"Wyrena?"

"Just one selfish thought on your behalf," Ten Ga'ar said. "If he goes to Lynx, in all likelihood you will never have to deal with him again."

Sujata was silent for a moment. "Does anyone have any fears that Wells is positioning himself for a coup?" she asked quietly.

"Just the reverse," Berberon said. "I would be more fearful of that if he stayed here."

"I agree," said Marshall. "Earth is the locus of power in the Affirmation. This is where the action is. Let him go, Chancellor. Let's be rid of him."

Sujata's gaze flicked in Berberon's direction. *Does this change the rules of our bargain?* her eyes asked. *Would this free me?*

Berberon answered with a slow nod. *Yes,* he thought. *And free me as well.*

"Very well," Sujata said. "Wyrena, please call Comitè Wells. Tell him I want to see him."

chapter 11

The Destinies
of Ships and Men

Harry Eugene Barnstable had been roaming the gangways of
Maintenance Yard 105 for a long time. He had come to the
orbiting shipyard at age twenty-two, fresh out of school, because he loved the deepships, found them achingly beautiful
in form and romantically compelling in function.

With a clarity of self-knowledge uncommon in the young,
Barnstable had understood that he lacked whatever it took to
wear the black ellipse of the deepship crews. Whether it was a
timidity of spirit or an addiction to comfort, Barnstable knew
he would never give up Earth and the normal life it represented to fly star to star in the deepships. But this close he
could get, like the landlubbers who once haunted the quays,
the earthbound whose spirits alone soared into the clouds on
silver wings.

Barnstable's first job was as an enviromental integrity engineer—a fancy name for someone who maintained pressure
enclosures and space doors. There were a lot of space doors in
Yard 105. The station boasted sixteen full-sized work bays
arrayed in a four-by-four grid, and each shipway had seven
interlocks—two for man-sized waldoids, two for the construction teleops, and three flying tunnels to provide shirt-

sleeve access to completed hulls. Yard 105 kept its EI engineers busy.

But being busy proved not to be enough for Barnstable. Feeling as though what he did was peripheral to the real work of the Yard, he returned to school quarter-time in a quest for new employment endorsements. Three years later he was fully qualified as a teleop assembler, enabling him for the first time to make a direct contribution. The highlight of that period was helping to lay the keelspine of a new packet destined for the Earth—Ba'ar Tell run.

Yet even in his new role there was still a distance between him and the ships he loved so much. He performed his duties in the comfort of the Yard's shirt-sleeve teleop center, isolated from the ships in the bays by a hundred metres of space and the very technology made his job possible. His robotic surrogates—welders, pushers, seamers—roamed all over the ships's hulls. His real hands never touched them.

By the time he was forty, Barnstable had found a way to cross that final barrier, graduating from the teleop room to the ranks of the integrations engineers. Then, at long last, he could board the deepships freely, and he learned them as well as the men who crewed them, and in some ways better.

Barnstable felt a pride in what he did that drove or shamed those who worked with him to ask more of themselves. And the word got out that when Barnstable's crew installed something, it worked; when they fixed something, it stayed fixed.

Then a freak accident—ironically, caused by a mismaintained hatch that cycled closed without warning—irreparably damaged nerves in his right leg, costing him both strength and mobility and bringing him back to the soft duty on-station. Barnstable could have sued or retired, or both. Instead he stayed on as the supervisor of F-bay.

In all, Barnstable had spent thirty-one years watching the ships come and go from Yard 105's bays. Some had taken shape there, and some had only been visitors, stopping for a time to rest and recoup. Packets and cruisers, tugs and freighters—he remembered them all by name, and many by the service he had done them.

As different as the ships and Barnstable's memories of them were, they had one thing in common: once a ship left Yard 105, Barnstable knew not to expect to see it again. Ships left Yard 105 for the craze and the long runs to the other Worlds. Those that were meant to return would not do so until many more years had passed, time eaten up by the long, empty light-years.

Of all the ships that Barnstable had seen riding at anchor in the shipways, only one had ever left and come back—and it had done so repeatedly. The ship had been in Yard 105 when he had first come there, and he had begun to think it would be there long after he had left. Its name was *Tilak Charan*.

As spanking new outside as *Charan* appeared to the eye, it was in fact a relic of an era, the feeling of which was almost impossible to recapture, when the frontier had represented challenge and mystery instead of terror and death. *Tilak Charan* was the third name the vessel had borne. When Barnstable had first crossed paths with it, it had been called *Weichsel*. When it had begun its life more than a century and a half ago, its name was *Taipeng*. Barnstable did not concern himself with the changing appellations, for he knew it best by the hull registration under which all the ship's work records were indexed—USS-96.

Like its sister ship the *Joanna Wesley* (formerly *Journa*, née *New York*), which was in the care of Yard 102, USS-96 was part of the Survey Branch's last great shipbuilding project. The sixteen vessels that had comprised the Cities Series were to have been the spearheads of the Survey Branch's Phase III search, fresh blood for the millennium-long pursuit of First Colonization Worlds. Aided by a much larger fleet of unmanned drones, the Cities vessels were to have pushed hard at the limits of the known, more than trebling the volume of explored space in the course of a five-hundred-year plan that would add four thousand new star systems to the catalogs of the astrographers.

But Thackery's Revision had intervened, abruptly halting the expansion and canceling the Survey Branch's plans. Of the sixteen Cities hulls, six were never more than engineering drawings, and three were abandoned with their keelspines freshly laid. Seven were completed as "generic" AVLO hulls and renamed for seven of the Unified Worlds. Five of those seven misbegotten survey ships now patrolled the Perimeter in their new identity as Sentinels.

Except for the journey inbound to Earth from the Centers where they had been built, the two remaining ships—USS-96 and USS-97—had spent the next hundred years as deepships in name only. In the decades immediately following the Revision, when the panic was most palpable, they had been flying archives, filled with nonvolatile memory cubes representing what was hoped would be a meaningful abstract of the species's collective knowledge and history.

Later, when fear of the Mizari had mellowed to paranoia, the memory cubes had been removed from USS-96 to make room for berths and accommodations intended for Earth's ruling elite and the Service's senior staff. When the list of those demanding to be part of the evacuation grew too long for USS-96 to accommodate them, the same had been done to USS-97. For thirty years the two ships were quietly held in reserve, ready to leave orbit literally on a day's notice. But the need had never arisen.

Three factors led to the next phase of the ships' careers. Progress on the Perimeter listening posts gradually erased the fear of a sudden, overwhelming attack by the Mizari. The Service withdrew from the evacuation plan, prompting a few key Terran officials, embarrassed by the suggestion of selfishness and cowardice, to remove their names from the list. And as the new Defense Branch matured, it began to exercise its claim on the resources of the Service, especially those it felt were being underutilized.

As a consequence, both ships underwent still another metamorphosis, this time to emerge as engineering test-beds. Every new development in deepship technology between the mid-500s and the early 600s was field-tested on USS-96 or USS-97, or both. The procedures for upgrading ships in the field were worked out, sometimes by trial and error, on their viscera. Toward the end experimentation overran development, and boths ships diverged sharply and in different directions from the standard internal plan for deepships.

That was how Barnstable had first found USS-96—its lines marred by the addition of experimental doughnut-shaped AVLO radiators forward and aft, its innards ravaged by a succession of tinkerers, all of whom had treated the ship as a disposable good.

It was Harmack Wells who had rescued the ships from slow death at the hands of the Office of Systems Research. Soon after Wells took office, USS-96 was moved into Barnstable's F-bay, USS-97 into Yard 102. In the six years since, both ships had been stripped down to the bone and then rebuilt with state-of-the-art components. Virtually the only original equipment left in place were the AVLO-L drives, and even those received new controllers and peripherals.

The thoroughness of USS-97's renovation and the degree of interest the Director's office expressed in its progress had long ago caused Barnstable to wonder if the ship were being readied for a role as fleet flagship. But it was not until five weeks ago that his suspicions were confirmed, when USS-96 and USS-97 were both assigned flag crews.

Even then it was not clear which of the two ships would be primary. Not until the recommission orders came through specifying that the ship in Barnstable's F-bay was to have *F-1 Tilak Charan* as its transponder ID was the picture complete. Wells was going to the Perimeter, and it was *Charan* that would take him there.

For Barnstable that news was the vindication for a lifetime of labor. Even learning that *Wesley*'s unreadiness—she was still six weeks from full flight certification—had been a factor in the choice did not dim his pride. "First and best," he had told the refit team at their final meeting that morning. "That's what *Charan* is—that's what we are."

As much as Barnstable was pleased for his own sake, he was even more pleased for *Charan*. Though he knew better than most that ships were mere technological artifacts, he was enough the romantic to also believe that each ship had a proper destiny conferred on it by the intent of the builder. When that destiny was frustrated or unfulfilled, it could only be viewed as a tragedy.

From his office greatport Barnstable watched as the black spider that was the base tug entered the spaceward end of F-bay and nosed close to *Charan*'s bow. Two waldoids were standing by in case of trouble, but the tug pilot was skilled at his job, The six slender grapple arms gracefully closed on the flared circular rim of the forward radiator. After a brief pause to be certain all was secure, the shipway's anchors released *Charan*, and the tug began to edge the flagship out of the yard.

For the last time, Barnstable thought. This time *Charan* would not return. At long last she would become what she had been built to be—a deepship, riding gravity's own wave between the stars.

"It's about damn time," Barnstable said to himself, watching the tug's chemical thrusters fire as it pointed *Charan* toward Unity Center. "About damn time." Then he turned away from the greatport, surprised to find his eyes bright with moisture. Tomorrow another ship would fill the empty bay, and he could not allow himself to think of *Charan* for very long.

". . . the mighty arm of the chosen people of God. O Benefactor, look with favor on the labors of those who follow the path You have shown us, that we might win back the promised lands and earn the right to live forever in the infinity of Your Creation. Give us strength and comfort as we prepare ourselves to face Your enemies. . . ."

Though Janell Sujata was standing just a few metres away from the Most Reverend Bishop of the Holy Redemption Church, she was not listening to his invocation. Looking out from the temporary rostrum at one edge of Unity Center's great central atrium at the overflow crowd gathered on the balconies and the main plaza, Sujata wondered just when she had lost complete control over the departure ceremonies.

Perhaps my failure was not anticipating the amount of fuss that could attend the sailing of a single ship, she thought. *If someone had told me a month ago, I would not have believed it.*

A month ago everything had seemed in order for a quick, quiet departure for Wells and his staff. The Committee had given its pro forma approval to the relocation of Wells and the command staff. Wells had accepted her requirement that the journey be made in the minimum time possible, forcing *Charan* to stay in the craze, incommunicado, until its approach to Lynx Center. Satisfactory arrangements had been worked out for the Deputy Director of Defense to report directly to the Chancellor in Wells's absence.

The first clue to what was coming, the significance of which Sujata unfortunately missed, was the attention that *Charan* garnered after being moved to a station-keeping zone adjacent to Unity Center. From the first day, buses jetted almost hourly between the Center and the ship. Some carried Earthnet and outworld journalists, others dignitaries who had requested tours.

Most often, of course, the buses carried members of *Charan*'s crew, who were readying her for departure but not yet ready to take up residence. Gradually those who needed to be there began to crowd out those who were merely curious, and after two weeks the tours were halted. The next day the crew began to occupy the ship on a continuous rotating schedule, serving notice that *Charan*'s sailing date was drawing near.

But by then the Defense Branch had forwarded to Sujata without comment more than fifty internal inquiries as to whether there would be any formal send-off for *Charan* and the command staff. Some of the inquiries, assuming that there would be a ceremony of some sort, merely asked for the schedule and other details. The referrals did not quite add up to an official request on Wells's part, but Sujata nonetheless took the hint. Conscious of the psychological aspects of the transfer, she saw no harm and some possible good in a quiet, in-house salute to those who were leaving.

Then Berberon had intervened, asking if he might have the chance to address Wells and his staff as a way of underlining the Terran government's support for a move over which the Nines were reportedly ecstatic. She could not refuse him. But Berberon's involvement brought with it demands for access to the ceremony by Earthnet and a flurry of requests for invitations for officials from other Observer missions. Suddenly the quiet leave-taking had become a major media event.

Her one victory had been to keep Wells himself off the podium and away from the microphones. Instead he stood as part of a neat pattern of human bodies a few metres in front of the rostrum in a reserved area on the plaza. Wells and his staff, wearing rust-colored, high-collared tunics that only could be considered officers' uniforms, formed the front rank. She had seen the tunics before, but there was one new detail. Each of the men in the front row wore above his right breast pocket a small gold trigon made up of three discontinuous bars.

Standing behind in four rows of ten abreast were the flag crews of *Charan* and *Wesley*, thirty-five men and five women dressed in the blue unisex jumpsuits that had been standard deepship garb since the Service's earliest days. Compared with the front row, the crews seemed almost painfully young. Even so, they had well learned the stoic soldier's mask: Their faces were as unmarked by emotion as they were untouched by time.

Berberon was at the podium now, and Sujata forced herself

to listen, though she knew that his words were riddled with insincerity.

"Every great civilization draws much of its greatness from the quality of the men and women who answer the call to defend it," Berberon was saying. "A city, a nation, a world, a species that does not enjoy the loyalty, does not inspire the sacrifice, of its strongest, brightest, and bravest men and women, cannot be called great no matter what its other accomplishments might be.

"Yet those who answer the call have been rarely accorded the depth of gratitude their service deserves. They perform their offtimes onerous duty in the twilight of our consciousness—we know they are there, but for some reason we do not see them. They do for the rest of us what we would have trouble doing for ourselves, asking nothing more than the opportunity to follow the dictates of honor. But they have earned much more.

"So it is altogether fitting that we take this occasion to say to the commanders and crews of the flagships *Tilak Charan* and *Joanna Wesley,* thank you. We thank you for what you have done and what you will do. We thank you for what you have already sacrificed and for what you will sacrifice. And we thank you for the courage you have shown, and the courage you will show as you face the challenge of keeping your homeworlds safe."

A well-constructed speech, Sujata thought as Berberon interrupted himself by leading the enthusiastic applause for the crews. All the magic words—*bravery, duty, sacrifice, honor*—a paraphrase of Eric Lange's famous quote about what the brightest and best mean to society. How could they doubt that you are their friend?

At Berberon's prompting, Wells acknowledged the applause with a raised hand. That gesture drove the intensity of the tumult a notch higher. It began to fade only when Berberon stepped away from the podium, making way for Sujata to replace him there. It was as if the crowd wanted there to be no mistake about who was the object of their acclaim.

She had struggled with her own role in the ceremony. In the end she decided to keep it simple—a few words that were meaningless because they were merely the public echo of agreements already made.

But she had not realized the context that Berberon and the others who had preceded her would create, the climate in which her words would be heard. As she came to the podium she discarded her planned remarks and cast about for the minimum she could say to satisfy the expectations of both Wells and his supporters.

"Harmack Wells."

Wells took one step forward and looked up at her.

"By the authority of the Chancellor's Office, I hereby appoint you Commander of the Perimeter Defense Force of the Unified Space Service."

The crowd roared its approval, and the sound rained down on Sujata as a tangible entity. Wells saluted, though whether he was answering Sujata or the crowd, she could not say.

"With the blessings of wisdom, may we have peace in our time," Sujata said. "Commander, your ship awaits you."

A second salute, this one clearly meant for Sujata, and Wells turned to face the uniformed assemblage. One row at a time, beginning with the rear rank, Wells's party marched down the aisle that had been kept clear for them, across the center of the plaza to the spiral slidewalk that led down to the shuttle terminal. The thunderous applause continued long after the last of them had vanished out of sight.

The atrium's high-intensity lights began to dim to permit the progress of the crew and the departure of the ship to be shown holographically in the middle of the atrium. Her presence no longer required, Sujata took advantage of the moment to descend from the rostrum and retreat to the privacy of her office. The only one who seemed to notice was Berberon, who fell in beside her wordlessly and escorted her out of the plaza and up-station to her office.

"Did you see that display?" Sujata demanded the moment the door closed behind them. She flung her jacket into a chair with an intensity that told her she was more disturbed than she had realized. "It isn't just the Nines—you're all crazy. What is it about you people that the prospect of a fight excites you instead of terrifying you?"

"I tried to tell you once," Berberon said. "You'll never understand us unless you embrace it."

"I resist your explanation," she said stiffly. "This has to be something you've taught yourselves, not something you inherit. You'd never have survived otherwise."

"We almost didn't," Berberon said idly. "Mind if I watch the departure?"

Sujata gestured with one hand. "I intended to watch. I just

had to get away from that crowd. Holo on," she said sharply. "Channel one. No audio."

The holo showed a twenty-place bus with blue-and-white Transport markings jetting across from the station to *Charan*, which was waiting two klicks away with a caretaker crew aboard. Though there was no video from the bus's passenger compartment, Sujata knew that it carried only half of those who had stood in the plaza. Against the small, but real, possibility that one ship or the other might be lost en route to Lynx Center, everything had been duplicated or divided, including personnel.

The Traffic Office's lane regulations required a minimum one-day spacing between AVLO ships on the same route, but it would be as much as a month before the second half of the expedition left. *Wesley* would not be ready to leave the Yard for five days, and final preparations could add up to four weeks to that. With Sujata's approval, Wells had chosen not to wait.

So *Wesley*'s crew and passengers—which included Farlad, the vice chairman of the Strategy Committee, and one of its members, as well as two senior command officers—had parted company with their mates somewhere between the plaza and the terminal. Along with Sujata, Berberon, and a large fraction of both the Service's million and Earth's billions, those assigned to *Wesley* were now merely spectators.

Its thrusters showing as tiny orange halos, the bus edged alongside *Charan* and extended its transfer tunnel to the forward three-o'clock entryway. One by one *Charan*'s crew drifted down the tunnel, caught the circular handrail just inside the hatch, and twisted as needed to bring them down upright on *Charan*'s gravity-ducted decking.

"Is what they do so much more admirable than what we do?" Sujata asked as the net changed feeds to show the bridge crew settling into their couches. "Absent the martial context, that crowd out there never would have responded to either of us with that kind of enthusiasm."

"A lesson learned by thousands of tottering dictators throughout history. No, of course they wouldn't," Berberon said. "There's nothing in the genome to fire them up over diplomats and administrators. Government was invented by man, not nature."

"You won't give up on that, will you?"

"Not when I know I'm right."

It did not take long for *Charan*'s crew to have her ready for departure, as the caretakers had already attended to everything that could not be handled by the crew and the ship herself in the last few minutes. As the scheduled power-up neared, Sujata walked to the greatport and opened the shade.

"Can you see *Charan* from there?" Berberon asked, crossing the room to join her.

Sujata waited until Berberon stood beside her, then pointed. "There—a couple of degrees southwest of Procyon, in Canis Major."

"I see it now," Berberon said. "Pretty thing, picking up the sunlight that way."

Just then, Procyon and the other background stars forward of *Charan*'s bow and aft of her stern seemed to jump to new positions as the AVLO drive suddenly came alive. The distortion caused by the twin gravitational lenses was the only evidence of the tremendous power being drawn from the spindle by the tiny vessel. Within a few seconds the ship was perceptibly moving, the ripple preceding it growing ever larger as the drive built up toward the craze.

"Until just now I didn't realize just how glad I am that he's leaving," Sujata said softly.

"I'm less pleased than I might be," Berberon said brightly. "Who knows what the Nines will be turning their attention to now? Whatever their choice, it will mean headaches for the Council." He glanced away from her and out the greatport. "Still, there is a certain satisfaction attached to the sight."

But it was a sight they did not get to enjoy for long. In less than a minute *Charan* crossed the star field and disappeared into it as a fading pinpoint. They turned away from the greatport as one.

"If you were so inclined, you could leave office now," Berberon said tentatively, less a suggestion than a question.

"I think not," Sujata said, collecting her cloak. "I wouldn't want to be responsible for cementing a tradition of midterm resignations."

"Commendable."

"But I do think I'll take my sabbaticals four times a year instead of three from here on," she added.

Berberon smiled and bowed graciously. "Since our most persistent nuisance just now courteously removed himself, you can do so in good conscience."

chapter 12

Diffidatio

How could we have been so stupid? Berberon demanded of himself as he stood at the terminal waiting for a response.

Sixteen days ago *Charan* had carried Wells off toward the Perimeter. For sixteen days Berberon had been enjoying not thinking about Wells, enjoying the sensation of a complex equation suddenly reduced to manageable dimensions. For sixteen days he had allowed himself to celebrate his victory. Suddenly, with no warning, matters were worse than ever.

A voice whispered in Berberon's ear, and he nodded to himself and turned away from the desk. "She's coming down," he said to his guest.

"I am very uncomfortable with this," said Teo Farlad. He rose from the chair where he had been seated. "I should leave now."

"You'll stay and you'll tell her what you told me," Berberon said forcefully. "She has to know the source. She has to understand that we're not guessing—that we know."

"You can't make any direct use of this."

"Your job is to collect the information, not to decide how it's to be used."

"We don't have the authority to put her in the picture."

Berberon poured himself an ample serving of anisette. "I'm taking the responsibility. You don't need to concern yourself on that account."

"I don't understand why you can't handle this the way you always have."

"Because she won't want to believe it," Berberon said bluntly. "Ever since the Erickson affair, Wells has been on his best behavior. He's never given her any real reason not to trust him. On top of which the Liamese rebellion served to pull them closer together than I'd have predicted they'd be."

Farlad nodded reluctant agreement. "Coming when it did, in her first year—"

"They worked very closely on how to handle that, and when the decision to enforce a general interdiction was made, Wells had the people in the right places to make it happen. You see, you have to tell her," Berberon said. "She'll be even less eager than me, to learn how stupid we both were."

"All right," Farlad said. "I accept what you say. But it isn't just Sujata. There's only six of us with access to these materials—three on *Charan* and three of us going on *Wesley*. If Sujata does anything openly because of what I tell her, it's inevitable that Wells will trace the leak back to me. My usefulness will be over."

Berberon could not let himself be swayed. "If that happens, it will be regrettable, but we have no choice. The situation is such that protecting you is a luxury we can't afford."

Farlad scowled.

Less than five minutes later the door opened to admit Sujata to the office.

"Teo," she said, acknowledging him with a nod. "All right, Felithe. I'm here. What's this about?"

The ambassador invited her toward a seat with a wave of his hand, then settled himself behind his desk. Farlad was standing stiffly by the chrome-steel sculpture in the center of the room, arms crossed over his chest as though hugging himself.

"Before I tell you, you need to know a little more about Teo and me," Berberon said.

Sujata's brows knit in puzzlement. "Is this something personal, then? I don't understand."

Berberon shook his head. "Teo, tell her who you are."

His expression sour, Farlad complied. "Chancellor Sujata, my real name is Kris March. I'm a captain in the World Council's Intelligence Operations Force."

Sujata gaped at Berberon unbelievingly. "He's a spy?"

"In a word, yes," said Beberon. "Teo has been my primary source inside Defense since the day Wells became Director."

"Which makes you—"

"A brevet major in the IOF, and coordinator of our operations here."

Any other Chancellor would have filled the room with their fury at that revelation. Sujata might have been furious, but there was no outward sign. "I suppose there are more, she said.

"Yes, but don't ask me to tell you who they are."

"In my office?"

"No. We place them where we need them. You've been open enough with me that it hasn't been necessary."

"I don't know that I should be comforted by that answer. How long has this been going on?"

"Chancellor, I resolved to tell you who we are so that you would take what we have to talk about seriously. But I'm not prepared to be quizzed about the IOF," Berberon said. "You know my reputation for knowing things I'm not supposed to. Now you know that my reputation is well founded."

"I always thought that you'd simply cultivated a network of contacts over the years—"

"In fact, I have," Berberon said. "It makes an excellent cover for the rest of my job."

"You'll have to leave the Service," Sujata said tersely, looking at Farlad. A chink, however small, in her emotional armor. That Maranit reserve will be tested today, Berberon thought sympathetically.

"We can talk about whether that would be prudent some other time," he said. "At this moment you need to listen to what Teo has to say."

Sujata folded her hands in her lap and sat back. "Go ahead."

"You need to understand the working relationship between the Director and myself," Farlad said, taking a step or two toward her and dropping his crossed arms to his abdomen. "Though I'm his top aide, my clearance has never been as high as his. There have always been things that he's done for himself or through others in the Branch, things that I've known nothing about until they were over with."

"Teo joined the Nines solely to increase the chances of Wells confiding in him," Berberon said. "It was only a partial success, unfortunately."

"You're a Nine too?" Sujata asked, taken aback.

Farlad nodded. "Fourth Tier."

"Is this what you asked me here to talk about, then? Something regarding the Nines?"

Farlad glanced sideways at Berberon before answering. "No, Chancellor. Major Berberon tells me that you had some doubts about Director Wells's motivations for moving the flag command. I think I know why he did it, and I think I know why he did it now."

"I'm listening."

"I didn't know anything about the move until Director Wells asked me to confirm my willingness to go. When I did, I seem to have passed some kind of test, because the next day I was promoted from Director's Adjutant to Chief of Staff for Defense, and my security rating was raised right to the top."

"Equal to Wells's?"

"Yes. I was given right-to-know on everything except personal datarecs, and invited to poke around. Wells himself even walked me through some of the new material the day before *Charan* left. He told me that he wanted me to be fully informed so that if something happened to him, I could be of assistance to Deputy Director Gaema."

"And you learned what?"

Farlad drew a long breath before answering. "Chancellor, were you aware that the Danfield Device has been successfully tested?"

Sujata blinked several times. "No."

"It has. It exists. It was tested five months ago, on a planetoid orbiting 41 Leo. The yield was 130 percent of design. The planetoid was nickel-iron and the deedee damn near melted it."

Sujata was still hiding whatever anger or alarm she was feeling behind her highwoman's mask. She looked at Berberon and said quietly, "I should have been told."

"Yes, you should have been," Berberon said. "But did the research authorization *require* them to tell you?"

"I don't remember, " Sujata said slowly. "That was years

ago. Perhaps it didn't." She looked at Farlad. "Is there more?"

"I'm afraid so. I know you were aware of the delays on Triad construction—"

"Yes. I understand the engineers were having trouble with the new series drive."

"The trouble they were having is making the AVLO-T blow like a deedee on command. They had to redesign it so that it can be made to open an uncontrolled aperture to the spindle. It wasn't easy to defeat the drive's tendency to just shut down and close the tap when something goes wrong."

"What are you saying?"

"That each element of the Triad will, in effect, *be* a Danfield Device."

Sujata brought her folded hands to her mouth and stared hard at the floor between her feet and where Farlad stood. Then she looked up and met his eyes again.

"I think I know what this has to do with," she said. "Harmack did discuss with me the difficulty of any sort of rescue operation at these distances and under battle conditions. I don't relish the thought of it ever having to be used, but it seems prudent and merciful to provide some sort of self-destruct. And we certainly wouldn't want our most advanced technology falling into the hands of the Mizari."

"Officially it's described in just those terms," Farlad said. "But I don't think Wells held up construction of something he considers so crucial just to get a particularly nasty method of self-destruction, not with other perfectly effective options available. I think he wanted every one of the nine ships to be capable of making a planetary assault on its own."

It took Sujata a moment to understand the implication. "But it would be a suicide attack."

"The crews call it 'volunteer's honor,'" Berberon interjected. "As though it were a privilege to throw away your life."

"But why? What possible use could they have for it?"

Farlad shrugged. "There are sixteen star systems in the Mizari Cluster, some as much as thirty cees from each other. You only gave Wells three Triads with which to cover them."

"I authorized a fourth last year—"

"Yes—to allow for downtime and make certain that three groups are on-station at any given time," Farlad said. "You gave him no more strength in the field, no more flexibility."

"Are you saying he would deploy the Triad elements individually?"

"He'll at least have that option now."

Sujata was shaking her head. "I can't believe he'd send them out alone. There has to be another reason."

"It may just be insurance," Farlad said. "Some of our studies show as much as a one-in-four chance that the carrier's weapon could be intercepted far enough out to nullify it. If you have four deedees to play with, the odds drop to one in a hundred, factoring in the loss of surprise on the follow-up attacks."

"So is this sort of death-dive in the Triad Force operational plan?"

"It's not forbidden. I don't know what kind of options Wells will allow the Triad commanders to load into their battle-management systems."

"No," Sujata said stubbornly. "I see nothing suspicious in this."

Farlad and Berberon exchanged glances. "Then let me tell you something that *is* in the Triad operational plan," Berberon said. "The Triads are going to be stationed at patrol circles ten cees beyond the Perimeter—inside the Mizari Cluster. They'll be fully armed and ready to move the moment they receive 'go' codes."

"Wells and I discussed this too. To have a credible deterrent you have to be in a position to make a quick response."

"Yes. Ordinarily I would agree," Berberon said. "Except I note that there is no provision for confirming an attack order with the Chancellor's office. The 'go' codes come from the Defense Director through Perimeter Defense Command."

"How else would you have it?" Sujata asked. "Wells can't order an attack without prior authorization from me."

The same benighted trust I so recently was forced to forgo, Berberon thought. *You are too much the legalist, Janell.* "Teo, would you give the Chancellor your appraisal of Director Wells's intentions?"

Her face still showing skepticism, Sujata turned toward the younger man.

"This is hard for me," Farlad said hoarsely, shifting his weight from one foot to the other as he stood with eyes averted downward. "You don't work closely with someone for a long time without developing strong feelings about them, one way or another. I like the Director. And I believe in what he said he believed in. I guess I resisted seeing what should have been obvious to me a lot sooner.

"All along he's had his sight set on one goal, and he's never wavered. There's been another purpose beyond the stated one to everything he's done. When he redirected weapons research from defensive systems to offensive. When he engineered the replacement of an activist Chancellor with —forgive me—a caretaker. When he used the communications crisis as a pretext for moving toward the Perimeter."

"What goal, Teo?"

"Isn't it obvious? To destroy the Mizari. He never meant to build us a defense against them. His talk of deterrence and a balance of terror was a smoke screen. Yes, theoretically you control the Defense forces. But you do it through Wells. You depend on him and his good faith. The Triad commanders will be looking to him, not to you."

"Wells won't start a war simply because he can," Sujata said with unwavering certainty. "He's extremely stable—conservative. You should know better than anyone that he's anything but reckless."

"Chancellor, I'm sorry, but you don't understand," Farlad said. "Have you forgotten that he is a Nine, what their mindset is? He *is* willing to start a war—because he's incapable of believing that we could lose. And he always meant to lead the charge himself. Triad is a first-strike weapon. It's a sneak-attack weapon. He'll use them as soon as they're ready—and they'll be ready when he reaches Lynx Center."

"But the Perimeter would be the worst place to be in a war," Sujata protested. "Why would he go there?"

"Because his concept of honor demands it," Farlad said quietly.

Reluctant though he had been to take part, Farlad had followed Berberon's script flawlessly. The timing, the delivery, the careful unfolding of the story in such a way to maximize its impact—all had been perfect. And yet still Sujata did not react.

Berberon would have wagered heavily that no one could listen to what Sujata had heard and not explode out of their chair with fury at having been betrayed. He could not believe that it was solely her Maranit heritage that was to blame, that she was capable of holding such feeling behind her mask. At some fundamental level she was discounting what she had heard. Thankfully, against that possibility he had held back one card, which he now played.

"For whatever reason, you do not seem to be taking what we say very seriously," Berberon said. "Would it make any difference to you to learn that there is something else that Wells kept from you? That the Triads not only now have a weapon but also have a target?"

He saw a flicker of dismay cross Sujata's face, but he did not stop to measure how deeply his words had pierced her. He continued on, driving the blade deeper. "The very first thing that Wells told Teo after raising his clearance was that eight and a half years ago a new generation of data analyzers in the Perimeter listening posts began to report weak and uncorrelated emissions from Mizar-Alcor. That coincides with the beginning of Wells's campaign for Triad.

"The Mizari are real, Chancellor. And Wells knows where they are."

Even Sujata's surrender, when it came, was controlled. As Berberon was speaking, her eyes had widened as though trying to absorb the enormity of the deception. Then suddenly she pressed her folded hands against her forehead, squeezed her eyes shut, and curled into a rigid ball in her chair. But her retreat could not shut out Berberon's words, and she shivered violently in reaction to his last sentence.

From his chair across the room Berberon looked on with genuine sympathy. He understood her pain, and her anger at his part in it. The fact that he felt the same humiliation did not reduce his responsibility. His empathy was empty of comfort, and so he made no attempt to communicate it to her.

"Thank you, Teo," was all he said. "You can go now."

Then, when Farlad was gone, Berberon himself withdrew to an adjoining room so that Sujata might have an opportunity to restore the privacy of self that he had been obliged to so rudely violate.

Ambushed.

There was no single word that could adequately describe what Sujata was feeling, but that one captured the highest points. Sujata felt victimized by those she had trusted, ambushed, and then cruelly misused by them. Everyone had lied to her. Wells had lied and she had failed to detect it. Berberon had lied and she had failed to detect it.

A feeble gift you have, she whispered to herself. *Too little for Maranit—too little even for here.*

But the cut that had gone the deepest was Farlad's. A "caretaker" Chancellor, he had called her. She could not deny it. She knew well her own selfish inclinations. They were her answer to her anger at being cornered into taking the Chancellorship, an anger that even six years of selfishness had not completely erased.

But she had a conscience as well, which demanded she give her position its due. She had not always placed herself first. In her six years she had canceled two sabbaticals and returned from a third early to deal with minor crises. Her conscience would leave her at peace only as long as the Service was functioning smoothly.

But Farlad's revelations were a brutal lesson that though she had attended to appearances and to the day-to-day detail, she had neglected larger concerns. She had not led the Service but had been content merely to manage it. And by doing so, she had given Wells his opportunity.

Curled up in her chair, eyes turned inward, Sujata had barely been aware of Farlad and Berberon leaving the room. She was only slightly more aware when Berberon returned. He walked toward her slowly but deliberately, stopping a polite distance from where she sat.

"You have to stop him," he said quietly.

His words roused Sujata out of her withdrawal. "Stop him!" she exclaimed, coming up out of her chair with a sudden, violent motion. "You slitter, you were the one who said to help him! Look where we are now."

"Sorting out the degrees of blame can wait for another time. Right now you need to decide what you're going to do."

She turned her back on him and walked toward the closed greatport. "What else? I'm going to have to recall *Charan,* order it to return here as quickly as possible."

Across the room she heard the deep breath Berberon took before answering. "I wish it were that easy. Did you forget she's flying deaf, in the craze? She won't rejoin the net until the approach to Lynx Center."

Sujata sighed, the outward sign of a sudden wave of self-recrimination that washed over her. "Of course, you're right. And I did that. I wanted Wells to be isolated from his network here. He wanted to have *Charan* make the run in pogo mode, coming out of the craze every few months to pick up dispatches. I insisted otherwise."

"It was a good decision with what you knew then," Berberon said. "Unfortunately, it just makes things more complicated now."

Sujata barely heard Berberon's reply. Her mind was busy casting about for another solution to the dilemma. "I'll have to remove him from the Directorship," she said at last, turning to face the Terran Observer. "Wells will arrive at Lynx Center to find he has no authority."

"How's it to be done?" Berberon asked. "The accused has the right of reply during a recall. How can Wells defend himself in absentia?"

"The Committee will surely allow an exception in this case—"

"Why should they? Don't you realize that what upsets you will please them? They *want* the Triads to have operational weapons. They assumed all along that the Mizari are real."

Sujata fought her own rising panic. "Then the only answer is to cancel Triad. He'll get there and he'll have nothing to start a war with—"

"Try, and you'll no longer be Chancellor," Berberon said gently. "The hawkish tilt of the Committee is worse now than it was when Erickson tried to stop Triad. One politically incorrect move on your part and Loughridge will move into your office."

"What's the answer, then?"

"Don't let him be out there alone," Berberon said simply.

Sujata shut out the unwelcome words. "I—I don't know what I was thinking. It doesn't matter if he can't return right away. I can still recall him," she said, the words tumbling out on top of each other. "The dispatch will be waiting for him when he gets there. He'll just have to turn around and come back. Or no, even better, we can conduct a hearing on his dismissal through the Kleine. He can have his say and then we'll be rid of him—"

Berberon shook his head slowly. "Two thirds of the people on Lynx are Defense personnel. They have seventeen years to think about him coming. More than time enough to create a powerful mythos about the man who'll lead them as they rise up to vanquish their enemy and reclaim their pride. They'll receive him as a soldier-messiah. He'll become something larger than life to them."

"No—"

"Just as Teo said, they won't be looking to you—they'll be looking to him. Once he's there alone, he doesn't have to obey you. And if he chooses to follow his conscience instead of the Service charter, there won't be anything you can do about it. You can't touch him there."

"He wouldn't do that," she said, a note of desperation in her voice.

"Teo says otherwise—and I agree with him. So do you, if you're honest with yourself."

Sujata threw her head back and stared up at the ceiling as a cascade of anger and indignation flooded through her. *No! Why should I have to pay the price again? I've only just gotten back what it cost me the first time. Damn it all, it isn't fair—it isn't fair—* Although those thoughts ravaged her, still she kept them bottled within her.

"The only answer I can see is for you to be even more imposing a figure and just as close at hand," Berberon continued. "You have to follow him, in *Wesley.* You have to enforce your objection in person."

"What good will that do?" she demanded. "You said Defense owns Lynx Center. If Wells has decided to break with the Service and follow his own path, he can refuse my orders as easily in person as he can with me here."

"I don't have the answer to that," Berberon said. "He may not listen to you." He hesitated briefly, then went on. "It may be necessary to remove Wells another way."

She stared disbelievingly. "You can't be serious—"

"I am perfectly serious. Teo will take care of it if we tell him it's necessary. But even so, it already may be too late to stop this war," Berberon said. "I'm going to have to tell my government to assume that war is coming."

At that moment she saw in his face and heard in his voice the fear he had been trying to hide from her: a helpless fear of the ending of things, of the inevitable loss of all that was worth saving. He did not fear for himself so much as for his people, and suddenly she thought of Maranit with a vividness she had not known for years.

Berberon's fear stilled the streets of her memories, and littered the burning maranax with bodies of her friends. Her knees suddenly weak beneath her, Sujata felt her way back to her chair. "The Committee will never permit me to leave."

Berberon came closer and crouched down within arm's reach. "Don't tell them you're going there to stop him. Tell them you're going there to join him, because of the gravity of the situation."

She pressed her palms to her temples and stared down at the floor. Each noisy breath carried the echoes of tears trapped within her. *I don't want to leave Earth!* she thought in one last furious, selfish cry. *I don't want to leave what I've found down there—*

As though he could read her, Berberon said softly, "Janell —I'm sorry. But it has to be you. There's no one else."

A heart-rending sound, half cry, half moan, escaped her lips as the mask shattered and the tears came. "God damn you," she said, sobbing. "You take and take and take. You— steal—*everything* that matters to me." Her face twisted into an ugly rictus as she fought to stem the flood of anguish and despair. Failing, she came up suddenly out of her chair and fled with quick strides to the far wall. She threw one forearm up against the wall at head height and buried her face in the crook of her elbow.

Presently, as her sobbing weakened and slowed, she turned her face toward Berberon. Her mask was not yet up: her eyes radiated hate.

"Fecuma. Ka'arrit. I'll go, God damn you," she snapped. "I'll catch your runaway soldier and I'll try to cage him. But you're coming with me, you slitter. You tell the Council whatever you have to, I don't care. But you're coming with me. This time it's going to cost you too."

chapter 13

So Long a Journey, So Little Joy

As a four-time veteran of the transplant trauma, Sujata knew exactly what it represented. It was not unlike extracting an ingrown wandering vine from the hedgerow. Given enough time and a patient hand, both the hedgerow and the vine could emerge from the sundering largely undamaged. Get the transplant into new soil soon enough and almost always it would smoothly recover from what shock it necessarily endured. And in most cases the hedgerow would never even notice it was gone.

But when time was short and the direct took precedence over the delicate, both organisms were going to suffer grievously. *Cut here, uproot there, and never mind the fragile new leaves. We can prune away the damage later—*

Sujata had begun the delicate business of disengaging her life from that of Wyrena Ten Ga'ar six years ago. But despite early success and the passage of time, she had never pressed the process to a conclusion. There came a time when the emotional price of the final break outweighed the gain to be had from making it. Equilibrium set in, a new equilibrium that found the circles of their lives still overlapping, but no longer congruent.

Ten Ga'ar had her own residence, her own friends, and the comfortable illusion that she was still first in Sujata's love. In truth, Ten Ga'ar had moved to the periphery of Sujata's emotional life. But respecting the illusion, Sujata made no effort to move anyone else into the space Ten Ga'ar had vacated.

For her part, Sujata kept her *xochaya* mates, Allianora and, later, a new émigré named Lochas—Ten Ga'ar did not know enough of the depth of those relationships to be jealous of them. And during her sabbaticals on the surface, Sujata merged herself with the mother, engaging her senses and her sensibility with the living fabric of a homeworld now more precious to her than her own. Between the two she saw to her own needs, or enough of them to keep her whole.

But she and Ten Ga'ar were still lovers; they were comfortable friends. And they were going to have to say good-bye.

Sujata had kept her decision to pursue Wells to herself as long as possible. There was no reason to deal with its ramifications until the Committee had spoken. Now, returning from the Committee chamber with that body's permission, there was every reason to hasten the unpleasantries. The grapevine would soon be humming with rumors, and it would be crueler by far if Ten Ga'ar heard it from another.

She briefly considered taking Ten Ga'ar home with her as a courtesy, breaking the news to her where they would have the privacy to fully and freely express their feelings. But she convinced herself that Ten Ga'ar would accept the decision more readily if the Service's needs were emphasized and the personal consequences downplayed. The impersonal atmosphere of her conference room was more conducive to such a strategy than the intimacy of her suite.

Ten Ga'ar arrived in the Chancellery Office a minute after Sujata, and they walked to the conference room together.

"How did your special session go?" Ten Ga'ar asked, stopping so that Sujata could enter the room first.

"It was—productive."

"Am I allowed to know yet what it was about?"

"That's why I wanted to see you."

They settled on opposite ends of a backless divan. "I don't quite know where to start," Sujata said. "Certain matters came to light yesterday that are going to mean a lot of changes. I don't want to go through what those matters were or what the changes will be now, because it would just delay getting to the point. What it all means in the end is that we made a mistake.

"I made a mistake," she corrected quickly. "I shouldn't have let Wells leave. And to correct the mistake I'm going to have to follow him out to Lynx in *Wesley*."

Ten Ga'ar's eyes cast randomly about for focus as she grappled with the implications of that statement. "All right," she said finally. "It'll be crowded, but we can find two berths —"

Please don't make this harder, Sujata begged silently. "Observer Berberon will be going with me."

"Three berths, then. We can double up some of the ratings —"

Sujata could not let the misapprehension take any stronger hold. "You won't be going."

A look of wounded surprise, like that of a dog whose nose has been smacked for no obvious reason, passed over Ten Ga'ar's face. "Why?" she asked plaintively.

"In the first place there isn't room. *Wesley* has combat accommodations. Even adding two people to the manifest will make for a miserable thirty days to Lynx."

"But I could stay with you, in your cabin—that wouldn't put anyone else out—"

"I'm only going to request a single command cabin, which Observer Berberon and I will share. There isn't room for a third person."

"You and I would only need one bunk—"

"Wy, I'm sorry—no. There's a more important reason, besides. I need you here. I had to agree that *Wesley* would run the leg in pogo mode. We're going to drop down for dispatches every second day, which means every nine months or so on this time track. I need someone I know and trust here to distill that nine months of activity down into something I can deal with in ninety minutes, and then to see that my decisions get carried out. Not to mention make all the little decisions that will need to be made on the spot."

"Regan can do that, just like he has during your sabbaticals."

"With you helping, as you have during my sabbaticals."

Ten Ga'ar hugged herself as her eyes brightened with moisture. "You don't want me to go. If you wanted me, these other things wouldn't even matter. You never even considered taking me."

The attempt at emotional blackmail triggered a rush of anger in Sujata. "No, Wy, I didn't. I've been thinking about trying to stop Wells from plunging the Worlds into war. In that kind of company our relationship moves pretty far down on my list of concerns."

Ten Ga'ar half turned away and stared down at her feet. She sat rigid and motionless except for her left hand, which played idly with a fastener on her blouse.

"I shouldn't be surprised, really," she said in a voice almost too faint to be heard. "You've been looking for a reason to break with me ever since you became Chancellor. I couldn't move with you to the Chancellor's suite—security, you said. I knew it was because you were embarrassed by me. The parties I wasn't welcome at—business, you said. I knew better. The sabbaticals you took alone—once you talked about us exploring Earth together. Then, I was afraid to. But you never asked me again. You made clear I wasn't welcome."

Ten Ga'ar raised her head and turned a tear-streaked face toward Sujata. "I kept waiting for you to push me all the way out. But you never did. I suppose you wanted me to decide I wouldn't stand for just a little of you and take that last step myself. Or maybe you were just reducing me to what you really wanted me for—a hand between your legs, a mouth on your breast—"

"Wyrena, stop," Sujata said, a command and a plea. "We were living on top of each other. I needed more room, and so did you. It was never that I didn't love you."

Ten Ga'ar's lost and distant look did not waver. "You never loved me as much as I loved you."

Sujata sighed. "I loved you as much and as well as I was able to."

"And I never asked for more, did I? Even though I wanted it. Wanted what you gave Allianora. No, don't be surprised. Even though you never talked about *xochaya*, did you think I couldn't find out elsewhere? That still hurts, Janell. I wanted to be part of all your secrets, but you never thought me good enough."

"It isn't something you teach someone in an afternoon," Sujata said helplessly. "You can't put on another person's culture like a change of clothing. It would have been empty of meaning."

"Not to me," Ten Ga'ar said, her eyes brimming over again. "Not to me."

Infected by the other woman's sadness, Sujata edged toward Ten Ga'ar and opened her arms. "Let me hold you."

But Ten Ga'ar drew back defensively. "No. No, I don't think so." She rose from the divan and retreated a few steps to the center of the room. "I guess when I think about it, you really haven't been very good to me—or for me—after all," she said, her back to Sujata. "I—I don't think I would care to go with you to Lynx, anyway. I'll make—I'll meet with the captain of the *Wesley* and arrange space for you and Observer Berberon."

"Regan and Captain Hirschfield are coming in at 13:00 to work out the final arrangements," Sujata said, though she hated having to do so. "I wasn't sure you'd feel like being involved—"

"I'm fine," Ten Ga'ar said stiffly, her back still turned. "It's part of my job, isn't it? I'll come back at 13:00, then." She moved toward the door.

Sujata realized then that she had chosen her office for the encounter, not in the hopes of inhibiting Ten Ga'ar's feelings, but to inhibit her own. She came to her feet and called after Ten Ga'ar, "Wy—please understand. I don't want to do this."

Ten Ga'ar stopped a step from the doorway but did not turn.

"Going to Lynx is the last thing I want," Sujata said pleadingly. "I would have been happy to stay here and keep you in my life. Wy, I did love you. I still love you. I didn't let you into my life lightly. I don't leave easily. And I'll never let go of the feeling." She held out her arms, an invitation to an embrace. "Please," she begged. "Please, Wy. Let me hold you."

But she knew it was too late. Ten Ga'ar's own wounds were still bleeding, rendering Sujata's pain irrelevant. "I'll be here at 13:00 with the others," Ten Ga'ar said with the barest shake of her head.

She never even looked back as she walked away.

"This is wonderful news you bring me for a change, Felithe," Tanvier said, pivoting slowly back and forth in his bowllike chair. Though the two men were alone, the World Council President wore the insincere half smile of contentment that was his public face. "The Service leadership squabbling at the highest levels—first Wells and now Chancellor Sujata hying off to the Perimeter—this almost warrants a celebration. Certainly it demands some careful reflection on the opportunities that might now open up."

"I am ever more convinced that you'll never understand anything I tell you correctly the first time," Berberon said sharply. "This is a disaster, Jean-Paul, the final failure of your attempt to neutralize the Nines."

"Final failure?" Tanvier said, reaching for his pipe and lighter. "My dear Felithe, you are so dramatic. What has changed except that the USS is now headless and will soon topple to the ground dead? By the time Wells's little convoy reaches Lynx, we will quite likely control the space over our heads again."

Berberon glowered in the direction of the pipe and circled Tanvier's desk to a spot where the room's air currents were taking the plume of pollution away from him instead of toward him. The pipe's contents were noncarcinogenic but far from nonallergenic; smoking the pipe was something Tanvier did specifically to annoy him.

"Enjoy your triumph while you can. Because when the Mizari return, I doubt you'll have the same cheery view of things."

Tanvier snorted. "Do you really believe that Wells means to start a war he can't win? The Nines are radicals, yes, but they're not insane—Wells least of all."

"We're all a little bit insane, Jean-Paul," Berberon said, leaning over the desk. "It's the reptile brain buried down there under all those cosmetic layers of cortex. It keeps asking us to do things that made perfect sense in the Cambrian Era but no sense at all in the world we occupy. Mostly we ignore the voice, but every now and then we say yes. Wells has already said yes to his beast. I knew that ten years ago. All he's been waiting for is the opportunity to follow through. Which, bloody goddamnit, we went and handed to him."

Tanvier leaned back and spread his hands wide. "What do you want from me, Felithe? You said the Chancellor was on to him. She'll put the bad genie back in the bottle."

"I don't think we can take that for granted."

"Then let Farlad loose. He'll handle it," Tanvier said with a shrug. "I'll place that option at your discretion."

"I've already claimed it myself, thank you. But the opportunity may not arise. And we have no one else positioned to take up the ball."

"None of our agents were tapped for *Charan?*"

"No. And, of course, we have no in-place assets at Lynx Center or Perimeter Command. Talk to the section head about that, not me," he added quickly.

"So we'll be spectators," Tanvier said sanguinely. "I ask you again—what do you want from me?"

"For one, leave the Service alone at least until this matter is resolved. If he gets to Lynx and finds that we're answering the phones at USS-Central, he'll figure this is his one and only chance and be all the more determined not to waste it. I don't care how good an opportunity this appears to be. We can't cut Janell's legs out from under her until Wells is under control."

Tanvier pursed his lips and drew deeply at his pipe. "You may have something there. Very well. The Service can muddle along without our interference—for now."

Berberon nodded gratefully and settled back into a chair. "That's a good decision, Jean-Paul. See that you stick with it."

"Felithe, have I ever pointed out to you that you're a pushy bastard?"

"Less often than you've thought it, I'm sure. So when I tell you the next part, I'm sure you're going to want to have that celebration, after all."

"Why? What's the next part?"

"I've promised to go with Chancellor Sujata to Lynx."

"Why in God's Earth would you do that? Wait—you're not—but I heard that she was—"

"Stop right there," Berberon snapped. "I'm going so I can try to help her pull your irons out of the fire, that's all."

Tanvier screwed up his face into a daunting frown. "You're the Terran Observer to the Steering Committee of the Unified Space Service. How can you fulfill that function from twenty-five cees away?"

"The only events that matter over the next fifty years are going to take place out there. Nothing even remotely as important is going to happen in the Earth locus. I assume that you'll want me to be where I at least have a chance to make a difference?"

Tanvier gestured with his pipe hand, disturbing a column of gray smoke. "We can send someone else along with Sujata, for appearances. It doesn't have to be you."

"I'm afraid I've already committed myself."

"Then I'm afraid I must insist you give up your post. I just can't embrace the idea of an absentee Observer. Rather oxy-moronic, don't you think?"

"So call me something else," Berberon said tersely. "Create a new position—Special Ambassador for Military Affairs, I don't care. Just make sure I have some authority to represent you. Give me some leverage to help Janell with Wells."

Tanvier nodded grudgingly. "I suppose we can come up with something suitably vague and ceremonial. But tell me— what exactly is it you think you're going to be able to do?"

"I'll know better when we reach Lynx," Berberon said with a shake of his head. "Maybe lend moral support. Maybe help Janell space the son of a bitch."

Laughing broadly, Tanvier leaned forward and set down his pipe. "Felithe, I'm going to miss you."

"Jean-Paul, you don't know how much it troubles me not to be able to say the same," Berberon said, rising. "I have to get back. They're moving up *Wesley*'s departure to try to make up for some of the time we'll lose dropping down for dispatches. We want to make sure we catch him at Lynx."

Tanvier struggled up from his chair. "Are there any matters down here that will need looking after? For instance, any pretty women being left behind?" he asked, flashing a grin. "Seriously, if there are things that you need—"

"Just my title and a draft of my authority, by sailing time—16:00 tomorrow."

"I'll see that you have it."

Berberon nodded and moved toward the door. He took two steps, then stopped and half turned toward Tanvier. His expression was grim. "This is a bad time, Jean-Paul, and a very dangerous business. Don't make any mistake about that."

His earlier amusement was no longer in evidence on Tanvier's face. "I won't, Felithe. Good luck to you. I have confidence that you and Chancellor Sujata will get the job done, one way or another."

Berberon grunted. "All the same, just in case we fail and Wells gets his war, I'd recommend you start digging a very deep hole to hide in. Because this time around I don't think the Mizari will settle for half measures."

Forty-one hours after Berberon had called her to his office to hear Farlad's story, Janell Sujata boarded the auxiliary flagship *Joanna Wesley* for the first time.

It had been forty-one hours of frantic activity, forty-one hours without sleep. Nearly six of those hours had been spent fighting with Captain Hirschfield, who had come as close as he could to refusing outright to recognize Sujata's claim on his command before finally capitulating. Even then Hirschfield had been barely less accommodating about hastening the sailing date. He had insisted, ultimately futilely, that the ship's defensive systems (which were not fully fault-tested) were as important as its propulsion and navigation systems (which were).

From Hirschfield she had gone to the Committee, informing them only that a Sterilizer nest had been detected and that the critical nature of the situation demanded her presence as well on the Perimeter. To her surprise the other Directors did not balk, perhaps because Wells's departure had conditioned them to the idea, perhaps because her absence promised to leave them more powerful, or perhaps even because they accepted her argument and their perception of the danger at face value.

There had been other long sessions with Ten Ga'ar and Marshall, working out the responsibilities of each in the ongoing management of the Service. Those meetings, formal and businesslike, had been all Sujata had seen of Ten Ga'ar. There had been no chance to try to tear down the wall that suddenly had sprung up between them.

As the time neared to board the bus for the trip to *Wesley,* Sujata had not even been able to locate her to say good-bye. Nor had she had time for a final *xochaya* with Allianora or Lochas, though her need was great. Stealing a few minutes to call them was the most she could manage.

The shipwrights had turned *Wesley* into an armored labyrinth, mechanical and claustrophobic. The thick energy-absorbing layer under her new mirror-finish skin had stolen some of her former living volume, and her new equipment, including the 1.5-terawatt lance, had stolen still more. The pressure walls and hatchways every few metres along the narrow climbways gave the illusion of shells within shells within shells.

Throughout the hull, human comfort had clearly been relegated to second place behind military functionality. The largest unobstructed volumes within *Wesley*'s hourglass hull were the new command bridge, just forward of the pinched "waist," and the drive and weapons engineers' systems center, just aft of the "waist." Cushioned between them amidships were the drive, the massive capacitance bank for the lance, and key elements of the ship's communications and computing facilities.

Ignored in the confused activity of final preparations for sailing, Sujata headed forward to find the cabin she would share with Berberon and see that her effects had been safely delivered aboard. She had been too busy even to see to something as personal but fundamentally trivial as selecting her own clothing. In fact, she had only returned to her suite once in the last two days, and then only long enough to retrieve her lifecord from its hiding place and add it to the things her aide had collected for her.

The cabin was essentially as she had expected, yet seemed almost intolerably crowded. It was narrow enough that she could span it with her outstretched arms, perhaps twice that deep, and had a low enough ceiling that Sujata was aware of it over her head. There were two bunks, the upper folded and latched against the wall, the lower providing the only seating; a tiny bath with shower and toilet, to be shared with the occupants of the adjacent cabin; and a floor-to-ceiling bank of swinging-door lockers of assorted sizes, serving as closet, bureau, and desk.

Her possessions were neatly arrayed in several lockers labeled with her name, though on scanning their contents she immediately thought of other things she would have liked instead of, or in addition to, what was there. But it was too late for such considerations. Sailing time was less than an hour away.

In the process of coming forward she had snagged the loose folds of her *daiiki* several times on projections and so took the opportunity to change into more close-fitting clothing. Then, since she had no part to play in the preparations for departure, she stole a few minutes to tour the rest of *Wesley*'s climbways and chambers.

When she reached the aftmost section, she instantly regretted her unspoken complaints about her cabin. The ratings' quarters located there made the command cabins seem palatial.

Ten sleeping cubicles, arrayed like cells in a honeycomb—

or crypts in a mausoleum—faced a small galley flanked by a two-stall shower on one side and a lavatory on the other. The cubicles, which were too small even to sit up straight in, consisted of a padded sleeping surface, a blank wall that cried out for decoration, a sliding wall that concealed storage for personal effects, and a bare ceiling with recessed lighting and a flatscreen terminal.

There would be little privacy here, Sujata saw. The ratings would eat, sleep, copulate, bathe, and excrete in close proximity to each other, the fundamental human functions colliding in the confined space. And, she knew, should any of them die while on patrol, the bodies would rest here as well, sealed in a cubicle flooded with tissue-preserving gases, awaiting return to the requested place of burial.

Leaving the crew quarters, she joined Berberon and Hirschfield on the command bridge. With its six egg-shaped battle couches arrayed in a circle, the bridge looked oddly like the nesting place for some great bird. The couches rested on a circular track; if *Wesley* were to begin spinning as a defense against energy weapons, the couches would rotate in the opposite direction along the track, protecting their occupants from any disorienting effects. In the center of the circle was a six-sided display not unlike that in the Committee chamber. The screen facing Sujata showed a graphlike gravigation track.

"I was just about to come looking for you," Berberon said, coming up to her. "Captain Hirschfield says that we can go forward—that there's really no place for us here."

"Even so, we can stay if we're so inclined," Sujata said, loudly enough for Hirschfield to hear. "Which I am."

They stood there together and listened to the chatter between the various bridge officers and the techs on the systems deck as 16:00 drew closer. Though much of what was said meant little to Sujata, she could see that Hirschfield was walking them through the final minutes in an unhurried, yet crisply disciplined, manner.

"Captain Hirschfield?" the comtech said at one point. "The off-watch is requesting a feed of the coverage from Earthnet. Any objection?"

Hirschfield shook his head. "No. You can put it on up here, too, on alternate screens."

Earthnet had learned a lesson from the sailing of *Charan*, namely that a deepship retreating against a background of stars is an unspectacular image on all but the largest and sharpest video displays. Unquestionably the most dramatic sight in Earth's region of space was Earth itself. So for *Wesley* the Net was trying another tack: covering the sailing from *Wesley*'s perspective and showing the receding Earth as it would be seen from the ship's observation deck—if it had one, which it did not.

The picture that came up on the screen facing Sujata was of swirling cloud tops and mottled blue oceans, zigzagging rivers and smooth, tan plains. The sight brought an involuntary smile to Sujata's face.

All that you've done these last two days, and nothing for yourself, she told herself. *You didn't even take a few minutes out to go down to the Earthdome, or even to take one long last look from the greatport in your office.*

All at once the true dimensions of what she was leaving behind were clear to her. Up until then she had been too busy to think of it, too busy and perhaps too wary of the emotions such thoughts would unleash. But fatigue had made her vulnerable, and as she stood there staring at the face of Earth, a devastating sense of loss welled up inside her.

"Wait," she said suddenly.

"What?" Hirschfield demanded.

"I said wait. Suspend the count."

"Listen, I asked you once to go forward to your cabin, that I didn't need your interference here," Hirschfield said crossly. "Now I have to insist—"

"No!" she said sharply, cutting him off. "I have to leave the ship. Recall the bus."

"You can't," Hirschfield protested. "We're programmed to sail in eighteen minutes."

"Recall the bus," she repeated. "I am sorry, but I have to do this."

Three strides carried her to the port climbway, and she started forward without looking to see if Hirschfield or Berberon were following. Ten metres on, the climbway merged with the corridor leading to one of the forward space doors. She stopped there and pressed the stub of her transceiver. "Joaquim? Where are you?"

"Uh—Chancellor, I'm here in Central. Seeing you off from the star dome, in fact, with a few friends from Transport."

"Joaquim, I need to go downwell one last time. Point of

Arches. Very quick—just down and back. Can you help me?"

"Of course, Chancellor," the pilot said cheerily. "No problem. We heard you recall the bus. I'll see that there's a shuttle ready to go by the time it gets you back here. And a skiff standing by in Seattle."

After Hirschfield's belligerence and Berberon's questioning looks, his unquestioning willingness to help her touched Sujata, nearly triggering tears. "Thank you, Joaquim," she said hoarsely. "I'll be waiting."

The bright landing lights of the skiff lit up a cloverleaf-shaped section of the sands like midday, sending nocturnal crabs scurrying in confusion for cover. Other creatures watched from their dark sanctuaries as the vehicle dipped to within a metre of the ground, gracefully rotated a half turn, then settled on the beach.

With a hiss and a faint metallic creak, the port hatch edged open. Almost immediately Sujata clambered out, clutching in one hand a small parcel wrapped in a thin red fabric.

"Give me ten minutes," she shouted over the whine of the turbines and the white noise of the surf.

"I'll just wander up the coastline to Cape Flattery and give the Makah Indians a scare," Joaquim called back. "Holler when you want me and I'll pop right back."

Waving her agreement, Sujata pushed the hatch closed, ducked her head against the flying sand, and moved away quickly. As she did, the skiff raised up and slewed northward. Its machine sounds faded gradually into the night, restoring peace to the beach and insuring privacy for Sujata's actions.

Compared to the harsh argon floodlights of the skiff, the light from the gibbous moon was pale and ghostly. Sujata fell to her knees in the sand and set her burden before her to unwrap it. The land breeze tugged at the corners of the light fabric, then swept the scrap away when she cradled the life-cord in both hands and raised it before her eyes. Slowly she ran the knotted cord with her fingertips, remembering. Then she draped it around her neck and clutched the heartstone fiercely in one hand.

So long a journey, with so little joy, she thought sadly.

Slipping her shoes from her feet, she stood and walked down the slope of the beach to the water's edge. The chill brine swirled around her ankles and made her shiver. She leaned down, scooped up a handful of water in her cupped palm, and brought it to her mouth to taste. Then, for a long moment, she stood still, listening to the Mother's voice, reaching out with all of her senses for Her face.

Then with a sudden, decisive movement, she slipped the lifecord from her neck and hurled it with all her strength out toward where the waves were expending themselves against the columns of black rock. She watched the lifecord arc over the near breakers, turning gracefully end over end, but lost sight of it in the shadow of a sea stack and did not see where it fell.

"*Selir bi'chentya,*" she began chanting in a voice that trembled and broke. "*Darnatir bi'maranya en bis losya. Ti bir naskya en bis pentaya. Loris bir rownya. Qoris nonitya—*"

Suddenly chilled through, she hugged herself and retreated a few steps from the surging water. *There,* she thought. *I'll never leave You now, Mother. I have given myself to You. Make me forever part of You—*

With an effort, she made herself turn away and walk back up the sloping beach. She picked up her shoes where she had discarded them and, surrendering to the sand clinging to her feet, tucked them under one arm. For just an instant she hesitated, stealing another glance back out to sea. Then she reached up and firmly pressed the stub of her transceiver.

"All right, Joaquim," she called in a voice husky with emotion. "You can come back for me. I'm ready to go now."

chapter 14

Mothball

"Coming up on the starboard side now is *Regal Bearing*, a typical yacht of the Adara yards," intoned Jeffrey Hawkins, *Viking*'s tour guide, in a cheery, practiced voice. "*Regal Bearing* was built in 312 A.R. for a Journan corporate collective and spent most of its active years legging from Journa to Advance Base Perseus. . . ."

It had been four hours since *Viking* had left its moorings, and more than a hour since the tour had begun. Already there was some restlessness among the tour cruiser's fifty-odd passengers, and some chatter among those who had already tired of Hawkins's ongoing narration. One or two were even sleeping in the dimly lit main cabin.

But others were listening and looking out through the viewports as raptly now as they had when the first great bulk had loomed up out of the darkness and suddenly been lit by *Viking*'s powerful spotlights. Among them was a towheaded three-year-old boy seated in the back row on the starboard side. At the announcement he squirmed in his chair and craned his head in an unsuccessful effort to see past the heads, shoulders, and backs between him and the viewport.

"Pick me up, Mommy, please?" he asked plaintively.

"Sssh. Be quiet, Matt," whispered the young woman to the child's right.

But an elderly man with a close-cropped white beard who was sitting on the child's left reached down with a pale, oddly scarred hand and hoisted the boy onto one shoulder. "There you go," he said. "Can you see it now?"

The boy's answer was a beaming smile and a gleeful, "Can you see it? Ye-ah!"

From his vantage point in the guide's booth Jeffrey Hawkins took note of the byplay. He smiled to himself as man and child together peered out through the synglass at the still and silent shapes of the Unified Planets Spacecraft Museum slipping past.

Hawkins knew them all: sprints and warships, freighters and yachts, scattered across the blackness as though painted in place. The stillness was illusion. In reality the Museum's exhibits were hurtling along in formation, a hundred-odd ships scattered through a hundred cubic kilometres, their hulls bronzed by light from the giant red star Arcturus. Moving as one, they traced an orbit between the habitable planet Cheia, home to the Arcturus New Colony, and the Jovian planet Chryseis.

It was Hawkins's third season as *Viking*'s tour guide. Three weeks out of every two years, the Museum passed close enough to Cheia for *Viking* to carry the curious for a visit. The tours were not run to provide a profit but rather a service. They were a way to say to the Service bureaucracy at Central, "Yes, we value what you've sent us—send us more."

In those three seasons Hawkins had come to know the two kinds of people who came to the Museum as well as he had the ships themselves. The first group, those Hawkins thought of as the believers, usually comprised the majority of the visitors. They were the ones who came to marvel at the technology, to steep themselves in the history. Like Hawkins, nearly all had been born on Cheia. Also like Hawkins, they had no real hope of ever leaving it.

The believers came to the Museum with a wistful longing and the conviction that circumstance had conspired to deprive them of something wonderful. For them the ships represented other worlds, other times, other lives. The bearded man with the child on his shoulder was one such; Hawkins could read the emotions on his face, could see it in the way he had treated the child's request as something important.

By contrast, the child's mother belonged to the category Hawkins called the skimmers. Some skimmers were tourists in the true sense: members of visiting packet crews who came to the Museum only to be able to say when they returned to Boötes Center or Earth that they had been to a place that was beyond the reach of their audience.

But most skimmers were native Cheians. They were the type of social gadflies who were only interested in championship games, finish lines, and opening nights. Their interest in an event or activity was related less to the inner satisfaction that might be derived from it than to its snob value and trendiness.

It was the skimmers who had packed *Viking* for this tour, just as they had every tour this season; ordinarily the four rows of seats would have been half full or less. It was the skimmers who were talking and dozing and shifting impatiently in their seats. They had no interest in a typical yacht of the Achernar yards, or the bulk-cargo packet retired from the Cygnus–Maranit run, or any of the Museum's proletarian vessels. They had come to see the royalty. They had come because of *Munin*.

Five years earlier *Munin* had arrived at Arcturus New Colony from Boötes Center carrying twenty-six emigrants and as great a volume of technological trade goods as could coexist with her human cargo. From the first, her presence had caused a sensation. While she was being unloaded at Equatorial Station so many people left their jobs elsewhere on the orbiting base to come see her that the station manager felt obliged to declare the docks restricted. Six hours later he surrendered in the face of a near mutiny and issued a visitation schedule instead.

However extreme, the interest in *Munin* was perfectly understandable. With *Pride of Earth* now a ground-based monument in the Journan capital, *Dove* destroyed, and *Hugin* scrapped, *Munin* was the oldest surviving pioneer survey ship, the last of the Pathfinders on whose exploits the entire Survey Branch had been founded.

But transcending even that, *Munin* was "Merritt Thackery's ship"—the instrument of the Revision, by extension a symbol of the D'shanna themselves. Such was her cachet that already several hundred Cheian colonists claimed to have emigrated aboard her, and the number was sure to grow in the years to come.

With such a pedigree *Munin* immediately had become the centerpiece of the Museum, most of the holdings of which were of little intrinsic value. They were there more or less by default; ships that, one step from being scrapped, had made one last journey as part of Arcturus New Colony's one-way lifeline. That was reflected in the care they were given; though their external appearances were maintained by the Museum staff, no effort was expended to keep their systems operational. Many could no longer even hold an atmosphere.

Munin had been treated very differently. When her last passengers had disembarked, her hold had been emptied, and her final crew had signed off, she had been turned over to the Museum historians. Their charge was to see that *Munin* was restored inside and out to match as closely as possible her appearance when, with Thackery commanding, she had crossed paths with the D'shanna among the stars of Ursa Major.

During the Museum's last close pass to Cheia the curators had still been at their task, their tug and work barge moored alongside and *Munin*'s exterior further hidden by work rigging. Many had come to see *Munin* then and gone back disappointed. Now *Munin* was ready, not only to be seen but also to be boarded. Hawkins was not surprised, then, that his show was now playing to a packed audience. But he also could not help but feel more kindly toward the believers aboard than toward the skimmers.

On this particular tour Hawkins had spotted someone he knew among the passengers, a man who did not qualify either as believer or skimmer: Colonel Ramiz. As second-in-command of the Defense Branch's small contingent on Cheia, the little man with the jet-black hair, pinched face, and unpleasant manner was a familiar sight around the Equatorial Station—much noticed but little regarded.

But why Ramiz was aboard *Viking* was something of a puzzlement to Hawkins. When *Munin* had come in, Ramiz had gone aboard in the company of a gaggle of shipwrights, trying to decide whether she could be turned into a sort of bargain-basement Defender for the ANC. Surely he had seen all that he needed to of her then—unless he had changed his mind about her usefulness?

"There she is," someone cried suddenly. "There's *Munin*!"

Fifty heads turned as fifty pairs of eyes searched space beyond the viewports. There was a chorus of oohs and ahs, and Hawkins forgot Ramiz. He liked to let his passengers spot *Munin* for themselves, tried to allow them that little thrill of discovery, but once they had, it was time to go to work.

"That's right, ladies and gentlemen. That giant ship coming up to starboard is none other than S3 *Munin*, last surviving Pathfinder, flagship of the Unified Worlds Museum, and still carrying an honorary commission from the Survey Branch of the USS. In just a few minutes we'll be going aboard, starting with those of you sitting on the portside—no, sorry, too late to change seats, but you'll all have your chance—"

As Hawkins had guessed, Colonel Raymond Ramiz was not aboard *Viking* for the tour. He was there to keep an eye on the bearded man who called himself J. M. Langston, but who years ago and cees away had had another name.

Ramiz's instructions had come not from the Defense hierarchy but from the Upper Tier, and they were simple. Langston was not to leave Cheia—ever. So long as he kept to himself and led a quiet life, Ramiz was to let him be. But if Langston tried to get near any ship capable of intersystem flight, he was to be stopped.

In the five months since his arrival, Langston had given every indication he intended nothing more than to disappear into the woodwork. Take the matter of *Fireside*; his first act had been to sell it to the Colony Manager's office, under terms that would make him comfortable on Cheia for as long as he might be expected to live.

Aside from what it said about his intentions, the sale also showed his willingness to adapt to local conventions. Though technically operating on the official Service currency, Arcturus New Colony was loath to embrace those who brought only paper wealth to the community. They took from the colony with their Coullars more than those Coullars could bring back to the colony, since the once-every-five-years packet schedule created a bottleneck that prevented exchanging the surplus for something useful.

So new Coullars brought from the outside could only cheapen old Coullars, and those who brought them and nothing else faced the community's approbium. Langston had that kind of wealth but left it untouched. He lived within the limits of his locally derived income and so escaped any unwelcome notoriety.

But the thought of Langston aboard *Munin*, even as a visitor, made Ramiz uncomfortable, and so he had tagged along. He was even more concerned after seeing how careless the Museum was about security. As each passenger had paid his fare the clerk had collected his name—but had not checked those names, even against their own identification. Ramiz knew that for certain, since the phony name he himself had given to test them had gone unchallenged. They did not know who they had aboard.

At least the young tour guide took the elementary precaution of tallying up with a hand counter the number going aboard. Ignoring the indignant looks from the other passengers, Ramiz edged his way forward until only two bodies separated him from Langston. He did not know what he thought Langston might do, but he was confident that he could stop him.

The group gathered briefly on the ed-rec deck to listen to Hawkins outline the ground rules for the tour. When Hawkins led the way downship, Ramiz made sure that Langston started down the climbway first, so that he would have him in sight at all times.

They paused for a short spiel at the drive-core access hatch, again at the contact lab, and ended their descent in the dress-out room and the gig bay. When they started back, by virtue of having been one of the last down, Ramiz found himself trapped into being one of the leaders going up. He comforted himself with the realization that there was really nowhere Langston could go.

On the way back up, Hawkins took them through the wardroom and allowed them to peek inside two of the restored cabins, including Thackery's. Then it was on to their last stop, the bridge.

A surprise was waiting on the bridge: animated holograms of the ship's crew moving in synchrony with the canned chatter. There was Thackery at his command station, and Amelia Koi, and Derrel Guerrieri, and Gwen Shinault. Chuckling to himself, Ramiz turned to catch Langston's reaction. But Langston was not there.

Pushing his way past the others, Ramiz rushed to the rail-

ing at the edge of the climbway and looked down. Neither of
the two tourists still climbing was Langston. Swinging himself
over the railing, Ramiz started back down.

He descended the climbway slowly, with catlike agility and
a light step, trying to sort out any unusual sounds from the
cacophony filtering down to him from Hawkins and the
others. He did not have to go far. Langston was standing facing one of the now-closed doors on B-deck, where the command cabins were. On the door before him was a small brass
plaque that read M. THACKERY, CMDR. in three-centimetre-tall
block letters.

"This is wrong. This wasn't here," the bearded man whispered to himself as he traced the grooves of the engraving
with a fingertip.

Ramiz had seen enough. "You," he barked, stepping off
the climbway. "What do you think you're doing? You've got
no special privileges here. Get upship with the others."

Langston started and looked back over his shoulder with a
frightened look in his eyes. As he did, Hawkins materialized
on the climbway just above and behind Ramiz. The tour guide
gave both Langston and Ramiz long, hard looks, then continued down past them. "Come along now, folks," he called back
up the climbway, "I'm sure your friends and companions back
on board *Viking* are mighty impatient for their turn."

Eyes downcast, Langston brushed past Ramiz and joined
the migration back to the entry port. Ramiz waited until the
last of the passengers was by, then took his time descending,
studying the ship's interior from a different perspective than
he had the last time he was aboard.

But as he reached the port and tried to pass Hawkins, the
tour guide stepped away from the wall and blocked the way.
"What are you doing here?"

"My job," Ramiz said curtly.

"It looks like you're trying to do mine. What did you think
he was going to do? Stow away? He's just an old man with a
fantasy. He couldn't hurt anything. There wasn't any need to
go after him like that."

Ramiz could not resist the temptation to parade his superior
knowledge before the youth. "You dumb little mouthpiece,"
he snarled. "What's he have to do, go sit in his chair before
you'd recognize him? He's an old man, all right, but he's not
here fantasizing. He's here remembering."

Better judgment finally silenced Ramiz before he said

Langston's former name. "Now get out of my way," he growled, "before I knock you down and walk out of here on your face."

He enjoyed the sight of Hawkins hastening to comply.

Back in the tour-guide booth, still fuming over Ramiz's presumption, Hawkins struggled with what the colonel had said. Could the bearded old man actually be Merritt Thackery? It seemed impossible. And yet who else could Ramiz have meant? Hawkins tried to study the face of the mystery passenger, but he sat sunken into his chair, chin down, head turned half away. The seat-assignment chart said the man's name was J. M. Langston, which proved nothing.

If it is Thackery, I can't let him leave without talking to him.

But how could it be? Yes, Thackery's deepyacht was here. The Museum had tried to acquire it but had been outbid by the Colony Manager's Office. Could it have been Thackery himself that brought it to Arcturus? *I thought he was dead. But even if he's not, why would he come here?*

The pale, scarred patches on the man's hand—Hawkins suddenly remembered a grisly sequence in the holoflick *Appointment With Destiny*. In the course of one of the landings he made while pursuing the D'shanna, Merritt Thackery had been bitten by a native organism and nearly died of poisoning, his skin turning black and splitting open to reveal raw red flesh. He did not know how much the makers of the film might have stretched the truth—but if there had been such an incident, surely it would have left its mark.

But he would have had the flaws corrected, surely—who would have worn such scars willingly?

By the time *Viking* returned on its berth at Equatorial Station, Hawkins was no more sure of his facts. But he was firmly determined not to let the matter end there.

Getting to Langston proved to be a test of patience, since Hawkins did not want Ramiz to know of his interest. Happily, all of Equatorial Station's dock facilities were concentrated in one area, with the Museum's offices located directly across from the boarding lounge for the Cheia shuttle. It was not difficult for Hawkins to find reasons to linger in the offices, and an easy matter to keep an eye on Langston from there.

Ramiz was also lingering and watching, though somewhat more obviously, almost as if he wanted Langston to be aware that he was there. Twice Langston shambled up the corridor toward the main station, with Ramiz following openly. Each time, he returned within twenty minutes, Ramiz dogging his heels, and took a seat in the shuttle boarding lounge.

Not until the gate attendant arrived and Langston lined up with the others to register for the 18:00 shuttle did Ramiz relax his vigilance. As Langston took his seat once more, the colonel approached the attendant, exchanged a few words with him, and then, apparently satisfied by what he had learned, headed off in the direction of the Defense Annex.

That was Hawkins's opportunity. Leaving the Museum offices, he double-checked the corridor for any sign of Ramiz, then headed for Langston. Using a side entrance to the lounge, he came up out of nowhere to take Langston by the shoulder with a firm grip.

"Would you come with me, please," he said in as authoritative a tone as he could muster.

As though he had no will left with which to resist, Langston allowed himself to be steered down the corridor to an unoccupied comfort station. When they were inside, Hawkins locked the door behind them, then gestured toward the single chair.

"Sit down, please," he said.

Moving slowly, Langston complied. Hawkins hopped up and sat on the edge of the sink facing him. "You're Merritt Thackery," he said, leaning forward.

Langston closed his eyes and his features seemed to sag.

"You are, aren't you?"

Eyes still closed, Langston nodded. "I didn't know that I was being watched, even here, until today," he said in a half whisper.

"You are. Not by me. By that man who caught you on B-deck. Colonel Ramiz, from the Defense Branch." Langston —Thackery—opened his eyes but still avoided looking at Hawkins. "I had hoped I had left all that behind me," was his tired answer.

"Why are you here? Did you come all this way just to see *Munin*?"

Thackery said nothing.

"What, do you think I'm working for Richardson?" Hawkins prodded. "I despise the man."

Still Thackery was silent, staring at the floor.

Hawkins frowned and rubbed his face with one long-fingered hand. "See, I keep trying to figure out why you came here, why a little backwater colony like Cheia. Somehow I don't think it's a coincidence that *Munin* is here too. And I keep trying to figure out what Colonel Ramiz was worried about. The answers keep coming out the same."

At that moment the first boarding call for the Cheia shuttle sounded through the comfort station's speaker. "My flight—" Thackery said, starting to rise out of his chair.

"Sit down. We have fifteen minutes, at least," Hawkins said sharply. When Thackery meekly acceded, Hawkins continued. "You know, I know a lot about these ships. Not just what I say during the tours. I've read most everything the curators can dig up. But there's one thing I'm not sure about, something you can answer. What if there'd been a disaster that left only one crew member alive—some kind of contamination, maybe? Would he have been stranded? Can one man handle a survey ship?"

Thackery shuddered violently and folded his hands in front of his mouth.

"It must bother you, all these strangers trampling through your ship," Hawkins said softly. "Peering into the room where you and Dr. Koi slept—listening to the ghosts on the bridge and thinking that's the way it was—"

"What do you want from me?" Thackery cried.

Hawkins flashed a quick, sympathetic smile. "I don't want anything from you. I want to *give* something to you. I want to tell you that if Captain Ramiz is right—if you came here to try to take *Munin*—that I'll help."

Thackery raised his eyes to meet Hawkins's and stared unbelievingly into them.

"I don't think you could manage it on your own," Hawkins said. "Not with Ramiz watching. Not without someone to tell you where to find the cutout box the curators installed to disable the controls during tours. But we could do it together, if that's what you want. I can handle Ramiz. I already know how I'll do it."

"Why would you do this?" Thackery asked wonderingly. "Why would you care?"

Hawkins smiled wryly. "You're Merritt Thackery. What more reason do I need?" But instead of warming up at the flattery, Thackery's expression frosted over again. "You wouldn't have left Earth and come all this way unless it was important," Hawkins went on anxiously. "And you wouldn't think of taking *Munin* unless you had a need that justified it."

"And what if my only reasons are selfish ones, if the only needs I care about now are my own?"

Shaking his head, Hawkins said, "Whatever she means to you, it's more than she means to us, to the Museum, *Munin* is yours if you want her—we owe you so much more. Will you take her?"

For a long moment there was silence, and Thackery would not meet Hawkins's eyes. "It—it was easier to leave Earth than you might think," Thackery said at last, slowly, as though the words were painful, as if the very act of self-disclosure required breaking deeply ingrained patterns. "I don't belong there—I never really have. It's been a lay-over, a breathing space between missions. *Tycho—Descartes —Munin—Fireside*—they were my real homes, the only places that life stood still long enough for me to understand the rules."

Thackery raised his head and their eyes met. In Thackery's blue-gray orbs Hawkins saw pain and vulnerability, a loneli-ness and weariness that he could not touch. They were eyes that seemed to remember everything they had ever seen in a life spanning half a millennium.

"Will you take her?" Hawkins repeated. "Will you let me help?"

Thackery drew a deep breath and released it as a sigh. "Yes," he said.

Hawkins hopped off the sink and onto his feet. "Friday is the last tour of the season," he said, moving to the door and unlocking it. "Come on the tour again. I'll hold a seat for you."

"As simple as that?"

"For you—yes." His hand on the door actuator, Hawkins turned to go, then turned back to Thackery. "If you could just tell me—where will you go that *Fireside* couldn't take you?"

"Out," Thackery said, his eyes misting. "Out where there are no colonels to watch me. Where there's no one that wants anything from me. *Munin* will take me where I can be alone. Where there are no stars in the sky, only galaxies—" Thack-ery's voice broke, and he looked away.

"I'll—I'll look for you Friday," Hawkins said, regretting

having asked. "You have about five minutes to catch your shuttle," he added. Then he slipped out the door quietly, feeling for all the world like an intruder in the other man's life.

Friday brought both Thackery and Ramiz back to *Viking*. The crucial first step was to seat them far enough apart so that Hawkins could draw the line separating the two tour groups for *Munin* somewhere between them.

Thackery had the first seat on the aisle, from which position he would be first in line when it was time to cross to *Munin*. Hawkins filled the seats around him with two families with eight children between them.

So when Ramiz came to the counter and demanded, "Put me as close to Langston—that one, there—as you can," Thackery was already insulated.

"I can get you across the aisle and one seat back," Hawkins said helpfully.

"No. Put me on the same side as him."

"Row H?"

"Fine."

Hawkins resisted the impulse to smile.

For the first time in three seasons the tour seemed interminable. *You're turning into a skimmer,* Hawkins thought, chiding himself. But he forgave himself his impatience, and even the flubs his inattention created, knowing the reason.

Finally *Munin* was in sight. Hawkins waited until *Viking* was alongside and the transfer tunnel extended before announcing, "The first group will consist of Rows A through G—"

For a moment Ramiz sat rooted in his chair by surprise. Then, after looking around the cabin as if to see who might try to stop him, he bounced up out of his seat and headed forward. But by then the aisle was full, and he had no choice but to bide his time at the end of the line.

At the head of the line Thackery's eyes locked with Hawkins's, asking a silent question. "Go right on aboard, sir," Hawkins said. "Follow the blue line and wait at the other end. F-5," he added in a whisper as Thackery brushed by him.

Hawkins had unlocked the isolation cabin at the end of the previous day's tour, and he trusted that Thackery understood he was to wait there. He passed him through without registering a tally on his counter, then turned his attention to the next face in line. "Brought the family out with you, eh?" he said brightly.

The counter showed twenty-seven when Ramiz rounded the corner from the main aisle to where Hawkins stood by the hatch.

"Excuse me, sir, but I believe you were seated in row H," Hawkins said, blocking the corridor. Hawkins and Ramiz were alone, but the fact that there could be an audience on *Viking*'s bridge—in truth, Hawkins hoped that there was— required carefully chosen words. "Wait your turn, please. I'll be back for the rest of the group in a few minutes."

"You little jerk, he came back for a reason. You don't know what he could do in there—"

"I don't know what you're talking about," Hawkins said innocently. "Now, if you'd just return to your seat—"

"Get out of my way," Ramiz snarled, placing one hand on Hawkins's chest and giving a shove.

Hawkins staggered back, but he had been prepared for it and kept his balance. His right hand went to his hip, and as Ramiz tried to pass, the hand came up in what must have seemed to Ramiz to be an attempt to ward off any further contact—except that Hawkins's hand was not empty.

In three seasons Hawkins had never had cause to use the small aerosol of Sub-Dew that rode unobtrusively on his belt, but he remembered all he needed to about how it worked and what to expect. There was a sharp hissing sound, and a narrowly focused jet of mist caught Ramiz full in the face. Almost between one step and the next, Ramiz slumped sideways against the bulkhead, his rubbery legs buckled, and he slid to the floor.

His own legs shaky, Hawkins leaned back against the bulkhead and tapped the shipnet. "Bridge, I had a little trouble with one of the passengers. If you could send a steward back to the transfer hatch—"

"We saw, Jeff," came the reply. "Are you all right?"

"Sure. I'm fine."

"Then go ahead with your tour. We'll take care of it."

Hawkins waited until the last passenger of the last tour had crossed back to *Viking* before paging Thackery in F-5. It was an unnecessary step; as though *Munin* were already his again, Thackery seemed to know the right time, appearing bare seconds later at the far end of the corridor.

"I don't have long. I'm supposed to be powering down for the season," Hawkins said. "The cutout box is under the panel at the gravigation station—nothing complicated, just turn everything off to on. The consumables reprocessor is still about a third full from when the curators moved out. The clothes in your cabin are your size, unless you've gained weight—the curators were very thorough. The drive hasn't been touched since she came in, except cosmetically."

"Should I wait, or—"

Hawkins shook his head. "Just long enough for *Viking* to get clear. If you don't leave quickly, you may not get a chance to."

"You're going to catch hell."

"For carelessness, maybe. Not for helping. I think I'm covered. Anyway, this isn't that great a job," he said without conviction. "I have to go. They'll be expecting my okay to separate."

Thackery nodded and advanced a few steps closer along the corridor as Hawkins stepped into the lock and cycled the outer hatch.

"I like to think that roaming in *Munin*, you'll outlive us all," Hawkins said as the door smoothly rotated out from the recessed position.

"I don't," Thackery said bluntly. "Outliving people has been my curse."

Feeling foolish again, Hawkins turned away and reached for the lock controls.

"Jeffrey—"

Hawkins looked back through the narrowing gap.

"Thank you," Thackery said simply.

The *thwwpp* of the hatch sealing itself precluded any reply.

The transfer tunnel returned to its cradle on the side of *Viking* with a muffled clang that made the floor panels under Hawkins's feet vibrate.

"Hawkins to bridge. We're all buttoned up."

"I make us one short on the count."

Hawkins looked up at the camera and shook his head. "Must have one in the john. How's our feisty guest feeling?"

"Still under. Resting comfortably," the bridge replied. "All right, Jeff. Find your own seat. We're about to get moving."

The great survey ship came clearly into view to starboard as *Viking* drifted sideways under the impetus of its station-keeping thrusters, then began a braking maneuver to start her journey back to Equatorial Station. Less than a kilometre separated the two ships when suddenly the stars fore and aft of *Munin* seemed to ripple, as though the very substance of space were being shaken by the energies of its drive. The cabin filled with cries of alarm and delight as those with the best view came up out of their chairs, pointing excitedly.

"What the hell is going on?" demanded *Viking*'s captain. "Hawk, what'd you do to her?"

Part of Hawkins longed to answer honestly, to share the pang of jealousy that came with seeing *Munin* under power, and the deep satisfaction that proceeded from knowing who was on her bridge. But an honest answer could only aggravate whatever difficulties lay ahead.

"Shit, I didn't do anything! Looks like we've got a runaway," Hawkins offered lamely, then tabbed the cabin circuit. "Nothing to concern yourself over, folks—just part of the show, a little surprise for the end of the season. Those survey ships sure can move, can't they? Nothing in the Universe can catch them—"

chapter 15

The Far Bank
of the Rubicon

There is simply no way, Sujata thought as she waited for the comtech to establish the link with Earth, to adjust to this insane time-twisting. The journey to Lynx Center was nearly over, and she had still not made peace with the fact that the ship's chronometers were lying to her. One minute was not one minute at all—it was two hours. While she slept a single night's sleep, forty days raced by. From noon to noon was four months.

Contrary to her expectations, her previous transplant experience had helped only until *Wesley* sailed. After that it counted for nothing. The other times, she had hit the craze and never had to look back. She had been able to say good-bye once and then break cleanly with her past.

But with *Wesley* diving down out of the craze every second day for contact with Central, Sujata felt as though she were always saying good-bye, and the check-in had become something to dread. It meant painful reminders of what she had given up. It meant deaths and resignations and retirements, always without warning, gradually replacing the little world she had known with one she did not.

The hardest defection to take had been Regan Marshall,

who resigned at the midway point of *Wesley*'s voyage. Though he had consulted with her on his replacement, it still left her depending heavily on someone who was a stranger. She was beginning to feel like a helpless spectator, cheated not only of any sense of accomplishment but even of any real feeling of involvement.

But even that was not as hard as watching Ten Ga'ar complete her metamorphosis from child to woman.

The first day Ten Ga'ar had stolen a moment of the link-time to say that she forgave Sujata, that she understood, that leaving her behind was the right decision, and that she had learned how to be happy without Sujata. Her words were jarring, and Sujata was taken completely by surprise. In one day of shiptime Ten Ga'ar had had more chance to work through her sadness, to heal the wound, than Sujata would have in the course of the entire voyage.

Still bitter that Ten Ga'ar had been so petty as to cheat her out of a chance to properly say good-bye, Sujata at first rebelled at being forgiven. It had taken her a few days to realize what Ten Ga'ar already knew by the first check-in—that they could not afford to sustain any emotion save a fond remembrance of the intimacy they had once shared. They were out of sync and growing apart, and there was nothing to do but accept it.

There were missteps, too, on the professional side. More than once in the first week Sujata came back the "next day" with suggestions and solutions for problems that had been either solved or made irrelevant by the months that passed between one afternoon and the next. To make it work, Ten Ga'ar had to learn to offer Sujata a decision to be confirmed rather than a situation to be analyzed, while Sujata had to agree to surrender more of her authority than she had initially thought necessary.

The sole thread of continuity across all seven weeks of the run was Garrard and Evanik's report. It had come to be the only part of the dispatch that commanded her attention when the link had been terminated. The duo now headed a team of fifteen researchers, who documented in both objective and subjective detail that the cultural shift Sujata had feared was continuing.

Both the economy of the system as a whole and the budget of the World Council were increasingly dominated by military expenditures. The time was not far off when the military would directly or indirectly employ the largest fraction of the system's work force. Questions of planetary security had moved permanently onto the World Council's agenda.

Those were the generalities: the specifics were equally disturbing. Eleven years ago the Nines had brought the concept of political parties back to global governance, coming out of the closet to promote Robert Chaisson for a vacancy on the World Council. Though he failed to gain appointment, Chaisson did gain a new platform for his views. As if to answer Chaisson's charge that the Council was jeopardizing Earth's security by entrusting its defense to the Service, the next year Tanvier initiated an ambitious and horrendously expensive effort to build ground-based defenses against a Mizari attack— defenses that Sujata's technical analysts regarded as worthless.

Three years later the Council authorized a special branch of the Peace Force that was in everything but name an army. The Exotics, as they came to be called, were meant to be the first on the scene if the Mizari attack took the form of an invasion. Their weapons included everything from teleoperated air armor to X-ray bombs and other nucleonics; their strategy embraced such concepts as "cauterization" and "nonstrategic personnel write-off." The Exotics did not need to recruit—there were ten applicants for every opening.

But that was no surprise, considering that the three most popular mass entertainments of the decade were jingoistic glories-of-war tales in which courageous men and women turned back the loathsome Mizari hordes. True, all three were independently produced (one with financial support from the Nines), and less inflammatory fare was still coming out of the Council's edu-entertainment arm, but the fact that they attained net distribution at all was in itself telling.

A light winked on the terminal before her, and Sujata roused herself from her gloomy ruminations. The check-in was fairly routine. In less than fifteen minutes Ten Ga'ar highlighted the contents of the main dispatch, being transmitted on the high band in compressed mode directly to *Wesley*'s library.

Evanik came on to outline the research unit's current projects, and to inform Sujata that Garrard had finally made good on his threats to resign, taking a position with the Council's sociometric division. Vice Chancellor Abram Walker came on to offer his usual empty assurances that everything was in hand and running smoothly.

There was nothing in any of their messages for Sujata even to respond to with more than a grunt and a nod until Ten Ga'ar came back on at the end.

"I wanted to remind you that this is the last opportunity for you to send a dispatch forward to Wells," she said, "something that'll be waiting for him when *Charan* comes out of the craze. The majority opinion here is that you need to take the offensive, because he's sure to. He's virtually certain to take the fact that you're right on his heels as a threat."

"I'm afraid I'm going to side with the minority, Wy," Sujata said, shaking her head. "Wells has to act before I can react. What he's done so far isn't enough to support coming down on him—if it was, we'd have gone through the Committee. Even though we're afraid he intends to, he hasn't crossed the line yet. I see no reason to force him to that point any sooner than necessary. I don't want to corner him into having to disobey an order.

"He'll hear through normal channels that I'm coming to Lynx, and the official reason for it. Beyond that, I'm content to let him wonder. Hitting him with an order to ground the Triads, or some such, isn't going to make him feel *less* threatened. Just the opposite—all it would do is spook him. I need to sit down with Wells and have this out before he does anything irreversible. I can't do that from here any better than I could from where you are. It's just going to have to wait until I catch up with him. Which won't be long now."

Ten Ga'ar received those words with a neutral expression, which confirmed for Sujata that the "reminder" actually had been someone else's idea. As the years had slipped by, the number of people willing to talk to her directly had dwindled to three. Sujata understood—she was a stranger to most of her own staff, a sort of technological oracle giving three audiences each year. In a recent nightmarish dream her face had appeared on terminals throughout Central, but no one had known who she was or wanted to talk to her.

"We understand your perspective, Chancellor," Ten Ga'ar was saying. "What you said parallels some of our discussions here. Is there anything else we can do for you today?"

"No," Sujata said. "Nothing you can do."

"Then I guess the next time we talk, you'll be out of the craze for good and inbound to Lynx. Our best to all of you until then. Central out."

"Wesley out," Sujata said, leaning back in her seat and rubbing her eyes. *No, nothing you can do to help me, Wy. And that's about the hardest part to accept—*

The sound of exuberant cheering was still ringing in Harmack Wells's ears as he settled into a chair in the office of Andrew Hogue, the governor of Lynx Center. Barely an hour ago Wells had led the crew of *Charan* out of the disembarkment tunnel to a reception that made the send-off from Central fifty-two days ago seem restrained.

"They really love us, don't they?" Captain Elizin had whispered. He was standing beside Wells on the cargo sled that had been pressed into service for the processional through the streets, which were thronged with thousands who had come out to welcome them.

Wells had nodded agreeably, but he did not take the acclaim personally. He took it instead as a sign of how badly the people wanted a champion, a hero. He accepted it graciously at the same time he discounted it, because he understood their need to find release from fear.

This is not for what we've done but for what you hope we'll do, he had thought, looking out at their faces. *I will try to do justice to your faith.*

Across the room, Onhki Yamakawa, the senior member of the Strategy Committee traveling with Wells on *Charan,* stood studying a directory of Lynx Central. "I am afraid that I will have no better luck finding a proper Japanese meal here than I had trying to coax one from *Charan*'s synthesizer," he said mournfully.

Before Wells could commiserate, the door opened to admit two men, both Lynx natives. The first through was Hogue, a broad-chested man with a pleasant face and fair hair that was so closely cropped he almost seemed bald.

"Governor," Wells said, coming to his feet and offering his hand.

"Very glad to meet you at last, Commander," Hogue said as they shook. "Sorry about all the commotion on the way over here. I thought it was best if we simply got that behind us all at once."

"Perfectly understandable," Wells said. "I'm sure the crew appreciated it."

Hogue introduced his companion, a rangy young man with

darting eyes that never seemed to look straight ahead, as Colonel Philip Shields, chief of the Defense Intelligence Office, Lynx Annex.

"I know this has already been a long day for you," Hogue said, "but Mr. Shields thought it important that you be put in the picture as quickly as possible."

"I agree entirely," Wells said, settling back into his chair. Hogue took the seat to Wells's right, and the others dragged chairs across the carpet to form a small circle.

"Did you have a chance on the way in to begin reviewing the news abstracts we sent over?" Hogue asked.

"A few minutes, no more."

"Then you know at least the good news: the Perimeter is quiet, the political situation is stable, and the Triads are on schedule. However, there are a couple of wrinkles that I'll let Mr. Shields discuss."

"What about *Wesley*?" Yamakawa interjected. "What's her status?"

"Due in thirty-eight days from now."

Wells wrinkled his brow at hearing that. "She was only supposed to be twenty-one days behind us. What happened? What delayed her?"

With a meaningful glance Hogue deferred to Shields.

"Commander, Chancellor Sujata and Ambassador Berberon are aboard *Wesley*," Shields said. "*Wesley*'s been pogoing in and out of the craze, which accounts for the slippage in her arrival time."

"This is bad," Yamakawa muttered. "Very bad."

"Why are they coming here?" Wells asked with honest puzzlement.

"Sir, I do not know. The official purpose is to observe. Our sources inside the Chancellery report that Sujata has described the situation on the Perimeter as 'critical.'"

"Even so, I don't understand why she should consider her physical presence necessary," Hogue said. "Communications with Unity haven't even been close to going down."

"Does anyone have any ideas?" Wells asked. "Colonel?"

"The one possibility I've considered is that she may wish to align herself more strongly with the pro-defense faction and thereby secure her own position."

"She's coming to meddle," Yamakawa said firmly. "She is coming to insinuate herself into matters she knows nothing about."

"Does that seem reasonable to you, Commander?" Hogue asked.

"No," Wells said. "She's kept her distance, and at the same time she's been very accommodating to our interests and concerns. I don't believe that she would suddenly decide that she needed to become more intimately involved."

"Unless something happened to make her lose confidence in the senior Defense administration," Yamakawa pointed out. He had been preparing to say more, but caught an admonitory glance from Wells and fell silent.

"Are there any messages waiting for me from the Chancellor?" Wells asked, turning to Hogue.

"None that I am aware of."

Wells frowned and shook his head. "This seems to me to be no cause for concern. Certainly Chancellor Sujata has every right to exercise oversight in person," he said. "Assuming that this is one of the wrinkles the Governor mentioned, what's the other?"

"I think you will find this a more serious matter. There is about to be a violation of the Perimeter. Not by the Mizari," Shields added quickly. "By one of our vessels—*Munin*, sir. Hijacked from the Unified Planets Museum at Arcturus."

"Hijacked?"

"Yes, sir. It gets stranger. The person responsible seems to be Merritt Thackery. As far as we've been able to determine, he's the only one aboard. The investigation showed that he had two accomplices at Cheia, one a Museum employee and the other one of our people, a Colonel Ramiz. Both served time, but that hasn't helped us get *Munin* or Thackery back."

"Well, I'll be damned," Wells said, settling back in his chair. "Where's he headed?"

"At first we had no idea. But after we made clear we knew who was on board, he filed a formal flight plan giving his destination as the Corona Borealis Cluster."

"I'm afraid I'm not familiar with that astrographical feature."

"No reason why you should be, sir. It's a galaxy cluster, one of the richest—more than five hundred of them, mostly ellipticals. Sir, that cluster lies more than a billion cees beyond the edge of our Galaxy. But he's in no hurry, considering how far he thinks he's going. *Munin* hasn't crazed since he made his getaway."

"*Munin* may not be crazed, but there seems ample evidence

her pilot is," Yamakawa said. "Why was the ship not intercepted?"

"No Sentinel was in a position to do so," Hogue said.

"If Triad One had been on-station, would it have been able to intercept?" Wells asked.

"I don't think anyone has worked it out," Hogue said. "My suspicion is yes, it would have."

"What is the point of entry into the Mizari Zone?" Yamakawa inquired.

"Indeterminate. *Munin* will not enter the Cluster proper. In fact, her general heading is carrying her away from the more sensitive areas. She'll cross the Perimeter somewhere in the Boötes-Corona Borealis area. Here's an odd note: He's been changing course to pass through or near systems which haven't yet been surveyed. He relays back the data collected by the ship's scientific instrumentation—or tries to."

"Tries to?"

"*Munin*'s communications gear was not updated for advanced error-checking. We lose a portion of his transmissions to interference."

"Then we *are* in contact with the ship?" Yamakawa asked.

"After a fashion. He's never answered any dispatch directed at him," Hogue said.

"Interference again?" Wells asked.

"Possibly," Shields said. "Possibly intransigence. I agree with Mr. Yamakawa—whoever he is, this man is not stable. And he is about to compound what is already a very serious list of offenses."

"Seems to me as though he has little to fear in the way of retribution," Wells said lightly. "Was there anything else, Governor?"

"No. Nothing of comparable urgency."

"Fine," Wells said. "I'll sleep on both these matters and take them up with you again tomorrow. I also want to tour the yards tomorrow and take a look at Triad Three."

"I'll arrange it," Hogue promised.

"Not too early," Wells added as he stood up. "Onhki? What do you say we go try to see what Lynx *does* have to offer in the way of civilized fare?"

"The effort should be made," Yamakawa said. "But I hold out little hope for fresh seafood."

• • •

Over a Daehne-style platter of sectioned fruits, seared meat cubes, and seasoned raw dough, Yamakawa and Wells continued the discussion.

"Are you truly concerned about the *Munin* matter?" Yamakawa asked.

"Why do you ask?"

Yamakawa twirled a meat cube in a cup of mustard sauce. "The ship is two hours west and twenty degrees south of Alcor. Colonel Shield's alarm seems excessive."

"There's a lesson in what happened," Wells said. "The fact that we couldn't prevent *Munin* from leaving means that in that same time frame we couldn't have prevented a Mizari ship from entering. It underlines the importance of getting the Triads on station.

"Still, to answer your question, no. I'm more concerned about Sujata. Why did you say what you did about her losing confidence in us—in me?"

Yamakawa chewed thoughtfully before answering. "As you well know, there are certain sensitive matters on which she was not fully informed. If she were to have been appraised of them, she would be forced to consider the Mizari threat more seriously than she was previously inclined to. At the same time she could well conclude that in order to have full and honest knowledge of the situation, she would have to be more directly involved. Either or both would account for her coming here."

"How do you imagine she came to be 'appraised' of those sensitive matters?"

Yamakawa shrugged. "This decision was clearly made in haste, after we sailed. The window of opportunity was small, the number of candidates limited."

Wells ticked them off on his fingers. "Captain Hirschfield. Mr. Rice and Mr. Scurlock of the Strategy Committee."

"And Farlad."

"Yes."

"Three of whom had access to that information for several months before we sailed," Yamakawa observed. "Surely if it were one of them, they would have acted sooner."

"So you think it was Teo?"

"I do."

Wells stared at Yamakawa for a long moment, then shook his head. "Why would he do it? Why would he betray me that way?"

"The motives of traitors and cowards are not particularly subtle. Money. Self-aggrandizement. Misplaced loyalties. Fear. Does it really matter?"

Wells laid down his fork, the food suddenly tasteless in his mouth. "I suppose not."

"He will have to be disciplined, of course."

Wells did not answer. *How many years must you wait?* he was thinking. *How well must you know someone before you can be sure of him?*

"If there is doubt in your mind, all four can be presumed guilty—" Yamakawa began.

"I want him out," Wells said harshly. "I want him gone."

Nodding, Yamakawa went on. "It is a court-martial offense. Even a capital offense. But difficult to prove. And a trial would be awkward, due to the Chancellor's involvement. We may wish to find other means to settle the account."

Wells was not listening. An old adversary, thought vanquished, had returned to the board, and he was busy assessing her position. *She can only be coming to stand in my way—if she believed in the cause, she would have stayed on Earth. She seeks to harry me, to distract me, to place her collar and leash around my neck. But to do that she will have to catch me—*

Despite a night of restless sleep and what he had told Hogue, Wells was up early the next morning, impatient to see at last the fruits of his labors. Wells had defined the mission, but he had been obliged to entrust the engineers with designing the ships themselves. He knew only the generalities; he was eager to learn the specifics.

The final contract had awarded Triad One to Boötes Center, Triad Two to Perimeter Base, and Triad Three to Lynx. The decision had turned not on politics or economics but on time. Any one of the Service's Earth-orbital shipyards could have built a Triad twenty percent faster for thirty percent less. But the price of those savings was an extra seventeen years journeying to the patrol circles located from eight to fifteen cees beyond the Perimeter.

Lynx Center's shipyard was an integral part of the station, occupying the equivalent of its nine lowest levels. Most of that volume was devoted to an enormous enclosed work bay with a one-tenth strength gravity field that was upside down in relation to the rest of the station. The inverted field, which turned what should have been the ceiling into the floor, was an innovation peculiar to the Lynx Center. It was necessary because the real floor was a multisectioned door several hectares in total area and quite complicated enough without gravity ducting.

Nearly one third of that door was at that moment retracted, and from the foreman's lookout where Wells was first taken he could see why: One of the Triad's two lineships was being towed away from the yard by a small tug. Wells knew at a glance that the ship under tow was part of the Triad. Its peculiar profile said it could be nothing else.

Each Triad ship had not one AVLO drive, but two—an axial drive with forward and aft field radiators, just as any deepship, and a translational drive, with a second set of radiators amidships oriented at right angles to the primary hull. The transverse hull gave the lineship the appearance of a flying Iron Cross.

Turning his attention inside the work bay, Wells saw that the effect was even more pronounced with the carrier. Its transverse hull was nearly as large as the primary in order to accommodate the cradles for the massive DDs, one on each side.

"I don't see how you shoehorned them all in here," Wells said to his guide. "The bay looks crowded even with one of them out."

"There hasn't been much room to spare since the hulls were completed," the guide agreed. "Ready to go aboard?"

"You bet I am."

Though the physical elements that made up the interior were familiar to anyone who had ever spent time on a Service deepship, the Triad as a whole had an alien feel to it. Most notably there was no bridge to speak of. Where Wells would have expected to find it, he found instead a ring of second-generation battle couches burrowed in among the hardware of the drives, each at the end of its own cavelike ejection chute.

The arrangement afforded the crew the maximum physical protection, but it also meant that they would go into battle fragmented, psychologically alone. They would never look across an open bridge and see dying and injured mates, but they also could never look out and catch a thumbs-up or a reassuring grin.

Absent a bridge, the largest "open" spaces aboard were the immersion tanks forward and aft. The tanks were there to protect the off-shift crew against the neck-snapping lateral accelerations that would come as the ship evaded incoming fire. The translational drive was nearly as powerful as the main. Test crews had opined that even with the couches and I-tanks, the brutal translational maneuvers—combining snap rolls and abrupt sideslips—were more punishing than taking fire would be.

As the tour proceeded, Wells tried to build in his head a picture of what life would be like aboard Triad, a picture that would keep the ships and their crews real to him when they were far removed from his sight in the Mizari Zone. But the picture refused to coalesce. Only the mechanical elements were in focus: he strained unsuccessfully to bring the human element to the forefront.

Presently Wells realized that he was responding to a design philosophy completely antithetical to that of all other deep-ships. The packets and surveyors, even the flagships, had been built as living places for human beings, tiny worlds cased in synthmesh and alumichrome. Triad was more akin to an intrasystem tug or mining ship, where every other consideration was subordinate to its function.

But even beyond that, Wells sensed that Triad had been designed and built as an integrated organism, a cyborg with interchangeable brains. The bridge stations were merely places to plug in key components, the tanks and berths merely places to store the spares.

Following his voluble guide from stern to bow, Wells had less a sense of being inside a hull than of crawling through the guts of a machine awaiting the installation of its animating force. Everything he saw said that the prospect for human pleasures was small, the possibility of death very real.

Wondering if he was asking too much of the men and women who wore the golden trigon, Wells continued his inspection. He sat in the captain's battle couch, peered into the heart of the drive, tasted the output of the food synthesizers. He tested the knowledge of the riggers aboard with his questions, and their workmanship with his eyes and hands.

After more than ninety minutes Wells and his guide left the carrier by the forward access hatch. On the bulkhead between the hatch's inner and outer doors, directly below the anodized plaque bearing the carrier's official designation "T 301," Wells discovered an unauthorized plastic sign that bore the legend AVENGER. The lettering was rendered in a bold free-hand style, the oversized *A* drawn as a pair of pincers, poised to crush a planet already in flames. "Where did this come from?" Wells asked, pointing.

"One of the riggers, probably. The Triads weren't given names by the Flight Office, so I'm afraid the crews come up with their own. I'll see that it's removed, sir," the guide said apologetically.

It was the first purely human touch Wells had seen that morning. But more than that, it was a welcome sign that the human spirit of *Avenger*'s crew would survive the privations their duty aboard her would enforce on them. "You'll do nothing of the kind," Wells said. "It's a good name. It stays."

"Certainly, sir. Would you like to see *Falcon*, sir?" the guide asked. "I understand that Mr. Yamakawa isn't expecting us for another forty minutes."

The armed and armored reconnaissance ship was moored in the adjacent refit bay; originally Wells had planned to include it in his tour.

"No," Wells said with a small, contented smile. "I've seen enough."

Wells spent the rest of the morning huddled with Yamakawa. That afternoon he called Hogue, Shields, and all the Lynx Annex department heads together for a war conference. He did not waste words.

"In three days the survey ship *Munin* will cross the Perimeter," Wells told them. "We can't prevent this violation. We can't predict whether the Mizari will detect the incursion or what reaction they might have if they do. So we have to ready ourselves for the worst. As of this moment I am officially placing the Defense Branch on a full war footing."

There was a stirring among those gathered, but Wells ignored it and went on. "I have already this morning ordered the Triads deployed to their patrol circles beyond the Perimeter as soon as they are operationally certified. Within six hours Triad One will sail from Boötes Center. I am assured that within four weeks Triad Three will be ready to sail from here. All Status-A mission rules are in effect—the ships will be armed and authorized to defend their sectors.

"I am also ordering the reconnaissance ships *Eagle* and *Kite*, now at Perimeter Base, to begin their intrusive survey of the members of the Ursa Major Cluster. *Kite*'s initial destination is Megrez. *Eagle* will attempt to make contact with Feghr, the isolate colony believed to be on 82 Lynx. As soon as its crew is complete, *Falcon* will leave here to join the mission—"

"Commander?" interrupted one of the department heads. "It seems to me that all this does is multiply the risk—"

"By the time the first survey is made, all three Triads will be positioned to respond swiftly to any threatened hostilities," Wells said firmly, shaking his head. "Believe me, we've analyzed the risks very carefully."

"I am counting on everyone's very best effort toward seeing that this transition comes off smoothly. Now, more than ever, we cannot afford any failures. The entire Defense Branch must function as a single, coordinated whole.

"Unfortunately our monitoring of transmissions from *Munin* provides further evidence that communications between here and the Perimeter are more severely affected by the interference than communications elsewhere within our territory. The situation is, in fact, now worse between here and the Perimeter than it was between Earth and Lynx when my staff and I decided to relocate here.

"So to guarantee that command integrity will not be compromised during the critical period ahead, I have decided to move my staff to Perimeter Base. We will take the next two or three days to work out any short-term logistical problems with you, and then we'll be heading out. Because of the possibility of significant developments while we're en route, we will run the leg in four-a-day pogo mode—more or less a monthly check-in schedule from your perspective.

"I'm sure that you have many questions, but most of them are particular to your specialty, so let's hold them for individual conferences. File your requests through the governor's office.

"One last matter," Wells said, standing. "Due to some reassignments related to these changes, I am going to need a new Chief of Staff for Defense. Colonel Shields, would you be interested in coming out to the Perimeter?"

Shields looked startled at first, then beamed. "Thank you, Commander Wells. I would be honored to have the opportunity to serve in that capacity."

"Then the job is yours. I'll see that your new orders are cut immediately," Wells said, and stood. "That's all, gentlemen. Let's get on it."

"I want an explanation," Chancellor Sujata said. Her tone was icy, the muscles of her face rigid.

Governor Hogue raised his hands in supplication. "Chancellor, I had no reason to think that Commander Wells was exceeding his authority by continuing on to the Perimeter. And even if I had known, it wasn't my place to stop him."

"How can you say that?" Berberon demanded. "Aren't you governor of this station? That makes you responsible for everything that happens."

Rising from his chair, Hogue turned his back on them and walked to the étagère on the facing wall. "Ambassador, I don't think you appreciate my position here," he said, absently adjusting the positions of the objects displayed on the shelves. "To the extent that I am an official of the Operations Branch, my job is to facilitate the work of our clients—the other branches of the Service. But beyond that I am a *military* governor. I have two masters. I am to treat instructions coming from the Defense Director as though they came from the Operations Director."

Hogue turned back toward them. "Now tell me where in there you find a basis for me to give orders to Commander Wells. No," he said, shaking his head, "if there are policy disagreements between the two branches, or between the Directors and yourself, they have to be settled on a higher level than a station governor."

"I accept your assessment of your authority, Governor," Sujata said placidly. "Now please give me your assessment of mine."

"Why, your authority here is absolute. You are the Chancellor."

"Very well. Triad Three is not to leave this station."

Hogue's face reddened. "Chancellor, I can't prevent it."

"Why not?"

"Triad's sailing orders come from Wells himself."

"I am countermanding them. I am ordering you as governor of this station to see that Triad Three remains in port."

"And I'm telling you, I can't issue such an order."

"The order comes from me, not you."

Hogue released an exasperated sigh. "I accept your authority, Chancellor. Probably the Defcom people here do too. But exercised through proper channels—through the Defense chain of command. Not through the likes of me."

"Are you saying you think they'll disregard that order?" Berberon asked.

"I know they will. Chancellor, they are well trained and well disciplined. And part of good discipline is knowing who's got the right to tell you to jump."

"But you do control station services," Berberon said. "Cut the power to the yards. Freeze them out. Disable the hangar doors. You can order that, can't you?"

"Yes," Hogue said. "I can do that. If that's what you really want."

"Why shouldn't we want it, if it will do the job?" Berberon asked.

"Triad One has already sailed. Triad Two is firmly in the hands of Defense. You won't be able to call either of those back unless you do it through Wells."

"So? We'll take our victories a piece at a time," Berberon said.

Hogue frowned. "It just seems to me that all you do by keeping Three here is weaken us just when we most need to be strong."

"Now you sound like Wells—" Berberon began, disgusted.

"Governor Hogue is right," Sujata said, unable to keep the tiredness out of her voice. "Wells doesn't need three Triads to start a war. Denying him this one won't solve the problem. It may even make it worse, because he will need all three and more to fight one." She sighed. "Would you leave us alone, please, Governor?"

"Of course," Hogue said.

The moment the door closed behind him, Sujata pitched forward in her chair and buried her face in her hands. Though she held back the tears, her own tortured breaths were loud in her ears.

"Janell—" Berberon said tentatively.

Though embarrassed by her display, she could not bottle up her despair any longer. "We'll never catch him," she said helplessly. "We'll never stop him. It was already too late when we started."

"You can't let yourself think like that," Berberon said, more stern than compassionate.

"What was it Teo told us Wells had said? 'When we find them, we will have to fight them. And we will find them.' That's the way it's going to be. It's no more complicated than that. Except that there's no way we can win."

"Where *is* Teo?" Berberon asked, nobly trying to change the subject. "I want to get his opinion of what Hogue said."

"He went to report to the Flight Office with the rest of the crew," she said, sitting upright and pressing her steepled fingers against her lips. "He'll be up presently."

Silence descended on the room, as though the mention of Farlad had constituted a pact not to continue until he was there. Sujata stared out at the arboretum Hogue's office overlooked and tried to summon up a semblance of enthusiasm.

"You know we're going to have to follow him to the Perimeter," Berberon said at last.

"I know," Sujata said. There was a long pause, and then she added with a resigned sigh, "I don't want to get back on that ship. But I suppose there's no good reason to postpone it."

"Governor Hogue said that *Charan* will be pogoing," Berberon said encouragingly. "There may even be a chance we can beat Wells to Perimeter Command."

Sujata nodded politely and reached for the com key. "Find Captain Hirschfield," she said. "I want to see him."

"Yes, Chancellor."

Sujata released the key, then suddenly tabbed it again.

"Yes, Chancellor?"

"Also, call the Security Annex and have them send up a couple of marshals. Put them somewhere Hirschfield won't see them and have them wait," she said. She looked up to find Berberon staring at her curiously, and smiled. "You know how we Maranit are when we don't get our way."

"Testy," Berberon said with a hint of a smile. "Can I be somewhere else?"

"You most certainly cannot."

When Hirschfield arrived twenty minutes later, it did not require a Maranit upbringing to be able to read his thoughts. There was a look in Hirschfield's eyes that said he resented being called there, a look that said, *I thought I was finished with you*. The set of his jaw telegraphed his determination not to cooperate.

Sujata read all that and more in him, but none of it mattered. It was no longer important to avoid conflict; indeed, she no longer had that luxury.

"Captain Hirschfield, how quickly can *Wesley* be ready to continue on to Perimeter Base?"

Hirschfield's gaze narrowed. "I don't understand your question. This is *Wesley*'s home port now. Or did you mean, how long would it take her to get there if needed?"

"Answer the question I asked. How much time will you need to get *Wesley* ready to sail for the Perimeter?"

Hirschfield was trying to guard his expression but with little success; his apprehension came through clearly. "The operational plan for *Wesley* specifies an alert response time of two hours—"

Glancing at the clock before she spoke, Sujata said, "Very well. Please return to the ship and supervise the preparations. Sailing time will be 11:30."

"Are you calling a drill, Chancellor?"

Sujata folded her hands on her lap. "No, Captain. I am telling you that in two hours we are continuing on to the Perimeter."

Hirschfield began shaking his head before Sujata was finished. "You don't understand. *Wesley* is the auxiliary fleet flagship. As such, her role is to be available to the command officers at the secondary command base, which is Lynx Center. *Wesley* is staying here."

"I understand perfectly. You seem to be the one having the difficulty. This is not a request or a suggestion. Ambassador Berberon and I are going to Perimeter Command. *Wesley* is taking us there."

"No, sir," Hirshfield said sharply. "Because you insisted on a quick getaway from Central, we left there without operational certification of *Wesley*'s weapons systems. *Wesley* has fifty man-weeks of final checkout due her, and she's going to get it here and now. I'm not about to take her farther out into the Perimeter without a fully operational lance."

"Captain Hirschfield, I am Chancellor of the Service. I am ordering you to take me to the Perimeter."

"I'm sorry, Chancellor. Adding yourself to the manifest back at Central was one thing. Even fiddling with our sailing date. But you're asking too much. We're under a Status-A alert. *Wesley* is staying here so that she can do the job she was built for."

"I'm not asking anything, Captain. That was an order."

"I take my orders from Commander Wells and the Flight Office, Chancellor. Not from you."

For a long moment they stared at each other with eyes that were hard and unyielding. Then Sujata raised one eyebrow questioningly as she turned away and touched the com key.

"Yes, Chancellor?"

"Please send in my other visitors."

"Yes, Chancellor."

A moment later the door opened and two lithe, well-muscled security officers came through the opening. They continued two steps into the room and then stood at attention, awaiting their orders.

"What is this?" Hirschfield demanded.

Sujata ignored him. "Captain Hirschfield is under arrest for willful insubordination," she told the officers. "He is to be held in custody until the mustering-out procedures are completed. The Ambassador and I will forward our depositions to the judge advocate by the end of the day."

"Yes, Chancellor," the taller officer said. "Captain?"

Hirschfield shot a black, putrescent look of pure will-to-harm in Sujata's direction, but allowed himself to be led away. When they were gone, Berberon made a clucking sound deep in his throat. "He didn't play that very smart."

"He didn't think he had to," Sujata said tersely. "He thought he had the better hand. Who's second-in-command?"

"Killea."

She reached for the com key.

"Yes, Chancellor?"

"Find Lieutenant Killea. Tell him what happened to Captain Hirschfield. Then tell him I want to see him." Sujata looked across at Berberon and managed a weak smile. "I hope we don't have to end up flying the ship ourselves because the crew is all in custody."

"Killea will get the message," Berberon said. "I only wish there was reason to think it would be that easy when we catch Wells."

Sujata frowned and shook her head. "Security is part of Operations. Those men work for Hogue. Where we're going, everyone works for Wells."

"As I was saying—I wish."

•   •   •

Farlad showed up just as Killea was leaving, making for a momentary traffic jam at the door to the office.

"Captain Killea is on his way to get the ship ready for a noon sailing," Sujata said. "We're continuing on to Perimeter Command."

Flashing a tight-lipped and troubled smile, Farlad said quietly, "I'm not."

"Why not?" Sujata asked.

"Wells left new orders for me. I'm to report for duty on board the recon ship *Falcon*. We're being sent into Sector Seven of the Mizari Zone—to begin surveying the black-flagged systems."

"Never mind that," Sujata said. "You're coming to the Perimeter with us."

Farlad shook his head. "This says that he knows, just as I told you he would. I can't be of any further use to you. But I can still be of some use to the Service."

"Teo, this is not necessary," Berberon said. "I am terminating your assignment. Resign your contract. You can return to Earth—"

"Can I?" he asked, holding his head cocked at an angle. "Return to who, or what? What use will the Council have for an agent whose training is thirty-five years out of date, who'll require not just retraining but a complete reeducation to be useful again?" He shook his head again slowly. "I don't want war to come. But if it is coming, I want to do my part to protect my homeworld. Do you understand?"

"Your attachment to Earth, yes," Sujata said. "The rest—no."

"I understand," Berberon said compassionately. "Teo—I'm sorry it worked out this way."

"Nothing to be sorry about," Farlad said. "But it would be all right with me if you manage somehow to make what *Falcon*'s going out there to do unnecessary."

"We'll keep that in mind," Berberon said with a wry smile.

After Farlad left, Sujata cast a weary glance in Berberon's direction. "We have about an hour. Do you need to talk to home before we head back out?"

"Yes."

"So do I," she said, standing. "You can use the terminal here. I'll let Hogue scare me up another one."

●   ●   ●

Even confined to a fifteen-centimetre screen, Tanvier managed to be imposing. Age had made his features cold, his sunken eyes remote. "There is no way that Farlad can carry out his instructions?"

"No," Berberon said. "He was right. Wells knows—or suspects. If Farlad shows up at Perimeter Command, all he'll manage to do is get himself busted down for not following the orders Wells left here for him."

"Then we will have to depend on you."

"Jean-Paul, I haven't the training—"

Tanvier's expression was hard and unyielding. "I will not let this insanity endanger what I've built. You went out there to solve a problem. The problem is still unsolved."

"What do you expect from me?" Berberon shouted. "You created the problem. You signed this devil's pact. This was never to be part of my responsibilities."

"I'm sure that when you have time to think about it, you'll realize your objections are foolish," Tanvier said, unmoved. "A lot of things that were never to happen, happened. You are on the scene. You will have to do what needs doing. Farlad's mission is now your mission. I have no doubt that you will accept that necessity before the time to do something about it is on you."

As the link was established, Sujata was shocked to see that Wyrena had cut her long, splendid hair, the symbol of her Ba'ar heritage. The woman staring back at her from the terminal was a stranger, not ten years younger than Sujata and refreshingly naïve but ten years older and serenely seasoned.

"Everything's coming apart," Sujata told the stranger. "Wells has gone on to the Perimeter, and we have to follow him. So that we have a chance to catch him, we're going to stay in the craze throughout the leg. You understand what that means—that you're going to have to do without any help from here for—I haven't even had time to figure out how long it will take us to run the leg."

Aware of her own weariness, Sujata plunged on. "Umm—we'll be leaving Rice and Scurlock and the rest of Wells's entourage here. They're no friends of ours, and there's no sense bringing them along. Oh, and I had to replace Captain Hirschfield—"

Sujata lost the thread of her thoughts and stopped. "I know there's five hundred things that need to be dealt with, and I can't think of the first one," she said finally. "I'm sorry. This has all happened so quickly, I'm still a little off-balance."

"It's all right," Ten Ga'ar said. "We'll manage."

"Vice Chancellor Walker will probably have to pick his own successor, without my approval. I suppose you'll need that authority in advance," Sujata rambled on. "And budget authority—"

"We'll deal with whatever needs doing," Ten Ga'ar said. "We have the mechanisms in place. You do what you need to. We'll keep the rest of the Service humming."

Her words made Sujata feel completely useless. "Of course you will. I don't know why I'm worrying about trying to help solve your problems when I can't even deal with my own," she said self-hatingly, and sighed. "We don't have much time before we have to board. Can you think of anything you need to know, anything I need to say to make what you do official?"

Ten Ga'ar shook her head slowly. "This is no different than when you were en route to Lynx. The Vice Chancellor will act in your name while you're out of touch."

Sujata found herself with nothing to say. "If it's that simple at your end, then I suppose it's time for good-bye. There are still one or two minor details here that require my attention—"

A compassionate look touched Ten Ga'ar's features. "Janell—don't stop believing in what you're doing. Wells is not beyond reaching. Remember the Canons."

"It seems like a very long time since you tried to teach them to me," Sujata said, unable to silence the defeated note in her voice.

Ten Ga'ar smiled affectionately. "For me, it not only seems, but is. But I believe in you, Janell. You have what is needed for this task. Only be certain that you know clearly what it is. Your goal is not to bend him to your will, to remake him as you would wish him to be. You must take him as he is. Know him, and you will have him. He is vulnerable to what he believes in. Remember that, and you will turn him."

Had her heart not been so filled with despair, Sujata would have found the reversal of roles amusing. "I wish I could hold you," she said, though what she meant was that she wanted to be held.

"I wish I could give you that," Ten Ga'ar said, as though

she understood. "But I know you will find the strength you need alone."

I'll have to, Sujata thought as she signed off. *Because that's what I am—alone.*

chapter 16

In the Palace
of the Immortals

In the three months he had been alone aboard *Munin*, Merritt Thackery had come to understand that he was losing a battle with madness. He knew that as certainly as he knew that the power to prevent it had already escaped him.

Since there was so little else to think of, he thought most often about the fragile structure of his own thoughts. But all his thinking, and all he had learned through it, had done nothing to stem the decline of his reason.

He understood that *Munin* was only a catalyst, not the cause. He had returned to her hopeful, in search of the sense of belonging he had last known aboard her. It was a vain hope, the kind that sprang from the heart to the will unexamined by the mind. He had been alone, and sought to end the aloneness. But now he was more alone than ever.

It could not have been otherwise. *Munin*'s compartments and climbways sang to him of the familiar, inundated him with images of times lost and faces forsaken. The curators of the Museum had been astonishingly thorough: either they had had the assistance of some of Thackery's former crew or the Service had known more about the details of life aboard its survey ships than he had realized.

His allovers, a bit snug now, were the size he had worn then; he had found them in the locker where he had always kept them. His food preferences were still programmed into the synthesizers. The ship's library contained nothing more recent than A.R. 538, the year of the Revision; nothing of the D'shanna, nothing of the Mizari, no word of the four colonies he had discovered—in fact, no mention of Thackery at all.

It was as though all the intervening years had simply not happened, as if it were still A.R. 538 and *Munin* was still searching for the beings who had stolen life from the Sennifi, still chasing the floating tomb of *Dove* among the stars of Lynx Octant. In a perversely fitting reversal it seemed as though, instead of being the one who had vanished, he had returned to the ship to find it suddenly empty of life. *Munin* screamed their absence to him, still bleeding from the wound made by that which had been torn from her—and from him.

The fact that he had not realized that it would be so told him that his madness had begun long before he had boarded her. But it had grown much worse in the days since. The evidence, perhaps even the cause, could be found in his changing reaction to the bridge holograms.

There were six of them, remarkably real, disturbingly faithful to Thackery's memories. Himself, of course, seated at the captain's station, one hand on his chin as he studied an image on the primary display. Derrel Guerrieri, who had been Thackery's shipmate from the time he left Earth as a novice surveyor until the day he left *Munin* to meet the D'shanna on the spindle. Feisty Gwen Shinault, whose engineering skill had rescued *Munin* from the scrap heap. Joel Nunn, the quiet, dependable astrographer. Elena Ryttn at the communications station.

And Amelia Koi—Amy, a gentle good spirit with whom he would have shared a lifetime. Duty had cut their days together abruptly short, had stolen any future that might have been. He had paid the price of conscience in the coin of her love, and from that day his conscience had never been at peace.

Five lost friends, near enough to touch yet forever beyond his reach. They spoke as well as moved—in their own voices, spliced or borrowed from recordings in the Service archives. To Thackery's eyes and ears they were real. Missing only was the tang of human habitation in the air, the hundred exhalations of life that made of the ship a friendly cave shared to escape a colder winter than *Homo neanderthalis* had ever known.

His first day aboard, Thackery stood by the climbway railing and watched the real-yet-not-real animations move through their five-minute ballet three times in succession. Then he broke down, crying. When he turned the projectors off, he vowed never to turn them on again. He knew the danger from the first. He sensed that to surround himself with such easy, but empty, comforts was to start down a road from which there would be no returning.

Yet on this day, three months later, he found himself well down that road. For there were six figures on *Munin*'s bridge: five ghosts and a man who was little more than that. Their motion stilled, their voices silenced, they stood as statues in a family gallery. One by one he had brought them back, first Derrel, then Elena, Joel, Gwen, and finally himself.

One place, though, was still empty. He could not, would not, try to bring Amy back that way, could not endure the reminder. And yet he could not ignore the message of the empty chair, nor stop himself from thinking of her. The conflict was yet another thread of his madness—a thread he had woven into the fabric himself.

Cognizant of the risk involved in his plan to return to Earth through the spindle, Thackery had thought it the merciful thing to allow Amy and the rest of *Munin*'s crew to think that he was dead—a goal accomplished when Gabriel allowed the corpse of *Dove* to plunge into the seething mass of a star.

But by that same act he had started an emotional time bomb ticking. After *Dove*'s destruction Amy had turned *Munin*, her captain and purpose gone, back toward home. By the time the Service came to grips with what Thackery had to tell them, *Munin* was already flying deaf, its crew believing a lie.

The lie could not endure. When *Munin* came out of the craze, Amy and the others would learn the truth—where he had been, what he had done, and that he was still alive. As inevitably as the sun must rise, someday the display would chime and a picture begin to form on the screen, a visage out of his past.

She would speak, and her words would destroy him. Either she would still love him, thirty years out of sync and twenty-five light-years out of reach, and her love would cost him the tenuous peace he had made with what he had done. Or she would hate him, and her hate would cost him the fond memories of the only woman with whom he had ever shared more than grief.

Thackery could not bear to face that day, that call, that accounting. So before it came, before it would come, he had taken a field assignment on Rena that he had no right to take and fled Earth in *Fireside*. Cocooned in the craze, he was safe from her, from the pain that could only come from connecting with her again.

But waiting for him when he reached Rena was the news that Amy had found she could bear to face it even less than he. While Thackery was in the craze, running from her in selfish cowardice, Amy had guided *Munin* into port, then resigned her Service contract. And when no one and nothing had call or claim on her, she had gone off alone and quietly taken her life.

Hearing that had cost Thackery more than peace or memories.

He wondered at times why he had not followed her lead and ended the pain. He did not fear death, confident as he was that it meant nothing more than the end of life, that darkness and not judgment awaited him. The only answer he could find to the riddle was that continuing to live was a punishment he inflicted on himself in expiation of his guilt.

Now Thackery shared the chair at his station with his own projection, the younger apparition poised in anticipation, the older submerged in dolor. Both gazed up at the bridge display, but only the ghost saw what appeared there. The images played on the real Thackery's retinas but were rarely perceived by his mind.

In that state, even the klaxonlike collision alarm did not quickly penetrate his consciousness. But when it did, he stirred in his seat and looked up at the screen hopefully, scanning for the reason for the alarm. He was not so far gone as to be beyond being rescued by novelty.

He was not sure at first what he was seeing. The star field began to shift as, having waited as long as it could for guidance, *Munin* moved to save itself. But the alarm continued to sound, and the star field continued to shift, as though *Munin*'s efforts were somehow being negated. Puzzlement gave birth to curiosity, and curiosity reclaimed for the moment the better faculties of his mind. His brow furrowed, Thackery studied the image intently, until at last he focused not on the glowing points of light but on what lay between them.

It was a growing sphere of darkness, a black destroyer rising from the shadows. Star after star winked out as the expanding edge of an emptiness more complete than space itself masked or swallowed them.

Thackery knew what the black star meant. He had seen it once before, from the spindle, and knew that there was little time. Even so, he stood staring openmouthed for long seconds before he realized that he was looking at his own death and that despite everything—this, his greatest madness—he did not want to die.

Moving slowly at first, his eyes riveted to the screen, he edged toward the climbway. When his hand brushed the cold metal of the railing, it seemed to galvanize him. Twisting away from the sight of the Mizari black star, he scrabbled down the rungs of the climbway until he reached the access door for the drive core. His mind was focused with a cold, crystal clarity it had not known for years.

For a terrifying moment the access door resisted. Then it swung free, and he dived through the opening recklessly, tearing a long gouge along one forearm. He did not even pause to notice the pain or blood. A touch on the engineering board, and the shield plates for coils sixteen and seventeen slid into their recesses, revealing a complex of spiral tubing seething with energy.

There was no time to do more than draw a deep breath and summon his will to live to the front of his consciousness. Reaching out with trembling arms, closing his eyes at the last instant, Thackery plunged his hands into the heart of the drive and seized hold of a whirlwind of fire.

Once his hands closed on the flesh of the demon, there was no releasing his grasp. Every muscle knotted in agony, every cell crying protest, he fought against the onslaught of energies seeking to steal his will. He clung there, huddled in a ball, screaming a scream that was at once a protest against his life and a howl of defiance.

His body was burning and he did not know whether from within or without. As his mind cried, *Where is the crossing*? *Where is the end*? the ship surrounding him dissolved into component atoms and vanished like a mist in sunlight. An instant later, oblivious to his fight for life and coherence, the universe of stars did the same.

• • •

The Defense Intelligence Data Analysis Center (DIDAC) was a mausoleumlike crypt within the bowels of Perimeter Command: one thousand locker-sized AI modules filling row upon row of floor-to-ceiling interface racks. Only the modules' rectangular faceplates were visible, featureless and identical except for the identifying number embossed in the upper right corner.

Quiet and dimly lit, DIDAC seemed to be a forgotten place, an electronic graveyard left over from some now completed task, an impression that cast the single data technician, moving quietly through the aisles with his cart of components and test gear, in the role of caretaker—or even undertaker.

But that impression, however outwardly justified, was wrong. The appearance of the modules belied both their capabilities and importance, and the restful peace of the corridors was in sharp contrast to the furious activity within the racks. For each of the modules was in fact a keen and highly specialized electronic mind, busily sorting through its share of the incessant deluge of data being gathered by the Defense Intelligence Office.

Operating under the dictum "You can never know too much or prepare too well," the Office eagerly monitored the output from every active Kleine unit within the Boötes and Lynx Octants. Each separate source was assigned a separate DIDAC module. A few modules were dedicated to major facilities such as Lynx Center, and a larger number to the various deep-ships patrolling in or simply traveling through the region.

But by far the majority of the modules were attending to the output of the eight hundred listening buoys that comprised the Shield. That was the task for which DIDAC had been built; all other functions merely reflected the Office's determination to find use for the system's consciously included reserve capacity.

Oblivious to tedium, undaunted by detail, the modules patiently panned the binary stream in a quest to find that most valuable commodity, information, among the wealth of valueless data. Though they could not be said to possess consciousness, they did possess curiosity—an insatiable curiosity for the irregular, the anomalous, the unexpected, the unexplained.

So the intelligence that was monitoring the dispatches from *Munin* was machine, not human. Until recently MOD 214 had been devoting its attention to the output of a buoy located in the Canes Venatici region of the Shield. But that particular buoy was currently being serviced by the Sentinel *Daehne*, and so MOD 214 had been assigned a secondary task.

That its new task was considered by the supervising human intelligences to be of less import than its old, MOD 214 had no awareness. It reviewed the complex of digitized data with the same perseverance it had devoted to its previous duty. And when it detected a discrepant event matrix, it reacted with no less urgency.

As clever and flexible as it was at sifting through the data, MOD 214 knew only three things to do in the event that its search was successful: to retrieve from downstream all previously passed-over data associated with the event; to route that data and any that followed to a save file; and to alert a human operator. MOD 214 did all three within a fraction of a second, then returned to its task. Curiosity about what happened next had not been included in its library of enablers.

The comtech who received MOD 214's alert was far from oblivious to tedium and only indifferently curious. In the first three hours of his four-hour shift, Paul Wilkins had been called on to examine nineteen discrepant event matrices detected by various DIDAC modules. None had been meaningful. In fact, during the five months he had served as a DIDAC operator, the most significant anomaly that had passed through his board was a minor buoy malfunction, which was only a Code Three event.

So when the alarm began sounding, Wilkins casually took the time to finish what he was saying to the operator on his right before turning lazily to his board.

"Tell me," he said, which silenced the alarm.

In the design of the DIDAC module, not much of its brainpower had been allocated for conversation. MOD 214's answer was typically terse. "Threat code, sector N15.30, survey ship *Munin*."

"Inference class?" Each DIDAC module monitored its own logic stream so that it could both reconstruct and evaluate the decision-making process. This provided the operators and the analysts in the Office with a tool for weighing conclusions that they could not hope to confirm independently. Class Five inferences were barely more than guesses: Class One, only fractionally less than certainty.

"Non-inferential. Direct observation."

"Show me," Wilkins said, suddenly chilled.

For several seconds he watched in stunned silence as the black star closed with *Munin*. He knew that he should act, but the sight transfixed him. They're coming out, he thought, and the thought paralyzed him. The Mizari are coming out.

The operator to Wilkins's right saved him, reaching across from his station to touch the com key. "Station 31 paging the watch commander—"

Wilkins took over in a shaky voice. "I have a Code One event in sector N15.30, survey ship *Munin* under attack—"

Before the watch commander could respond, it was over. A flare of energy from the black star seemed to burn out *Munin*'s eyes, followed a few seconds later by a dispassionate announcement from MOD 214: "Active mode gone. Transponder gone. *Munin* LOS. Munin destroyed."

"Inference class?"

"Class One."

"Aggressor ID?" asked Wilkins's neighbor, now standing over him.

Even knowing the answer, it was a jolt to hear it: "Mizari."

"Inference class?" Wilkins whispered.

"Class One."

Before the day was over, the record of *Munin*'s final moments would be replayed a score of times—for the watch commander, for the head of the Defense Intelligence Office, for the station commander. For the captains of all the Sentinels and tenders on the Perimeter. For Governor Hogue at Lynx and Deputy Director Barnes at Central. And for Acting Commander of Perimeter Defense Osten Venngst, who was reponsible, with Wells incommunicado in the craze, for ordering the Service's response.

No matter where the dispatch was played, or for whom it was played, always it ended the same: "*Munin* destroyed. Aggressor ID: Mizari."

By such simple words did they learn that the fighting had begun.

Cocooned in the tissue of his own consciousness, Thackery allowed himself to be tossed and buffeted by the tides and currents of the spindle. He had no energy to spare for rejoicing that he was, in at least an abstract sense, still alive.

The crossing had been difficult, and he was acutely aware of the savaging the finer elements of his new structure had suffered. Shielding himself from the turbulence with the strongest surviving elements of his personality, Thackery endeavored to restore what he could.

Where an echo, fast fading, or a shimmering fragment, fast dissipating, remained to remind him of the elegant shape and complex synergy of the element it represented, there was hope. But that which had been torn free and swept away, without even a pale, harmonic ripple to show something had been there, these things he could not reconstruct. He could not even catalog what had been lost.

The wounds had been grievous, and for the most part, his repairs were crude. He felt as though he were struggling to assemble with maul and mallet the delicate parts of a fine and complex watch. With every well-intentioned movement he sent the tiny gears and catches scattering, losing three for every one he captured.

But still he persisted, tracing down each thread of his consciousness, weaving loose ends back into the pattern, forging connections where it seemed proper to do so. And presently there came a point at which he had recouped enough of his faculties to spare some small portion for other concerns, among them wondering how he had survived.

Thackery was unable to summon concrete remembrances of the moments in which he had passed from *Munin*'s drive core to the spindle. He sensed that, rather than projecting himself by a simple act of will, he had been drawn across the barrier when the drive was destroyed and the aperture closed. His achievement had been to maintain the integrity of his consciousness long enough for that moment arrive.

Because I remembered. Because I have been here before. The thoughts formed clearly and easily, and their resonances were true.

Time passed and his understanding grew. He saw that the bulwark surrounding him was nothing less than his will to live, bolstered by the clean, simple structure of his reason. Within that shell he found, drifting free, pale threads of his curiosity and a mote that was a memory of a word. He restored both to their station and felt himself grow.

I am D'shanna now, he thought, and unfolded.

He had remembered the spindle as a place of great beauty —a place where currents of energy—like long, gentle swells, each with its own hue and timbre and taste—collided miscibly and immiscibly in a rhythm that seemed random and chaotic until the mind's far eye abstracted the pattern.

But this time Thackery opened his senses to a landscape full of fury. He had not realized the strength of his shield, nor the violence of the assault against it, and for long moments he wavered on the brink of retreating. But the need to see, to know, was complete in him, while fear was a shrunken fragment. He steeled himself against the battering and looked outward into infinity.

The resonance that was Thackery was drifting like a mote in a great Brownian sea near the interface between the matter-matrix he knew as the Universe and the energy-matrix of the spindle. The interface, propagating like a slow-moving ripple from the cataclysm of origin in which the two matrices had been separated to the cataclysm of terminus in which they would be reunited, marked what those he had left behind called the present. Downtime, there were only echoes; uptime, only anticipations.

There had been turbulence here before, he remembered. Every ship's drive was a whirling sinkhole, every Kleine message a hard-edged resonance slicing through the fibers of the spindle. There were more ships and more messages now, and so a greater disturbance.

But there was also a powerful tide from uptime, an incursion of discordant energies whose shadowy dark colors blocked the far view. Thackery could name neither its source nor its substance, but it proclaimed its own power to his eyes. It was the shadow tide that drove the storm holding the spindle in its grip.

Thackery was abruptly aware of his isolation. As far as his senses could reach, even deep into the quiet downtime, he perceived no other resonances like his own. If the D'shanna could be said to have a birthplace, it was here, cradled between future and past. This was the one point at which the constructs of both matrices could be said to be real, real enough to manipulate, and yet not so real as to be unchangeable.

When last he had come there, the exodus uptime had already begun, tens of thousands of D'shanna migrating away from the intruding human presence. But even so, Thackery had known the presence of many of Gabriel's kind, and now he felt their absence.

Gabriel. Each thought Thackery formed seemed to contain reflected in its fine resonances a dozen more, and so the healing continued. This was a good thought, a strong thought, rich in implication and memory.

Gabriel . . . He sent the namepattern out into the chaos with little hope of answer. If Gabriel still endured, he was with the other D'shanna in the far uptime near terminus, beyond the chaos of nearer tomorrows. Thackery was alone in the interface zone, alone and uncertain of what next to do . . .

. . . for one of the threads that had eluded him in the course of his self-resurrection was purpose. He had found the place where it belonged, the anchor points that cried out for its presence, but the wounds there were nearly healed, as though purpose had been lost not in the transition but sometime long before.

He remembered how time had weighed on him, on Earth, in *Munin*. Now he had nothing but time. There was death on the spindle, or at least nonexistence. All he need do is let go, open himself to the dark currents and let them scatter his energies. It would be an easy death, without pain, without rancor. But he could not let go. That which had protected him through transition and rebirth also protected him against the impulse to die.

So time remained, perhaps time without ending. In the absence of purpose Thackery could at least indulge his curiosity, for he had conceived a question, and a question demanded an answer.

All the Universe was spread below him, all the past stretched out behind him. The art of seeing was still within him, and he opened himself to let the echoes of reality pour into him. Patiently—for he had time in abundance—he sifted through the echoes for familiar images, for places and moments congruent with the resonance of memory. He reached with his senses across the barrier and surrounded himself with the Universe, seeking the creatures that had driven him here, searching for the face of the enemy.

Hard by the thin nebulosity that had been *Munin,* two stars whirled in an oscillating ballet. The dancers were ill-matched, the larger a brilliant white, the smaller a pale yellow. They were joined in their dance by a small, rocky world tracing what seemed a perilous course between them. The planet's echoes said nothing of life, and yet there was something.

Thackery focused his sight and scanned the face of the whirling mote. It was a desolate place, hard-edged, dry, airless. Nowhere on its surface could he find the signature of life. Nowhere was there a sign that this was the world that had launched the black star. And yet there was something— Something more—

A sound heard at the periphery of sensation—

Not sound but muted song. Not voice but discordant chorus. He listened with ears newly opened to a clacking, whining sound that made him think of swarming nests of ants and flights of angry bees. But where was the source? Nothing moved on the dead planet's surface.

The sound seemed to emanate from the planet's entire surface, but not uniformly so. He let his senses follow the voice of one of the loudest singers and found there, set in the cold stone surface of the planet, a shallow crystalline dome. He probed past its smooth, unmarked surface and sensed a confusion of electrical currents within the solid mass of silica-quartz, of energies received and transmuted, then emitted again.

Was this life? Could this be life? But he sensed no pattern in the currents, no sense to the song. If there was Mind here, he could not touch it. Life, perhaps, but not intelligence— merely the pointless stirring of matter in obedience to the impulse from within. These sun-eaters could not be the builders of the black star.

Thackery widened the focus of his viewing both across and below the planet's surface. There were many of the crystal creatures, and he sensed the synergy among them. Even life without purpose obeys the imperative of interdependency. A whole ecology of meaninglessness—

But as he stretched himself in an effort to absorb the ecology of this strange world in its entirety, a new and shocking perception forced itself on him without warning. For a brief instant he brushed up against the energies of a powerful Mind, powerful enough that he flinched from the contact defensively.

Even so, that moment was enough to show him what he had seen without seeing—a Mind that harnessed energy directly in the substance of its body, without the need for mechanical contrivance. A Mind that embraced an entire world and looked out from it with one sight that embraced an entire Universe.

Such were the Mizari. Such were the enemies of humanity. Thackery did not need to probe the Mind of this Mizari nest to discover its self-name, for he knew that it would carry the same thread of meaning as all self-names: *We are that which is worthy—we are life*.

How came you here? he asked of the Mind. *How long ago did you make your claim*?

He did not expect nor receive answers and so began to search for them on his own.

Leaving the turmoil of the interface behind, Thackery began to push his way downtime, against the steady past-to-future current of the spindle. His senses, still focused on the Mizari world, now embraced echoes that were true but not real.

Bare moments after he began his sojourn he was a spectator to his own death, the only witness as the black star appeared, closed on *Munin* and destroyed her, and then vanished. But even from his privileged position he could not see whence the black star came or to where it went. He shrugged his puzzlement aside and continued on.

The years unrolled before his eyes, the worlds spinning backward in their courses, a hundred, a thousand, a hundred thousand years, and still the Mizari owned the barren planet. A million years, ten million, and still the Mizari persisted, their song declaring their presence. It seemed as though as long as there had been a planet, the Mizari had been there. They were more than visitors. They were part of its substance.

An ancient species they are—old already when humankind was being born. If they had wanted it, the galaxy could have been theirs. They had time, and the black stars to carry them—

Still farther back Thackery flew, until the stars in that region of space began to converge and the nebula out of which they had formed to reappear. As they came together he heard across the unimaginable distances another Mizari voice, and a third, and a fourth, each singing the same song, yet each singing a song all its own.

Like great whales cruising the black depths of the sea, each alone save for the distant voice of its kin—

Thackery realized with sudden certainty where he was, what he was witnessing. He knew the names of these newly young stars and the shape they would one day make in Earth's night skies: Alioth. Merak. Megrez. Phad. Alcor. Mizar. But there were a hundred more, spawn of the same mother but not the same litter, returning from haunts more widely scattered in space: Menkalinan. Sirius. Aldhafera. Ras Alhague.

As the stars and their planets dissolved into whirling disks of gas and dust, and as the disks merged into a great coalescing cloud, the Mizari song was finally stilled, and Thackery understood at last. This glorious unnamed nebula, alive with turbulence, had given birth not only to the Ursa Major Cluster but to the Mizari as well.

The evolutionary pressure that had shaped their nature and their powers was the same that had shaped the planets that were their homes. The same process had bound them inextricably to those worlds. No new Mizari nests had been founded since the cluster had dispersed. Those that existed in Thackery's time had existed since the beginning. These were not creatures oriented to dominion and conquest. By their very essence they were creatures shaped by the single imperative of survival.

Thackery tried to form the namepattern for an intelligence that had known fifty million years without death, whose body massed ten million times that of the largest life-forms Earth had ever known, whose perspective embraced the spectacle of the Universe from every direction and across immense spans of time. He failed. It was a conception too great for Thackery as he was. He would have to grow before he could accept it into himself.

There was one riddle left unanswered—the black star. But with what he now knew, Thackery understood what it must be. A species existing on a planetary scale could only be endangered by a catastrophe on the same scale. The black star was the reason the airless Mizari world he had studied was oddly unscarred by craters. It was the means by which a handful of Mizari nests had survived the violence of planet-making. Guardian, shield, it stood between the Mizari and a deadly fall of stones.

Drifting uptime along a different fiber of the spindle, Thackery acquired the proof he did not require. He watched the two Mizari worlds of Alcor turn aside a thousand wayward planetoids, vaporize a hundred wandering comets—even, in time, shatter whole planets and drive their fragments into the sun—until the system was swept clean of all that might endanger them.

The black star appeared when needed, disappeared when

its task was done. For it was neither star nor ship, nor could it even be said to be real. It was a weapon without substance, which could not be destroyed because it did not exist at the point where it appeared to the senses. It was an instrumentality for their collective will, a receiver for their energies. And the channel for those energies led through the spindle.

Panthers had their claws, piranha their teeth. The Mizari had the Mind's Shout—an ancient reflex still slumbering within them, a terrible savage power still at their command.

Sixty thousand years ago the Mizari had swept away the *Weichsel,* not in retribution but in response to an imperative as deeply ingrained in them as the will to live. Now Thackery had unwittingly repeated the transgression of the Weichsel iceship so long ago. Withdrawing his senses from beyond the spindle, he hastened to rejoin the present, wondering as he flew across the years how high the price would be this time.

chapter 17

The Provider's Voice

Midway between Lynx Center and Perimeter Command, *Tilak Charan* emerged from the craze at the leading edge of the gravitational track that betrayed its position among the stars of Leo Minor. At the bidding of its comtech *Charan*'s instruments reached out and snatched from the ether the recognition sign and ready-to-link signal of its destination, toward which the ship continued to hurtle with barely less urgency than before.

In the privacy of his cabin Wells waited patiently for the pale blue WAITING FOR CARRIER message to vanish from the display. Two minutes of waiting exhausted his patience, and he touched the com key. "Problem, Mr. Stevens?"

"Sorry, sir. A little trouble picking it out of the scruff, that's all," the comtech said. "Should be coming up now."

A moment later the pallid-skinned, mustachioed face of Osten Venngst appeared on the screen. Venngst glanced to his left, as though listening to someone standing there out of view, then nodded and looked down at his lap as though consulting a slate. "Time mark, 710.245. Defense status: We are at Code One alert throughout the entire Perimeter—"

"What's happened?" Wells demanded, unable to contain

his alarm. "Why are we in a war alert?"

"Sir, two months ago we received a positive confirmation on an active Mizari nest in the One Corona Borealis system," Venngst said. "The rogue ship *Munin* was entering the system on a survey run and was destroyed by a hostile by means of an intense burst of black-body radiation. Fortunately *Munin* was relaying data right up until the end, so we did get a good look at their weapons. But since the attack came so quickly, the system survey is very sketchy and we could not establish where within the system the Mizari are based."

For the first time since he had set his course fifteen years ago, Wells felt the stabbing chill of uncertainty. A touch on the terminal command board brought a map of the Boötes and Lynx Octants up in place of Venngst's face. "One Corona Borealis—that's Alphecca, yes? What the hell are the Mizari doing there at all? That's way outside the cluster. If they've gotten that far, they could be anywhere."

"Yes, sir. The strategy staff here is *very* concerned, as you might imagine."

This is my own damn fault. Thackery wouldn't have been out there if I hadn't been feeling soft about him. Damn, damn, damn. These always come back to bite you. Wells chased the map from the screen with a touch. "What action have you taken?"

Venngst acknowledged the question with a nod. "I immediately placed all elements of the Perimeter Defense on highest alert. I also exercised my preemptive authority under Status-A mission rules to divert Triad One from its patrol circle. Triad One is now in the high craze to Alphecca with instructions to locate and destroy the Mizari nest."

Wells frowned and sat forward in his chair. "I presume these attack orders conform to the specifications of the Strategy Committee."

"Yes, sir. As per your instructions, Captain Lieter's orders are presumptive-go, and he was given full command discretion. Triad One will come out of the craze twelve hours before system contact to pick up the most current intelligence and to provide a final opportunity for a wave-off—you'll be on-station by then, incidentally. Absent a recall at that time, he will go back into the craze and not drop out again until beginning the actual assault run."

"Very good, Osten."

"There is one other matter," Venngst said. "I took the liberty of amending the standard battle order to provide an additional opportunity for a wave-off, approximately six weeks from now on the PerCom time track. The command lineship only will come out of the craze for a twenty-minute Kleine troll—"

Wells slammed his palm down on the console beside him. "Damn it, Osten, all that does is give them a chance to get two fixes on our ships and a track back to our facilities on this side of the Perimeter."

"I thought this additional exposure was justified," Venngst said defensively. "Sir, I ordered Triad One to Alphecca with serious reservations about the wisdom of doing so. Yes, it was the response dictated by the strategic plan—except the strategic plan didn't anticipate a target so far removed from what we always considered the primary front. I wanted you to have an opportunity to countermand my attack authorization if you thought it more important to keep Triad One at home than to make a swift, punitive response."

Venngst hesitated, then glanced down at his lap again. "I understand that you may wish to convene the Strategy Committee to discuss this, so we are prepared to hold this link open as long as necessary."

"Has there been any additional activity in or near the One Cor Bor sector?"

"No, sir. We have sixteen buoys focused on the hot zone, and they've seen nothing. However, we are somewhat limited by the fact that the buoys out on the fringe have never been upgraded since their original deployment. At the moment we can't even pick up the Mizari EM signature *Munin* was monitoring."

"Status of the other Triads?"

"Fully operational and on their patrol circles."

"And the recon ships?" Wells asked, calling back the map.

"No change. *Eagle* is inbound to the 285 Lynx system, to make contact with the Feghr colony. *Kite* has completed a survey of the Megrez system, negative outcome, and is continuing on to Alioth. *Falcon* is headed for 17919 UMa. All this is in the report we high-banded to you at the top of the link. We'll stand by while you and the Committee review it."

"Not necessary," Wells said. "Your ambivalence about the Alphecca mission was unnecessary. I'm confirming your attack orders for Triad One. Send Lieter a scram signal so that he'll get his ship back up in the craze as quickly as possible."

Venngst seemed relieved. "Yes, Commander."

"But you didn't go far enough," Wells continued. "It's strategic suicide to sit around waiting for them to take the first swing on the primary front too."

Swallowing hard, Venngst said, "We thought that considering the length of the run to Alphecca, we could afford to defer on that until you'd been put in the picture."

"You shouldn't have," Wells said bluntly. "I assume you'd have told me if we'd picked up any additional probables?"

"There are none, sir. Mizar-Alcor and Phad are the only systems displaying the EM signature."

"All right—what follows are formal command orders, to be abstracted into both *Charan's* command log and your command log there. *Eagle* is to be redirected from the Feghr contact to survey 21 Leo Minor. We can't offer the people of Feghr any protection, so there's no point in possibly betraying their presence to the Mizari. *Kite* is ordered to proceed directly to Phad and conduct a pre-assault recon. *Falcon* is to proceed directly to Mizar-Alcor and do likewise there. All best speed and minimum exposure."

"Confirming, *Eagle* to 21 Leo Minor, *Kite* to Phad, *Falcon* to Mizar-Alcor, Code One rules."

"Yes," Wells said, settling back in his chair. He felt strangely calm. "On my authority you are also instructed to deploy Triad Two on a presumptive-go mission to Mizar-Alcor, ditto Triad Three to Phad. I want the wave-offs scheduled so that they get every last bit of data from the recons, and I want the assaults as tightly scheduled as possible, so the Mizari don't have a chance to learn from experience. Clear?"

"Yes, Commander Wells. Clear. We're going in after them."

Oh, certainly—the vainglorious quest for honor, the challenge and glory of combat, Wells thought. *All the easier to embrace because you will not huddle in the tunneled dark spaces of a Triad hull bargaining with Death. But what choice do we have? What choice have we ever had?*

But his thoughts were thoughts to which no Commander could admit ownership, and he stilled their voice inside him. What were needed now were words that Venngst could pass to the crews of the Triads, words that conformed to image and expectation.

"Damn right we are," Wells said. "It's time to hit back."

• • •

On a long leg in the high craze there was little to do aboard *Wesley* except mark time. The crew found the long watches tedious and the time between them a challenge to their capacity for self-amusement. Nothing changed except money from one hand to another and bodies from one bed to another.

With neither those diversions nor even the alternative of work available to her, Sujata's days were even longer and harder to fill. She and Berberon were outsiders: out of deference or vindictiveness or both, the crew had effectively closed them off from ship life.

Oh, they recognized her right to go anywhere without being challenged, but her presence was accepted rather than welcomed. When she appeared in a compartment, conversations came to a halt, and they regarded her with looks that were wary at their core. They acknowledged her right to inquire into any aspect of ship operation, but she knew only that which she asked about. Except for an occasional tidbit from Captain Killea, nothing was ever volunteered.

Perhaps they thought that she wanted nothing more than that. A few probably thought that Berberon filled whatever social needs she had—the same few who kept alive the ugly jokes about the nature of their relationship. Killea had said nothing to Sujata about it—she learned of it directly from ship's records—but he had already disciplined two crew members for "propagation of salacious and unsubstantiated anecdotes disrespectful of the office of Chancellor generally, and Chancellor Sujata personally." Rather than putting an end to it, no doubt Killea's action had simply taught the crew not to repeat such jokes in his presence.

In truth, Berberon had been very poor company since *Wesley* had left Lynx three weeks ago. His characteristic cheeriness and volubility had vanished without warning in the wake of their failure to catch Wells there. The removal of Wells's staffers from *Wesley* left them with separate cabins, and Berberon rarely left his. He would sit quietly in the dark for hours, thinking unimaginable thoughts.

When he did emerge, Berberon was at best polite and cooperative. It was as though he no longer felt the need or could summon the energy to raise the smiling mask he formerly wore. But he offered no explanations, and for a time Sujata respected his privacy.

But one evening when the empty hours and the silence were wearing on her, she came to his cabin to find him sitting on the far end of the lower bunk, chin propped on his steepled hands, staring vacantly at the wall. Settling at the opposite end of the bunk, she broached the issue with an attempt at humor.

"What have you done with the real Felithe Berberon?" she asked. "Did you replace him at Lynx, or is he still on board somewhere?"

He responded to her words as though being called back from somewhere, his eyes seeking hers, his face suddenly reanimated. "I'm afraid my thoughts have been largely unhappy ones, and I have never seen much point in sharing unhappiness."

"Why unhappy?"

Berberon glanced upward at the cabin ceiling. "Such a little world this is, this ship," he said. "Coming out from Earth we had the daily dispatches to unite us with the rest of humanity, to give us new things to think about. But flying deaf in the craze this way, all the way to PerCom—"

"It's the only way to be certain we catch Wells."

"I know that," Berberon said. "But he could have changed his plans, his schedule, even his destination when he learned that we were still following him. They could be fighting the war even now. I don't know how you deal with the uncertainty."

"Wells will be there," Sujata said with the confidence of the desperate. "We will have a chance to change his mind."

Berberon sighed. "When I am not feeling any more than my normal measure of cynicism, I, too, think that he will be there. But I can take no comfort in that, because I hold little hope that you will succeed in dissuading him,.."

Sujata's eyebrows narrowed in surprise. "Once you told me that you thought I was the only one who could persuade Wells not to do this. Or what else was that long harangue on the biology of aggression about?"

"About nothing, it seems. You'll recall that I was unable to convince you."

"Which doesn't mean that I ignored what you said."

"Yes—your research project. From which you learned too little or learned it too late. It doesn't matter now," Berberon said tiredly. "Besides, you misremember what I said. I thought you had promise as one who could stop Wells. I never believed that you could change him."

"It isn't necessary to change Wells—just this particular decision."

Berberon slapped the cot with his right hand. "But don't you see, what he's doing comes from what he is. He's listening to voices he doesn't know how to say no to, voices that have been working on him all his life. You can't hope to turn him around with a few well-chosen words." He let his head tip back until it rested against the bulkhead and he was staring up at the ceiling. "This is pointless. You don't believe it even now."

Sighing, Berberon closed his eyes. "It isn't your fault," he went on. "Admitting that we have an animal nature is not easy. Harder still is the truth that it controls us as much or more than we control it. We are too proud, we humans, too attached to the idea of our own free will. It took generations for the simple truth of evolution to become part of the educated concept of who and what we are."

Sujata allowed an affectionate smile to touch her lips briefly. "I liked the old Felithe better—the silver-tongued schemer who always had five angles on the situation and smiled so much, you knew right away you couldn't trust him."

Berberon straightened up and met her eyes squarely. "If you see him," he said dourly, "tell him he can have his job back."

"Felithe," Sujata said gently, reaching out to pat Berberon's knee. "I did listen to you back then. I listened then, and I've been listening ever since, everywhere, to everyone. Trying to hear what's not said, to find the common threads that you said linked so much together. I found something—not what you said I would find but something all the same. Will you let me take you away from your misery long enough to tell you what I learned? I think perhaps I can promise you a little hope."

Shifting to a more comfortable position, Berberon managed a weak smile and a weaker joke. "Very well, Janell. But only a little hope, please. I am afraid that in my condition, I might suffer an allergic reaction to the full dose."

The energy resonance that called itself Merritt Thackery had learned much since returning uptime from the birthplace

of the Mizari. He knew now the cause of the storm that raged
in the near uptime. He had learned how to hear the echoes of
Mizari thoughts and to resolve the patterns of their unimaginable antiquity and fundamental alienness. He carried within
him as new harmonics the imperatives that were integral to the
Mizari mind.

What he did not know was if he would ever be able to tell
another human what he knew.

While roaming the interface and garnering new understanding, he had been confident that he knew how to reach
across the barrier. The Kleine units on every ship and station
were linked through the spindle. The subharmonic that carried
the coded patterns of communication was as open and exposed
as an unshielded cable, vulnerable to the tumult of the interface, open to Thackery's touch.

He had thought it would be a simple matter to manipulate
the Kleine waves, to reshape them to carry his message
throughout the net. They would not be able to ignore the
image and message of a dead man, images originating from
nowhere, invading the system from somewhere outside reality,
messages comprised of warnings and portents.

But when he tried, he failed. He thought at first that the
waves were too subtle and his efforts too clumsy. But when he
focused his senses more clearly on the Kleine harmonic, he
saw that his touch was deft enough. Following the altered
waves outward, he learned that the fault was not his. Every
change he effected, every thought he injected, lasted only
until the waves dived back beyond the barrier and reached the
machines that waited patiently in the loop to sift the wheat
from the electronic chaff. To those machines his messages
were merely noise to be suppressed.

The only possibility remaining in Thackery's limited inventory of ideas was to drive himself down to the barrier and
reach across to plant his thoughts directly into the mind of a
chosen individual, echoing the way Gabriel had reached out
and touched the mind of a young Merritt Thackery.

But Thackery was determined not to make the mistake that
Gabriel nearly had. He had searched across time and space to
discover the one who could act on what she would learn from
him, and then had searched again to find her. Now he looked
down on the ship that carried her, looked down into the swirling vortex of its drive, down through the hull and bulkheads.

He found her young and vibrant resonance cocooned within a cabin with a second, more subdued. She was speaking, and Thackery opened his senses to hear both her words and the inner voice that declared her namepattern.

Her words said, "It's as if there are two distinct ethics in the human ethos—a provider ethic and a preserver ethic. The provider ethic is about acquiring. It says that if one slain deer is good, two is better. The preserver ethic is about keeping. It says that there is a point at which it is more important to protect what you have than to run the risks involved in acquiring more."

Focusing his substance and energy, Thackery drove himself downward in an attempt to project himself into the cabin between them. If he could stretch the barrier until it touched her, if she could hear his echoes the way he heard hers—

Chancellor Sujata—listen to me. What we are—you are— means nothing now. What matters is what the Mizari are. Listen and I will tell you. They harness the energy of the spindle through their Mind's Shout. They destroy out of a reflex twenty times older and more finely honed than any you may carry in your bodies.

But Sujata showed no awareness of Thackery's nearness. "I hear the provider ethic in the words said over fallen soldiers: He died for a good reason, in a good cause," she was saying. "And you rarely question the claim. How can you? You are the ones left behind, the ones for whom they sought to provide. You must honor them or demean yourselves.

"When a capitalist talks about defending market share or evaluating a return on investment, I hear the provider fretting over poaching in his traditional hunting ground and deciding whether the fur of a black bear is worth the risk of dying trying to take it. When an engineer wonders how to use a new discovery, when a runner celebrates his victory over the pack, when an explorer plants a flag in the ice of an uninhabitable mountaintop—I hear the provider ethic in all of these.

"The provider ethic is always looking forward to tomorrow, to the next challenge, the next conquest. The preserver ethic is more interested in savoring today—"

Listen, won't you listen! Close your mouth and open your mind. It was the Mind's Shout that crushed the Weichsel, that sterilized the planet. And they are stronger now than they were then.

But Sujata was listening to her companion rather than to Thackery. "What you are saying is nothing more than what I said to you, dressed up in different clothing," Sujata's companion was saying. "You've found new words to describe the urging of the reptile hindbrain to fight and of the limbic system to love. I *am* heartened by your enlightenment, even though it's much overdue. But I see no reason yet to hope that Wells will suddenly become tractable."

"Perhaps there is a genetic root to all this, as you say," Sujata said. "But if there is, the genes reside not on the sex chromosomes but somewhere else in our genome. This is the key difference, and the reason to hope. Aggression is not the exclusive province of the male. Nurturing is not the exclusive province of the female. They are complementary principles, not only within the species but within each individual.

"Yes, for most people, one or the other dominates their outward behavior. But those who embrace one ethic to the exclusion of the other cannot survive. The provider dies a death of reckless courage. The preserver dies a death of unchecked fear. Both ethics coexist in everyone. Which means that Wells, provider archetype though he is, has within him the capacity to understand an argument couched in the preservation ethic."

The proximity of the drive taphole and its turbulence, the struggle to stand against the currents near the barrier between matter-matrix and energy-matrix, the sustained effort to project himself beyond it and seize Sujata's consciousness, all were taking their toll on Thackery. He sensed the weakening of his will, his mind, his substance, and sensed, too, the imminent necessity to abandon his effort and retreat to repair himself once again.

There was enough time left for one last effort, all his energy concentrated on opening a single infinitesimally small passage, all his consciousness focused on forming simple concrete thoughts of great internal coherence:

Listen to me!
The Mizari want nothing we have.
They are not demons.
They are not destroyers.
Leave them be and live.
Disturb them and die.

Sujata suddenly looked ceilingward. "How very strange," she said. "Felithe—come feel this. It's been getting hotter where I'm sitting—it must be fifteen degrees hotter right here than in the rest of the room. Can you feel the air moving? Like a breeze. But there's no vent overhead. Do you think there could be a fire somewhere behind the ceiling plates?" she said, fretting.

The channel was minute, the link fragile. But it was real, and Thackery called on the last of his reserve to force his thoughts across to Sujata.

Yes, touch me, listen! They can find us anywhere if they have reason to. They watch the sky with their whole being. They hear the whispers of their kin across the light-years. There is no defense. There will be no warning. The black star will simply appear, and there will be death.

Then, abruptly, it was over. Drained, battered, Thackery was torn away from the point of contact by the surging currents. Instantly the normal balance between the matrices reasserted itself, and the channel vanished as thoroughly as if it had never existed.

Thackery could not afford to concern himself with the loss. It was all he could do to keep from being drawn into the drive vortex and consumed. Tacking away from the dangerous eddies, he cocooned himself within his life-will and allowed the currents to bear him inward, away from the barrier.

He did not look back. He could not. He did not need to. He had sensed no answering recognition from Sujata's inner voice. She had not heard.

Kneeling on the end of the bunk, Sujata passed her right hand slowly through the air above her head. "This is so odd —can you feel it at all? Perhaps I should find the ship's med-tech instead of the environmental engineer—"

"It does seem a little warm," Berberon said politely.

"It's fading now," Sujata said, frowning and shaking her head. She waved her hand experimentally a few more times, then sat back on her heels. "Whatever it was, it's gone." She looked toward Berberon and smiled ruefully. "I'm sorry. You were about to say something and I interrupted you."

With a slight shrug and a shake of his head, Berberon demurred. "Nothing of consequence."

"Tell me at least if you share my hope."

"I wish I could say yes—"

"But you can't. Why?"

Berberon sighed and looked down at his folded hands. "Because even if you are right in everything you say, even if my view has been too mechanistic and I took too little account of heart and mind, all you can offer is talk. And it's too late for talk. It was too late already once Wells left Earth. He's committed too much. Even if there was a time when he would have listened, when he could have understood, that chance was lost. He won't listen now."

"I don't understand," Sujata said, her brow furrowed. "If you believe that, then why are you here? Why did you come? Oh, I know I insisted, but I couldn't have forced you. If you thought we had no chance, why put yourself through this?"

Berberon raised his head and held her gaze with sad and tired eyes. "A simple reason," he said. "There is something that, if it can be done at all, I am the only one who can do. You see, Janell, if you fail, then I must try to kill him." He smiled self-mockingly. "Tell me, if you can, in which ethic I will find comfort if I succeed."

chapter 18

Koan

Sujata and Berberon made a point of being on *Wesley*'s bridge as the ship made its inbound exit from the craze. Since they had no responsibilities there, they also had no stations at which to sit. Ignored, they stood together in the observer's dais a few steps behind Killea's command couch, Sujata with arms crossed over her chest, Berberon nervously plucking at the skin below his lower lip with the thumb and forefinger of his right hand.

Until the moment that *Wesley*'s space velocity dipped below cee, there was little to watch. But as soon as that moment came and the forward telecam view began to form behind the navigation graphics on the primary display, it seemed as though everyone were talking at once.

"Kleine carrier acquired," reported the comtech. "Time mark: 715.288."

"Hey—it's my birthday," one of the defense systems techs said with surprised pleasure.

Her mate at the defense board offered a less prosaic observation. "Captain, we're being scanned by PerCom picket radar—taking transponder query now."

"Acknowledged," Killea said.

"Just think of all the lances being zeroed on us right now," Berberon whispered to Sujata.

"I'd rather not."

A moment later the comtech announced, "PerCom Traffic Office has accepted our ID and cleared us through to dock."

"Navigation signal acquired," the gravigator added. "PerCom Traffic Office requests we hand over control to them."

"Do so," Killea said.

"Yes, sir."

The comtech was not done. "Acquiring PerCom net carrier, five bands. Mail coming in now—top of the stack is formal welcome, Acting Commander Osten Venngst and Station Governor William White to Captain Killea and all hands." He turned toward Sujata. "Chancellor, Commander Wells also extends his greetings."

Sujata nodded expressionlessly.

"The son of a bitch beat us here," Berberon said in a harsh whisper.

"I never expected anything different," Sujata said with a slight shrug. "He knows what happened to Captain Hirschfield. He wasn't about to let us get here first, and he had the edge. All he had to do was pass over one or two check-ins to stay ahead."

"Any reply, Chancellor?" asked the comtech.

"No," Sujata said with a shake of her head. "But find out for me how long *Charan*'s been in port."

"Yes, sir."

"But now he's had a chance to reaffirm his claim to these people's loyalty," Berberon said, fretting. "Now PerCom's even more clearly his fiefdom, the staff his retainers, and you the unwelcome visitor."

"Thirty-six hours, Chancellor," the comtech said. "She came in yesterday morning."

"Thank you."

"Add a week lost during the approach," Berberon said. "More than enough time for Wells to establish his hold on the station."

"What's important is that he's still here," Sujata said. "Mr. Morris, let me know when the library updates are all in."

The comtech shook his head. "Sorry, Chancellor. We won't be getting any until we're on-station. The net operator says by the time they push it all through to us, we won't have time to do anything with it, anyway."

Sujata nodded absently. "Thank you, Mr. Morris."

"Another Wells gambit?" Berberon asked Sujata.

"Of course."

"There is mail for both you and the Ambassador, though," the comtech added.

Sujata closed her eyes momentarily. *Of course there is. But I don't want to look at it*— She opened her eyes to find Berberon looking at her curiously, his eyes expressing concern.

"We'll both want privacy while we catch up," she said. "Why don't you go use the terminal in your cabin first?"

"I'd be happy to wait until you've—"

"I want us to maintain a presence on the bridge," she said, gracefully lowering herself to her knees, sitting on her heels in the center of the dais. Berberon frowned uncertainly, then bobbed his head in reluctant agreement. "If you insist. I'll come back down as soon as I'm finished."

"Fine," she said, avoiding looking at him by focusing her gaze at the display. "Mr. Morris, please tie my transceiver to the Kleine audio for PerCom."

"Of course. But it's pretty dull stuff—"

"I would rather be the judge of that myself." But a half hour of eavesdropping on the primary voice-link to Perimeter Command vindicated Morris's judgment—when there was any traffic at all, it was stultifyingly practical and proper.

The approach to Perimeter Command seemed interminable, and that perception did not proceed entirely from Sujata's impatience. The inbound flight profile thrust *Wesley* into playing out a variation of Zeno's paradox—the closer they drew to the station, the slower their progress, until it seemed as though they would never get there at all. It was always that way, Sujata realized, but she had never sat and done nothing but wait it out before.

Berberon was gone nearly two hours. By the time he returned, Perimeter Command had graduated from invisibility to an indistinct gray oblong in the center of the primary display.

"Sorry I was so long," Berberon said as he joined her in the center of the bridge. "I needed to discuss some matters with home."

"Perfectly understandable," Sujata said, taking Berberon's hand to help herself up. "You'll stay here?"

"If you wish."

"Just keep an eye on things for me."

• • •

There were several long messages in Sujata's mail queue, and little enough good news between them. Most of the mail had been sent under familiar headers but unfamiliar names, for both Vice Chancellor Walker and Ten Ga'ar had resigned, the latter shortly after *Wesley* had left Lynx. Sujata had fully expected Wyrena to go, and read Walker's notice concerning it as the Ba'ar woman's long-overdue declaration of independence.

Even so, the news enforced Sujata's sense of isolation and the perversity of AVLO flight. The twenty-two-year-old girl who had followed Sujata to Earth was now a mature woman of eighty. *How did you spend those years, and were they good ones?* she wondered. *Did I ever cross your mind in a fond memory, and did you ever find someone who could accept what you tried to give me?*

Sujata skimmed the reports from Pierce, the new Vice Chancellor, with little enthusiasm. The events and developments detailed therein were the sort of concerns that make up life but not history. The changing names and faces and the work done by those to whom they belonged seemed fundamentally irrelevant to her or to her problems: Transport had X number of packets operating on Y schedule to destination Z; Resource had begun recovering high quality ore A from new mine B; and on and on.

It was clear that Pierce was confident of his own authority and was reporting to her almost more out of courtesy than obligation. He neither asked her opinion on anything nor felt obliged to explain the rationale for his actions. As she read, she came to understand that she was Chancellor of the USS now in name only. At best, she was the Chancellor of the Defense Branch. And perhaps not even that—despite the fact that Pierce seemed unable to separate her from Wells.

". . . you and Director Wells . . ."

". . . you both understand . . ."

". . . if either of you . . ."

The tone of the reports raised grave concerns in Sujata's mind about how much authority she still retained. Not one of those whom she had left on the Committee remained. Pierce, exercising administrative power in her name, was a complete stranger—chosen not by Walker but by Walker's successor, another stranger. How would they react to orders from the Chancellor Emeritus thirty years after her abdication? Sujata thought she knew, but there was no comfort in the answer.

Nor was there any comfort in the realization that Wells was in the same situation. Wells did not need any help from Central; he had all the allies he needed here on the Perimeter. It was Sujata who needed allies—who needed somewhere to turn if persuasion failed. Something other than an ambassador-assassin to fall back on—

But it was hard to convince herself that allies would be forthcoming: *I don't even think there's anyone left there who understands what's at stake out here—and it's too late to educate them*.

Thinking such thoughts, Sujata was slightly heartened to find one familiar name, that of Katrina Evanik, attached to the last and lengthiest item in the queue. Instructions for Evanik had been one of several things that had been overlooked in the haste to leave Lynx. In retrospect Sujata wished she had told Evanik to wrap up the project and disband the research unit; she had learned what she needed to from it. But Evanik had carried on faithfully, making Sujata's project her life's work.

Out of a sense of duty Sujata began to review Evanik's summary. There was much in it that once would have commanded Sujata's rapt attention, including the news that the Nines were at last on the decline. In her summary Evanik alluded to two primary reasons for the shift: a rejection, because of the oppressive cost, of the defensive buildup with which they were so closely identified; and the perception, formed from his zealous public advocacy of the Nines' agenda, of Chaisson as an extremist and an elitist.

The expanded files with their amplifying details beckoned, but despite the guilt she felt doing it, Sujata saved the report to her personal library without reading further. No doubt it contained much good work and would be an important supplement to the Council's own studies when the histories of the Revision era were written.

But as uncertain as she was that those histories would ever be written, she could generate no more interest in the shifting tides of Terran politics than she had in the reorganization of the Transport Branch. With what could be the final war hanging over the species, it just did not seem to matter.

When Sujata finally returned to the bridge, she expected to see the primary display filled edge-to-edge with the image of

Perimeter Command. But the display was nearly blank, offering only systems status indicators in place of the customary star view and position plot.

She crossed the bridge to the communications station. "Mr. Morris? Are we having problems with the forward telecam?"

"No, Chancellor."

"Then put its output back up on the board."

Killea's battle couch rotated toward them. "Chancellor, I ordered the video suppressed because it contains sensitive information," he said.

"Oh?"

"Chancellor, information on the configuration and defensive capabilities of Perimeter Command carries the highest security restriction. That restriction includes video images."

"What's your point, Captain?"

Killea glanced sideways at Berberon. "Not everyone present on the bridge holds a clearance equal to that restriction, sir."

"Are you referring to Ambassador Berberon?"

"I am."

After a calculated pause Sujata turned back to the comtech. "Restore the video, mister."

Looking past Sujata toward Killea, the comtech began, "But the ambassador doesn't have—"

Sujata moved neatly sideways until her body blocked the line of sight between the tech and the captain. "He does now, Mr. Morris. Log it and restore the video to the board."

The comtech drew a deep breath and turned back to his console. "Yes, Chancellor."

Facing the display, head cocked slightly to one side, Sujata studied the image that appeared there. The station was shaped like an *H* that had toppled on its back, with a long, rectilinear central section and two smaller wings attached perpendicular to it on either end. Eight lance towers bristled from the lateral wings, each consisting of a silver ball of aperture lenses at the end of a slender stalk.

The lower half of the central section contained the service shipways, arrayed like cells in a honeycomb and open to space on both sides. Sujata gauged the size of the station by the shipways—the central section was wide enough for its lowest level to include three Triad-sized work bays, all of which were empty. The next level up had six Sentinel-sized bays, two of which were occupied by metallic pupae—*Charan* and one of the Sentinels.

Nodding to herself, Sujata turned and moved toward the climbway. "Thank you, Mr. Morris. I'll take that feed in my cabin now. Ambassador, will you accompany me?"

"You didn't have to do that," Berberon said when he caught up to her on the corridor leading to their cabin.

"Yes, I did," Sujata said.

"I mean it. Teo got me several files on the station."

Sujata shook her head as she unlocked the cabin. "That's not why I did it. Obedience is a habit. They need practice. Now—was there anything in your mail that you can or need to tell me about?"

Sujata and Berberon returned to the bridge in time for the final stages of the berthing. They joined the bridge crew as spectators, since *Wesley*'s drive was idling and her movements were controlled by the pilot computers of the spider tugs locked on her bow and stern. Accustomed to the conservative pace of the human tug pilots working the Terran yards, Sujata marveled at the efficiency of the double-tug arrangement. It took bare minutes, rather than the hour or more she had expected, to guide *Wesley* into one of the tunnellike bays.

As soon as the all-secure message came, Sujata strode to the center of the bridge as though she were walking onstage.

"Captain Killea."

Killea rotated his couch toward her and met her hard gaze.

"Command log, record," she said.

"Recording," the library station acknowledged.

"Captain Killea, you are instructed to disregard any deployment orders you may receive from the PerCom Flight Office or any part of the Defense hierarchy. In simple terms, *Wesley* is not to budge from here without my explicit authorization. Further, I want this ship available to move on five minutes' notice. Don't shut down any systems that take longer than that to checklist."

"Yes, Chancellor," Killea said. "What about the final certification work on the lance?"

"Have it taken care of. But don't let any station personnel on board unsupervised. If there's maintenance work that needs doing, have your own techs do it, or make sure they're right there watching to see that it's done right."

"I understand. May I authorize station leave?"

"For up to six of your crew at a time—but make sure you always have a full watch on board."

"That's the accepted procedure, Chancellor."

"Fine. Report to me on ship's status daily at noon." She turned her gaze on Berberon. "Ambassador?"

"Ready."

"Then let's go visiting."

Waiting for them at the end of the access tunnel was a fresh-faced lieutenant wearing the gold eagle's feather emblem of the command staff on the collar of his blouse. "Chancellor Sujata, Ambassador Berberon," he said with a slight bow. "I'm Lieutenant Baines. Commander Wells asked me to extend his greetings and to escort you to his office."

Oh, no, Harmack—the game doesn't start until the field is level, Sujata thought. She summoned up her best baleful look and released it full force on the lieutenant. "Has saluting a superior officer gone out of fashion on this station, mister?"

Taken aback, Baines blinked twice, then offered a brisk salute. "My apologies, Chancellor."

"Accepted. You can show us our quarters now."

"But the Commander said—"

"Commander Wells will understand that the Ambassador and I have just completed a long leg in the craze and would need an opportunity to unwind and acclimate ourselves. Now —which way?"

Baines frowned unhappily. "I don't know, Chancellor. We'll have to stop at Operations."

"Fine," she said briskly. "Let's go."

At Operations they picked up the housing officer, a sunken-cheeked man of forty who seemed faintly annoyed at the inconvenience of having to leave his desk. He led them in silence through the central section to Blue Wing, then up three levels to a dormitory block.

"Chancellor Sujata, this room has been cleared for you," the housing officer said, opening a door marked 301 and then stepping aside.

"And what about the Ambassador?" she asked as she brushed by him and into the room.

"The next room on this side of the block—303."

Stopping at the foot of the single bed, Sujata gave the room and its furnishings a protracted silent scrutiny, then turned to the housing officer. "I don't know—is anything larger available on-station?"

"No, sir. A room this size is usually a quad."

Pursing her lips, Sujata nodded. "This will do, then. Now, where is my office?"

The housing officer exchanged worried glances with Baines. "I was only given authority to allocate housing space—"

"Do you expect the Chancellor of the Service to live out of her suitcase and work out of her quarters?" Sujata asked with heavy irony.

Baines drew a deep breath and answered for the housing officer. "No, sir. Will you excuse us while we see to the arrangements?"

"Of course."

This time Baines remembered to salute, and the housing officer followed his lead.

"Testing the waters?" Berberon asked with a grin when they were alone.

"No," Sujata said, settling down on the edge of the bed. "Stirring them up a bit."

Berberon's grin widened. "Speaking of water, I *would* like a real shower, if you think we have the time."

"Go ahead," Sujata said. "Wells will wait."

Baines was back within half an hour. Berberon was still enjoying the relative comforts of his quarters, and Sujata did not disturb him. She went with Baines back to the central section, where he showed her a five-by-three-metre cubicle with the hopeful attitude of a real-estate agent showing off a choice property.

En route they had passed enough other office areas for Sujata to be able to gauge what amenities the station boasted in that regard. "This is acceptable," she said after glancing around the room briefly. She gestured toward the desk. "This terminal—will I have full access to the station library through it? Fleet deployments, general and command logs—"

"No, Chancellor. Only safe-room terminals—"

"See thet it gets such access."

"I can't do that, Chancellor. Only the Commander—"

"Lieutenant," Sujata said with exaggerated patience,

"please make an effort to think before you speak. I am Chancellor of the Unified Space Service. I have final administrative authority over every action taken by any Branch. There can't be any question about *my* clearance, now can there? Or do you think that I should need to go to the Directors and ask permission to see the information I require to carry out my responsibilities?"

"No—" Baines said hesitantly.

"Then my access code in your system should reflect that, yes?"

"I only know that—"

"Lieutenant—" Sujata said warningly.

"I don't have the authority to change access parameters myself. But I'll convey your request—"

"Order."

"Your order to those who can."

"I trust you'll show enough initiative to do so without needlessly troubling the Director. As recently as he's arrived on-station, I'm certain he has enough important business to occupy him."

"Yes, sir."

Left alone, she posted a message to Berberon telling him where to find her and then settled back to wait. Shortly before Berberon joined her, the terminal began to treat her queries more responsively.

"Do you think they really gave you access to everything?" Berberon asked skeptically when he had heard the story.

"No," Sujata said in a relaxed tone. "But they probably opened up everything they thought I would know they were hiding—which is exactly what I wanted to see. Sit down and let's go through it."

What little amusement they had derived from confounding the station bureaucracy vanished quickly as they learned of the destruction of *Munin* and the subsequent mobilization. Their long faces grew even longer as they studied the timetable. *Falcon* was due to survey Mizar-Alcor in just two days, *Kite* to reach Phad shortly afterward. The Triads would begin hitting their final wave-off points within the week, beginning with Triad One at Alphecca. A month later they would begin their assaults.

"No wonder he didn't mind us catching up to him," Berberon said somberly.

Her lips a small, tight line across her face, Sujata gave no reply. For the next two hours she silently studied record after record, report after report, her attention never wavering from the terminal, her concentration never breaking.

"All right," she said finally, pushing back from the desk. "I'm ready."

"Going to invite him down here?"

Sujata shook her head. "Those kind of games won't rattle Wells. No, I'll go to see him."

"I, singular?"

"This time," she said, and reached for the com key. "Lieutenant Baines—this is Chancellor Sujata. To my office, please."

The folds of her *daiiki* flaring out behind her, her face a mask of determination, Sujata strode into the outer office of Wells's suite with Baines at her heels.

"Which door?" she asked, slowing momentarily to let Baines come up beside her.

"Commander Wells's office is straight ahead," Baines said, then looked to the puzzled aide-de-camp, who had risen half out of his chair at their entrance. "Is the Commander in?"

"You can't—" the aide began, but Baines silenced him with a look and a cutting motion of his left hand.

"This is Chancellor Sujata," Baines said sharply.

The aide saluted in slow motion, as though his confusion had driven motor functions to a lower level of priority. "Yes," the aide said meekly. "The Commander's with Mr. Shields."

Baines nodded. "Should I wait for you here, Chancellor?" he asked, turning back to Sujata.

"No," she said with a shake of the head. "I don't know how long this will take. You may go. But consider yourself still on call."

"Yes, sir," Baines said, saluting.

Some of the conversation had clearly filtered through the door, for both Wells and the stranger who had to be Shields were both staring in the direction of the door when Sujata entered. For a long moment no one spoke. It was as though Sujata and Wells were trying to stare the other down, while Shields suspiciously sized up the newcomer.

"Leave us, Philip," Wells said at last.

Shields glanced back and forth twice between Sujata and Wells, then frowned crossly and stalked out with his head lowered. As the door closed, a faint, wry smile creased

Wells's face. "Welcome to the Perimeter, Chancellor."

"If I thought you really welcomed my presence, I'd thank you," Sujata said, circling to the right, her eyes locked on Wells's.

"Why shouldn't I welcome you?" Wells asked, easing a step to his left and resting his hands on the back of a chair.

"Can we dispense with the fencing?"

Wells slipped around to the front of the chair and settled himself in it. "Certainly," he said.

"I'm here to find out why you're doing this. I'm here to find out why the Triads are on their way to attack the Mizari."

"Is it such a mystery?" Wells asked, raising his hands and turning them palms-up. "They've destroyed one of our vessels and, in the process, murdered one of our most revered statesmen."

"An old ship and a forgotten hero. Does that justify the deaths of millions on both sides?"

"There's no deterrence if they don't know what we can do," Wells said firmly. "Since we have no way to tell them, we have to show them. We can't let what they did go unanswered. Do sit down, Chancellor—"

Sujata ignored the invitation. "Why is it necessary that we answer with warships? Why not send an ambassador ship instead, a new *Pride of Earth*?"

Smiling tolerantly, Wells shook his head. "The only way to negotiate with them is from a position of strength."

"Why does mutual survival have to be negotiated?" she demanded. "The concept of war is predicated on the belief that there are worse things than being dead. Nothing is worse than being dead."

"Would you rather that we were in a position where we had no choice but to submit to their demands?"

"What could they want from us? What could the Weichsel have given them?"

"Nothing less than the Galaxy, it would seem. Would you rather they simply overwhelmed us?"

"No, but I don't think that's the choice. How hard you've worked this last century to meet them in battle!" she said earnestly, extending a hand toward him, then snatching it back. "How little you've done to embrace other possibilities. We haven't talked to them. We don't even know if we can talk to them." She opened her arms wide, which the loose-sleeved robe made into a dramatic gesture. "All we really know of them is what they did. We don't know what their reason was. We don't know if the conditions that prompted them to do it are still in place."

"Come, now, Chancellor. Isn't it obvious that they operate from an incompatible ethic?"

"We have to believe that they're enough like us to understand. We have to believe that there's another answer."

Wells twisted sideways in his chair and hooked his folded hands over one knee. "We have no reason to believe that—which is why we have to be ready to destroy them."

Crossing her arms over her chest, Sujata turned half away and cast her gaze downward. "You're more than ready," she said angrily. "You're eager. It's time to drop the fiction of deterrence. What you really want is to lay waste to their world and their culture."

Wells came up out of his chair and took a step toward her. "Neither the Weichsel iceship nor *Munin* posed any threat to them, and both were destroyed without warning. Isn't it clear that there can never be any rapprochement between their kind and ours?"

"They are *just* like us," she said sharply, turning on him. "They have one set of rules for treating those they consider brothers, and a second set for 'the others.' Why can't we just recognize each other's right to exist?"

"This isn't about existence. It's about empery." Wells turned away and stared out the greatport at the stars of the Ursa Major cluster. "We might be willing to concede them what they occupy. They might even be willing to do the same for us. But how much of what no one holds will they be willing to grant us? Or us them?" He looked back over his shoulder at Sujata. "I'll give you the answer to that one—neither side will give away anything until we know what it is we're giving, and maybe not then. No, Chancellor. Our survival is predicated on their destruction."

The words of the provider, over and over. "So you believe. And a few weeks from now you'll give them reason to believe the same. But do either of you know if you're right?"

"I do," he said with simple confidence.

Frowning, Sujata circled the room clockwise, forcing Wells to turn away from the greatport to keep her in sight. "And how will you carry out your intent? *Munin* was barely within the heliosphere of the Alphecca system when it was attacked. How much time did it have, two minutes, three? The

Triads won't get close enough for their wreckage to fall on the Mizari, much less their weapons."

It was Wells's turn to cross his arms over his chest defensively. "In fact, Chancellor, our analysis of the attack on *Munin* has made us more confident, not less. *Munin* had no defensive systems, no energy-absorbing shield, no systems hardening. A Triad would have survived that attack. Even a recon ship would have come through it in good shape."

Sujata realized that it was a mistake to have begun arguing tactics, but she could not go back. "And if the Mizari used only as much force against *Munin* as was necessary to destroy it, if they're capable of much more?"

"The weapons and energies used in the attack on *Munin* were consistent with our models of the attack on the Weichsel," Wells said stiffly.

"The same principle applies. You still only know what they did, not what they're capable of."

"We're not fools, Janell. The recon ships are going in first. We'll adjust our tactics according to what they learn."

"I have a more fundamental adjustment in mind," Sujata said, her eyes boring into his. "Cancel the attack orders. Bring the fleet back."

Wells did not flinch from her gaze. "No," he said. "I'm sorry."

"Commander Wells—you've gone a half step over the line," she said, drawing closer to him. "That's not too far for you to step back."

He shook his head. "It has always been the responsibility of those who most clearly perceive the danger to respond to it. I didn't plan *Munin*'s intrusion. But I would be remiss in my duties if I did nothing in its wake. Not to move against the Mizari would be the reckless act now."

"You're talking about trying to avoid losing a war," she said pleadingly. "I'm trying to avoid fighting one."

"That's no longer possible."

"It's always possible. The answer is in you, Harmack. Don't resist it because it seems obvious. Wage peace. Turn away from war."

"I wish that it were that easy," he said wistfully. "I truly do."

"It can be. Call back *Falcon* and *Kite*. Call back the Triads."

Wells shook his head slowly. "I am sorry, Chancellor. What you ask is impossible."

"Then you leave me no choice but to recall them myself."

"I'm afraid that you will find that just as impossible. They will not accept such an order from you."

Sujata squeezed her hands into fists and shook them at Wells. "Who owns you, damnit? How can you do this?"

"My conscience owns me, Chancellor. You never have understood that."

"Your power is out of balance with your responsibility. You speak for yourself, but what you say endangers everyone. Who gives you the right? Who gives you the authority?"

"And whom do you represent, Janell Sujata?" he asked, his eyes flashing anger for the first time. "What plebiscite put you in office? When did the Unified Worlds designate you to represent them? One coward selected you, and three more put you here—and even they're dead now. An impressive mandate, indeed. Necessity gives me the *right,* Chancellor. *I* give myself the authority."

Sujata knew she should challenge Wells's pronouncement, but she felt drained, her determination blunted, her optimism sapped. *He isn't listening. Not to me. He never wavered, not for a moment.*

To retreat was to concede defeat, but she lacked the will to continue. *I did lose. I did lose, but I'll try again. Another day, another tack—perhaps with Yamakawa here, or Venngst. They might listen. There's still a little time. With an audience he wouldn't dare defy me openly—*

She heard the desperation in her own thoughts and turned away before it could show on her face. Mustering what dignity she could in straight shoulders and an erect head, she stalked out of the office. But her fleeing steps were not swift enough to keep helplessness from closing in on her, nor to catch up with her departed hope.

Though she had left Berberon in her office awaiting her return and report, that commitment had fled her consciousness by the time the moment to fulfill it arrived. Instead Sujata went to her room and sought refuge in the embrace of bed covers and the dark freedom of sleep. But her dreams were disturbed and disturbing, bringing restlessness rather than peace. She moved back and forth between sleep and consciousness, hardly knowing the difference between them, for her reality had become a nightmare from which there was no awakening.

So when the page alarm sounded from her transceiver, Sujata was more tired than when she had turned in. It was a jarring way to be awakened—the sound seemed to drill through the bones of her skull. By habit she placed the implant off-line, but new surroundings and the grim circumstances had broken many habits. She fumbled for the stem and pressed it once to acknowledge, then lay wide-eyed in the dark and tried to gather her wits.

"Chancellor?" It was Berberon's voice.

Sujata managed a grunt of assent.

"I wondered if you were finished with Commander Wells. It's been almost four hours."

This time she managed words, though they were slurred. "Yes," she said. "Yes, we're finished."

Berberon waited a moment, as though expecting Sujata to amplify her answer, then cautiously asked, "What success did you have?"

"None."

"Ah." Berberon managed to make that single syllable ring with compassion. "I thought that might be the case when you didn't come back." He paused. "Do you want me to go see him?"

An ally, a fresh reinforcement, Sujata's clouded mind told her. "We have nothing to lose by it," she said sleepily. "I think you do understand him better than I do."

"I wish it were otherwise," Berberon said, his words strangely clipped. "You try to think of other things now. It's my turn to carry the freight—my turn and long overdue." There was a long silence, then he added, "Take care of yourself, Janell."

Sujata murmured a good-bye and placed her transceiver off-line, then turned on her side and drew the extra pillow under her arm. Sleep was inviting her back, teasing her with the promise that she would not have to think at all.

Surrendering to the exhortations, she shrugged aside the tiny voice of alarm, the warning that she had missed something important in the conversation that had just ended. The pleadings of her body for a surcease of feeling, an end to her mind's pain, were too strong, and she slept, blissfully unaware that in the days ahead sleep would be very hard indeed to come by.

The weariness Berberon had heard in Sujata's voice was only an echo of that which he felt in his entire being. It was not simple fatigue but something much deeper and much harder to eradicate. He was weary of the stratagems and the secrets, weary of the double-dealing, the intrigue, the responsibility.

Most of all he was weary of the guilt. Tanvier had been the architect of the appeasement plan, but it was he, Berberon, who had supervised construction. Little matter that he had done so reluctantly, that he had seen the flaws in the design and worried over them. Now that the edifice stood poised to collapse, he was as culpable as Tanvier—more so, perhaps, for having swallowed his objections and surrendered his conscience to the dictates of duty.

He had undertaken this journey solely to expiate his guilt, a goal he had not yet come close to achieving. Now there was a strangeness to everything around him that told him the end of his journey was near. The end of the corridor seemed to recede farther into the distance with each step he took toward it, and the sound of his footsteps echoed hollowly in his ears. All other sounds were hushed except the hammering of his heart within his chest.

As he made the turn from the corridor into the anteroom of the Office of the Commander, Perimeter Defense, the oddly focused feeling persisted. He had time enough to calmly note the three identical unmarked doors leading to inner offices, the fish-eyed scanner high in one corner, the golden-hued broken triangle prominent on the facing wall, and a hundred other details before the aide behind the desk turned a questioning eye in his direction.

"I'm here to see the Commander," Berberon said, summoning a well-practiced air of authority.

"Your name, please?"

"Berberon. Felithe Berberon, representing the World Council of Earth as Special Observer for Defense."

The aide nodded and gestured toward the chairs on the opposite side of the room. "Thank you. If you'll give me a moment, I'll see if Mr. Shields is available or can work you into his schedule."

Berberon rested his hands on the edge of the aide's desk and leaned across it. "I'm afraid you misunderstood. I want to see Wells, not this Shields."

"I'm sorry, Ambassador Berberon," the aide said unblinkingly. "Your name doesn't appear on the Commander's cleared list."

"Of course it doesn't," Berberon said with an engaging smile. "Chancellor Sujata and I have only just arrived on *Wesley*. If you'll just advise the Commander that I'm here, I assure you he'll want to see me."

While Berberon was speaking, the middle door opened and a rangily built man in a black dress allover emerged. "A problem, Lieutenant?"

"Colonel Shields, this is Ambassador Berberon. He's requested to see the Commander, but he's not on the cleared list."

"Obviously an oversight—" Berberon began.

"If the Commander wants to see you, Mr. Berberon, be assured that he knows where to find you," Shields said coldly. "If you have a concern, you can relay it through me."

Berberon bit back a sigh that would have verged on a sob and glanced away from Shields with what he hoped was an indignant look on his face. *Is this what I've come to, unable even to finesse my way past a flunky and a supernumerary?* Berberon was addled by indecision: to threaten, to wheedle, to make a show of displeasure and storm off, to accede—the seconds were passing, and with them the initiative.

Then the door on the left opened and Wells himself emerged, engaged in conversation with a man Berberon did not know. Berberon took two steps toward them, then stopped short when Shields began to move to intercept him.

"Commander Wells, I really must see you," he blurted out, more anxiously than he would have wished.

Wells glanced his way in surprise and his steps slowed. "I'm sorry, Observer Berberon," he said. "I haven't the time." Then he continued on, passing behind Shields and heading for the rightmost door, the stranger trailing behind him.

"But you met privately with Janell—" Berberon cried out in protest.

Wells slowed, stopped, and turned to face Berberon. "I have certain responsibilities with respect to the Chancellor. I have none toward you. You have no authority here, no official status whatsoever. I tolerate your presence on this station as a courtesy to the Chancellor. But I feel no obligation to allow you to waste my time with inanities."

"How dare you talk to me like that—" Berberon sputtered.

"Besides," Wells continued, the stiffness going out of his pose. "I can find reasons to respect Sujata. The same has never been true of you. You're smarmy and weak, Berberon, a perfect argument for breeding control."

The man standing beyond Wells looked embarrassed for Berberon, while Shields was clearly enjoying the skewering. Berberon's mouth worked soundlessly as he struggled to compose a retort.

"Please save your breath," Wells said. "I feel nothing but contempt for you. It's a continuing irritant to me that in protecting what's good about our species I have to protect the likes of you as well." Shaking his head disgustedly, Wells turned away.

Berberon had resolved not to take the first opportunity but to wait patiently for the best one. Now it seemed as though the first would be not only the best but also the last. Oblivious to anything but Wells's retreating figure, Berberon reached into the pocket that concealed the tiny fletchette gun.

He had barely drawn the weapon clear when a tremendous blow to the side of his face sent his head snapping to the right, and the impulsive clench on the trigger released a wild flurry of darts. There was a sharp cry, but Berberon did not know from whom.

Shields. I was too close to Shields—

Staggering back toward the entrance to the anteroom, Berberon tried to turn the gun on the Chief of Staff. But the younger man's reflexes were quicker, and Shields stepped in close, a look of grim pleasure on his face. A sweeping blow with the left hand sent the weapon spinning out of Berberon's grip, and then a quick thrust with the right drove fingers as rigid as iron rods up under Berberon's sternum. The final blow was a stiff-knuckled shot to the larynx, the cracking and splitting of his own cartilage loud in Berberon's ears.

Wide-eyed at the sudden pain that possessed him, Berberon toppled backward, sucking air with strangled, rasping sounds, the periphery of his vision graying. By the time his head struck the hard surface of the corridor floor with teeth-jarring force, Berberon's limbs were already numb and cold, and the shuddering spasms that shook his body as it lay there were only the last protests of a mind that was already gone.

chapter 19

No Call to Die

"I am the family face
Flesh perishes, I live on . . .
The eternal thing in man,
That heeds no call to die."

—Thomas Hardy

Sujata's eyes flew open suddenly, her sleep-addled mind attempting to focus on that which had disturbed her. Knocking —a loud, impatient knocking on the door of her quarters. Loud enough to drag her up from a deep and dreamless sleep; impatient enough that when she did not answer immediately, the door slid open to admit a cascade of light and two tan-uniformed security officers. The younger of the two, an ensign, advanced as far as the end of her bed. The other, a lieutenant, remained by the door.

Lying flat on her back was a poor position from which to enforce a sense of indignation, so Sujata struggled to a sitting position, gathering the blanket around her torso to hide her nudity. "What are you doing?" she demanded.

The ensign squinted in her direction and said, "Chancellor Sujata, you are to come with us."

"Where? Why?"

"Chancellor, all I know is that we were told to escort you if you were cooperative and drag you if you weren't," the lieutenant said from the entryway.

"Whose orders are these? Surely I have a right to know that much."

After a moment's hesitation the lieutenant said, "Commander Wells's." He added, "Chancellor, since I'm not entirely comfortable with the idea of dragging you, I'd be grateful for your cooperation."

Sujata's first impulse was anything but cooperative. But since her grievance was with him who had given the orders, not those who carried them out, she bit her tongue. Keeping the blanket wrapped around her, she swung her feet over the side of the bed. "I have to dress."

The ensign nodded stiffly. "We were told to wait."

"You can do so outside."

"With all due apologies, Chancellor," the lieutenant said, "we were instructed not to leave you alone or turn our backs on you."

A half-remembered conversation flashed through her mind, and suddenly Sujata knew with a horrible certainty why she was being summoned. *No, Felithe, not that, not now. Even in failing you could have cost me my last chance, and if you'd succeeded—*

Sujata stood, letting the blanket fall away. Shrugging off her visitors' watching eyes with the knowledge that they could not invade her truly private self, she crossed the room to the wardrobe.

"Be quick, please," the ensign added.

To be summoned like this, to be subjected to this kind of invasion— Slipping into a russet *daiiki,* she reflected, *Wells wants to humiliate me. He is angry, angry enough to make him reckless.* She reached for a brush to quickly erase the snarls and tangles of a restless sleep, then stopped in mid-motion. *No—let him see me this way. Let him think he has won his little game. Perhaps I can do more with him by surrendering the advantage than by trying to reclaim it. There is something about that in the Canons, isn't there, Wyrena?*

She turned to the officers and planted her hands on her hips. "I'm ready."

To her surprise, they led her not toward Wells's suite but into an area of the station she had not yet seen. Much of the signage along the way was cryptic, number and letter codes without obvious meaning, and it was difficult even to keep herself oriented to station compass points. But presently they came to a block that—wherever it was located—unambiguously housed the station's medical services.

But who's hurt? Felithe? Or Wells? Perhaps it was something other than anger that had given his orders their urgency, she thought. She was led through the triage area with its express lift—from the docks? she wondered—and into a corridor lined with double-doored examination rooms.

Standing outside the last room on the left were two more station security officers, a male colonel and a female ensign. Notwithstanding the precautions Sujata's escort had taken while she dressed, the ensign searched her—not politely—before standing aside to admit her to the room.

Two steps inside, Sujata stopped short, her breath catching in her throat at what she saw. In one of the far corners stood Wells, half turned away from her, arms crossed over his chest, shoulders hunched. There was a padded bulge at his right calf, as though his trousers were concealing a bandage.

Shields sat casually in a chair, one leg hooked over the other, a smoking stick in one hand. And lying on his back on an examination table, naked and still, was Berberon. Or, more precisely, Berberon's corpse. The ambassador's open eyes, as lifeless as tinted glass, stared up at the ceiling.

One small part of Sujata's consciousness had been preparing for this possibility since she had left her room. Even so, the sight suffused her thoughts with a wave of regret and outrage. Stepping forward to the table, Sujata touched the purple bruise in the middle of Berberon's chest and felt the clamminess of the cooling flesh.

"What happened?" she asked in a small voice.

Wells whirled in place to face her, raising his right arm to point a small weapon at her face. When his arm was fully raised and extended, the mesh opening of the gun's rectangular barrel was only a few centimetres from her face.

"Do you really need explanations, Chancellor?" he snapped. "He failed in his assignment. Now he's dead instead of me. What do you think, Chancellor? Do you like looking down the barrel?"

Sujata almost did not hear the words. The moment Wells turned, she saw with astonishment that his mask was down. Felithe had surprised him. No, more than that—he had shaken him, she thought, reading a hundred nuances in Wells's face and tone and posture that she had never seen in him before. *I would not have expected this. Perhaps there is something here—*

"I don't especially like it," she said with a practiced casualness, looking past the gun to Wells's face. "Do you like seeing the man who paved the way for you to become Director lying there like a trophy kill?"

Slowly Wells lowered the weapon and passed it into Shields's hands. "He came to my office and tried to murder me," he said. Deprived of the camouflage of anger, his voice betrayed his shock with an uncharacteristic tremble. "Tried to shoot me in the back, right outside my own office. He came closer to succeeding than I like to think about. If Colonel Shields hadn't been there—"

Though Wells would not admit to it, it was obvious that he was favoring his right leg, bearing most of his weight on his left. *A little pain, perhaps, Harmack? There's a message in it if you'll listen.* Sujata glanced momentarily at Shields, then looked back to Wells. "Am I to assume from the way you had me rousted out that you expect me to try to follow his example?"

Wells laughed without humor. "I expected you to try to tell me that he did this on his own—"

"Far from it. If you believed that, it would be easier for you to shrug this off, which is just what you should not do," Sujata said, resting both hands on the table at Berberon's side. "Of course he had orders—orders from the World Council. They're frightened of you. This tells you how much. Don't blame Felithe. Blame yourself and what you're doing here. You closed off all the other options."

It was Shields who answered, stepping in as though protecting Wells. "I'm afraid that the blame points more toward you, Chancellor. Yes, the Ambassador received such orders from President Tanvier before you left Lynx. But the new President, Dailey, countermanded them after *Wesley* came out of the craze."

"Felithe said nothing—how can you know that? You monitored his calls?"

"This is a sensitive military installation, Chancellor. Everyone's communications are monitored," Shields said. "Outgoing *and* internal. Oh, don't try to hide behind your indignation. Your responsibility for what Berberon tried to do is obvious."

Sujata looked at Wells. "I could not have given him such an order, nor would I if I had the authority. I came here to try to prevent needless death, not to be a party to it."

"Then why did Berberon call you for instructions before he acted?" Wells demanded.

Taking Berberon's hand in hers, Sujata looked down at his slack-muscled face wistfully. "He called me for information, not instructions. Perhaps I should have known what he was thinking. I wish I had, because then I would have stopped him, and he might still be alive." She glanced up at Wells. "But I gave him no orders, Harmack. If his orders from the Council truly were withdrawn, then he did what he did for his own reasons."

"Or your reasons," Shields persisted.

"No," Sujata said firmly. "Even if I thought as you do, Colonel—which I'm grateful I do not—what Commander Wells told me yesterday would stop me. I want the Triads recalled. Since he seems to be the only one who can do that, it would be insane to have him killed. And contrary to what Chaisson has been telling your homeworld, hoping for peace with the Mizari does not automatically mean one is insane."

Wells's face, still open to her reading, told her that her argument had persuaded him. But she had no fund of shared experience with Shields to draw on, and he remained unimpressed.

"You can plead your case when you're tried," he said. "Which, unfortunately, can't be immediately. Who you are and where we are poses certain technical problems—as I'm sure you took into account beforehand."

"A complaint against a Chancellor has to be presented before the full Service Court," she said.

"Yes. Which, of course, is based at Central. But we may not have to ship you back there—we've requested an opinion on whether the trial can be conducted through a Kleine link."

"So I'm not under Clause 34 suspension?" she asked, referring to the relevant part of the Service contract.

"Until we have the Court's answer, technically not. But that doesn't mean you're going to have your run of the station. Governor White has more than sufficient authority on this station to restrict you to your quarters."

She looked to Wells. "Harmack, this is unnecessary. You know that I'm no threat to you."

Scratching the back of his neck with one hand, Wells turned away from her. "Perhaps not. But you still could disrupt this station at a critical juncture. Governor White is concerned, and it's his decision. I'm here to exercise operational command, not logistical. Don't look for me to interfere."

Sujata pursed her lips and nodded. She had expected nothing less, and yet she needed something more. "If you don't object, I'll contact the Council and tell them of Felithe's death."

"No communications," Shields said sharply.

But Wells overruled him with a wave of his hand. "You can't stop the Chancellor from talking to Central, Philip. She has that right. And if she wants the unhappy task of reporting the Ambassador's death, I see no reason we can't oblige."

"She may have coded messages to deliver—"

"All she can tell them is the truth. I have nothing to fear from the truth."

"They could have other agents here," Shields insisted. "Remember Farlad—"

"If there are other agents here, no doubt they will take the Chancellor's cautions to heart," Wells said. "Authorize a link with President Dailey for her."

"Thank you, Commander," she said.

Shields scowled, then rose from the chair. Pocketing Berberon's weapon, the Chief of Staff circled the examination table and moved to the doors. He stopped there and looked back expectantly at Sujata. "Come along, then," he said.

Sujata gave Berberon's flaccid fingers one last squeeze and then released his hand. You didn't kill him, Felithe, she thought as she followed Shields out the door. But perhaps you showed him that he's mortal, and that might be enough. Enough to make him understand what there is to be afraid of—

Roland Dailey, 107th President of a World Council just concluding its 694th annual session, was a younger man than Sujata had hoped he would be. All that tradition was in the hands of a man who wore less than four decades of living on his face.

The young pretend that death only happens to others until the truth is forced on them, she thought as she studied him. Have you had your revelation yet, Roland Dailey? Through what set of preconceptions will you filter what you hear?

She could study him at her leisure, for Dailey's image was frozen due to interference between Perimeter Command and Earth. Her greeting block had gone out and she was waiting for a reply; in the meantime the terminal was holding the last complete data frame on the screen. The net operator had warned her she would spend half her time waiting and recommended a text link. But she had insisted on a full bimodal link.

I need to see his face and hear him, and he to see and hear me, she thought. *I need every edge I can get—*

Dailey's image was abruptly reanimated as the next data block got through. "Chancellor Sujata, what a pleasure to make your acquaintance. I wonder if you might not have known my grandfather, Commissioner Brant Dailey. I understand that that was your era."

"You'll forgive me, President Dailey, if I forgo the reminiscences," she said with courtly curtness. "I have a great deal to talk about and a limited amount of time in which to do so. To begin with, I must tell you that this conversation is being monitored by the military forces here under the command of Harmack Wells, Director of the Defense Branch. You should consider any interruption that occurs to be an attempt at censorship rather than the result of interference, which I am assured the techs can cope with if we're willing to be patient."

This time the wait was only a few seconds, as though a screen-before-transmission delay had been removed from the loop. Shields had reluctantly left her alone at her office terminal, but she had no doubt he was listening in. "I understand, Chancellor—at least I understand what you said, not why it should be so."

"I hope to make that clear," she replied. "I don't know you, President Dailey, but I must depend on you. You don't know me, but you must trust me. If I can't depend on you, or if you decide you can't believe what I tell you, then the last chance to prevent a foolish and unnecessary war will slip away from us.

"I understand fully that it may be difficult for you to credit what I tell you. I am a woman, and I know that there are still many men who hear the same words differently from a woman's mouth than from a man's. Even more, I am a Maranit woman, and so doubly suspect. But though I am not of your world, I love it better than my own. You must believe that we have a common stake in preserving the life it embraces. I have done as much as I can. Now I need help."

Dailey's expression and tone were both guarded, but there was a flicker of curiosity in his eyes. "You make this all sound very ominous. All right, Chancellor. I am listening."

"Before I can tell you anything, there's something I have to know," Sujata said. "President Tanvier had authorized Ambassador Berberon to kill Commander Wells if circumstances dictated. Though I didn't approve of the method, I did understand the reasoning. You withdrew that authorization. Why? I need an honest and complete answer. Why aren't you as troubled by the situation here as President Tanvier was? What do you understand the situation here to be?"

There was a long delay, and Sujata had no way of knowing whether it originated with Dailey or somewhere in the loop. "I don't know if you know the circumstances of my succession," Dailey said. "President Tanvier held on to this office for fifty-seven years, which virtually everyone but Tanvier himself and the Nines agreed was twenty years too long. He was President when I was born, and he was President when he died three years ago. I was elected by the Council to replace him precisely because I reject his Machiavellian approach to governance.

"I inherited from Tanvier a rather large file detailing the attempts by him and Ambassador Berberon to manipulate the internal affairs of the Service. I don't know how aware you were of these attempts. I do know that I was shocked to read of them. Perhaps before we had our own independent planetary defenses there might have been some justification for concern, if not for meddling.

"But I don't share the paranoiac obsession with the Service's Defense plans that typified Tanvier and his supporters. And there can be no justification for the kind of orders Tanvier gave the Ambassador. Ever since I learned what they were, I've been most eager for a chance to countermand them. Which I finally got when your ship arrived at Perimeter Command.

"I was glad to hear you say that you disapproved of the assassination order. I don't like this kind of business, Chancellor. I also don't like the kind of people who employ it. Which is why when we spoke the other day, I gave Ambassador Berberon seventy-two hours to submit his resignation or be fired."

Dailey's prideful revelation answered one of Sujata's nag-

ging questions. *Now I understand why Felithe didn't wait,*
Sujata thought. *His time was running out even faster than
ours. If he were no longer Ambassador, Wells would have no
reason to see him.*

"President Dailey, you've judged a man you didn't know
more harshly than he deserves," she said. "There's no point in
trying to persuade you of that, because it's now a moot issue.
Orders or not, Felithe Berberon was killed a few hours ago
attempting to assassinate Commander Wells. I don't expect
you to mourn, though I will. But despite what you think of
him, I do need to persuade you that he wasn't paranoid but
justifiably frightened. And the reason he was frightened is that
Wells is about to begin a war he can't win."

Dailey's face screamed his resistance to that news. "What
has this to do with me or the Council?" Dailey protested.
"Why are you coming to me with your complaints? You're
Chancellor of the Service. If you disagree with your commander's judgments, overrule him. Order him to stop. Or am I
missing something?"

Sujata sighed. "Regrettably Commander Wells no longer
accepts my authority. In his mind, he's not here on behalf of
the Service. He thinks he's representing all humanity. And
since there is no one delegated to speak for humanity, he's
following his conscience."

"I don't understand why you gave such a man command in
the first place—" Dailey began.

"Then Tanvier's file was incomplete," Sujata said angrily
without waiting for the clear-to-send. "Or are you trying to
pretend the Council had no part in creating this problem?"

"—and what do you mean that he's about to start a war?
And how do you know he can't win? Why would he do such a
thing? Or are you trying to pull me in on your side of an
internal power struggle? If you were friends with Ambassador
Berberon, perhaps you share more of his philosophy than you
care to admit."

"President Dailey, you deserve specific strategic details,"
Sujata said, sighing. "But I have no doubt that the moment I
begin to provide them to you, this connection will be broken.
All I can risk are the naked assertions, and you must somehow
find a way to believe me. War is imminent. The Triads cannot
protect you. The Defenders cannot protect you. Your Exotics
cannot protect you. If war comes, Earth will be put to ruin just

as it was when the Weichsel called it home."

"I simply can't accept such a claim. Our strategic advisers—"

"Your strategic advisers are just like Wells's," Sujata said. "They find it impossible to credit the Mizari with powers on any level other than our own. You impose our limitations on them without knowing anything more about them than that they exist."

She paused to catch her breath and collect her thoughts, then continued. "Perhaps your advisers are right. Perhaps Wells is right. But do you understand the price of being wrong? Do you have any concept of the level on which this war will be fought, the energies each side has harnessed? Do you have any concept what these weapons can do to the body of life on our worlds and theirs? How can you allow him to make this decision for you?"

President Dailey's expression had turned cross, as though he had stopped resisting and begun resenting. "If he won't listen to you, then why would he listen to me? I don't see where you've presented me with an alternative. If your Commander Wells is as reckless as you say, what can I do to rein him in? Do you expect me to appeal to him as a planet-kin? It's your china shop he's broken loose in, not mine. If you can't stop him, how can I?"

"I think he would like a reason to stop," Sujata said, measuring her words carefully. "I think you can give him that reason. Wells is not out of control, you have to understand that. He's a principled man. He's doing what he thinks is his duty, according to the code that he's lived his life by. But that perception—of duty, that code he subscribes to, that gives us one chance to reach him.

"But to do it you have to create an authority greater than that of the Service and the Chancellery, one equal to the level of the principle Wells is following."

"You expect the Council to seize control of the Service? Or are you offering to surrender it to us?"

"That wouldn't be enough," Sujata said. "You have to create an authority that is nothing less than all the Worlds united, which offers a way for you to reclaim collectively the power Wells believes he's exercising in your best interest. You must make a credible way for the Worlds to say, 'No, this is our decision to make, not yours.'"

Dailey was shaking his head even before Sujata finished. "No, Chancellor, no. This is impossible. Do you understand the political cost—the entrenchment against any sort of inter-system federalism, a legacy left by the Nines? How can you even ask me to surrender Earth's sovereignty—"

"If I were there with you, I'd wring your neck for a fool! What value is there in the sovereign right to die a meaningless death?" Sujata exploded. "Do you think you can escape the consequences just by telling yourself it's the Service's problem? Do you think that by helping pay for the Triads you've discharged your duty, like some medieval knight paying scutage?

"This is the way it is, President Dailey, as unhappy a choice as you gave Felithe. You can have war, or you can have the responsibility you've been shirking since the Revision. You have three days to make it happen. Because that's all the time left before Wells's fleet takes us past a point of no return—"

The screen went blank, and Sujata fell silent, knowing what it meant. Less than half a minute later a breathless Shields materialized in the doorway, his chest heaving as he glowered blackly at her.

"I don't care what the Commander said, that's the end of it," he said fiercely. "You'd do anything to stop us, wouldn't you?" Betray the Commander, sell out the Service—"

"Yes," she said, rising from her seat uncowed. "And if you understood what was really about to happen, you'd be helping me. But you don't have it in you to understand that you're being loyal to the wrong man and the wrong idea."

"Yours is the wrong idea, Chancellor—that it's somehow more moral to be a victim than a victor. Ensign!" he barked, and a moment later a security officer appeared behind him. "Escort Chancellor Sujata to her quarters and post yourself outside the door until you're relieved. She is not to leave or have visitors."

He looked back to Sujata with a grim, but self-satisfied, smile on his face. "You were right about one thing, though, Chancellor. Time is running out for you. When the Triads conclude their final wave-off checks, it will be too late for anyone, including President Dailey, to interfere."

Though there were no bars in her makeshift cell, Sujata's imprisonment was complete. The room terminal was locked out of the station net, and her slate had been taken from her. She had no way of reaching Dailey or even Wells, and no friends on-station to argue for her in her stead.

Each time a meal was brought, she asked the bearer to pass a message to Wells: "Please tell Commander Wells that I would like to see him." But none of her messengers wore the command emblem or ranked higher than specialist. So none were positioned to pass that message directly to Wells, and she was certain that Shields would never relay it to him. In any event, there was no answer.

She could not sleep, and yet awake there was nothing to do but wonder. The mind-eating uncertainty drove her to converse with her guards, sitting on the entryway floor with her back propped against the inside of the door. But though it saved her from endlessly reviewing her catalog of missed opportunities and outright mistakes, the guards were no less vigilant for her having reached out to them.

One day ground by, then a second, and a third began, days counted by the cycle of meals since even the terminal clock had been disabled. When she tired of the guards or they of her, her mind kept returning to images of ships in the high craze, drawing closer and closer to worlds teeming with life. Terrible weapons nested under the wings of the carriers— more terrible weapons waited on the planet's surface. In the darkness and silence of her quarters she could see them clearly, sense their imminent unleashing.

She saw the wholeness of life shattered—the delicate fabric of ancient ecologies rent. The shock and confusion in the last moments, not only in sentient minds but also in the minds of a thousand species with a glimmer of self-awareness and in the collective mind of the Mother. The soul-searing knowledge that this specter, this moment, was death, death final and terrible, death cold and inescapable. And the world she kept seeing in flames was Earth.

Sujata knew with a certainty not justified by any facts she could marshal that Wells's ships could not win, and that certainty puzzled her. She could not recall when that certainty had displaced prudent apprehension, personal affront, and cultural opprobrium as her motivation. Sometime after *Wesley* sailed from Earth orbit, sometime before it docked at this station—she could fix it no more firmly than that.

But her inner conviction meant no more to Wells and those who shared his viewpoint than her apprehension. It was the lesson Berberon had tried so hard to teach her and which she had learned too late. If she had understood Wells the way Felithe had, she would have understood how hopeless her mission had been.

She saw now that Wells was incapable of the leap of trust required for her to succeed. He was what he had to be. He could be nothing else, think no other way. War was inevitable not because Wells wanted war, but because he saw it as inevitable. He could not allow himself to hope the Mizari were capable of mercy or wisdom or even simple sanity. No victories had ever been won by thinking the best of an enemy, and many defeats had been avoided by thinking the worst.

The only way out was to take the decision out of his hands. But the best opportunity to do that had been lost when she had left Central. If she had understood then, and stayed behind, there would have been time at least to try to push the Worlds together. Wells understood power, respected power. He would have listened to the massed voice of the Affirmation, she was sure of it.

But that understanding had come too late, and there was not enough power in her ideas alone to reach him. Her vision was nobler and more ennobling than his, but she could not force him to embrace it. Felithe had made more of an impression on Wells with his futile, fatal gesture than she ever could hope to make with words. But even that had come too late.

Sujata was working such thoughts into a fine web of despair when she was interrupted by the sound of the door page. The sound puzzled her, for the guards never troubled to use it when allowing her meals to be brought in. She raised her head and looked toward the door just as it slid open. To her surprise, it was Wells who stepped through the doorway.

"Falcon is about to begin its survey of the Mizar-Alcor system," he said. "I thought perhaps you might like to monitor the pass with us in the situation room."

Unspoken was the coda, *So you can see that I'm right.* She almost laughed. *The True Believer—still thinking he can convert me. I've given up on him, but he hasn't had a comparable awakening.*

But she quickly suppressed her bitter thoughts. It was a gesture Wells did not have to make, and her sense of resignation had not erased her curiosity. Beyond which, it was a chance to escape her prison for a little while.

"Thank you. I *would* like that," she said, and followed him out into the corridor.

There he surprised her again, dismissing the security contingent. When they were alone, he turned to her. "Chancellor, I'm embarrassed to say that I didn't realize until now how severe the restrictions placed on you were," he said. "I don't think they were justified, and I've instructed Governor White to lift them. I've also reviewed the evidence Colonel Shields intended to use in his complaint against you, and I didn't find it persuasive. No complaint will be made."

It was probably as close to an apology as Wells was capable of offering, but it was not enough. "Does this mean that you will recall the Triads?"

Wells avoided looking directly at her. "Let's leave that discussion until after *Falcon*'s recon," he said, starting down the corridor. He took a few steps, then stopped and looked back at her. "Oh, and Captain Killea has been rather anxiously trying to reach you for three days. Because he couldn't, he's got that ship and crew locked up as tight as if they were in Contact quarantine. When we get to the situation room, would you please call over to him and free the slaves?"

Though it was not immediately obvious, the system map on the curved screen of Teo Farlad's battle couch was among the most complicated in the ship's library. Within the small region of the Galaxy explored by humankind there were binary and trinary suns aplenty, and no shortage of stars with ten, twelve, or fifteen major satellites. But the seven elements included on Farlad's map were all suns—seven suns clustered in one tiny area of the sky, so closely that to an observer on Earth they merged into what the eye saw as only two lights, a lesser and a greater.

But Farlad and *Falcon* saw them as they really were—not two stars but two families of stars. The two brightest of the seven, brilliant emerald-white twins orbiting each other so closely that they would easily have fit inside the orbit of Mercury, formed the core of one cluster. A trio of dimmer stars orbited the twins at a distance of more than two light-days. In the millennia since the Mizari attack on the Weichsel, the trio had completed only five leisurely circuits of the central pair. This was Anak al Banat, Zeta Ursae Majoris, The Horse— Mizar.

Lying a quarter cee to the east but sharing the same motion through space were two white stars, each only a few times brighter than Sol—Alcor, The Rider, The Lost One. Here, as from Earth, it was clearly the lesser member of the stellar partnership. Even so, it was *Falcon*'s primary destination, for Alcor was the apparent source of the discordant radio signature thought to betray the Mizari's presence.

The Alcor signature was three times as energetic as that emanating from Phad and several dozen times more powerful than the emissions from the Alphecca nest. Even so, it was but a whisper, a flickering candle in the night.

Until a few days ago there had been some question whether the signature arose from the twin suns themselves somehow or from a body orbiting them. Viewed from the observatory at Lynx, Alcor showed no planetary spoor, even though astrophysical modeling of the system showed that it was stable enough to have allowed planets to form. There were limits to the resolving power of the Lynx instruments, but even so, some quietly started to wonder about the admittedly remote possibility of star-based life.

Falcon had ended that debate when it dropped briefly out of the craze for a pre-survey navigation hack. From half a cee away it was clear that the signature was coming from a planet orbiting the twin suns at a distance of eleven light-minutes. They had taken its measure as best they could, plotted its orbit, and given it a name—6UMa-A1. Then *Falcon* had hied back into the craze while its crew worked out the details of its appointment with the Mizari.

The ship was on her way to keep that appointment now. Farlad touched a key with his right index finger, and a fourth of his display was filled with the telecam image of Alcor B. The main sequence sun lay just five light-minutes ahead on *Falcon*'s track. With its portrait digitally processed for maximum clarity, Alcor B showed a face marred by great magnetic storms and a limb made ragged by fiery prominences.

Spanning a quarter of a million kilometres each second, *Falcon* continued to dive directly toward Alcor B at a velocity that, unchanged, would take it deep into the star's turbulent photosphere. But that was not *Falcon*'s destiny. Already the ship's main drive was singing as it drew energy from the spindle, killing off velocity at a twelve-gee rate.

Farlad was aware that his back muscles were knotted with

tension. Coming out of the craze so close to a star, and at as shallow an angle to the system ecliptic as *Falcon* had, was a high-risk maneuver—but a purposeful one. *Falcon* was using Alcor B as a shield, masking its presence as long as possible from the inhabitants of 6UMa-A1. By hiding in Alcor B's optical and radar shadow until the last moment, then translating just enough to skim the photosphere, *Falcon* would remain undetectable almost up until the moment the survey began.

For any other Service vessel except a Triad lineship, the planetary detritus encountered during the headlong dive through the system, together with the furious radiation absorbed during the stellar pass, would likely have meant its destruction. But *Falcon* had been built to withstand that and more.

Almost before Farlad was ready, the gyros altered the ship's attitude, and the programmed deflection around Alcor B began. The stellar pass was harrowing, even though the shields and radiators dealt easily with all but a tiny fraction of the complex incoming radiation. Farlad could not shake the image of *Falcon* as a moth dancing too near the flame. To his great relief the pass was over in a matter of ninety seconds, and 6UMa-A1 replaced Alcor B on the displays.

Unless there was a serious gap in the data collected the first time, because of instrument failure or interference from the ground, there would be only one flyby. Twenty minutes inbound—twenty minutes outbound. There was no time to waste, and the increased traffic on the ship's command net reflected that urgency.

"Instrument pods, deploy."

"Track and timeline nominal."

"Nav hack, on the mark."

Though he was nominally in charge of data management, there was little for Farlad to do at this juncture but watch to see that the system followed the rules programmed into it. Data from the dozens of passive instruments focused on 6UMa-A1 was being funneled directly into the multiband Kleine link. The data cache was less than ten percent full, and that only due to data held for retransmission.

But the cache would quickly fill when the link reached its capacity and a backlog began to build. As *Falcon* drew closer to the planet the improving resolution would increase the data load, as would the entry of the active instruments into the system. Due to the lag at this distance, there was as yet no data from the mapping radar or other active instruments, but during the last third of the approach they would pick up the echoes of the energies they were now focusing on the Mizari world. Then Farlad would have to take a more active role.

With every passing moment *Falcon* moved closer to meeting the primary criterion for a successful mission: relaying good data to DIDAC. Farlad listened to the chatter as the survey techs plucked bits of data from the stream. An oxysilicate world with a cold inert core and one large moon. Nothing distinctive—but there were puzzles.

"Frosty down there—280 absolute. But it shouldn't even be that warm—"

"Picking up indications of a nonpolar magnetic field. Damn, how can they generate that—"

"Atmospheric pressure 285 millibars—an easy ride down for the deedees. But a rock that size should have held more air—"

"The EM detectors are picking up the signature from all over the surface of the planet—from the surface of the moon too—"

"Where are the rest of the planets? There should be more planets—"

The Kleine link was at capacity now, and the data cache was filling. Looking at the data that had already gone out, Farlad adjusted the priorities assigned to the various instruments so the more critical observations went directly into the link. Top priority went to the active instruments, which caught the echoes of their first probings as *Falcon* closed to within a million kilometres of the planet. At the same time the sending portion of those instruments shut down, lest they provide Mizari gunners with an easy means of tracking their target.

As *Falcon* raced on toward its closest approach to 6UMa-A1, Farlad began to allow himself to think about the chances of meeting the secondary criterion for success: survival. If the ship got as far as the outbound phase, her chances of survival were markedly better. Outbound, her speed would work for her, not against her. Outbound, Captain Rukekin had the authority to break off the survey and run—

But a bare three minutes from close-approach, almost as though Farlad had jinxed the mission by his presumption, the contact alarm sounded. Immediately Farlad reshuffled the priorities to make sure the battle-management data got through to DIDAC. Almost as immediately the throughput on the relay link plummeted. It was as dramatic a drop as might have been caused by all the high-band channels crashing at once. But there was nothing wrong with the hardware.

Farlad had no other duties under a contact alert, so he eavesdropped on the command net, looking for answers. The fear and barely contained panic he heard there brought him no comfort.

"Where the hell did it come from, that sector was clear—"

"I get no range vector, our probe's passing right through it as if it weren't there—"

Farlad heard the high-energy crackle of the lance firing, once, twice, again, and still again. The ship seemed to shudder, and the tumult on the command net devolved into raw static. Farlad suddenly knew that the egglike couch was about to become his coffin. He wanted to throw back the overhead hatch and climb off his back and into the access corridor, to run downship to the tanks and so not die alone. But it was already too late—the ejection countdown was flashing on his display, and the couch had begun to rotate from the vertical to the horizontal in preparation.

But it was also too late for that. In consecutive instants the couch ground to a stop halfway through its translation, and the access corridor lights went dark. There was heat without fire and Farlad's body screamed, but his mind watched detachedly as his own skin browned and blackened and crinkled. Then his eyes burned, too, and he was blind for the last long moment of agony that preceded the end of all sensation.

Shocked silence reigned in the situation room when *Falcon*'s transmission abruptly terminated. The expressions on the faces of the senior command staff ranged from Yamakawa's disgruntled frown to Captain Elizin's mask of horror. Sujata had to fight with herself not to turn away from the sight of her waking nightmare becoming real. Now she steadied herself with a hand on a nearby wall and fought to control her self-betraying panting breaths and racing heart.

"All right," Yamakawa said finally. "We've lost a ship and some good men. Let's dig in and find out what we got in exchange. We have one hour to figure out what to tell *Kite* when she reaches Phad, and five hours until Triad One hits its wave-off."

"There's only one thing to tell *Kite*," Sujata said, stepping forward. "To abort her mission. And the same for Triad One. Tell them to come home."

Yamakawa regarded her with a curiously impersonal gaze, as though she were a thing that had had the impertinence to step outside of its place. Then he turned his back on her and ignored her, as he had since Wells had brought her into the room forty minutes earlier.

"The attack came approximately eight minutes after the first opportunity for the Mizari to detect *Falcon* emerging from the stellar shadow," he said, addressing Wells. "That puts the upper limit on their response time. We ought to be able to get some idea of their sensing capability by looking at the *Munin* incident in that light."

"*Kite*'s target orbits tighter to its star than *Falcon*'s did to Alcor," Venngst said, consulting his slate. "If *Kite* makes its pass at, oh, seventy-cee instead of fifty-cee, she should be able to reach her breakaway point safely, with only a modest degradation of the data quality—"

Sujata could scarcely believe what she was witnessing, how easily they wrote off *Falcon*'s dead as the price for what they'd learned. Only Elizin still seemed to be shaken, and no one seemed to notice. And yet they seemed blind to the meaning of the truths blood had bought.

"What more do you need to know?" she demanded, advancing on Yamakawa. "What's the point of risking the crew of *Kite*? Mr. Brodini," she said, turning on the Strategy Committee's tactics expert. "If *Falcon* had been a Triad carrier, would she have been close enough to release her deedees?"

Brodini glanced nervously in Yamakawa's direction before answering. "No, Chancellor. But a carrier would have had support from its lineships—"

"For how long? Eight minutes? Five? Three? Who's to say they can't atomize three ships at that distance as easily as they did one?"

Venngst began, "I see no reason for consistently undervaluing our capabilities and overvaluing theirs—"

Sujata whirled to face Wells. "How are you going to fight that?" she demanded, pointing a finger at the image of the black star frozen on a display. "You heard *Falcon*'s crew—it came out of nowhere. The lances couldn't touch it. It destroyed a heavily shielded recon ship as easily as it did *Munin*. Whatever it is, it had enough power in it to cross eighty light-years and still destroy most of life on Earth. How can you think of fighting it?"

Wells looked away from her and up at the display. "We have options. There has to be a way," he said.

"What would you have us do, Chancellor?" Shields asked in a hard-edged voice. "Surrender without fighting? They've destroyed two of our ships—killed thirty-one of our people. We can't let them get away with that."

"Why not?" Sujata asked. "Why do you have to try to make every death mean something? Why can't those deaths have been our mistake instead of their crime? Humans used to know that losing and living was better than losing and dying. But you have this insane idea that pride and revenge are worth dying for."

"Life is worth dying for," Wells said. "That's what this is about, Chancellor. Survival—and the freedom to make the most of living. Millions have died gladly for that cause."

She felt Wells's ambivalence and at the same time sensed the pressure the expectant audience was exerting on him. Yamakawa, Venngst, Brodini, Captain Elizin, Shields—their faces demanded nothing less from Wells than confirmation of their most deeply held beliefs. Beliefs she had to keep trying to break down, at least in Wells's mind—

"Those aren't noble deaths," she said angrily. "They're the deaths of cowards—cowards who couldn't face walking away from a confrontation not the winner. Don't you understand? You're not snarling and waving your fists across a water hole. You're talking about a war that can only end with one of our species destroyed. Even if we win, it's wrong."

That was the ultimate heresy, and voicing it only hardened them further against her. "Commander, it's obvious that this is hopeless," Shields said. "I warned you a Maranit could never understand."

Wells tore his gaze away from Sujata's face to glance at Shields, then began to turn his back on Sujata as though dismissing her.

"Why do you want this war?" she shouted across the room at him. "Why can't you let go?"

"I *don't* want it," he snapped back. "Don't you understand? I never wanted it."

"Then do you have the courage for peace?"

"How do you know that they want what we want?" There

was something in his voice that pleaded for a persuasive answer.

"If they're living things, they must have a drive to preserve themselves," she said with breathless earnestness. "I count on nothing more than that."

Wells's anguish was now evident to everyone in the room. "Do you understand what you'd be risking?"

"Yes," Sujata said bluntly. "Do you understand what you already are?"

Slowly drawing a deep breath, Wells averted his eyes downward. Sujata waited and said nothing, sensing he had reached a delicate cusp.

Yamakawa sensed the same thing. "Commander," he said firmly. "Time is slipping away from us. The Phad recon— *Kite* will need guidance—"

Sujata pounced. "That's right—tell *Kite* what happened to *Falcon*. Tell them you've decided to wait until the same thing happens to them to be convinced." Her tone changed abruptly from biting to soothing. "Harmack, it doesn't matter what they think. It doesn't matter if we don't have all the answers. If a thing is right, it's right no matter what. How many reasons do you need?"

Wells pursed his lips and slowly shook his head.

Despair flooded Sujata's being. "Commander Wells, as Chancellor of the Service I am ordering you to recall all ships to the Perimeter. I understand your reservations. But the responsibility is mine. Call them back."

He slowly raised his head and met her eyes. She knew the answer he would give, and she knew, too, that no one in the room would question his defiance. And yet he hesitated, holding her gaze for a long, frozen moment.

"I'm sorry—" he began in a soft voice.

Just then a trilling sound from one of the consoles interrupted. "Basenet," announced a com operator. "I have a priority request for conference from President Roland Dailey."

Sujata suddenly perked up.

"Refuse it," Wells said. "I can't take the time."

"Commander, this is Senior Specialist Marlenberg," said a new voice. "Sir, President Dailey is most insistent—he promised to arrange for the evisceration of the duty tech if he didn't refer the request to higher-ups. I've already refused a request in your name. This request reminds you that you claim Terran citizenship and orders you to respond immediately or face charges under Council law."

"What is this?" Yamakawa demanded.

"I guess we should find out," Wells said. "All right, Mr. Marlenberg. We'll accept the conference." With a sideways glance at Sujata, Wells walked to the conference ring at the far end of the room. As he stepped inside the circle, holographic images began to appear opposite him: first Dailey, then a man wearing the imperial robes of Liam-Won, a Maranit woman in high dress, and on until seven semisolid human shapes stood there. Slight differences in density among the figures and the faint auroralike modulation patterns between them showed that each was originating from a different location.

"Commander Wells, is Chancellor Sujata present?"

"She is."

"Chancellor, would you enter the circle, please?"

Sujata picked her way between Yamakawa and Shields and came forward to stand beside Wells.

"Thank you," Dailey said. "Chancellor, I call on you today not as President of the World Council of Earth but as Chief Delegate of the Concordat of Worlds, currently in session by means of this conference you have joined—"

chapter 20

Footsteps of the Dawn

"The bear that prowled all night about the fold
   Of the North Star hath shrunk into his den,
Scared by the blithsome footstaeps of the dawn . . ."

—James Russell Lowell

"Is this a joke? What in bloody hell is the Concordat of Worlds?" Colonel Shields demanded from where he stood in the middle of the situation room.

If the conference relay picked up Shields's words, Dailey paid them no notice. He went on to introduce the other delegates, who proved to be the heads of state of the six most populous First Colonization worlds: the Journan Elector, the High Councilor of Ba'ar Tell, the First Mistress of Maranit, the King of Liam-Won, the Renan Elder, the Dzuban Life Father.

Dailey continued, "Seats are being held open for all the other home worlds—including Feghr—pending their unification. We will not consider the Concordat complete until all the worlds are represented. In the meantime it's true that a number of our brothers and sisters will be, in effect, disenfranchised. However, I want to note that our seven worlds are home to the vast majority of the human population. The worlds not yet seated boast a total population of barely two hundred and fifty million—three percent of the total census.

"Chancellor, the Concordat is a voluntary federation not unlike the former Pangaean Consortium of Earth. Under the charter that each of the delegates has signed on behalf of his world, the individual worlds surrender to the Concordat the right to exercise dominion over certain matters of common interest, while retaining autonomy on all matters of strictly local concern. Among those functions we intend to address collectively are those which heretofore have been administered by the Service—transportation, trade, and security."

Behind her, Sujata heard Elizin's hostile whisper: "What's going on here? Why is he talking to her?"

"I understand," Sujata said, stealing a sideways glance at Wells. The Director's expression was passive and unrevealing.

"I want to assure you that the Concordat is prepared to assume the contractual obligations incurred by the Service, both toward the individual employees and its trading partners," Dailey said. "You also have the right to know some of our specific intentions. The Arcturus New Colony on Cheia will be asked to decide whether it wishes to be admitted as a voting member or continue to be administered by central authority.

"Where the various facilities of the Resource Branch are located in an inhabited system, they will be sold at a fair value to the local government. The remainder will be held by the Concordat and administered for the general welfare. Finally, the ships and forward stations of the Survey, Transport, and Defense Branches will be merged into a provisional Space Authority under the direct supervision of the Concordat.

"Chancellor, we make this claim lawfully and would prefer to exercise it peacefully, but we are prepared to take all necessary measures to enforce it. Will you recognize our authority and release the assets of the Service to us, or will it be necessary for us to seize them?"

"I recognize your authority," Sujata said, no hesitation in her voice.

"Nobody cares what you say, bitch," Brodini said, raging. "Let them try to seize us. They'll wish they'd left us alone—"

"That remark is out of order, Mr. Brodini," Wells said sharply.

"I mean it. She'll see just what the Triads are capable of when we send one to Maranit—"

"Shut up or remove yourself, Mr. Brodini," Wells said, underlining his words with a hard look of rebuke.

Brodini fell silent, but he was not the only objector. "This is a setup, a sham," Shields declared. "This imaginary Concordat has no power over us. We have the right to—"

"To do what?" Wells asked, sending the Chief of Staff the same withering look. "Please consider your words, Mr. Shields. What exactly are you defending?"

Dailey had to be hearing the altercation, but he chose not to wait for it to end. "So that the Concordat has the opportunity to be served by executives of its own choosing, I ask that you submit your open resignation," he said to Sujata. "I might add that this doesn't mean that you may not be retained in this or some other capacity."

"I understand, and I'll respect that request."

"Thank you, Chancellor, for your sense of honor. Commander Wells?"

"Yes," Wells said, turning back.

"Commander Wells, under the legal and uncoerced transfer of power you just witnessed, you are now an employee of the Concordat's provisional Space Authority. Twenty minutes ago the Concordat voted unanimously to order the recall of all of its vessels to the Perimeter pending a complete review of the consequences of past Service policies. You are directed to facilitate that recall. Please acknowledge."

"Tell them to go to hell," Yamakawa demanded angrily. "This is nothing but a hijacking dressed up in legalisms."

"I have to agree, sir," Venngst volunteered. "Without seeing the Charter, knowing the circumstances—I don't know how they can expect us simply to hand over the sort of power our ships represent. The other worlds may be holding out, and the Concordat may be planning to use the Service to enforce their power. I don't think your duty here is at all clear."

Wells drew a deep breath and released it in a sigh. "When a thing is right, it's right no matter what sort of clothing it's wearing," he said softly. He glanced down at Sujata, and she saw something new—call it relief—in his eyes. Then he turned his back on Venngst to face Dailey.

"Acknowledged, Mr. Chief Delegate," Wells said in a clear, strong voice. "I will recall the ships. I assume you will want my resignation as well?"

"Yes, for the same reason."

Wells nodded. "I will tender it directly, along with those of my senior staff."

It was over that quickly. Her knees suddenly weak, Sujata

released the breath she had been holding as a shivery sigh of relief. She closed her eyes and saw the shadow lifting from the surface of her adopted homeworld, saw life stirring anew in the light. She heard someone say, "Thank you, Harmack," in a fervent voice. Only later did she realize it had been hers.

Translating intent into action took a little longer. The clock was still running on *Kite,* which gave issuing its recall the highest priority. But before Wells could deal with that, he had to deal with a minor revolt among his staff.

There was no trouble with Yamakawa, a pragmatic man, or Venngst, a consummate professional who knew his place. Even Shields, though surly, seemed ready to accept the new reality.

Brodini and Elizin were another matter. As soon as Sujata and Wells left the conference and the continuing session of the Concordat, Brodini flatly refused to do anything to help carry out Dailey's instructions. Since as a member of the strategy committee Brodini had neither command authority nor operational responsibility, it was something of an empty vow.

But Wells reacted to the symbolic meaning of the refusal rather than its substantive value. "I'll accept your resignation now, then, Mr. Brodini," he said curtly.

"I'm not resigning, either," Brodini said defiantly. "Do you think I'm just going to go quietly and let this happen? Somebody has to speak out. I'm going to make sure the station staff knows what's happening."

For all the bold words Brodini's protest ended meekly. His security clearance was dropped all the way to R-1 and he, himself, was frog-marched by two Security officers to confinement in the housing block. Instead of a fight, Brodini settled for shouting imprecations against Sujata and the Concordat all the way down the corridor.

But Brodini's ineffectual gesture seemed to embolden Elizin, who had taken the loss of *Falcon* harder than any of them. Ever since then he had stood alone, unnoticed, near the back of the room, head hanging, silent, lost inside himself. When Brodini was gone and Wells announced he would make the recall in person from the Flight Office Command Center, Elizin suddenly sprang to life, rushing with long strides from where he had been lingering to intercept Wells.

"Mack— you can't do this. You owe them," Elizin said, blocking the way to the door with his body. "I had friends on *Falcon*. So did most of my men. I ate dinner with Captain Hardesty the night before we left Lynx. He was telling me about a place he'd bought near Benamira. To retire to, you know?"

"Stand aside, Captain," Wells said, firmly but not without a note of sympathy.

Elizin backed a step or two toward the door but made no move to get out of the way. "Those monsters fried him and you're going to let them get away with it. It isn't right, Mack," he said with an earnest and deeply felt anguish. "It just isn't right. You let them go out there thinking the Service was behind them, believing we were gonna back them up. You've gotta do something, Mack. You can't just leave them out there. You've gotta bring them back, at least—"

There was too little time to be diplomatic. "There's nothing to bring back. I'm sorry, Captain," Wells said, and tried to brush past the captain.

On surprise alone, Wells made it to within two steps of the door. Then Elizin grabbed him by the arm with an iron-fingered grip and swung him around. "Didn't you hear me?" he shouted, waving his free arm wildly, the hand balled in a menacing fist.

The move had put Elizin's back to both Shields and Sujata. Sujata looked expectantly at Shields, expecting him to intervene. When he did not, she did, stepping forward and grasping Elizin's neck from behind in a sure-handed grip that took both the fight out of Elizin and the starch out of his legs. He collapsed heavily to the floor and lay still where he fell.

"Carotid artery and motor ganglia," Sujata said, looking down at her handiwork. "He'll be all right in a minute or so."

"See he's taken to the infirmary," Wells said to Shields. "He's not dangerous. He's not even wrong. He's just upset." Then he turned to Sujata. "We've got to move."

She fell in beside him in the corridor, keeping pace with his long, uneven strides.

"I didn't know you had that kind of trick available to you," Wells said. There was a grudging respect in his tone.

"Just something we Maranit bitches came up with to keep the herd docile," she said lightly.

Surprised, he laughed. "Please don't make me like you,"

he said soberly. "It's bad enough having to concede that you were right."

Sujata stayed with Wells in the Flight Office Command Center until *Kite* acknowledged the recall and made good its escape from the Phad system by climbing immediately back into the craze. After that it would be four hours until the next message had to go out, to Triad One nearing Alphecca. Sujata took advantage of the lull to excuse herself and go off alone to pay the first installment of gratitude on some sizable debts.

Unescorted for the first time on the station, she quite predictably got lost. But she had been cooped up in her quarters long enough that the freedom to get lost was a pleasure in itself. When she found her way again, her first stop was *Wesley,* where she found Captain Killea supervising the long delayed housecleaning of his now empty ship.

"Thank you," she said when she had separated him from the dock foreman.

He shrugged. "We didn't do anything. In fact, I'm still wondering what it is we were going to have to do."

"You followed my directions. You sent a message, just by doing your job."

Killea nodded thoughtfully. "I guess I understand that, with the stories I've heard since we opened up. I could still do with something more concrete to tell the crew."

"Did you have any trouble with them?"

"Trouble?" he asked, cocking his head to one side. "No, Trouble is the second watch laying me out with a fitting wrench and making for the hatch. But I've had my fill of raised eyebrows and sidewise looks for a while."

"I'll give you something more concrete for the crew—like a Service citation you can drop into their personnel files."

"That would help," he said. He inclined his head toward the dock foreman. "I've got to see to some things, if you'll excuse me."

"In a moment," she said. "Captain Killea, I may yet need more from you and *Wesley* than sitting locked-out in dock."

He folded his arms across his chest. "How soon? The lance stills needs certification work."

"Don't worry about that. Where we'll be going we won't need it. In fact, I'd prefer the lance disabled. I presume it's not practical to think about removing it."

It was Killea's turn to raise an eyebrow. "No, Chancellor, it wouldn't be."

"What *Wesley* does need is the very best linguacomp available, on-station or elsewhere. I'll authorize a priority link if it needs to be downloaded from Central. Your librarian will have to make a partition in the ship's library for the inference processor and knowledge bank. And the battle strategist's station on the bridge is to be modified for the operator."

"I'm not sure that the displays are compatible—"

"Then have your systems people replace them. Rip out the whole battle couch if necessary. We won't be needing that, either."

"It'll take some time."

"I understand that. Give yourself a couple of days off, then get on it."

"Yes, Chancellor," he said, brightening. He started to turn away, then stopped. "Chancellor, are we ever going to know what really went on in there?"

She smiled faintly. "I doubt it, Captain."

"But it's over, right? Everything's back on keel now?"

"Not quite, Captain. Not quite."

Returning to her office, Sujata tried to call Dailey, only to be told he was not available. The Concordat was still in session. It was the same an hour later, and an hour after that.

It was not surprising that the first session of the Concordat should be a lengthy one. But there was something novel in the experience of trying to contact someone who had more important things to do than to talk to her. It impressed upon her in a way that merely saying the words had not that she was no longer the final arbiter.

The discovery was at once liberating and jarring. For six and a half years she had been the person to whom people came for permission. In her ingrained habit of thinking she had planned out her afternoon: *First I will see Killea, then I will talk to Dailey, then return to the Flight Command Center for the wave-off of the Triads.* Now she was serving at someone else's pleasure, and though there was some relief in having given up responsibility with authority, it was irritating to be made to while away time waiting for Dailey to make himself available.

She spent most of that time looking over the shoulders of

various DIDAC specialists as they reviewed the data *Falcon* had managed to gather in the minutes before its death. Everything she saw, everything she learned from and with the specialists, convinced her that her still unspoken resolve was right-minded.

Studying the images of the crystallike domes scattered over the surface of both the planet and its moon, Sujata tried to embrace the totality of their existence, their unity to each other and with their worlds. The integration of the Mizari to their homeworld was even more total than that of the Mother to the motherworld, and she marveled at it. When she listened to the modulations of their life signature, the unique expressions arising from each of the two Alcor nests, she tried to infuse them with meaning.

So hard even to think of it as life, even for me. So hard to identity with—so easy to discount. Nothing here to love or even to know empathy with—

It was not until after the successful Triad One wave-off, which she went ahead and witnessed as planned, that she made contact with Dailey. Though there was weariness in his eyes, there was also an inner glow of satisfaction illuminating his features.

"My greetings and apologies, Chancellor," he said cheerily. "I was notified of your messages, but I simply could not break away until now."

"I understand," she said. "I realize that you had a lot of business to attend to—and probably still do."

"Indeed," Dailey said, tipping backward in his chair. "It was quite exciting, actually. The Elder of Rena-Kiri put forth the proposition that since the crisis had been averted, the Concordat should therefore be dissolved and everything would return to the way it was. In short, he wanted to turn it into the sham Commander Wells's advisers were saying it was. It was rather a challenge to turn him away from that idea."

"I'm happy to hear that you succeeded," Sujata said. "I have some good news for you as well. *Kite* has been recalled from her survey of Phad, and Triad One from its attack on Alphecca. The other recalls should be completed shortly."

"Excellent! You seem to have managed to make the most of our meager assistance. I *am* sorry that we could only muster seven worlds," Dailey said. "I was concerned that that would be a problem for you."

Sujata shook her head. "I'm amazed that you managed that much in as little time as you had. And you gave Wells the opportunity, the out he needed, at just the right time."

"In truth I'm rather amazed. But we—Earth, that is—had more influence than I would have thought before trying. Journa and Maranit were with us from the start, Journa because of the special affection they have always felt for us and your world as a matter of principle—your involvement may well have been a factor too. But the Ba'ar were more than a little reluctant to play the mouse bedding down with the elephant, which is why we ended up with a one-world, one-vote system.

"Of course, the prospect of the Renans or the Liamese getting the upper hand then scared the Dzubans so badly that they threw in with Journa and Maranit to see that I became Chief Delegate." Dailey laughed to himself. "Oh, it is going to be a challenge, I can see that already. I intend to go back and read everything Devaraja Rashuri wrote on the subject of statecraft. I will need all the help I can get to keep the worlds from flying apart again like marbles on a spin-table. But I can postpone such concerns until tomorrow. Tonight is a night for celebrating. Do you have something to drink at hand? I would like to toast you for bringing us back from the brink, for preserving the delicate peace."

Sujata shook her head. "I would have to refuse the toast, Chief Delegate. This isn't peace—it isn't even a stalemate. It isn't enough just to go back to what and where we were before. The status quo represents sterility, not stability."

Dailey frowned. "I'm sorry, Chancellor, I don't understand why so."

"I wonder even if you can. You see one moment in time, and nothing of the path that's brought us here. This whole business of the Mizari and the endless, unfought war has arrested us, diverted our creative energies into engineering destruction. We've become so numbed by the prospect of death that we no longer feel the life within us.

"You see, Wells and the Nines were right, at least in part. We need a solution that will reopen the Galaxy to us," she said with a passion she had not realized she felt. "Until we find one we're blocked not only physically but emotionally. We don't know how to turn inward on ourselves. We need the frontier. We need the capacity to grow, to conceive of hopeful futures."

"I find nothing to quarrel with in that," Dailey said easily.

"But that's a vision for a tomorrow still a long way away."

"No, sir," she said. "It has to be a vision for today. Knowing that the Mizari exist and something of what they are and what they can do does nothing to erase the fear we feel. All it does is give it a clearer focus. Unless there's a change, there'll be more like Wells. And eventually one of them will get what he doesn't want but is always working toward—war."

"I thought you said we couldn't win."

"Not now. But you know the way we are. Some of these people are already working their endlessly inventive little brains overtime trying to find a way to overcome the Mizari advantage. Perhaps there's some way to blind the Mizari. Or perhaps we'll learn how to graviate accurately enough to bring a robot bomber out of the craze ten clicks above the surface of one of their nests. There'll either be a way or we'll convince ourselves there is."

Dailey sighed. "Agreed. But what can be done to prevent it? What is it you want me to do?"

"All you need to do is give permission. I'm ready to do the rest."

"Permission for what?"

"I want to take *Wesley* to Alcor. Not to spy on the Mizari or to try to take their measure. To reach out to them as best we can. To try to show them that we, too, are life, worthy of surviving."

"And if they destroy your ship, as they did *Falcon* and *Munin?*"

"I hope you'll send another, building on whatever I learn. Ships and staff are cheap enough when it's the future you're trying to buy back."

Dailey considered for several moments before answering. "I don't think we could approve it without some reason to hope for success."

"I wouldn't offer to go if I didn't think there was one," Sujata said quickly. "The Alphecca and Alcor systems have both been heavily altered by Mizari efforts. The only bodies in them are stars and the Mizari nests—we didn't pick up a bit of debris larger than a fist. They've swept their homes clean, as it were—planets, moons, asteroids, everything—using this energy instrumentality we've been calling the black star."

"You're not encouraging me," Dailey said. "That's a terrifying power."

"Agreed," she said. "But ask yourself why the two nests in

this system left each other alone while they cleared out everything else. Why don't they mutually annihilate each other, or at least the larger destroy the smaller? Why make this one exception? Because they know the other is there. This low-frequency signature we used to find them—it's how they talk to each other, or at least how they identify each other."

"So you think you can dress like a lion and walk among them?"

"Munin had no EM output, and it was destroyed, probably as soon as it was detected. *Falcon* got much closer, but after it shut down its EM output it was also destroyed. If we go in there broadcasting the signature of the Phad or Alphecca nest, I know they'll leave us alone."

Dailey pursed his lips. "Write up a proposal. Something I can show the other Delegates—"

Before Dailey was finished, the screen blanked, cutting him off in mid-sentence. A moment later Yamakawa appeared in his place.

"Chancellor, you're needed in the situation room immediately," Yamakawa said.

"Why? What's wrong?"

"Triad Two didn't acknowledge the wave-off," he said grimly. "It's still on its way to Alcor."

"How the hell could this happen?" Sujata demanded, thrusting her face close to Wells's. "If this is some kind of trick to commit us, to go back on your word—"

"I suppose I shouldn't be surprised that you would think that," Wells said tiredly. "The fact is that we did everything the same for Triad Two as we did for Triad One. Except Triad Two never acknowledged. We never even picked up their transponder signal."

Sujata turned away and hugged herself. "Maybe because there was nothing to pick up. Maybe something went wrong."

"Chancellor, each Triad command ship has dual backups for the Kleine system," Yamakawa said. "It's unlikely that any technical failure would render it mute."

"Unless it had been destroyed."

Wells shook his head. "I'm afraid we have a good idea why they didn't hear us. Mr. Marshall?"

One of the comtechs cleared his throat nervously. "Chancellor, I was reviewing the transmission from *Falcon* just before it—before the link was broken. At the moment the black star first appeared, the interference jumped up fifteen points and kept climbing through to the end of the encounter. Even if *Falcon* had survived, we would have lost contact with it in a matter of a few more seconds."

"What about the *Munin* encounter?"

"The same pattern, though less severe—proportional to the black star's release of energy."

Sujata's brow furrowed as she looked back and forth between the tech and Wells. "How can that be? I understood that the Kleine link was direct through the spindle. How can anything happening on our side of the fence cause interference?"

Yamakawa answered. "It appears that the spindle *is* the source of the black star's energy. Or to put it more accurately, the black star is the manifestation of a corridor to the spindle. The Data Analysis Office confirms that the spectrum of radiation directed against the *Falcon* and *Munin* is identical to the raw energy flux tapped by the AVLO drive."

"They can tap the spindle, just as we can—"

"Yes," Yamakawa said. "It explains the sudden appearance of the black star on both occasions. It also explains the interference. Their weapon disturbs the spindle. After it's used, it leaves a zone of"—he paused, looking for the right word, then shrugged—"a zone that the relatively low-energy Kleine carrier can't penetrate."

"Why wasn't I told?"

"Chancellor, all these pieces have fallen together in the last few minutes," Wells said. "No one kept any secrets."

Her back to everyone, Sujata retreated a half dozen nervous paces, then turned and looked at Wells. "So, what now? The Triad commander was expecting to hear something, right? What are they supposed to do when they don't hear it?"

Wells nodded to Marshall, who cleared his throat again before answering. "The procedure is that if they don't acquire our carrier in the first ninety seconds, they extend the exposure—their time out of the craze—to a total of three minutes. If they don't have it by the end of that time, they go back up."

"And do what?"

"Carry out their standing orders," Wells said. "That's what presumptive-go mission rules are all about—the possibility that the command structure may be impacted by enemy activity, leaving the battle group to carry out its mission without support. Triad Two is on its way to attack the Alcor nests."

Sujata stared at him for a long moment, then searched the faces of the others, each in turn: Yamakawa, Venngst, Shields, Marshall, and the other auxiliaries. What she read there frightened her. "Why isn't anybody doing anything?" she demanded, throwing her hands in the air.

"There's nothing we can do," Wells said quietly. "Nothing to stop them, anyway."

"When they begin their attack, we can catch them then, though, just as we did *Kite*."

Wells lowered his eyes and shook his head slightly. "Triad Two is heading *into* the zone of interference. There's very little reason to hope it will abate enough by the time it gets to Alcor for us to reach them."

A small spark of hope manifested itself in Marshall's eyes. "Chancellor, if the black star really is a spindle manifestation —" he began tentatively.

"Yes?"

"I've been thinking about the fact that it's been eleven years since the *Munin* incident, and there hasn't been any retaliation. If they can respond as quickly as it seems they can—maybe they can't track an AVLO ship through the craze back to its point of origin the way they could a *Weichsel* ice-ship. It *is* a much more difficult feat, even for us, and they're our ships. Maybe they don't yet know where to find us."

"Maybe not," Sujata said. "But if Triad Two reaches Alcor, we're going to be giving them three more reasons to keep looking." She turned to Wells. "When will they reach Alcor? How long do we have?"

"Three months."

Sujata stared blankly. "I have to talk to Dailey," she said at last.

"I can make that link for you here," Marshall said.

"Chancellor, be sure to ask him if he still wants us to recall Triad Three," Yamakawa said pointedly.

She understood immediately the implication, and the realization chilled her. *To think we may end up stumbling off the precipice after deciding to turn and walk away—the true mistake was made when we walked up to the edge in the first place. Too late now for regrets—or for much of anything else.*

"Chancellor, I have the Chief Delegate now."

Sujata drew a deep breath and started across the room toward the com station without knowing what it was she was going to say. Already fevered by her distress, she did not notice the swirling pool of warm air she passed through on the way.

Wait.

"No," Sujata said. "I don't think anyone here is to blame, at least not for the specific failure. There's plenty of blame to pass around for creating the circumstances in which it's taking place."

Do nothing.

"My recommendation is going to sound like a non-decision."

Trust.

"I say we hold our breath and ride it out. Maybe we can't stop Triad Two, but we don't have to help them."

It is my turn.

"Yes, three months is a long time for us to hold our breath. But we know what will happen with the other option. It's a choice between the chance of them striking back and the certainty of it."

In his newest metamorphosis he knew himself to be even more of the spindle and less of his former existence. Much that was old and no longer useful had been stripped away, and he had learned much that was new. The most important lesson he had learned was that he could channel the spindle's energies and did not need to risk his own. Understanding that, he had power; understanding himself, he had the skill.

Thackery had sensed the wrongness the moment he brought his once-again-restored resonance back to the focus of disturbance. He listened and then reached out and touched

Sujata's mind, this time with a delicate, sure touch that left pale, quavery shadows on her thoughts:

> *Wait.*
> *Do nothing.*
> *Trust.*

Then he moved off, riding the currents of the spindle with the same grace he had once seen in Gabriel, his sight focused far across the fibers to where a trio of wormholes betrayed the presence of three infinitesimally small cylinders enclosing the ordered energies of life. There was no haste in his movement, for he knew the moment and the means and that both were within reach. Doubt was not part of him, nor fear. He had given those up forever.

At one time he had garnered acclaim for doing that which any of thousands could have done as well. Now there was a service that only he could perform but which none would ever know about. They would know only, in time, that the ships and their crews never emerged from the craze, never completed their mission.

He did not even regret their sacrifice, not only because regret, too, had been excised from his substance. He saw that those ships were the center, the source, of the dark anticipations that clouded the near uptime and confused the present. It was within his power to erase those anticipations, and the price paid, even the death of those who had once been his kin, could not begin to compare with the value received.

Calling on knowledge both new and old, Thackery reached out, down toward the boundary, and extended his essence and control into all three wormholes at once, into the hearts of the three ships. It required only a mere shrug, a twist *so*, and a flood of energy poured through him and into the fragile drives. Irreplaceable circuits fused, then melted. There was a sudden flowering of energy where the ships had been, a flowering of such dimensions that the watching eyes on the matter-matrix could not help but detect it and know its meaning.

It was done.

He lingered there to watch the cautious approach of a single ship singing the song of the Mizari to the system of seven suns, to savor the meeting of mind and Mind, and to listen to messages meant for other hearers.

"We will never stand face-to-face to take each other's measure," the woman told those whom she served, "for what we are is as far outside their grasp as what they are is outside ours. We will never join hands in friendship, for they have nothing to offer us or we them. But neither will we make war on each other again. We will never share a world with them, but we can share a Galaxy."

In his new state Thackery could no longer feel, save for those two feelings that all intelligence cannot help but know: amusement at the absurdity of existence, and respect for the finality of nonexistence. But he still had the memory of other emotions, and the heart he no longer possessed swelled with a joy his new body could not have mustered.

For the disturbance in the spindle was vanishing even as he watched, and at long last, the way uptime was clear. And in the tranquil far future, he saw a wondrous vision in the matrix, a living resonance of such delicacy and beauty that merely to embrace it Thackery was required to grow in himself.

=*Gabriel* . . . =

>I heard your call and came down from terminus, but the turbulence blocked the way to you. Are you in need?<

The touch of the D'shannan's answer on Thackery's being was rapture, a taste of reunion, of completion. =*No. I am whole.*=

>Are you finished here?<

Before answering, Thackery looked out across the barrier to the matter-matrix that had been home and hell, that had created him and then destroyed him. He saw the restless activity of the ships and their crews, the worlds newly astir with unleashed ambition. There was no place among them for him, no part in their strivings for him. He was done with that now.

=*Yes. I am finished here.*=

>Then will you come uptime with me, to await the end in communion?<

=*I will, Gabriel,*= Thackery answered eagerly. =*Do you know this timbre? Do you understand my joy?*=

>I understand. Come, Merritt Thackery. Come and be one with us.<

ABOUT THE AUTHOR

Michael P. Kube-McDowell has at various times called New Jersey, Indiana, and Michigan home. He holds a master's degree in science education, and was honored for teaching excellence by the 1985 White House Commission on Presidential Scholars. Mr. Kube-McDowell's stories have appeared in such magazines as *Analog, Asimov's, Amazing, Twilight Zone,* and *Fantasy and Science Fiction,* as well as in various anthologies published in the U.S. and Europe. Three of his stories have been adapted as episodes of the television series "Tales From the Darkside."

EMPRISE, the critically-praised first book of the "Trigon Disunity" future history, was a Phillip K. Dick Award finalist. Mr. Kube-McDowell's other books include *After the Flames* and *Enigma;* he is currently at work on a new novel, *Alternities,* for The Berkley Publishing Group.